THE
BREADCRUMB GAME

LAUREN KRISTEN ROBERTS

BOOKS

Also by Lauren Kristen Roberts

Gemini Divided

For Jean-Leon Bouchenoire (1941-2023) with love.

Chapter 1
Ella

E LLA'S HOUSE WAS FULL of ghosts.

Not the ghosts from campfire stories or haunted houses, or the ones that sent messages from beyond the grave. Other people would've called the ghosts memories, but Ella disagreed. Memories could be forgotten, but try as she might, Ella could not forget. Years ago, she'd lived in this house with three other people, but most days, that felt like another lifetime.

She knew she would've been better off in therapy, but she didn't like to confide in anyone. Most people in her shoes probably would've moved out of the two-story house she'd lived in all her life, but she couldn't bring herself to let go of her past, painful as it was.

Each morning, she got up before the sun and drank her coffee while listening to the news anchors drone on about war, disease, and social unrest. Hearing about everyone else's struggles put her own First World problems in perspective. Compared to them, she was fine. She had food, shelter, and a good job.

After an hour of the news, her interior design business swallowed up the hours from morning until night. Every project for every client was like a puzzle to solve – what designs would fit best with a particular client's needs and wants? Today, she was preparing options for a seven-year-old girl's bedroom—the front runners were giant fuchsia polka dots or abstract shapes with a light pink shimmer. Glancing at the samples, she smiled, knowing that her seven-year-old self would've chosen the polka dots.

Next up, she would select furniture for another client's Cape Cod style living room. Her clients sent her their lists of likes and dislikes, and she used those to select pieces they would like that worked in their space. With every job, she had a new challenge. When her mind was busy, her ghosts retreated to the shadows, and she did everything she could to keep them there.

Since she concentrated best without music or noise while she worked, on nice days like today she left her windows open, and her daily soundtrack was the comings and goings of her neighbors. She was deep in thought when a familiar metallic screech broke her concentration. Without looking up, she knew it was the worn-out brakes on her neighborhood postal carrier's delivery truck. Sheila had been delivering her mail since Ella was a kid, and almost always passed by within the same ten-minute window.

The pale-yellow walls of her sunny kitchen re-materialized around her and she took a sip of the iced tea on the table beside her and stood, stretching her tense muscles. Today's mail might just hold something she'd been waiting for, so she padded to the front door and slipped on her shoes. Pulling the door closed behind her, she squinted into the sunshine, waving to Sheila as the square vehicle pulled away from the curb.

In the mailbox she found a wad of advertisements, several bills, and on top, a small, padded envelope. Her stomach turned over at the sight of the innocent-looking package. That was not what she'd been hoping to see, but she knew what it was. The messy scrawl was the same as always, and there was a cluster of colorful stamps in the top right corner. The ink stamped over them had smeared enough to be illegible, and there were no other clues about the sender. Every time one arrived, she told herself she wouldn't open it, but curiosity always got the better of her.

Back inside, she dropped the other mail on the hall table and slowly tore open the padded envelope. These parcels containing tiny clues arrived every few months, and while they never had a note with them, she knew they were from Mal. They hadn't spoken since their last fight, twenty years before. The trinkets started arriving after ten years of radio silence. She knew what Mal was doing, she just didn't know why.

She tilted the envelope, and into her hand dropped two lime green dice, the kind used by serious gamers. Unlike regular dice, these had more than six sides.

Ella had loved solving logic puzzles since she was a child, but this one required no effort to figure out. Her mind bounced backwards through time, dragging her back to blinding sunshine and scorching heat outside a convention center.

People in strange costumes streamed around her toward the entrance. One of them bumped her shoulder, turning back to scowl at her.

Her father was there, laughter dancing in his eyes. "Do you want to go check it out, girls?"

Mal was there, too, her expression mocking. "If Ella's not too scared," she said, and Ella gave her a dirty look.

After pushing their way through the crowded entryway, the two young teens and their father gazed with awe out over the sea of costumed humanity. The memory of the fan convention (or "nerd convention," as Mal had called it) floated hazily behind her eyelids.That family trip to Arizona had been the last time she'd seen the style of dice that now sat in her palm.

"Come find me!" An even younger, less moody version of Mal shrieked with delight inside Ella's head, and Ella shivered. From the time she'd been old enough for hide-and-seek, Mal had insisted they play the game her way, and she'd left clues to where she was hiding. For the past ten years, Ella had received trinkets like this in the mail, and she'd thrown away every single one. She had no idea why Mal had started sending them, but she wished she would stop.

So you're in Arizona, she thought as she tossed the dice and the envelope into the recycling bin. *Good for you. Why won't you leave me alone?*

Chapter 2
Ella
FRIDAY

IT WAS A DAY like all the others. Ella woke up early and listened to the evils of the world dissected on the news while getting ready for her day, ate her Chocolate Cheerios, then turned her thoughts to work. The morning flew by, as it usually did; she would've worked through lunch again, but for once, her stomach rumbled a reminder. She reheated the leftover Chinese food from the night before and ate it in front of her laptop. Work-life balance wasn't really her thing, but that was okay with her. She loved her job.

She was in the middle of a phone call with an important client when the doorbell rang several times in a row. Eager to make the noise stop, she rushed to the door as her client barreled on, undeterred. A man in a reflective vest and hard hat stood on her doorstep, saying something about a water main break and pointing at her back yard. Nodding, she waved him toward the gate on the side of the house, turning her attention back to her call.

A distant screech broke her concentration mid-afternoon, as it so often did, letting her know she'd been absorbed in her work for hours. Sheila was nearly ten minutes off schedule with the mail that day, but that was still within her normal window. Ella pushed her chair back and stood. Two birds chirped greetings to each other outside her kitchen window, alternating their songs as if in conversation. The wind chimes that had been a souvenir from a trip to Hawaii filled the air with gentle music.

Today she was expecting a large check from an eccentric client who insisted on sending her payment through the mail rather than via electronic transfer, so she was eager for the mail to come. Once that money arrived, she'd start planning a trip to Bermuda for next Christmas.

Sheila was gone by the time Ella walked out the front door. She picked up a small box from her doorstep with a printed label addressed to her, but no return address or postage. She knew who it was from, so she didn't bother to open it yet. Her next-door neighbor's black and white cat threaded herself between Ella's ankles, circling her leg and purring. She bent down to pet the soft ball of fur, speaking softly. "Hey Domino," Ella cooed to the cat, who was rubbing herself against Ella's legs. "How're you doing today? How's my favorite cat in the world?"

Ella continued to the mailbox with the small box in her hand and Domino at her heels, waving to her elderly neighbor, Miss Rosa, and her daughter, Celeste, in the driveway across the street. Ella stopped to watch Celeste and Miss Rosa hugging goodbye, a pain in her chest hitting her without warning. What she wouldn't give for her own mother to still be around for her to hug.

She watched as Domino took off at a run towards Celeste, who scratched the cat's head and then got into her car. As Celeste turned the corner at the end of the block and Miss Rosa disappeared back inside her house, Domino scampered along the curb across the street. Ella scanned the otherwise quiet, tree-lined street fondly. Except for the four years she'd lived in a college dorm, this house had been her home all her life—thirty-five out of thirty-nine years.

Imperfect as her life was, there was nowhere she would rather live.

She smiled to herself as she tugged the mailbox door open and was surprised to find it empty.

That's weird... I know I heard the mail truck.

She reached in to see if Sheila had pushed the mail to the back, out of view. Her hand had not yet reached the back of the mailbox when the ground rumbled as a blast of hot, smoky air flung her backwards like a rag doll and slammed her against the pavement.

Momentarily blinded by the explosion, she lay still in the eerie silence, coughing and struggling to breathe amid a cloud of dust and debris. Panic zinged through her veins.

Once she caught her breath, she focused on what her brain insisted she'd just seen. She recalled a flash, but couldn't reconstruct what had caused it.

The shifting wind cleared the air little by little, and a few minutes later, when she could finally see across her yard, she choked on a mix of despair and lingering particulates. Her house was now nothing but a pile of mangled siding, broken glass, and smoking embers. A foul taste coated her tongue and in seconds, the edges of her vision went fuzzy. Light-headed, she watched her surroundings tunnel to a prick of light as the darkness swallowed her.

When her eyes blinked open again, she was sprawled in the middle of her street, her limbs heavy. She sat up slowly and inspected her hands, which were raw and scraped. Domino was nuzzling her head against Ella's arm. She could feel the vibration of the cat's purr, but heard nothing. She noted that fact but, being completely overstimulated, simply filed it away for future analysis.

She brushed her palms together, and the tiny pebbles that had embedded themselves in her skin when she'd hit the ground fell away, revealing pinpricks of blood. Somehow, she didn't feel them.

A fine layer of gray powder floated down, covering her and everything else like newly fallen snow. Spots of red showed on her arms where her skin had been broken. Swiping a finger across a small area above her wrist, she exposed a strip of bare skin, but whatever was falling through the air quickly covered it again.

Raising her eyes, she held up a hand to catch the weightless powder. The mysterious substance's slow-motion descent was beautiful—until it hit her that this was ash made from the remains of her house and all her belongings. Bile rose in her throat, and she brushed her hands together, trying in vain to clean them. She closed her eyes to shut it out, but the explosion replayed behind her eyelids.

Ella took another deep breath, sucking in a mouthful of ash and doubling over coughing. She imagined her possessions burning one by one. The teddy bear she'd had since birth. The vividly colored landscape paintings that had been her mother's specialty. The long letter her father had written to her the day before he died. The delicate fan she'd brought back from a family trip to Japan. The lavender blanket she'd knitted amid her grief years ago. And maybe worst of all, every single one of her family photos. She'd grown up before digital pictures, and hadn't scanned most of hers, so they were irreplaceable. With every item she envisioned on fire, the imaginary knife twisted tighter in her chest.

She opened her eyes and turned away from the pile of rubble where her house had been. Miss Rosa was standing on her porch across the street, gaping at the scene. The older woman's lips moved, but Ella heard nothing.

Sirens wailed in the distance, the first sound to pierce the silence in her head since the explosion.

"Whoa, Miss Ella, are you okay? Let me help you out of the street."

The voice was faint and wobbly, as if it came from underwater. She raised her head to find Mason, a high school senior who lived a few houses down, towering over her. The faces of several other neighbors bobbed behind him, concern etched in their frowns. Mason helped her to her feet, wrapping an arm around her back to help her limp to the curb in front of Miss Rosa's house. After lowering her to the ground, he kneeled in front of her, his face creased with worry.

"What happened?"

Her ears still weren't working right, and the murmurs of her neighbors wavered like a videoconference with a faulty microphone. When she replied, too loudly, her own voice sounded strange to her. "I don't know."

Domino appeared out of nowhere, pressing herself against Ella's side until she unconsciously stroked her soft fur.

Mason looked around, bewildered. "I just got home from school and heard the explosion." His gaze moved from her face to her temple.

Inside her head, the blast played on repeat. If he said anything else, she didn't hear him.

She spoke haltingly, her voice still too loud. "I reached into my mailbox, and... my house... blew up." She closed her eyes again and took a deep breath, this time getting clearer air. Beside her, Domino mewed.

When she opened her eyes, Mason was staring over his shoulder at what had been her house. The mob of spectators had grown, their focus split between her and the wreckage.

Mason turned back to Ella, frowning at her temple. "Looks like something got you pretty good there. Does it hurt?"

"What?" She touched her forehead, pulling her hand back when she felt wetness. The sight of her own blood on her fingertips made her inhale sharply.

Mason repeated himself, louder this time. "Does it hurt?"

Ella stared at her fingers in confusion, then wiped them on her jeans. "No. Not at all."

While she was not in physical pain, an intense ache radiated through her. She'd experienced heartbreak many times before, but never like this.

The sirens had been a distant hum a moment before, but now they screamed, announcing their arrival and drowning out everything else. Domino ducked out from under her hand, fleeing down the sidewalk, away from the noise.

She folded her arms across her knees, let her forehead drop against her arms, and tuned out everything and everyone around her. But this wasn't better, because in her mind, all she saw was a never-ending loop of her house blowing up.

When she raised her head, she noticed the stain her wounded forehead had left on her sleeve, and the pounding inside her came louder and faster.

Emergency vehicles' flashing lights and radio chatter from their drivers' walkie talkies had replaced the screaming sirens. Several police cars were now parked down the street, and a fire truck had mercifully pulled up to block the sight of her property. Sadly, there wasn't much for the firefighters to do but douse water on the smoldering mess.

If there's anything left that the explosion didn't destroy, the water is ruining it.

An ambulance came to a stop along the curb, and the sea of neighbors parted to allow the EMTs to get to her. Mason stood up and joined the mass of spectators.

"Ma'am, are you alright?" She peered up at a young man with close cropped hair and a freckled, redheaded woman closer to her own age.

"Let's get you checked out," the man said soothingly when Ella didn't respond. She told her muscles to nod, but they didn't comply.

"Was anyone in the house?" the woman asked.

"No," she said weakly.

Crime scene tape now marked the perimeter of her yard, and the flashing lights of the many first responders' vehicles combined into a blinding kaleidoscope. Police vans, unmarked cars, black SUVs and various emergency vehicles blocked the road and part of the sidewalk.

A middle-aged police officer approached and looked squarely at Ella. "Ma'am, are you the owner of this house?" He gestured toward the pile of rubble.

She gave him her statement, and he took her cell phone number and promised to be in touch. As he walked away, she realized her number was no longer connected to a phone, but didn't have the energy to call him back.

"Let's get you to the hospital," the younger EMT said, snapping her back to reality. "Head injuries are nothing to take lightly."

The ambulance doors slammed, limiting her view of the outside world. It was a relief to be inside this compact vehicle, where the flashing lights were much dimmer and the commotion was muted. She watched the familiar streets of her neighborhood out the back window of the ambulance as she waited to wake up from the nightmare that refused to end.

Chapter 3
Ella

FRIDAY

ALMOST AN HOUR LATER, Ella had made it through the waiting area and triage room, and now lay in a double room on the third floor in a short-sleeved hospital gown. She was being kept overnight for observation, which was fine because it wasn't as though she had anywhere else to go. Apparently not only did she have a head injury, but she had symptoms of shock.

The other occupant of the narrow space snored softly behind the curtain a few feet away. Under normal circumstances, Ella hated needles, but when a nurse came in and put an IV in her arm, she didn't even flinch.

Closing her eyes, she begged to wake up in her own house.

The volume on the TV on the wall was low, playing some outdoorsy reality show. She welcomed the show's mindless distraction, because noise happening outside her head was exactly what she needed to distract her from the noise inside her head.

Before leaving the room, the nurse pointed to the phone beside the bed, telling her how to reach an outside line, then showed her the buzzer behind her head to call the nurses' station.

Sure, I could call someone. If all their numbers weren't stored in my phone. If Mal hadn't stopped speaking to me twenty years ago—not that I've ever had her phone number. If Mom and Dad were still around. If I wanted a thousand-question inquiry from any of my neighbors. If Caitlyn hadn't just left for two weeks in Greece and wasn't too busy to talk to me even when she's here.

With a heavy sigh, she reminded herself that she was perfectly okay on her own, and she had been for a long time. *Still, it would be nice to have someone who cared that I was here.*

After a visit from another serious-faced police officer, she leaned back against her pillow, too exhausted to feel anything. She turned onto her side and dropped into a fitful sleep.

Less than two hours later, she woke to a rustling at her bedside.

"Good morning. Sorry, I didn't mean to wake you," said a nurse in light blue scrubs. This was not the same woman who'd asked her to rate her pain and given her ibuprofen two hours before. Ella smiled, already drifting off again when the nurse's voice pulled her attention back from the brink of sleep.

"I want you to have this," the woman whispered. She closed a simple, silver bracelet with a flower charm around Ella's wrist. "I just lost my daughter. She was about your age, and you look so much like her. I bought this for her, but..." The woman sniffled, forcing a watery smile.

"Oh no, I couldn't take that." Ella shook her head.

"Please," said the woman, who was growing fuzzier by the second as Ella drifted back to sleep. "It would mean a lot to me."

Not having the energy to argue, Ella gave in tiredly. "Okay. Thank you."

As the nurse opened the door, Ella heard her say to someone, "She's awake. You can talk to her now. But please make it quick."

Ella opened her eyes again and looked up as a man in navy pants and a white button-down shirt stepped inside her hospital room and closed the door. The tailored fit of his clothes went in direct opposition to the state of his hair, which stuck up at odd angles, as if he'd recently woken up from a nap. It was too dark to call blonde, but too light to call brown.

His blue eyes fixed on her with an intensity that forbade her from looking away. For a few seconds, she forgot her inner turmoil, her surroundings fading into the background. Even though he wasn't smiling, his focused attention on her made her heart beat a little harder. A voice in her head exclaimed, "That man has good face karma!" A pang of sadness hit her squarely in her chest then, because that had been one of her mother's favorite ways to say that someone was attractive.

Ella guessed that he was in his early forties, though the bags under his eyes could have skewed her estimate. Looking at him, it was clear that he was long overdue for a good night's sleep. He walked right up to the edge of the bed, unblinking, and she was annoyed to realize that based on the heat in her cheeks, she was probably blushing.

Get a hold of yourself! He's probably from the insurance company. A claims adjuster or something. He's not here to flirt with you.

"Annabella Madson?"

His voice was deeper than she'd expected, and she chastised herself for liking the way he said her name with a growl. This was not at all who she was. Whose personality had she suddenly stolen?

"Yes. Call me Ella, please."

She was trying to psych herself up to discuss the loss of every piece of her personal property and not to focus on the fact that he was standing unapologetically inside her personal space, but she was finding it hard to focus on anything when he smelled so good. Like cedar and sandalwood and some kind of sweet fruit.

He took out what looked like a black leather wallet and flipped it open. "I'm Sam Donnelly, with the FBI. The Bureau has taken over the investigation of the explosion at your house because of potential connections with another case, which has national security implications. I have some questions for you."

She stiffened. *FBI? National security implications?*

"Where were you on Wednesday morning between 4:30 and 5:30 am?"

For half a second, she couldn't remember, even though the answer would've been the same no matter what day it was. "Um, I was at home, asleep. Like I am every day at that time."

"Can anyone verify that?"

"What?" she asked, taken aback. "Verify that I was sleeping in my own bed? No. I live alone. No one else was there... Not that that's any of your business." She took deep breaths to calm the emotional whiplash of switching from attraction to anger within seconds.

He watched her without blinking, as if she might bolt the moment he looked away. "Just before 5:00 on Wednesday morning, there was a break-in at a data security firm in Reston, Virginia. They have large contracts with several government agencies. A team of three people broke in, killed a security guard, and hacked into the system. They stole over ten million dollars. Do you know anything about this?"

"What? No, of course not! Why would I know anything about that?"

He crossed his arms over his chest, looking smug. "Maybe you were a part of it, and someone wanted to get back at you."

She stared at him open-mouthed, eyes catching on his muscular forearms before narrowing her eyes at his stupid, skeptical, and annoyingly attractive face. "What are you talking about? Why would you think I'd do something like that?" The heat in her cheeks now was caused by annoyance. Mostly.

"You're a match for the woman we captured on CCTV footage near the scene of the crime. I don't suppose you can explain that?"

"What? No. I can't be. I was..."

Oh.

It had been so long since Mal had caused her trouble, she'd forgotten what it felt like.

She sighed heavily, indignation draining out of her. *Not this again.* When she continued, she sounded tired.

"I have a younger sister, Mallory. We're not twins, but people always thought we were. Because she could pass for me, one of her favorite hobbies was making my life miserable. She was the poster child for juvenile delinquents. By the time she graduated from high school, her criminal record was a mile long. Breaking and entering, DUI, assault and battery, drugs... Probably more. I'm surprised the FBI has never come to ask me about her before. I guess she hasn't changed."

Ella checked the bedside table for her phone out of habit, forgetting briefly that it was gone. "If I had my phone, I'd show you a picture of how alike we were, but... it was blown up with everything else." Slumping back against the pillow behind her, she deflated.

Agent Donnelly's expression was unreadable, but his accusatory glare softened.

Annoyingly, it made him even more handsome. "I see," he said.

For several long seconds, she stared at this man whose features seemed to be made of stone. It was a shame that his good looks were wasted on someone so grumpy. Then again, wasn't that always the way it was? The hot ones were always moody, at best.

"Her name is Mallory? Last name Madson?" he asked, making notes on a small pad of paper.

"Yes." The accusation in his voice had faded, and his stare was making her blush again.

"What else can you tell me about her?"

"Her hair was always a little straighter than mine. Her eyes were lighter brown. She liked it when I was mistaken for her, because it bothered me, so she went out of her way to copy my hairstyle so she'd look as much like me as possible. That way, she could claim she wasn't the guilty one if someone spotted her."

He let out a long sigh. "Is there any chance you could tell me anything useful?" She stared in surprise at his sudden rudeness. Taking his tone down only a fraction, he added, "Did you ever take advantage of your resemblance in the same way?"

Ella scoffed. "No!" When he raised an eyebrow, she added softly, "Looking like her wasn't an advantage for me."

"Is there a reason you're talking about her in the past tense? Is she dead?"

"Not that I know of. But we don't talk anymore."

"Why not?"

"Does she sound like someone you'd want to keep in touch with?" she snapped, immediately regretting it. Antagonizing him wasn't going to help her, no matter how annoying he was.

She focused on her lap, but his stare bored into her.

He cleared his throat. "So, as you stated, you cannot account for your whereabouts between 4:30 and 5:30 am on Wednesday. Is that correct?"

"No! I can tell you exactly where I was. At home. Asleep. By myself. Because I live alone. Is that a crime now?"

"And your sister... do you think she did it?"

Ella sighed. "Don't get me wrong, she was horrible as a kid. I don't know if she'd go so far as to blow up my house." At least, she wanted to believe that Mal wouldn't go that far.

"She was a juvenile delinquent." It was a statement, not a question. "And by your own admission, you don't know her as an adult."

"That's true." Despite their painful history, she hated the feeling that she was betraying Mal all over again. She'd done it once before, years ago, and she still blamed herself for Mal's downward spiral afterwards.

Glaring up at him, she said, "I don't know what you want me to tell you." She stared into his annoyingly chiseled features, searching for a hint of humanity. He'd shown only faint glimmers of it so far, but enough for her to see that it might be in there somewhere. Deep, deep down.

He frowned and patted his pockets, his face creasing in annoyance, appearing to have lost something. Finally he pulled his phone out of his back pocket and tapped the screen, typing for several seconds before turning it off again. "I'm going to check into this sister of yours. I'll be in touch." He started toward the door.

"Wait!" She cringed at the desperation in her voice, and he turned back to her, his disinterest changing to impatience.

He let out an exaggerated sigh. "What?"

"I have nowhere to go when they discharge me. What am I supposed to do?" Her voice broke on her last few words, and she gritted her teeth, hating to be so vulnerable around someone who was so impossibly cold.

His hands clenched at his sides and for a second, she swore emotion flashed in his eyes, but his hands relaxed and the spark disappeared before she could identify it. "That's not my department," he said. "I'm sure someone else will work that out for you." He stared at her for a beat as if he'd paused mid-thought, then added, with a touch less hostility, "If I find out anything else, I'll be back."

Was that a threat? A promise? And what if he didn't find out anything else? The urge to throw something at him overtook her, but the door had already closed behind him. Grabbing a pillow from behind her, she pressed her face into it and screamed until she ran out of air. Her frustration morphed into tears, the trickle quickly becoming a torrent. Turning over on her side, she pulled herself into a ball, crying into her pillow.

Over the next three hours, her waking moments were filled with worry about her future and how and why her house had blown up. It could have been as innocent as a gas leak, after all... if she'd had gas lines running to her house. That left either mysterious "natural causes," or an intentionally planted explosive device. It wouldn't have been Mal. It *couldn't* have...

From the time she closed her eyes and then as she teetered over the edge into sleep, she watched the only home she'd ever known being blown to bits again and again. In her dreams, there were variations. Sometimes she was inside the house, or she was outside but saw Mal, or even one or both her parents, through a window, burning up in the explosion before her eyes.

She was immensely grateful for every one of the doctors' and nurses' sporadic visits, which woke her enough to pull her out of her dreams. Unsurprisingly, her frame of mind was unsteady at best when Agent Donnelly reappeared hours later, opening the door without attempting to be quiet—though he at least had the decency to look sheepish for a few seconds when she jolted awake at the noise.

He skipped any greetings. "I looked into the explosion at your house." Despite his less than friendly tone, a light in his eyes kept her from looking away. "It's still early, but it looks like it was intentionally set. Arson investigations take days, or even weeks, but I'm working on getting it expedited." He narrowed his eyes at her. "Did you do it? You may as well tell me now, because I will find out." He spoke without a hint of irony or sarcasm. "You'd save us all a lot of trouble by admitting it."

"What? No! Of course I didn't do it." Her skin flushed with anger all over again. "Is that what you think of me?"

"It's just a question. I don't know you."

His expression was perfectly blank. Detached. She glared at him, but he ignored her and kept talking.

"I believe you know more than you think you do. I'd like us to have a lengthy chat, so I'll need you to come in for questioning. There are too many distractions here." As if to prove his point, there was a crash of metal hitting the floor and raised voices from the hall.

She started at the noise, turning toward the door, and then back to him. "What? Now? It's not even morning yet!"

"You're not badly injured. You won't be here long. We need to make progress on this case as soon as possible."

Ella exhaled slowly. "Do I need a lawyer?"

"You're not under arrest. We just need to know exactly what you know."

She swallowed her annoyance. "Fine. It's not as though I have anything to hide. But I'm not cleared to leave here yet. The doctor I saw wanted me to stay overnight, and after that, I don't know. You'll have to take that up with him."

With a slight nod, he stood up and headed for the door. "I'll do that." Without another look back, he was gone again.

Ella willed the tension to follow him out, but the agent's impatient words had poisoned the air, remaining even after he was gone.

Eventually, she stopped listening for his return and focused on the small TV screen across the room, which was now playing a program about aliens. Her roommate snored softly from the other side of the room, and Ella's eyes soon drooped as well.

It felt like seconds later when rays of sunshine poked at her eyelids, as if the sun was being aimed directly into her eyes and held there to intensify. She turned her head to escape it and heard a grunt from the direction she was now facing.

"Wake up."

She'd only met him the day before, but she already prickled at the sound of Agent Donnelly's voice.

Ella opened her eyes slowly, squinting at the overhead lights, to find him in the chair beside her bed. The clock read 6:30 am.

She was still processing being awake when he started talking.

"I flipped through your case for connections between your sister and the explosion. I conferred with a colleague at the fire department—"

She rubbed her eyes. "In the middle of the night?"

His jaw tightened and he ran a hand through his hair.

That explains how it got so messy.

"Our work doesn't stop for beauty sleep, princess. Anyway, the charges that were detonated at your house were highly specialized."

"What does that mean?"

"That means they're used for very specific purposes, so only a few people have any reason to buy them. That should make it easier to follow the trail. If I find your arsonist, I might also find my thief." When she didn't answer, he added, "So like it or not, you're stuck with me."

She'd been awake all of two minutes, and this day had already gone from bad to worse.

Chapter 4
Mal

U SUALLY SHE LIKED THE chaos of airports, but ever since Bri had failed to meet them at their agreed-upon spot at noon, Mal had not relaxed. Bri wasn't answering her phone, either. It wasn't that Mal thought the third member of their trio would've ratted them out for the data breach job they'd pulled off two days before, but the uncertainty of the situation made her glad that she and Jimmy were on their way out of town. He attracted enough attention even on a normal day with his whole '80s UK cyber punk look—complete with the spiked hair, leather jacket, and British accent.

Those had been the things that had attracted her to him in the first place, that night in the tiny London club, and once she'd found out what he did for a living it had been all over for her. He was sexy, annoyingly smart, and had plenty of plans that would make him—and her, if she stuck around as his "muscle"—very rich. Sure, cybercrime was illegal, but it wasn't as though she'd never been on the wrong side of the law before, and Jimmy knew what he was doing.

His unique look and accent, which she liked so much, were the same things that made him stand out rather easily in a crowd, however. It would be safer to be off the radar for a while. Bri was probably with Ray, as usual.

Mal's foot tapped impatiently against the dull gray carpeting until Jimmy rested his hand on her knee to still it. When the college student across from them smacked his companion in the arm and gasped, "Whoa, look at that," Mal turned, already panicking.

She didn't find a stampede of police on their way to pick them up, as she'd feared. Instead, on a large TV monitor, video footage zoomed in on a pile of rubble. The closed captions flashed across the screen as the camera panned farther out, and Mal's brown eyes opened wide.

"Shit," she said under her breath.

"What's wrong?" Jimmy followed Mal's gaze towards the monitor. "Where's that?"

Mal was too busy reading the text to respond.

"A fiery explosion shook Rockville, Maryland this afternoon, when a two-story house on the 2500 block of Warfield Drive exploded without warning. There were no fatalities in the blast, though the owner, who was not inside at the time, was transported to a local hospital with minor injuries. She is reported to be in stable condition. The investigation is ongoing, and authorities would not speculate on the cause."

After only a few more seconds on the screen, the picture disappeared and the news report moved on to the next story.

"That's the house where I grew up. Or it was," said Mal.

"Well, good thing you weren't living there anymore, right?" He said it as if it was a joke, and Mal had to bite her tongue to stop from snapping at him. She'd mailed those dice to Ella at that address just the week before, and the house had been perfectly intact when she'd set the box on the doorstep that morning.

"I haven't set foot in that house since my parents died. That was almost twenty years ago." It was technically not a lie, since she hadn't actually gone farther than the porch that morning.

Was Ella the one who'd gone to the hospital?

He kissed her on the cheek. "So, where are we going?" Jimmy's eyes darted to the boarding pass on his phone, eyebrows raised. "Why Michigan, of all places?"

Pushing the past out of her mind, Mal lowered her voice and said, "There's a lake in northwestern Michigan where we used to go when I was a kid. My grandparents owned a house there. It's a tiny town. I have a friend who got us a place there under her name. We can stay until things cool down."

Jimmy tensed. "What friend?"

"Don't worry. She has no idea what I do now." She leaned in to whisper, "It's under control," then gave him a kiss that did not belong in an airport, ignoring the murmurs of disapproval from other travelers.

Mal scanned the other waiting passengers, but no one looked out of place. When she turned to check the row behind them, a man in a baseball cap looked up from his phone, eyeing her up and down. She gave him a flirtatious smile before turning away to reassure Jimmy once again that everything was fine.

Chapter 5
Mal and Ella

AGES 4 AND 5
(34 YEARS AGO)

A S THE HAZY SUNSHINE of mid-summer morning beat down on them, two little girls chased each other around the otherwise empty playground. The older one's dark hair stuck out in long pigtails on the sides of her head while the younger one's low ponytail of the same color was halfway out of its elastic. A thick layer of sunblock gave both girls' fair complexions a ghostly hue.

Nearby, a young mother rested her head on her hand, her elbow propped against the back of the worn wooden bench. She watched them, squinting against the sunlight and sipping coffee from a travel mug as if the caffeine it contained would solve all her problems. Late July days were hot and humid in Maryland, so Valerie Madson brought her girls outside early to burn off their endless energy.

"Count to twenty!" shrieked Mal with delight. As soon as her older sister closed her eyes and started counting, Mal put down a scrap of paper at Ella's feet and ran to the far side of the play set. Instead of just crouching, she flattened herself on the ground, burrowing into the mulch and squeezing herself under the end of the structure.

The first time they'd done this, their mother had been both confused about where Mal had gotten the drawing and concerned that she would end up hurt. However, while most of their other games dissolved into screaming and occasionally punching, if not worse, to Valerie's amusement, they got along while playing this one.

"Find me!" yelled Mal, unable to wait while Ella counted all the way to twenty, as instructed.

To Ella's credit, she acted genuinely surprised to find Mal every time, even when Mal insisted they play five or more times in a row and always hid in the same spot.

"Mal! Come up here!" called Ella from the platform, only three feet off the ground. "I'm on a pirate ship!"

Mal scrambled up the stairs to join her. "Is that a whale?" Ella pointed into the distance. For a few seconds, they squinted at the horizon.

"No!" Mal said excitedly. "It's a shark! And more sharks! It must be their family reunion!" The girls had recently been to their father's family reunion, and consequently, every large gathering was now a family reunion.

"Oh no," said Ella.

"I'm going to swim with them!" Mal hopped up and down.

"Ella, don't let Mal jump off the edge." It was a vain hope that Ella could stop Mal from doing anything she decided to do. The younger girl had always been a daredevil.

As predicted, Mallory bent her knees and launched herself into the air, yelling, "Here I come, sharks!" Their mother crossed the playground in seconds, but not fast enough to prevent her daughter's face-first landing in the mulch.

"Mal, are you okay? Are you hurt?"

The younger girl rolled over, a grin plastered across her face. "That was awesome! I'm a shark now, too!"

Valerie sighed with relief. Mal would give her a heart attack one of these days.

"Ella!" Mal called from the ground. "Come swim with your shark family! It's so much fun!"

Ever the cautious one, Ella took a step back from the edge of the low play structure.

"Come on! Don't be a chicken!" When Ella didn't move, Mal squawked at the top of her lungs. "Bawk bawk! Chicken chicken! The sharks will eat the chicken."

Ella's face scrunched in determination, and a second later, she launched herself off the platform and landed unsteadily in front of Mal. Before Ella could get her balance, she tipped forward and landed with all her weight on Mal's stomach. Predictably, Mal screamed. She grabbed Ella by the legs, clawing at her as Ella tried to kick her away.

Valerie wiggled in between her daughters, who were now wrestling in the mulch. Most of their games devolved into something like this, so she hadn't been far away.

"Mommy! She jumped on me!" Mal sputtered between sobs as she lashed out, trying to retaliate.

Ella shrieked as well. "It's not *my* fault! You told me to jump!"

"Mallory! Annabella! Stop it or we will not come back to this park."

This got their attention—the park was one of their favorite destinations. They sprang apart, though Ella slapped Mal on the shoulder one more time for good measure.

"Enough!" said Valerie, before they could start again. "Stand up."

Both girls got to their feet slowly, glaring at the other. Mal stuck her tongue out at Ella, which made Ella stick her tongue out in return.

"Tongues in, or those tongues will get no ice cream for a week."

Both tongues went back in.

"Now, what do we say? Ella?"

Ella huffed dramatically. "I'm sorry for falling on you. It was an accident."

Their mother nodded. "Very good. Mal?"

"I'm sorry."

"For what?" Valerie asked.

"For calling you a chicken."

"Put it together."

"I'm sorry for calling you a chicken."

"Anything else?"

"For... attacking you like a shark?"

It was close enough.

"In a sentence, please," said their mother.

"I'm sorry for attacking you like a shark."

"Better. And who should apologize for fighting?"

Ella and Mal pointed at each other with equal seriousness, and it took a lot of willpower for Valerie not to smile. The girls were covered in mulch, their eyes wide, convinced they were innocent. Valerie wished she could have taken their picture.

"You should both apologize."

Their identical glare reflected between them until Mal muttered, "Sorry for fighting," and before she'd finished, Ella was repeating it back to her.

"Let's go home and get you two cleaned up," said Valerie.

"In the pool?" asked Mal. The girls would spend all day in their blow-up pool if allowed, though they'd probably try to drown each other at least once. Valerie shook her head.

"No, in the bathtub. If you want to go in the pool, you need to get along nicely for three hours. In a row. And take a nap first."

Each girl took one of their mother's hands as they started for home. As they crossed the grass and the concrete plaza beyond it, they discussed for the thousandth time what they thought the abstract statue at the center of the plaza looked like, and after that, the terms of their required three hours of peace.

Chapter 6

Ella

SATURDAY

AFTER BEING RELEASED FROM the hospital and a tense ride to FBI headquarters, Agent Donnelly unlocked a stark white room with a metal table in the center. From what she'd seen on TV, Ella assumed it was an interrogation room.

"Have a seat. I'll be right back," he said behind her as she took a step over the threshold into the room. For once, his tone was almost friendly, but before she could turn around in surprise to look at him, the door slammed and he was gone. A startled whimper escaped her.

She examined the room as she slowly walked to the table. A mirrored window filled one wall, and she imagined numerous agents watching her from the other side. Cameras were mounted in the corners at the ceiling, pointed inward and down to record even the smallest movement. She wearily lowered herself into a chair.

So this is what it's like to sit inside a fishbowl.

Propping her elbows on the table, she put her head in her hands.

Her head snapped up when the door clicked loudly, swinging open as Agent Donnelly entered the room, looking as disheveled as he had the night before. His light brown hair stuck up unevenly, but not in an unattractive way. It made him look like he'd just rolled out of bed—

Okay, seriously, get a grip.

An older man walked in behind Agent Donnelly. The newcomer's charcoal hair was graying at the temples, with the odd lighter strands beginning to infiltrate the rest. He reminded her of her friend Caitlyn's father.

He looks a lot more like a high school guidance counselor than an FBI agent.

"Ms. Madson, I'm Agent Harrison. Agent Donnelly and I just need to ask you some questions." A few days before, she would've been surprised by his thick mid-western accent, but today she was just grateful for his lack of hostility.

"I assume you're the good cop."

Amusement flitted across Agent Harrison's face, but he did not respond. Agent Donnelly coughed, holding the side of his fist up to cover his mouth. He met her eyes with an expression that seemed to acknowledge the dig at him, after which he nodded slightly, blew out a breath through his mouth, and looked at the floor before fixing his eyes on her again.

Had he just called a truce? Or was she imagining it?

She looked back at Agent Harrison, who smiled at her. At least he seemed to understand the rules of professional interactions. "As I told Agent Donnelly, I really don't know anything else."

Agent Harrison leaned forward, nodding sympathetically. "I know it doesn't feel like it, but in our experience, people usually know more than they think. I understand that you've been over this a few times already, but if you could, please tell me exactly what happened yesterday. Start with what you were doing before the explosion."

Ella gave the same summary of the day preceding the explosion that she'd given to Agent Donnelly. At the end, she sniffled twice and paused before continuing. "I grew up in that house. I inherited it years ago when my parents died. Everything I owned was inside, and then it was all just... gone." She took a deep breath to steady herself.

Agent Harrison nodded sympathetically. He pushed a box of tissues towards her on the table, and she took one to dab at her eyes.

Agent Donnelly cleared his throat as if he was about to speak, but for a few seconds he just looked at her in silence. Something about his demeanor had changed. "I'm sorry," he said finally, but it came out in barely a whisper.

Agent Harrison looked at his partner, raised his eyebrows, and angled his head toward the door, but Agent Donnelly shook his head. With a shrug, Agent

Harrison turned back to Ella and started again. "You say you heard the post office vehicle?" He tapped the end of a pen against a file on the table.

"Yes."

"Is it possible that you actually heard something else?"

She paused to consider the question. "It's possible. It was a little early for the mail. Our mail carrier is usually prompt. But she's occasionally early, so I assumed..." She tilted her head, willing herself to remember the exact sound.

"Was there anything in the mailbox?" Agent Donnelly asked.

She answered slowly. "No, that was the strange thing. I swore I'd heard the mail truck."

"Do you usually collect the mail as soon as it arrives?" asked Agent Harrison.

"Not necessarily. But as I said, I was waiting for a check, so that day I was listening for it."

"What do you do for a living?" asked Agent Donnelly.

"I own an interior design company."

"So, Ms. Madson..." Agent Harrison checked his notes.

"Please call me Ella."

"Alright, Ella," said Agent Harrison patiently. "Let's look at this a different way. Would you say it's possible that it wasn't the postal vehicle you heard?"

"Yes... it's possible."

"Thank you for humoring me," he said. "Could you describe the sound?"

She narrowed her eyes, concentrating hard. "It was like... a squeak, but with a thump at the end. Now that you mention it, it wasn't as loud as the mail truck usually is." Closing her eyes, she replayed the moment, searching for another way to describe it.

"And are you certain the sound came from the front yard?" Agent Harrison's tone remained even and calm.

"Well, I assumed it did, because I thought it was the mail... but the windows were open in the front and the back, so I would've heard either. I'm not sure."

"According to a preliminary report, the blast was set in the back of the house. You didn't notice anything else unusual in the few days before the explosion?"

"No, I... Wait. Actually, yes." She thought for a moment, and both men leaned forward. "A few hours earlier, a contractor in a bright orange vest and hardhat rang my doorbell. I wouldn't have answered, but he rang it three times in a row, which made me assume it was important. He said he was from the water company and he asked to access my backyard. I was on the phone with my most important client, so I was only half listening. I waved him toward the gate."

"Your gate was unlocked?" asked Agent Harrison.

"Yes."

Agent Donnelly slapped the table hard enough to startle her. "You let a stranger into your yard? Unescorted? You didn't ask him for ID or what he was doing?"

Apparently the truce was over. Or there'd never been one.

Ella glared at him. "I had no reason to suspect him of anything! He said something about the water main in the backyard and flooding in my neighbor's yard. I don't live in a high crime neighborhood, and it's not as though I can see the future."

Underneath her defensiveness, she cringed at the thought that she might've been face to face with someone who had clearly meant her harm.

Agent Harrison held up both hands, one toward each of them. "Okay, let's take a breath."

Agent Donnelly stared down at his notes, jotting down unintelligible markings and grumbling to himself—the words "ridiculous" and "naïve" were the only ones Ella caught. She couldn't help but think of the only other person to have called her both those things to her face—Mal. Her sister had done much worse, though.

Ella's mind jumped backward to the time Mal had tried to strangle her when they were ten and eleven. As always, Mal had insisted that she wouldn't have gone through with it, and that she'd only been fooling around. Her parents hadn't known what to believe, but they'd taken Mal for yet another visit to the psychologist.

A few years before that, she'd held Ella's head underwater in the lake at their grandparents' summer house, though Mal had denied trying to kill her. That time they'd been young enough—seven and eight, maybe?—that their parents had chalked it up to a lack of understanding of cause and effect.

There had been a few other close calls, but their parents had dismissed them as sibling rivalry gone wrong—Ella failing to set a good example, and Mal having poor decision-making skills and wanting attention. They didn't seem to believe that either of the girls wished actual harm on the other. Ella shivered, pushing the memories away.

As the sound of blood thundering in her ears abated, she realized both men were watching her intently, waiting.

"Sorry. What was the question?"

"Do you have any enemies?"

She scoffed. "Enemies? I'm an interior designer. How would I..."

Agent Donnelly met her eyes, and she stopped talking, feeling ridiculous and indignant. "No," she shot back. "I don't have any enemies." Her tone told him exactly how ridiculous his question was.

Ella rubbed her temples, suddenly exhausted.

"You mentioned that you have a sister," said Agent Harrison. "Mallory Madson."

"Yes. We've had no contact in over twenty years. She has no reason to want me dead that she wouldn't have had all along."

He glanced up from his notepad. "Unless it's related to the data breach. Especially because someone who meets your description was spotted on the CCTV footage. And Mallory looks a lot like you." He slid a tablet across the table to her, on which Mal's enlarged driver's license photo scowled back at her. It was the first time she'd ever seen Mal as an adult, and it proved that they still looked eerily alike. Ella shivered, looking back up at the agents in front of her.

"We're very interested in talking to Mallory," said Agent Donnelly. His voice was calmer now. "Do you know where we can find her?"

"I haven't spoken to her in two decades. The place I used to find her was at my house, where we grew up, but she moved out when she graduated from high school, the year after I did. Where she is now, I have no idea."

"Why don't you tell us about Mallory?" said Agent Harrison. "Whatever you do know."

Chapter 7
Ella
SATURDAY

"MAL AND I NEVER got along. It went beyond sibling rivalry. I was no angel, and I'm sure she'd say I was the horrible one, but... no matter how cruel she was to me, she seemed like she was enjoying herself. It got worse and worse until..." She shook her head. She couldn't go there. Not yet.

"She was malicious towards everyone, not just me. She got herself in trouble with the police, too..." Ella looked at the floor, then back up to Agent Harrison, not giving in to the weight of Agent Donnelly's stare.

"What kind of trouble?" asked Agent Harrison quietly.

"I'm assuming you've seen her record. The first time the police picked her up, she was in middle school, but even in elementary school, she was always in trouble. I'm not even sure how many times the police had brought her home by the time she graduated—which she barely managed. When my mom died, I stopped getting updates, so I don't know what she's done as an adult."

"We pulled up her record. It's... extensive."

Ella scoffed. "That's a diplomatic way to say it." She studied the shiny metal table in front of her, pausing before she continued.

"Everything was a joke to her. And when something was important to me, she got a special, twisted pleasure out of taking it away. Including my boyfriend, when I was a senior in high school. I was no angel, and I sometimes antagonized her, but she had no conscience. It wouldn't surprise me if she preyed on other people the same way."

Agent Donnelly finally spoke up again. "If it was Mallory we saw on the CCTV cameras at the break in, her plan may be to frame you. Otherwise, it would be stupid of her to involve you at all. Not when it leaves us a trail to follow, and you're able to identify her. You might still be in danger."

"You think she's trying to frame me and then what? Kill me?"

"You can't tell your side of the story if you're dead," said Agent Donnelly. She looked up at him, startled by the bluntness of his statement. "She could leave you with the blame for whatever she did, and you wouldn't be there to defend yourself."

Ella was suddenly very tired, and she had the urge to curl up in a ball. Rehashing her childhood dysfunctional relationship with Mal was exhausting, but the thought that Mal still harbored so much malice towards her was even worse.

Can I really blame her, though?

She squinted at the agents skeptically, the wheels turning in her head. "Mal was always malicious and stubborn, but I wouldn't call her smart. I'm not sure she'd think of something like that. She was manipulative with a side of violence. My parents put us in self-defense class hoping it would instill discipline in her, but it backfired. She used those moves against anyone who pissed her off. It made her feel powerful. I can see her hurting people without a second thought, but she wouldn't be the one to plan some sort of heist or to blame it on someone else."

"Fair enough. But if she's working with a partner, they could be the brains behind the operation," said Agent Donnelly.

Agent Harrison made notes to himself, not looking up.

"I wish I could help you, but I've had no contact with my sister since the day I moved out twenty-one years ago. Even when I came home from college and she technically still lived there, I didn't see her—she'd disappear for days or weeks at a time. Didn't tell my parents where she was going. They barely saw her, either."

The older man frowned. "Any idea why your sister was so angry?"

Ella shrugged. "The million-dollar question. We fought a lot. Siblings fight, of course, but at some point it became more than that. She saw bad in everyone, even if it didn't exist. The few times she seemed well-adjusted, she was pretending so she could get something."

"Did she stop speaking to your parents as well?"

"No. She needed them to bail her out—both out of jail and financially—from time to time. But she was horrible to them. I hated that they let her treat them like that, but I guess they kept hoping she'd come around." Ella stopped, remembering how many times she'd heard her mother agonize over where she'd gone wrong with Mallory.

"And you've had no contact with her in all those years?" Agent Donnelly looked skeptical.

"No. But she likes to... send me things."

Agent Harrison opened his mouth, looking interested, but before he could ask a follow up question, Agent Donnelly snapped, "I thought you said you'd had no contact!"

Ella sighed loudly, clenching her fists. "It's only one-way. She sends me things. Sometimes it's a postcard with a random picture, sometimes it's an actual object. We used to play this game when we were kids. My mom had just read us Hansel and Gretel, so Mal called it The Breadcrumb Game. It was like hide-and-seek but with clues. Her clues were the breadcrumbs. She'd leave me a clue, sometimes a few clues, and expect me to find her. Sometimes they were just normal things. A pile of blueberries meant she was hiding by the blueberry plant in the backyard. Sometimes it was... not normal. Once it was my Barbie doll's head."

Agent Harrison coughed, his eyebrows raised. "What did that mean?"

"That Mal was in my toy box."

Agent Donnelly cleared his throat. "What do you do when she sends you these trinkets?"

"Nothing. I throw them away. She wants to manipulate me, but I'm not playing her game. If she wants to talk to me, she knows where to find me..." The words were already out of her mouth when she realized what she'd said, and hopelessness hit her all over again. "...or she did before the house blew up."

Agent Donnelly looked skeptical. "You never engaged with her? Even once?"

"No! Would it matter? I'm not the one blowing up people's houses."

Making notes in the file in front of him, Agent Donnelly said nothing.

A loud buzz broke the silence, and Agent Donnelly pulled out his phone, standing quickly. "Excuse me for a minute."

Once the door closed behind him, Ella relaxed in her chair, some of the tension leaving her shoulders.

Agent Harrison gave her a knowing smile. "You're doing great, Ella. Can you think of anything else that might help us?"

"I wish I could tell you something more than, 'My sister is a criminal who was a nightmare to grow up with and likes to send me random crap because she thinks it's funny.' But like I said, I don't even know her as an adult. Every once in a while I read a news article about a crime and wonder if she was involved, but nothing more than that." She couldn't meet his eyes, knowing how pathetic it sounded that she didn't know her own sister.

"Your parents are deceased?"

"Yes. My dad had cancer, and my mom had a heart attack. Both within a few years after I graduated from college... a long time ago." A sigh escaped her. Even after so many years, the sadness pressed on her from all directions.

"I'm sorry. Do you have any other siblings?"

Ella shook her head.

"Any other close family members?"

"No. My grandparents have all been gone for a while. My dad was an only child, and my mom's only sister died in a car accident ten years ago. I get a card from my uncle and my cousins at Christmas, but that's it. They live in North Dakota, and we don't really keep in touch. I have neighbors I've known all my life, but... I wouldn't say I'm close to them." She shrugged.

"That sounds lonely," said Agent Harrison.

She inhaled a shaky breath. She worked hard to be happy with what she had. Okay, she wasn't close to anyone, and yes, most people thought that was something to be pitied. As far as she was concerned, though, that was the best way to protect herself, so it had been a conscious decision. She'd had people she was close to in the past, and losing them had almost crushed her. She couldn't bear the thought of it happening again.

"Yeah," she whispered. Pressing her lips tightly together, she tried and failed to smile.

The door opened, and Agent Donnelly stepped halfway into the room. "This is Agent Donna Tipton, our sketch artist. She's going to use your description of the contractor who came to your door to create a sketch of him. We'll see if we can ID him that way."

Agent Harrison moved toward the door as a woman with grey hair cut into a stylish bob stepped in. An aura of calm surrounded her.

"You really think he was the one who blew up my house?" Ella glanced back and forth between Agents Harrison and Donnelly.

"It's too early to say anything except that he's a lead we need to follow up on," said Agent Donnelly. The lack of impatience in his voice caught her attention. "We'll see what happens when we run his sketch through facial recognition."

Donna smiled warmly. "Thank you, Sam. Don't stay on my account. I know you have work to do." To Ella, she said, "It's nice to meet you, Ella. Please call me Donna."

"Nice to meet you, too," Ella said, looking past the woman as the men moved toward the door. Agent Donnelly stopped in the doorway and looked back at her over his shoulder, and for a few seconds they held eye contact before he followed Agent Harrison out of the room. The door clicking loudly behind him and she returned her attention to the woman in front of her.

Agent Tipton took the chair Agent Donnelly had vacated and laid a sketchpad on the table.

"You don't do this on the computer?" asked Ella, glancing down at the paper.

"The new tools have their uses, but I prefer the old-fashioned way," said Donna. "Now, Ella, why don't you tell me as much as you can about the man who came to your door?"

Ella shuddered as her mind replayed the explosion again before she could direct it back to the contractor.

"I know this is difficult for you," said Donna, leaning forward across the table. "Just take a deep breath."

Ella nodded, centering herself and focusing on the hazy memory of the man. "I'm sorry. The day I saw him, I didn't know there would be a quiz."

Donna chuckled, and Ella cleared her mind, trying to see the man's features one at a time. "He was a few inches taller than me. He had a long face, light eyes... and a scar on his cheek."

Donna sketched as Ella talked. The agent asked questions about the man's appearance, and even when Ella had only vague answers, she didn't show a hint of sarcasm or annoyance. She asked Ella to look through a book with different facial structures and features. Now and then, she asked her to pick the image where the shape of the jaw or forehead looked the most like the man's. Even with these aids, Ella doubted the sketch would look like the man had in person.

Ella didn't watch Donna's progress. She just kept talking until several hours later, when Donna turned the sketchbook over on the table. "I think that just about does it."

The tension in Ella's shoulders eased, and she sighed with relief; but it was short-lived. "I'm going to have to look at it, aren't I?"

"Well, yes, but we can wait until the others come back. You deserve a break. Do you need anything? Maybe something to drink?" Donna tapped the screen of her phone quickly and then turned it off.

"No, thank you. I'm okay," Ella said quietly. She didn't really feel okay, but she didn't want the agent to go to any trouble for her.

They chatted for a few minutes, until the door creaked open and Agents Harrison and Donnelly returned.

"So, how'd it go?" asked Agent Harrison.

"Quite well, I think. Though Ella will have the final say on that," said Donna.

Agent Donnelly looked at Ella with interest, but before he could speak, Donna added, "I haven't shown her yet." To Ella, Donna said, "Remember, it's only a sketch. Just look long enough to tell us if it's a usable likeness, then you never have to see it again. Okay?"

Ella blew out a breath and nodded. It was only a sketch to them. To her, it could be the sketch of the person who'd stolen her whole life from her. She braced herself, clenching her teeth.

Donna turned the notebook over and laid it on the table in front of Ella, and for a few seconds, her other senses dulled and everything around her disappeared. The image was so accurate, it sent shivers down her back. "That's him," she said, looking away quickly.

"Great," said Agent Harrison. "We'll see what facial recognition turns up. Thanks again, Donna. Especially for being available on such short notice." He stood up and walked with her to the door.

Agent Donnelly sat down across from Ella, watching her even as she avoided his eyes. "Are you okay?" he asked.

For the first time ever, she heard actual concern in his voice, and she looked up at him in surprise.

Agent Harrison settled himself at the table once again before she could respond. He flipped through his notes, but Agent Donnelly continued to watch her, waiting for an answer. She looked up at him and they watched each other. It was only when she nodded slightly that he glanced at his partner, apparently satisfied, then back at her.

"Agent Harrison and I are with a specialized division of the FBI investigating a network of assassins."

Her eyebrows shot up. "A network of *assassins*?" she asked slowly. She was starting to feel like she was in a spy movie. "So you think...?"

Agent Donnelly shook his head. "Right now, we don't know. Our team has been analyzing the data we've collected so far. The explosion at your property gave us reason to believe that an organization we call The Network may be involved. And with the connection between you and Mal, and Mal and the data breach... we're still working out how it's all related, assuming that it is. We'd like to put you into protective custody for your own safety. We need to speak with Mal, and you are the one who's most qualified to help us find her. No matter who's responsible for the explosion at your house, Mal is a person of interest. For the time being, that will be my team's primary focus."

In theory, protection should have been a good thing, but she felt like she was suffocating. *But what about—*

"One more thing," said Agent Donnelly before her mind could spiral into panic at the idea of protective custody. He pulled something out of his pocket and set it on the table with a loud *thunk*. "What can you tell me about this?"

Ella leaned forward hesitantly to examine a spotted rock sealed in a plastic bag. "It's a Petoskey Stone. You can tell from the pattern—that's fossilized coral. I used to collect them as a kid. We found them in the lake at my grandparents' house in northern Michigan. Why is it in a bag?"

"It's in an evidence bag because it's evidence," Agent Donnelly said, crossing his arms.

Once again, she glanced between the agents. "Evidence of what?"

Agent Donnelly leaned forward, hands folded on the table. He'd rolled the ends of his sleeves up partway, revealing muscular forearms. "Well, it was in a small box that was addressed to you, in the street in front of your house, so I was hoping you could tell us."

Ella met his eyes in surprise and opened her mouth, but for a moment, nothing came out. She looked away, once again trying to peel back the layers of her hazy memory. "There was a box on my porch when I went out to the mailbox. I picked it up but I didn't open it. I must have dropped it when the explosion knocked me over."

"You didn't answer the question. Why was there a Petoskey stone in a box with your name on it?" Agent Donnelly asked.

She thought back to the various trinkets that had arrived in her mailbox, mostly in plain envelopes but a few in small boxes, over the years. The items had all had one thing in common—each one made her remember something specific from her childhood, which had led her to assume they were from Mal. A Petoskey stone fit the pattern.

"I don't know for sure, but if I had to guess, I would assume it's from Mal. I told you, she likes to... send me things. At least I think it's her doing it, because I don't know who else it would be. The things that arrive are always from places we went as kids, or things I remember from my childhood. If it is Mal, maybe it means she's going to Michigan, to the lake where we used to go on vacation. My grandparents had a house there. That's where we always found those stones."

"What's the name of the lake?"

"Walloon Lake. If this is Michigan..." She held up her left hand, fingers together, to give an approximation of the shape of the state. "Then it's about... here." She pointed to the top knuckle on her ring finger.

Agent Donnelly nodded, his face expressionless, and headed for the door, while Agent Harrison smiled. "Thanks, Ella. We'll see if that gets us anywhere. In the meantime, we need an hour to have a safe house prepared. We'll be back soon."

Before she could protest being left alone in the cold, sterile room, they were gone again. With a heavy sigh, she folded her arms in front of her and rested her head on them, alone in the endless silence.

Almost immediately, it started again—the explosion playing on repeat, just as it did whenever she closed her eyes. Her eyes flew open and she sat up quickly, breathing hard. Staring at the mirrored wall, she tried to look beyond it, willing herself to see the people behind it who were watching her.

With nothing to do but stare into space, time passed excruciatingly slowly. When the door finally opened again thirty minutes later, Agent Donnelly stepped into the room alone. "I come in peace," he said, adding, "I thought you might be hungry." For a second time, there was no hostility in his voice.

He was almost smiling at her. Not quite, but almost.

Setting a coffee cup and a white paper bag down in front of her, he sat back down in the same chair he'd occupied earlier.

"Thanks," she mumbled as he looked down at his phone.

She ate in silence, trying not to watch him as, she was pretty sure, he tried not to watch her. Every once in a while they both looked up at the same time, her stomach flipping as their eyes immediately darted anywhere else.

As much as she hadn't exactly been glad to see him when he'd arrived, when he picked up the trash and headed for the door, a twinge of panic ignited inside her.

"Hey, what's happening with the safe house?"

He stopped moving and looked back at her. "I'm going to check on that now." His words were a simple statement of fact, given matter-of-factly. It wasn't a promise that everything would be okay. Still, coming from him, even a neutral tone was an improvement.

"Oh, okay. Thanks."

He paused, his eyes locked on hers again. "I'll be back."

She was so surprised when he gave her the faintest hint of a smile, she didn't react until it was too late. "Could I..." The door clicked loudly behind him, and she finished her sentence in a whisper to the empty air. "...wait somewhere else?"

She checked her watch. Just after noon. It was going to be a long day. With a heavy sigh, she rested her forehead on the table again, but kept her eyes open this time.

This would make a great movie plot, but it sucks to live through it.

When the door clicked open again forty-five minutes later, Ella raised her head only enough to put her chin on her hands, lifting her eyes the rest of the way. Once again, Agent Donnelly stood there alone. They watched each other for a few seconds before his features softened the slightest bit.

"Let's go," he said.

She stood slowly. It took all her effort to convince her exhausted, sore body to walk across the room to the door. This time he held the door for her until she caught up, stepping out into the large bullpen crammed with desks. After the prolonged silence of the interrogation room, the din was jarring.

Ella followed Agent Donnelly to the elevator, where they stood and stared at the numbers above the elevator as they slowly moved closer. While it was an improvement from her initial impression of him, his complete detachment at that moment was both unnerving and also made her curious.

What happened to him that made him end up like this?

Between the illness and deaths of her parents and the many dysfunctional years with Mal before they'd cut ties completely, she'd known her share of grief and trauma, and it made her wonder about his past. If nothing else, focusing on Agent Donnelly's quirks was better than dwelling on her own mess of a life.

As the elevator doors creaked open and the two of them stepped forward, a petite young woman in a dark suit came barreling around a corner and right up to Agent Donnelly, completely out of breath. Several strands of light hair had come loose from the bun at the back of her head.

"Agent Donnelly, wait." It took a few seconds before she could get anything else out, and the muscles in his face tightened in impatience.

At least I'm not the only one who annoys him.

The young woman finally spit out what she'd come to say. "Agent Martin needs you. There's a new lead."

Chapter 8
Mal and Ella

AGES 5 AND 6
(33 YEARS AGO)

ELLA SQUINTED AT THE piece of mulch, trying to decipher Mal's clue. This wasn't one of their regular parks, so it was a little trickier than usual.

"Where's Mal?" asked their mother, coming to stand beside Ella. "You're not playing that game again, are you?"

"The Breadcrumb Game. Yes. It's her favorite. This is the clue she left. I just have to figure out—"

Concern swept across Valerie's face as she scanned the area for her mischievous five-year-old.

"I know where she is!" Ella cried out in triumph and made a beeline for the large tree at the edge of the agreed-upon hiding zone, ducking around it triumphantly. "Found you!"

Both girls emerged from behind the tree, laughing and hopping up and down with glee. They took off running back towards their mother, who watched in dismay as Ella's sandal clipped the side of Mal's. She tripped, falling flat on her face in the grass. Ella, who hadn't noticed her sister go down, continued at top speed, reaching Valerie with a grin as her mother passed her on her way to Mal.

"She tripped me!" Mal screamed, beating her fists against the ground. "She always trips me!"

Valerie kneeled in the grass and helped Mal sit up, ensuring that she was unhurt before crossing her legs and pulling Mal into her lap. "You're okay, aren't you?"

Mal gave a tearful nod, hiccupping.

"I saw the whole thing. Ella did not trip you on purpose. You were just too close together when you were running, and her sandal got caught on your sandal. It was an accident." She turned to look at Ella, who approached them cautiously.

"I'm sorry Mal. I didn't mean to trip you."

"Apology NOT accepted!" Mal squirmed in her mother's arms. "Let me go!"

Valerie looked up at her husband for help, and the two of them had a brief, silent conversation as Valerie released Mal from her lap. Mal scrambled to her feet, stomped over to Ella, and shoved her backwards as she walked by. She ignored both her sister's shriek and her parents' admonitions as she strode across the grass.

Her father's voice boomed after her. "Mallory Jane Madson, stop right there."

When he caught up with her a few seconds later, he put out his hand. "Let's take a walk."

Mal ignored his hand, instead walking beside him, arms crossed and fuming.

"Let's talk about what's happening in there." Her father tapped her forehead gently.

"I'm feeling angry."

"What did we talk about this morning?"

Mal sighed. "Big anger and little anger."

"That's right. What kinds of things are big anger for?"

"Bad guys. People who do terrible things. Things you would go to jail for."

"Should Ella go to jail because you tripped on her foot?"

Mal's eyes gleamed, as if she was imagining that very thing happening. Her father looked at her sternly. "Mal..."

"No," she grumbled.

"It's okay to be annoyed. It was a surprise when you fell, and not a good surprise. But can you recover from tripping on someone's foot?"

Mal scoffed. "Yes. I'm not a baby."

"So even if she did it on purpose, which I don't believe she did, should she get your big anger or your little anger?"

"Little anger."

"What can we do with little anger?"

"We can say 'thanks for visiting, but it's time to go.' And then open the door for it to leave." Mal paused. "But sometimes it's hard to get it to go."

"I know. People are like that sometimes, too. And just like with people, you have to be firm, and let it know you mean business. Anger doesn't get to control you. Right?"

When Mal didn't answer immediately, her father pretended to knock on an imaginary door in front of them. In a gruff voice, he said, "Hello, I'm Anger. I'm here and I'm not leaving."

Mal's smile immediately widened. "Would you like tea, Mr. Anger?"

"No!" huffed her father. "I just want to stay here with you and be angry."

Mal shook her head with pretend remorse. "I'm sorry, but I have plans today. You have to go."

"No! I love it here. You have a comfy chair and great snacks."

Mal glanced around them with a grin, as if the comfy chair and snacks might materialize. She remained firm. "I'm sorry, but no. Please go now."

Her father huffed again, this time louder. "Okay fine. I'll go. But I'll be back another day."

"I know. You can come back another day. I just need you to go for right now."

Her bad mood forgotten, Mal beamed up at her father. "How'd I do, daddy?"

"Well, that depends. How do you feel?"

Mal stopped walking and looked down at herself, deep in thought, her smile widening. "I feel better!"

"Fantastic! And if you weren't feeling better, what would you have done?"

"Count to ten. And if I'm still mad, I count to ten with a funny accent. And then in Spanish."

"What if that still doesn't work?"

"French."

"It's a good thing you're so smart. Otherwise, I don't know how you'd memorize all the numbers in two other languages."

Pride shone in Mal's face. "It's easy."

"Should we learn another one?"

"Yes!"

"Which one?"

Mal thought for a minute. "Chinese!"

Her father raised his eyebrows dramatically. "Chinese? Wow! I've heard that's a hard one."

Mal stood up taller. "I can do it, daddy. If you have trouble, I'll help you."

He beamed down at her fondly. "I would love that, Moosh."

"That's not my name!" She giggled.

He looked thoughtful for a moment, then said, "Maybe it's your Chinese name." His eyes twinkled mischievously.

"Daddy, you're so silly."

"I do need help with one thing that's very, very important, though." He squatted down to her eye level, his face serious.

She rolled her eyes and sighed dramatically again. "I know."

"What am I going to say?"

She recited the words that they'd gone over together many, many times before. "You need me to get along with Ella, because we're sisters and sisters are forever, and even if I think I don't like her, I really do and I just don't know it yet."

Her father smiled. "I'm so glad you have that fantastic memory."

"But Daddy..."

"I've made up my mind. You can't change it. Not unless you learn some magic spells and maybe turn me into a toad."

"Can I really do that?" Mal's eyes widened in wonder.

"Maybe. But only if you're nice to Ella."

Mal giggled again. "So if I'm nice to her, you'll teach me magic spells?"

"Oh no, I don't know any magic spells. But if we find a wizard, maybe he'll teach you some magic spells."

"Daddy, you're a nut."

Ella and her mother approached them then, Ella looking solemn.

"I'm sorry I tripped you, Mal. It was an accident."

"That's okay. I'm sorry for yelling at you," said Mal.

As they continued walking, Ella stuck her foot a little farther out than necessary, causing Mal to trip. "Oh no, watch out!" Ella called, catching Mal before she hit the ground. "Are you okay?"

Mal's eyes narrowed. "You did that on purpose!"

"I did not!"

"Girls, enough," said their mother.

"But she tripped me!"

"I stopped you from tripping!"

"I think it's time to think about how the other person feels in this situation," their father said seriously.

Both girls looked at the ground, deep in concentration, then mumbled, "Sorry."

Ella put her hand in her pocket, bringing it back out closed around something. "I was going to give you this later, but here. It's for you." She handed Mal a tiny elephant statue. "I know they're your favorite."

Mal's face lit up as Ella put the elephant in her hand. She looked from the figure to Ella and back, squeezed her hand around it and then grabbed her sister in a hug. "Thank you! I love it!"

Their parents looked on, pleased but wary. The girls' interactions could deteriorate in seconds, and being that close could be a recipe for disaster.

"How nice of you, Ella! I thought you were saving him for Mal's birthday," said Valerie.

"I know, but I just didn't want to wait that long." Ella beamed with pleasure, and for once, Mal did, too.

Mal stared at the elephant again before declaring, "He says his name is Skip, and he also says we should get ice cream." She looked up at her mother. "Please?"

"Great idea, Skip," said Valerie.

"Skip is happy that we are happy," said Mal as they headed for the ice cream shop at the end of the next block. She continued to chatter away as Skip's interpreter for the rest of the afternoon.

Chapter 9
Ella

SATURDAY

Agent Donnelly raised his eyebrows at the younger agent as she caught her breath.

"When you didn't answer her texts, Agent Martin sent me to find you before you could leave."

Agent Donnelly said nothing, only glanced at Ella, then back to his colleague, who shook her head. "You go see Agent Martin. I'll take her to the safe house."

"Fine." With that, he disappeared down a side corridor Ella hadn't noticed before. She stared after him, once again in awe at his lack of social skills.

"Hi, Annabella. I'm Agent Jacobs."

Agent Jacobs looked at least ten years younger than Ella. After dealing with Agent Donnelly, her warm demeanor was a welcome change.

"Nice to meet you. Call me Ella, please. Do they really have a lead?"

"It looks like it, but don't get too excited. It could easily turn out to be nothing. For now, let's get you out of here. If it's something, we'll hear about it."

Agent Jacobs was the opposite of Agent Donnelly; she chatted the entire way to the safe house. By the time they arrived, Ella almost missed Agent Donnelly's silence. Almost.

The safe house was a narrow end-unit townhouse, almost identical to the one attached to it on the left. The matchbox sized yards were neat and well-kept, the brick building in relatively good shape, neither brand new nor old.

Agent Jacobs went inside first, and Ella stopped on the threshold behind her. The exterior was basic but fine, but on the inside—as an interior designer, her job was to prevent a house from turning out like this one.

She tried to hide her disappointment, but her eyes gave her away.

"I know, it's depressing. But you'll be safe here."

Ella nodded, but said nothing.

"Let's look around and make a list of what you'll need. Agent Donnelly has already requested copies of your documents to be expedited—your birth certificate, driver's license, passport... Did he tell you that?"

"No."

"Yeah, he never misses a detail. Other than his questionable taste in music, I've never had a reason to doubt his judgement. You're lucky he's on your case."

Ella raised her eyebrows, and Agent Jacobs nodded. "I know. He wasn't always so moody. My first couple years, he was a fantastic mentor. I never would have thought..." She shook her head. "Anyway, he's the best at his job. He's just had a rough time."

Ella couldn't imagine that Agent Donnelly had ever excelled at anything involving people.

She followed Agent Jacobs through the living room and into the kitchen, where the agent grimaced at the almost empty refrigerator. "We'll write 'food' as the first item on the list. You can put down what items you want on the online order form."

"I don't need much. I can live on cereal. Especially Chocolate Cheerios."

Agent Jacobs smiled. "We can probably do better than that."

The two women continued room by room, but the list didn't get too much longer. As depressing and empty as it was, Ella couldn't bring herself to care about any of it. She would've happily laid down on the bed and gone to sleep in her only set of clothes and not worried about things like milk or deodorant or pajamas.

In the end, they agreed that the main things she needed were food, toiletries, and underwear. A wallet and a purse. A jacket. A cell phone. The clothes in the dresser were bland, but there were enough of the basics to make do for now.

Be grateful. You're alive. It could be worse.

She needed to suck it up and move on, like she'd always done. Yes, she'd lost everything, but they were only things. Maybe this was better. After all, she knew all too well that when you had nothing, you had nothing to lose. It had been the same way with people. No connections or genuine happiness, but no crushing loss either.

A few hours later, the dining room table in the safe house was full of shopping bags, everything procured by the FBI. Agent Jacobs' phone buzzed as she set the last of them down. "Sorry, I need to get back," she said.

"Of course. Thank you for everything." Ella's eyes flicked to the table full of bags. She no longer had to say she had nothing.

"You're welcome. One of us will be in touch. Probably him. He's not big on delegating tasks. But let me give you both of our numbers, just in case." Ella saved the agents' numbers in her new phone. "Now you're not stranded. The other emergency numbers are on the fridge."

"Thank you again."

Agent Jacobs headed for the door, smiling back over her shoulder. "Hang in there. We're going to figure this out."

Ella smiled at her, but it didn't reach her eyes. "Bye."

"Bye."

The door lock engaged from the outside, the *click* reminding Ella of being locked in the interrogation room at the FBI. Swallowing hard, she turned around to face the mound of shopping bags piled on the dining room table.

Once she'd put everything away, she took a hot shower and felt almost human again, though still sore all over. Sitting at the kitchen table with a cup of coffee an hour after Agent Jacobs had let herself out, Ella exhaled slowly, finally beginning to relax. That was when two things happened at once.

Chapter 10
Mal
SATURDAY

"JIMMY, I HAVE A bad feeling." They'd been sitting on the deck that overlooked the water, listening to the quiet of the late evening. Besides the occasional couple out for a walk, the only sounds were insects and birds chirping, squirrels foraging in the underbrush or scampering through the trees, and the gentle lapping of the lake.

"What's that, luv?" He'd been gazing out into the distance, lost in thought.

"It's too quiet here."

Jimmy looked at her, squinting slightly in confusion. "You picked this place because it was quiet."

"I know, but—"

"But now quiet is a bad thing?"

Mal rolled her eyes. "I can't explain it. Something just feels off."

A twig snapped in the underbrush nearby, and Mal straightened with a start.

"I don't think the squirrels are out to get us, but we can go inside if you like."

They soaked in the quiet for a few more minutes, and Mal flinched each time the smallest sound came from the darkness beyond the deck.

"What are you sitting there worrying about?" asked Jimmy.

"Bri. Have you heard from her? Because I still haven't."

Jimmy sighed. "No, not yet. I'm sure she's fine. The job's over. She's probably passed out somewhere, enjoying her split of the money. Maybe she's just being cautious. We could do a little better at that, you know." He gave her a pointed look.

"She usually sends something cryptic but ridiculous when she gets to wherever she's hiding out. Complete radio silence isn't like her."

"Let me ask around and see what I can dig up before you get worried. Alright?"

Mal nodded, her mouth a tight line. She stood up from the cushioned deck chair, not bothering to slip into her sandals, and padded down the stairs to the narrow walkway that ran beside the house.

The concrete was still warm from the day's heat, and she stepped off it into the grassy front yard, remembering a game they used to play with the neighbors' grandkids across their front yards. *What was it called?* She couldn't remember. It had involved running down the sidewalk, moving fast to avoid burning her bare feet on the hot pavement. At the same time, she'd had to avoid being tagged long enough to jump into the cool grass, where she'd run some more.

She continued across the lawn, down to the dock. The boards creaked under her weight as she walked out over the water. At the end of the dock, she gazed across the lake. Her dad had always said it was a mile across, but it looked much farther. Maybe he'd made that up.

Despite having seen no sign of anyone following them to this middle-of-nowhere haven of her childhood, Mal could not relax. *I never should have let Jimmy talk me into that last job.*

A crunching sound in the foliage on the shore to her left made her spin around, nearly slipping on the worn-out boards of the dock. She swayed on her feet just enough to make her fear ending up in the water. While she knew from experience that the water was shallow here, she still didn't want to fall in head-first.

Goosebumps broke out on her arms, and she fixed her eyes on the trees surrounding the house next door, suddenly feeling exposed. *Calm down.*

Flinching when her phone buzzed in her pocket, she cursed herself under her breath for being so jumpy. Something about the quiet here was unnerving. The notification was a text from Jimmy. Gazing up at the house, she saw him waving. She looked back down and opened the message.

Time to eat? What do you feel like?

She let out a sigh, chiding herself. *I'm really getting paranoid.*

Her bad feeling remained. The wooded lake that had felt peaceful when they'd arrived was closing in around her, and she took off toward the house at a run.

Chapter 11
Ella
SATURDAY

S ITTING AT THE SMALL dining room table in her safe house with her coffee, Ella was startled when the wooden table in front of her vibrated with her phone's notification. At the same time, a knock sounded loudly on the door. Leaving her phone on the table, she went to the door and looked out the peephole, but saw nothing—not even her tiny porch. Confused, she pulled the door open a crack to get a better look.

As soon as she did, someone shoved the door open, knocking her off balance. Unable to get her footing, she fell backwards the few steps of the entryway until her back slammed hard against the wall, and she fell to the floor with a hard landing that sent a jolt of pain from her lower back.

Someone had just broken into her safe house!

She raised her arms to shield herself from whatever blows were coming.

What have I done?

When no further attacks came, she opened her eyes to find that it was not an intruder standing over her, but Agent Donnelly. He was breathing hard, his face flushed, and his eyes were wide with an unsettling intensity. After a long second he turned to secure the door.

The silence of her last few hours alone made his angry shouts feel even louder. "You answered the door with no idea who it was! Don't you understand what's going on? You're here because you're in danger." He stopped and closed his eyes, taking deep breaths.

He'd scared her, but Ella's fear faded slowly, replaced by confusion over his reaction. It reminded her of an episode of a TV show she liked, *Gemini Divided*.

One of the lead characters had acted that way toward the other when they'd narrowly escaped danger. But that didn't make sense. The two characters liked each other—a lot. She was pretty sure that was not the case here.

After a few seconds, he looked down at her, eyes narrowed. "If you get yourself killed, how are we supposed to solve this case?"

Oh, okay. That makes sense, then. It wasn't as though his animosity towards her was a surprise, even though she didn't know where it came from.

"I..." Ella started, but he cut her off, barely in control of his anger.

"Never open the door without confirming the identity of the person on the other side. Do you understand?" She sat still and waited for what he would do next.

"Do you understand?" he repeated when she didn't respond.

She nodded quickly.

Agent Donnelly looked at her with a stormy expression for several more seconds before stomping off to the kitchen. Only when he'd disappeared did she realize she was shaking. She hugged her knees and gulped air into her lungs.

Her breathing had just slowed back to normal two minutes later when slow footsteps approached from the kitchen. She rested her chin on her knees, watching him as he approached. He stopped directly in front of her, and lowered himself to the floor so he was sitting with his legs crossed in front of her, his back against the front door.

After what appeared to be a great deal of thought and effort, he said, "I'm sorry, Ms. Madson. I overreacted." His combative tone was gone, and in its place was uncertainty, remorse, —maybe sadness.

Her iron grip on her knees loosened.

"The problem is, if you open the door for just anyone, well... It's my job to protect you. And I can't do that if you take unnecessary risks."

Yes, he'd been unnecessarily aggressive, but he was right that she'd been careless. Her eyes darted back to the floor, and she released some of the tension in her back.

"My reaction was inappropriate," he said. "Under the circumstances, I imagine you'd like another lead agent to take over your case."

All she'd wanted since they met was to be rid of him, and she opened her mouth to tell him that yes, it would be for the best if he withdrew from the case. But before she said a word, Agent Jacobs' voice played in her head, repeating her earlier words. *"He's the best at his job. He's just had a rough time."* She had to admit that he seemed like the kind of person who got things done because he had no patience for excuses. She needed someone like that. And she could certainly relate to having a rough time.

Hoping she wouldn't regret her split-second decision, she shook her head. "No. I'd like you to stay on my case."

"You would?" He looked as surprised as she was, but it felt like the right decision.

"I'm told you're the best, and I need answers." Growing bolder at having a choice in the matter, she added, "As long as you never yell at me like that again."

He gave only the faintest tilt of his head before she added, "You don't need to scare me into compliance. I'm scared enough." Her voice shook slightly on her last few words.

When he nodded that time, he looked chagrined. "Anything else?"

She thought for a second. "No."

"Fine. I'll check in with you tomorrow, then." He stood and turned toward the door, but stopped and twisted back around towards her. "If you need anything, let me know. Or tell Agent Jacobs. You have our numbers. Also, I'm going to assign a protective detail to be outside this unit, on the street."

She scoffed. "You think that's necessary?"

"Until you learn how to take safety precautions, I believe it is."

She recognized that for the dig it was, and let out another heavy sigh. "Fine."

"If anything out of the ordinary happens, let me know. And for God's sake, don't open the door for anyone except me or Agent Jacobs."

He opened the door and walked out without a goodbye. Though she'd wanted him to leave at first, she had to suppress the urge to call him back. She wanted another look at the person she'd caught a glance of under the impenetrable armor. Disappointed yet relieved, she forced herself to her feet to lock the door behind him.

It was 3:45 pm—the day was far from over, but until she got a new computer, she couldn't do any work. This was unsettling for a workaholic like her.

She retrieved her phone from the kitchen table and read the text she had ignored when she'd gotten up to answer the door. It was from Agent Jacobs.

Agent Donnelly is on his way over. He's probably going to test your security-consciousness.

"That's an understatement," she said to the silence.

A knock on the door made her jump. It had only been five minutes since Agent Donnelly had left, and after his stunt, she considered not even going to the door, but her curiosity won out. She winced when a board creaked under her feet as she tiptoed to the door. Tentatively checking the peephole, she saw not Agent Donnelly, but a woman with long black hair. Dressed in jeans and a black leather jacket, she looked normal. Harmless. But Agent Donnelly had been right. She needed to be much more cautious.

Ella stepped back from the peephole and started to walk away.

She'd taken three steps when the sound of a fist pounding on the door made Ella jump. Bringing her eye to the peephole again, she was surprised to see Agent Donnelly. Annoyed to feel relieved to see him, she opened the door just wide enough to glare at him.

"She was with you, wasn't she?" Ella asked.

"Yep." He glanced back at the woman, giving her a wave as she pulled away from the curb in a black sedan.

"So, was that some kind of test?"

He nodded solemnly. "It was."

"And did I pass?" she asked sarcastically.

"You did." He didn't smile at her, but his expression lacked hostility, and he turned to leave without another word.

Was that his version of a compliment? "That's all you came back for?" she called as he retreated down the sidewalk.

He turned and walked backwards as he spoke. "Yep. You did better this time. Now get back in there and lock the door."

"So stupid," she muttered, annoyed to find that she was smiling as she secured the bolt. She peeked through the peephole to see him get into his car at the curb and didn't look away until he was out of sight.

Lumpy as the couch was, she curled up in the corner, suddenly tired. With nothing else to do but distract herself with her newly backed up phone, she scrolled back through the few old pictures that she had—all pictures she'd taken on her phone of old prints, which meant the quality was terrible. They included scenery from trips she'd taken, including the occasional selfie. Older, grainier images of her parents that she seldom allowed herself to look at, lest she fall down the rabbit hole of nostalgia. Even a few of herself and Mal from when they were kids that she couldn't bring herself to delete. The four of them, a family unit in another lifetime.

She stopped on one, taken when they'd been in high school, in which she and Mal sat on a bright orange blanket in the sunshine, their father between them to act as referee. Behind them was a bush overflowing with white flowers. Ella and her dad both wore tie-dyed t-shirts and beamed at the camera, while Mal was dressed all in black and wore her usual stony glare. Still, the resemblance between the girls was remarkable. That picture was a perfect example of why so many people had mistaken them for identical twins. She would show it to Agent Donnelly later.

Her stomach clenched at the thought of Agent Donnelly.

Did I do the right thing, saying I wanted him to stay on my case?

The rest of the evening felt like it would never end. She made a peanut butter and jelly sandwich for dinner and downloaded a mystery novel onto her phone, curling up on the couch to read until she finally started nodding off.

The next morning, Ella woke to the sun streaming into her bedroom, neither the plastic blinds nor the thin curtains doing anything to block out the light. The mattress had seen better days, and her back screamed in protest. Giving up on sleep, she dragged herself out of bed and stumbled to the window to peek between the slats of the blinds. A slight movement in a car at the curb caught her eye.

That must be the security detail Agent Donnelly mentioned.

Showered and dressed in a too-big t-shirt and yoga pants, she poured herself a bowl of cereal and tried not to look around at her bleak surroundings.

She'd called her bank and her credit card company for replacement cards, and she'd filed a claim with her homeowner's insurance company. She'd spoken to each of her clients, and explained that she would be back to work as soon as she could. As difficult as it was for her, she had no choice but to relax—she'd done every productive thing she could do for now. She didn't want to watch TV, but she put it on for noise.

About thirty minutes into her forced relaxation, a knock on the door made her sit up. She grabbed the remote control and turned off the TV, and her eyes flew to her phone. No texts.

Another test?

The knocking came again, echoing through the still house.

She crept across the room, phone in hand, to the front door. Bringing her face to the peephole, she expected to find another of Agent Donnelly's tests. But her porch was empty, and she couldn't decide if she was relieved or disappointed. The car by the curb was gone, as well.

On her way back toward the living room, she opened a blank text to Agent Donnelly.

This is Ella. Did that protective detail start already? I thought I saw them outside earlier this morning, but no one's out there now.

A squeak made her look up, her eyes darting around but finding nothing out of place. It must have been in the adjoining unit. She looked back down at her phone when a new text popped up.

Paperwork is in, but it doesn't work that fast. Should be later today

Someone just knocked on the door. Twice. I thought it was you. I just checked and no one's there now

LOCK YOURSELF IN THE BATHROOM. I'M ON MY WAY

A *creak* sounded from above her—she recognized it as the sound triggered by pressure on the loose board on the third step from the top of her staircase. Her eyes snapped up and she froze.

Someone else is in the house.

For several heartbeats, her feet remained planted.

Move! Now!

She nearly made it to the bathroom door before another creak cut through the silence. This softer one told her that in about two seconds she'd be directly in the intruder's line of sight. No longer concerned with stealth, she scrambled forward the last few feet, threw herself inside the bathroom and slammed the door as footsteps suddenly pounded down the last few stairs. She pushed in the lock button on the door a fraction of a second before a heavy weight thudded against it.

Holding her breath that the door would hold, she backed away. They'd gotten into her house without using the front door, so it made sense that they could also break down the flimsy bathroom door without too much trouble.

She spun around, frantically searching for options. The window on the far wall was much too small for her to fit through, and too high to reach, anyway. In the cabinet below the sink, she found nothing remotely useful for defending herself. The only thing she could think to do was to press herself into the corner beside a narrow shelf and sit down, making herself as small as possible.

The doorknob jiggled, and she squeezed her eyes shut.

Chapter 12

Ella

SUNDAY

THE JIGGLING ON THE door grew louder and faster. Then it stopped for a second, followed by a *thud* when the person outside slammed against the door.

Ella winced, pulling her arms tighter around herself and squeezing her eyes closed. In the distance, the faint whine of sirens teased her. Surely they'd never get there in time.

But the sirens grew louder by the second, and all at once she heard footsteps retreating and a door slam. She waited, her entire body clenched in apprehension as the sirens suddenly shrieked.

When the sirens stopped, fear surged through her again. No one was coming to save her, after all. Her panic was back, but a thousand times worse.

An insistent pounding on the front door made her jump. Keys jingled. The outer door banged open, and the panicked shouting of a voice she knew all too well filled the house.

"Ms. Madson! Ms. Madson, it's Agent Donnelly. Open the door!" More pounding, another loud *thud* as Agent Donnelly also threw himself against the bathroom door, but still she couldn't move.

The sound of a gunshot rang in her ears and her entire body flinched, pulling into an even smaller ball as tears streamed from her eyes. The door burst inward, sending splinters of wood flying toward her. Though Agent Donnelly had already identified himself, she gasped, ducking her head and shaking.

"Ella!" His voice filled the room, no longer muffled by the walls, but she remained compressed in the corner. He didn't touch her, but his voice now came from only inches away and she smelled his cologne.

"Are you okay?" If she didn't know better, she'd say he sounded afraid. Terrified, even. Without raising her head, she shook it back and forth, sniffling.

"Are you hurt?" The concern in his voice made it difficult to believe he was the same man she'd known up to this point.

"No," she whispered.

When he spoke next, he was calmer. "Good. Was someone here?"

Ella nodded.

"Did you get a look at them?"

She ignored the question, her response muffled by her arms. "The stairs squeaked. I barely made it in here..." Her body convulsed at the thought of what had almost happened. "I didn't see them."

"It's okay. They're gone."

Her head snapped up. "They got away?" she asked in dismay.

His mouth made a thin line as he nodded slightly. "Unfortunately, yes. But you're safe now."

"I'm never going to be safe." Her voice trembled, and she put her head back down against her knees. Tears soaked into the sleeves of her shirt as her whole body shuddered.

Hands landed on her upper arms, and she flinched, muscles tight and ready to fight for her life.

"Sorry," he said softly, his grip releasing.

The contact with him had startled her, but as soon as he withdrew, she missed it. Little by little, she leaned her head forward until it rested lightly against his chest.

His arms had been resting on either side of her, and now they shifted into the most tentative of hugs, with his hands slowly settling on her back. "Okay?"

She nodded against him.

"It's okay now. Breathe."

Her pulse slowed, and her gasping breaths became farther apart. When she shifted the slightest bit, he released her and moved back, sitting on his knees in front of her. His chagrined expression was the only evidence the hug had taken place.

"You got here just in time," she said.

The muscles in his face tightened, as if the words had caused him pain, before giving way to a tired smile—the first real one he'd ever given her.

An unfamiliar voice broke the silence of the bathroom. "Agent Donnelly, there's something you need to see."

"I'll be right there," he said tersely over his shoulder. There was the agent she'd known until now. His tone made her grit her teeth. When he turned back to Ella, however, he spoke as gently as before. "I'll be back in a second. There are at least ten other agents here besides me. I swear to you, you're safe now." He held eye contact with her until she nodded, then hesitantly stood.

She focused on the small beige squares of the tile floor. His voice mixed with others, and with the chatter of police radios, until, lulled by the white noise and the need to shut out everything that had just happened, her eyes drifted closed.

An eternity passed before his voice broke through the static. "Ms. Madson?"

She opened her eyes as he squatted in front of her.

"I'm sorry this happened. This is a safe house. You should have been safe here."

Taking advantage of the newfound peace between them, she said, "I told you, call me Ella."

Once again, his mouth curled into a small smile, and some of the numbness inside her faded.

"Okay, Ella. Are you sure you can't tell me what the person who was here looked like?"

Her face immediately fell. "No, I never saw them. I didn't look back. I didn't even think to—"

He shook his head, cutting her off. His hand landed lightly over both of hers, and her galloping thoughts crashed to a halt. Only then did she realize she'd been clenching and unclenching them in her lap.

"No, that's okay. Tell me what you remember. As much as you can."

She had a longstanding rule—she held people at a distance on purpose, and yet, here he was, invading her personal space. His hand was still on top of hers, which made it hard to focus on anything else. She didn't hate it, which set off alarm bells in her head. Her chin tipped up little by little, and their eyes locked on each other.

"Sorry," he mumbled, letting go of her hands and sitting back.

Helped along by some gentle prodding questions, she recounted what had happened. When she was done, they both fell silent for long enough that the dripping water from the sink became a pattern in her head.

This was the first time she wished she had Mal's ability to disconnect from her emotions. Being emotional and scared all the time was exhausting.

As the adrenaline drained out of her, she rested her head against the wall beside her and closed her eyes.

He stood and turned the knob on the faucet to stop the drips. "What do you say we get out of here?"

She nodded without opening her eyes.

"Truce?" he asked uncertainly.

She opened her eyes and whispered, "Truce."

"Let's get your stuff. You're not coming back."

She hesitated before trailing behind him through the doorway into the living room, which was noisy and crowded with agents. They all went about their business as if it was an average day. Maybe to them, it was. Agent Donnelly stopped and glanced back, tipping his head to tell her to follow him.

With her few newly acquired belongings shoved back into shopping bags, they left the chaos behind.

"We'll get you a real bag for your things. Today," he said as they emerged into the sunshine, where a tangle of vehicles blocked the sidewalk and part of the road. Agent Donnelly unlocked the black SUV parked a few feet from the door. Dark skid marks behind the tires showed just how fast he'd slammed on the brakes when he'd arrived. He opened the door for her and waited patiently until she was settled, then closed it. The difference in him from just the day before was night and day. Her first question was whether it would last. Her second question was *why had he suddenly become a different person?* But those questions could wait.

"Where are we going?"

"Back to FBI headquarters."

"Am I staying there instead of a safe house?" She imagined herself living in a cell that was otherwise for prisoners, and shuddered.

"No, nothing like that. I have something to show you, then we'll get a new safe house figured out."

"And what about... the person who just tried to kill me? Won't they try again?"

"You won't be left unguarded again. I will personally assure your safety."

The energy around him was intense, but for the first time, his irritation wasn't directed at her. They drove in silence back to the FBI building in downtown Washington, DC.

Inside, she hesitated before getting on the elevator. Her last experience at the building hadn't been great.

As if reading her mind, he said, "Don't worry. No interrogation room this time."

She followed him to the far end of a long bullpen, where multiple large screens were mounted over a long desk. A woman in her thirties with a deep bronze complexion sat at a computer in front of the screens, her tight brown curls gathered loosely in an elastic.

"Agent Donnelly, I was about to call you," she said, her fingers flying over the keyboard. "Look at this." With one final tap she brought up several grainy enlargements from surveillance video.

Ella gaped as the images popped up rapidly, forming a loose collage with their edges overlapping. All of them featured the same brunette—or at least, a woman who could have been the same brunette.

Ella reminded herself to breathe, not taking her eyes off the screen. "You think that's Mal?"

"Yes. Our analysts have used several algorithms. This is from footage taken in the Detroit airport, so it tracks with your theory about the Petoskey stone meaning that she was going to that lake in Michigan."

Ella studied the images one by one. They were so fuzzy, it surprised her that even the FBI could identify Mal out of a sea of random people.

"We used to go there every summer when we were growing up. We stopped going in our teens, after my dad got sick, but I'll never forget it."

The agent at the keyboard typed "Walloon Lake" into a search bar, and the screens flooded with pictures. Ella inhaled sharply as familiar visions of her childhood appeared before her eyes. The shots were mostly of scenery from various parts of the lake and the surrounding area, but her mind filled it in.

She pushed away the sting of nostalgia. This was why she locked her memories up tight. "It's all... it looks... Wow. I haven't been back there in... it must be almost twenty-five years. My grandparents owned a house on the lake. I don't remember the address, but I'll never forget what it looked like."

"What are your grandparents' names?" asked the woman whose name Ella still didn't know.

"Marie and John Madson."

"I'll dig into it. And since this guy isn't going to introduce us, I'm Agent Martin. Call me Ayanna." She stuck out her hand to Ella and smiled, then gave Agent Donnelly a teasing grin. He rolled his eyes at her.

"Ella Madson," Ella replied automatically. "But you know that."

"If you need any dirt on this guy, I know it all. Like the fact that he loves karaoke, but should not be allowed to sing." She grinned at Agent Donnelly, who sighed and rolled his eyes like a teenager whose mother was telling his secrets.

Agent Martin turned back to the screens. "You two get out of here and let me work. I'll let you know if I find anything else."

"Thanks, Ayanna." To Ella, Agent Donnelly tipped his head to the side. "Come on."

She followed him down the hall to an empty, glass-walled conference room. "What are we doing here?"

"I need you to wait here while I figure out the safe house situation. I'm going to go talk to my boss about that, among other things, right now."

She lowered herself into a stiffly upholstered chair, eyeing her surroundings warily.

"Okay... but I thought you said..."

An agent with a no-nonsense expression and a military-style haircut stopped in the hall, facing them, nodding at Agent Donnelly.

"Agent Kopak will make sure no one bothers you," Agent Donnelly said as he pushed the door open. The other agent had taken up a position in the hall, facing her but not making eye contact.

Before letting the door close behind him, he looked over his shoulder at her. She pulled her feet up into the chair and hugged her legs to her, as she'd done in the bathroom of the safehouse. As soon as she did, he let go of the door and strode back across the room toward her, squatting down in front of her chair. "I can promise you that Agent Kopak will keep you safe until I get back, okay?"

She nodded, biting her lip and really hating how much she didn't want him to go anywhere.

Ella spent the next hour and a half curled up in a chair pushed against the far wall so no one could sneak up behind her, jumping at the slightest noise. When Agent Donnelly finally reappeared at the glass door, relief washed over her. He was staring down at his phone and paused in the doorway, then looked up at her and said, "Come on."

"Where are we going?"

"Looks like Agent Martin has a lead. Let's go see what she found."

With her handful of shopping bags in tow, they retraced their steps back to Agent Martin. This time, the other agent had even more shots of Walloon Lake, and of Mal, on her screens.

"Agent Donnelly, long time no see." The young woman was undeterred by the raised eyebrow and unamused expression her joke received.

"Agent Martin is our resident comedian. Please don't encourage her."

Ayanna grinned. "Fun fact," she said to Ella, "Agent Donnelly collects seashells."

Ella looked from one of them to the other, wondering if Ayanna was just trying to get under his skin. She'd have to file that away for later.

"Anyway," Agent Donnelly prompted.

"Anyway," said Agent Martin, then pointed at the screen. "I think this might be Mal."

She played a blurry doorbell video in which a man and a woman strolled arm-in-arm through the frame. Both wore baseball caps and kept their heads down, and the video caught their profiles, so it was hard to say for sure. The pair walked along a narrow path, and in the video's background, the land sloped down to a small beach and a dock leading out over the water.

Ella tilted her head and squinted slightly. It was impossible to say exactly where it had been taken based on her memory alone.

"See how they're huddled together with their hats down low? If we didn't know to search this specific town, we probably never would've found them."

Agent Donnelly studied the footage. "Do you have an address?"

Agent Martin's head bobbed from side to side. "I have the address for the house where this video was recorded, but they're just walking by. So it narrows down the area, but it's not as exact as we'd like. The houses face the water, and the road that runs behind them is narrow and mostly obscured by trees on the satellite view. That makes it significantly more difficult to get street view data than it is in a lot of other places."

Ella stepped toward the screen. "Wait, was it on... North Shore Drive?"

Agent Martin checked her notes. "It was. Maybe it's coming back to you."

"I remember that the downtown there was tiny. It only had a few buildings. A post office, a general store, a marina, and two souvenir stores. A hotel that had a restaurant. Oh, and a playground. At least, that's what was there when I was a teenager. Most days we'd walk there, and the path went right through everyone's front yards, just like on the video. We said we were 'walking to the foot,' because the village was at the foot of the lake."

Agent Donnelly regarded her strangely.

"What? That's what we called it."

"Your team is scheduled to leave for Michigan in two hours," Agent Martin told Agent Donnelly.

Ella glanced back and forth between them, stopping on Agent Donnelly. "Let me come with you," she said. "Please, I can help. I'm really good at logic puzzles, and I'm the one who grew up with her. I'm the one who remembers that place!"

"Out of the question. That's not the way things work." He folded his arms over his chest.

"But I—"

"No."

Ella's face reddened. "I'm useful to you! You know I am. You never would've known they were going to Michigan at all if not for me."

He'd opened his mouth to speak again, but she beat him to it. "Don't leave me here! I'm not even safe in a safe house, and you know it!"

The space went silent as the agents at nearby workstations stopped what they were doing to stare, as if they expected an explosion. To be honest, she did, too.

His stern features relaxed, but he shook his head, pained. "I don't have the authority to make that decision."

Tears formed despite her best efforts to contain them. "Oh. Okay," she said between sniffles. He glared at her.

You will not cry in front of all these people.

He sighed loudly. "But I'll make sure it happens."

Ella blinked, dazed from emotional whiplash. "You will?"

Agent Martin frowned skeptically. "Do you really think Barker will...?"

"She just walked into a meeting with the Director of National Intelligence, and can't be disturbed for the next three hours. I'll handle it. You don't have to be involved."

The other agent nodded. "Right, okay. Well, I'll send you everything I found. I already texted the rest of the team. They're en route."

Agent Donnelly turned to Ella, his face revealing nothing. "Let's get you a real bag."

Still in shock, Ella grabbed her things from the floor and kept pace with him down the hall.

For years she'd refused to dwell on her past, and yet she'd just insisted that the FBI take her back to the scene of some of her happiest childhood memories. It seemed contradictory, but her happiest memories hurt the most to relive by herself, so it remained to be seen if it would be as painful as she feared. But it was the only way.

She gritted her teeth through the drive to the airport, unable to relax.

Chapter 13
Mal and Ella

AGES 7 AND 8
(31 YEARS AGO)

"WHY IS IT CALLED a Swan Boat? Do swans pull it?" Even at seven, Mal had a gift for heavy sarcasm. With her arms crossed, she squirmed beside her mother in the line for Swan Boats tickets in Boston's Public Garden.

Valerie Madson smiled down at her as others around them in line tried to hide their amusement. "No, but there are some real swans in the lagoon. There's one over there. See it? It's called a Swan Boat because there's a giant cutout of a swan at the back. The guide sits back there to pedal, and that's how the boat moves."

"Yeah, I see it. That's dumb. They should call it a pedal boat."

"Well, I'm sure they considered that. But I guess they thought Swan Boats sounded nicer." She smoothed Mal's hair, but Mal jerked her head away.

"Don't, Mommy."

"Sorry." Valerie was unruffled by her younger daughter's surliness. "Even if you don't like the name, it might still be fun to ride it. Don't you think?"

Mal eyed the water warily. "I don't know. How deep is the water?"

"Deep enough so the bottom of the boat doesn't get stuck. But it's a small lagoon, so I don't think it goes too far down."

"Not as deep as the ocean, right?"

People in line around them stifled their laughter, and Valerie smiled. "No Mal, it's not as deep as the ocean. You have nothing to worry about."

Ella had been talking to her father, and now turned to Mal. "What's wrong? Are you scared to go on the Swan Boat?" Ella wasn't smiling, but she also didn't look sympathetic.

"No, that's dumb. Of course not."

As they often did, the two parents put themselves between the girls during the Swan Boat ride.

At the end of their picnic lunch near the Public Garden lagoon, Mal stood and gathered everyone's trash.

"I'll throw this away before the swans come after it," she said, glancing over her shoulder.

"Why thank you, Mal. How thoughtful," said Valerie.

As Mal took Ella's trash, she leaned down to whisper to her, "Count to thirty, then look under the corner of the blanket."

By the time Ella looked up at her, momentarily confused, her sister was skipping off toward the trash can nearby. *She wants to play HERE? Mom will not like that.*

But Mal had already taken off.

Ella glanced at her parents, who had not yet noticed that Mal had disappeared. When she got to thirty in her head, she crawled to the corner of the blanket where Mal had been and flipped it over. Underneath it, there was a Swan Boat ticket from their ride.

"Ella, do you know where Mal is?" There was panic in her mother's voice.

"She's playing the game again." Ella held up the ticket. "I think she's behind the ticket booth. I'll go check."

Ella scampered back toward the ticket booth, not far from their picnic spot. Before she rounded the narrow building, she heard a man's voice ask, "Are you lost, sweetheart?"

"No," Mal said, annoyed.

That was when Ella arrived. "There you are. Come on. Mom's not happy."

Their mother caught up with them, as well. "Mal, thank goodness. We've talked about this. Let's go." She thanked the man in the park employee uniform and took her younger daughter tightly by the hand. "Now."

"That was way too easy," Ella whispered to Mal, who gave her a devilish smile.

"Ella, please come walk on the other side of me before you two start fighting," said Valerie.

Ella skipped around to her mother's other side as they made their way back to their picnic blanket. As they walked, they had yet another serious discussion about why they did not play any form of hide and seek in public places.

Chapter 14
Ella

SUNDAY

ELLA SHIFTED THE BLACK backpack containing all her worldly possessions higher on her shoulder as she boarded the small charter plane bound for northern Michigan. Agent Donnelly was a step behind her. The open interior of the cabin was a surprise—she'd never been on a private jet before. At the back of the cabin, Agents Harrison and Jacobs were deep in conversation on either side of a table.

Ella stopped in the aisle. "Sit anywhere," said Agent Donnelly from behind her. Of the ten seats, she chose the first row by the window, while Agent Donnelly joined his team at the table. As soon as they were all seated, a single flight attendant closed the door and the others took their seats so they could push back from the gate.

Ella switched her phone into airplane mode. With nothing to distract her, all she could do was stew over her situation again, along with her dislike for flying. After years of self-analysis, she'd accepted that her need for control of her surroundings may have been part of why she disliked flying. Leaning forward and pressing her elbows into her knees, she lowered her face into her hands.

They'd leveled off when a rustling to her right told her that someone had joined her. The voice gave him away immediately.

"How are you holding up?"

She sat up and looked at Agent Harrison. His smile was genuine, and she relaxed slightly, despite a strange twinge of disappointment.

"I used to be terrified of flying. Now I wouldn't say I'm scared of it, only that I don't like it. But after everything else that's happened this week, flying doesn't seem as scary." She shrugged uncomfortably at the look of sympathy on his face, grasping for a new topic so she could change the subject.

Before either of them spoke, Agent Jacobs motioned for his attention from across the aisle. "Hang in there," he said as he unfolded himself from the seat.

She wasn't sure how long she'd been watching the clouds out the window, her mind drifting off, when a throat cleared loudly above her.

"I spoke with Agent Martin," Agent Donnelly said, looking down at her from where he stood in the aisle. "May I?" He looked down at the seat beside her.

"Of course."

He lowered himself into the seat beside her. "I also spoke with the team looking into who blew up your house. They're still following up on leads, but it looks like Mal is part of a trio who are suspected to be behind the data breach. Apparently, they left behind a digital signature."

Ella nodded. "I wish I could say 'Mal would never do that.' But..."

"Our research suggests that she hasn't changed."

Ella bit her lip, her hands fidgeting in her lap.

"So, how do you feel about this trip back to a place where you have so much history?"

She turned towards him in surprise at the change in topic. "I don't know. It's what needs to happen, because going there is how we find her. And I remember the times I spent there as happy..."

"But they were happy times with people who aren't around anymore, which is why I asked." The observation came out gently.

"Well, yes. I guess you could say the same about my house, too. It was the house I grew up in. But I'd lived there by myself for so many years... I was used to it. You're right, this probably won't be easy. I don't dwell on the past if I can help it. It's easier that way."

He studied her, his expression blank except for a touch of something she couldn't quite identify.

Unlike all those times years ago when she'd gotten pitying looks from well-meaning friends and extended family members after her parents' deaths, his kindness didn't bother her. Perhaps because he gave so little of it, and so reluctantly, it didn't feel like pity.

"Just take it one minute at a time," he said.

Her expression didn't change, but she wondered if her eyes gave away her surprise. She'd spent many years repeating those words to herself. It was strange to have it repeated back to her.

"Yeah," she said, looking down.

For a minute, neither of them spoke, but the silence wasn't uncomfortable. "Do you like your job?" she asked, looking back up at him.

"I do," he said thoughtfully. "No two cases are the same. I like knowing I've taken criminals off the street, and I like helping people find answers when other people couldn't."

She nodded.

"I assume you like your job, since you own your own business," he said.

"I like making order out of chaos," she said. "And giving people a space they can feel comfortable in. Making their home suit them."

And now I don't have one. The words popped into her head before she could stop them, and a sigh escaped her involuntarily.

"One minute at a time," he said softly, as if reading her mind. He reclined his chair, leaned back, and closed his eyes. Equal parts unease and warmth stirred inside her, and she turned back to focus on the clouds beyond the thick glass. They were quiet after that, but strangely, there was something comforting about his presence.

It was early afternoon when they landed at the tiny airport in Boyne City, Michigan, where they were directed to an area off to one end of the tarmac. Two black SUVs were dots in the distance, quickly growing to full size and pulling up in front of them.

The two men who'd just arrived flashed their badges, and after a signature and a few words, Agent Donnelly had the keys. The two men departed in the second SUV as Ella and Agent Donnelly's team walked toward theirs. Agent Jacobs walked up beside Ella, mumbling, "Take the front. Believe it or not, he's less grumpy with you than us."

Before Ella could disagree, Agent Jacobs was climbing into the back seat, and Agent Harrison had disappeared around the driver's side behind Agent Donnelly.

Agent Donnelly was setting the GPS on his phone and didn't look up as Ella settled into the passenger seat. Before she could close the door, he grumbled, "Come on, kids. Seatbelts. We don't have all day."

Ella clicked her seatbelt and peeked behind her to find the two 'kids' now buckled in, Agent Jacobs rolling her eyes and mouthing, "I told you."

"Do you mind if I turn on some music?" Ella asked.

"Knock yourself out."

She couldn't tell if the request annoyed him or not.

A country song blasted out of the radio when she turned it on, and she gave him an amused glance, eyebrows raised. He responded with a low grunt, eyes narrowed at her for a split second as if to say, "Do you have a problem with it?" Flattening her lips so she didn't smile, she flipped through the channels, settling on a pop song she hadn't heard in years. His mouth twitched, but otherwise he didn't react.

The drive to the little village at one end of Walloon Lake took only ten minutes. The road wound through the trees, and the music faded into the background as Ella went back in time. Suddenly, she was sitting in the back seat of her parents' old station wagon. A young Mal was beside her, and they flung themselves from one side of the car to the other, straining against their seatbelts as they exaggerated the curves of the winding road. They'd called this stretch, "The Walloon Lake Whip." Driving it now, as an adult, was strange because the curves weren't nearly as sharp as she'd remembered them.

What else will be different?

Her breath caught as they emerged from the trees on a short section of road that she recognized in a heartbeat. They were at the foot of the lake. Present-day Ella was both thrilled and on edge at the same time.

The sun was moving lower in the afternoon sky as they parked in the lot between the playground and the General Store. The first thing Ella noted was that the play equipment was new.

Of course it is. It's been twenty-four years. Time only stood still in your head.

To Ella, the current incarnation of "downtown Walloon Lake" was blasphemously overgrown, even though there were still only a handful of buildings. It all fit neatly into approximately two blocks, between a neighborhood at one end and a small bridge across the dam at the end of the lake at the other.

Outside the car, the three agents conferred. Both their suits and their vehicle marked them as comically out of place here, and Ella imagined what her younger self would have thought if she'd seen them. Her attention caught on the lake, and the sound of their voices fell away. She crossed the narrow, curbless street to the small patch of beach on the other side as if pulled by a magnet.

Lowering herself onto the metal bench halfway between the road and the water, she stared out at the lake spreading out before her. She knew that it went on for many miles, a long, irregular shape stretching north towards Lake Michigan. Not too far along the shore to her right, somewhere behind the trees, lay the building her family had called a cottage. She knew better now—it had been a large house.

Agent Donnelly sat down next to her on the bench, and she twisted in her seat to find the other two agents back across the street in the parking lot, gazing in their direction but keeping their distance.

She stiffened, waiting for a clue about his mood. His face gave away nothing.

"It's beautiful here," he said. No frustration, no impatience.

Ella relaxed, glancing at him before looking back out at the lake. "Yeah. The lake, at least, is just like I remember it."

He cleared his throat. "It's time to go. We'll start canvasing the locals before things close for the day."

Her head bobbed in agreement, but her eyes remained fixed on the water. He got up and started back toward the parking lot, but she couldn't bring herself to follow him. She'd missed this place desperately, and now here she was.

Just another minute, a voice in the back of her head begged, and her chest ached.

She stood on shaky legs and took her phone out of her pocket, opening the camera app and holding it up so the lake appeared on the screen.

It's like taking a picture of my past.

The last time she'd been there, every single part of her life had been different. There had been so many times over the years when she would've given everything for a moment like this, bittersweet as it was.

Inhaling slowly, she dragged her eyes away from the water, forcing her feet to walk past Agent Donnelly, who was waiting for her by the road. She couldn't risk meeting his eyes—if the flicker of emotion she'd seen in his face a moment before was still there, it would push her over the edge.

Their first stop was the General Store. A bell chimed over the door as they walked in, and a young blonde in a white t-shirt and jeans leaned against the counter reading a magazine. Ella's eyes darted from one corner of the store to another, amazed that it almost matched her memory. She saw a younger version of herself skipping gleefully towards the shelf of candy that had been on the wall across from the register.

"Please, Daddy? May I get one?" Younger Ella gazed over her shoulder at her father, batting her eyelashes.

"Alright Bella, but it's our secret, okay?"

As quickly as it had appeared, the scene disappeared before her eyes, leaving her wanting to laugh and cry at the same time.

When her surroundings faded back in, she found the agents watching her, and the cashier understandably unsure what to make of their group. Agent Donnelly raised an eyebrow at Ella, but said nothing.

She nodded, then turned to the cashier. "Hi, we're looking for my sister. She looks a lot like me. Same hair and eyes, and she would've been in here in the last few days."

The young woman, probably still a teenager, tilted her head in thought. "Oh wow, at first I thought you were the same person. You really look like her. She's been here a few times in the last couple days. Always with a British guy. The last time I saw them was this morning."

"Did you hear them saying anything in particular? Like where they were staying?"

The blonde shook her head. "Nothing like that. This morning they bought a bunch of food. Mostly snacks. That's all I know. You can't just call her?"

"No. I'm... here to surprise her. Anyway, thanks." She forced herself to smile even as a heavy blanket of disappointment draped itself over her. What was she thinking? Of course, Mal hadn't announced where they were staying in the middle of a store.

She had to get out of there. Without caring whether the others followed, she burst through the front door into the fresh air. Agent Jacobs was only a step behind her.

Ella leaned against the wall, catching her breath.

"You did great in there," said the agent.

Ella sighed. "I didn't think it would be so hard."

Before they could say any more, the other agents emerged from the building. "Let's keep going," Agent Donnelly said. He focused on Ella, his usual blank expression firmly in place.

She stood up straight and tried to appear more determined than she felt.

"You want one of us to take the lead?" Agent Harrison asked.

It was an appealing thought, but she shook her head. "No, I'm okay."

As they approached the next building, Ella stopped short on the sidewalk. "Wait. Where's the post office? Why is it a pastry shop?"

She read and reread the sign above the door, where the word "Pastries" taunted her. It had always been a post office. Always. It was supposed to be a post office. Blinking back tears, she fought to catch up with her racing mind, and to convince herself that it didn't matter.

Stop it. It's a stupid reason to cry.

No.

She wasn't sure if she'd said it aloud, or only in her head.

This time, Agent Donnelly waved the other two on toward the door, remaining behind with her on the sidewalk.

Her face twitched, and she took a deep breath, leaning her back against the wall by the door. She really didn't want to break down in front of Agent Donnelly. Fighting hard to control her emotions, she continued to avoid his eyes. "I know, I'm being ridiculous. Things change. But..." Her voice broke and she bit her lip, unwilling to risk saying more and opening the floodgates.

"But it's not fair," he said, and the kindness in his voice threatened to undo what little control of her emotions remained. At that moment, she missed the Agent Donnelly she'd hated, the one who'd made her so angry. Anger was so much easier than sadness.

She tried to smile, but the tensing of the muscles around her eyes pressed tears even closer to falling.

What am I doing here? Why did I think tagging along was a good idea?

"I'm sorry. I shouldn't have insisted on coming here. I should've stayed in DC."

He laid a hand gently on her shoulder before she could turn away. "No, you were right. Even if my boss isn't convinced. Who knows what being here will help you remember? Any detail might help us." He paused, and she glanced at him through glassy eyes. "And this way, I can be sure you're safe."

His confession distracted her from the pounding in her head and from the urge to cry. She didn't know what to say, or how to explain why his words hooked inside her chest and tugged. Inside the glass doors of the pastry shop, the other two agents talked to the man at the counter.

Again, she didn't risk looking at him—even the slightest trace of sympathy would be more than she could handle. "We should get in there," she said. Forcing her feet to move, she didn't stop until she entered the small pastry shop with Agent Donnelly behind her.

"Ah, this is the one. Yes, the woman who was here was definitely your sister," said the man behind the counter. "They were here yesterday. She was with the man with the accent. British, I think. I haven't seen them today, though."

Ella absorbed this information. At least two people had seen Mal. The voices of the agents and the cashier faded into an echo as she waited for the conversation to be over. When the others turned toward the door, she followed, still not listening.

After that, Ella let the agents lead, tuning their voices out. It was all she could do to stand and let strangers study her.

Agent Donnelly stayed back with her when she fell behind. He didn't smile or act overly sympathetic, but he also showed no impatience. That was surprising, because by the last building she was annoyed with herself.

Mal had made an impression on everyone she'd met, but no one had seen them since that morning.

"My grandparents' cottage... er, house... should be just a few minutes down the path, if you want me to show you." She bit her lip and hoped she wouldn't regret making that offer.

"Lead the way," said Agent Donnelly.

They took the narrow path two by two. As a child, Ella recalled walking it single file, mostly because she and Mal couldn't be within arm's-length without fighting. Mal always had to be first, but Ella hadn't minded—that way, Mal couldn't step on her heels or kick the backs of her legs.

The path narrowed and widened from yard to yard, houses on their right and the lake on the left. The size of the houses varied widely, and some properties had their own small beach, while others simply had a dock extending out over the water. Some had both, and a few even had a small boathouse, or a rocky overlook with lawn chairs set up near the edge.

Some houses had been upgraded so much in the years since Ella's last visit, they were unrecognizable. She did her best to look away.

When the path passed through a dense cluster of trees separating one property from another, Ella had a distinct flash of nostalgia. The "woods" were only about five feet from end to end—much smaller than the spooky "mini-forest" she'd remembered them to be. They walked through it in seconds.

A few more houses down, they left the unpaved path in front of a heavily wooded property, and stepped onto a paved sidewalk in front of a house with floor to ceiling windows that would have been described as 'modern' in the

1970s. She would've known this house anywhere—it had belonged to her grandparents' next-door neighbors, and it matched her memories exactly.

Gazing across the yard toward the water, she saw her young self and the neighbors' four or five grandchildren playing a game they'd invented together. Their course stretched between the two properties, the participants running in a large circle across both lawns and then up five steps made of weathered railroad ties onto the neighbors' sidewalk, moving as fast as they could across the scorching concrete in bare feet before jumping into the cool grass in front of her grandparents' house again. She watched her younger self squeal with glee as she scored a point for her team by making it to the finish line, marked by the two huge evergreens between their properties, without being hit by the beach balls the other team carried.

The game had been a mix of obstacle course, tag and baseball. She wanted to say they'd called it "Chase," but she couldn't be sure.

Keeping her eyes on the ground ahead, she swallowed hard.

"It's the next house."

Chapter 15
Ella

SUNDAY

E LLA PASSED THE TOWERING evergreens at the property line, gazing first towards the lake as she stepped off the left side of the sidewalk onto the grass. The sapling they'd planted the summer she'd been eleven was now a full-grown tree. This change didn't bother her—trees were expected to grow. A gentle slope led down towards the water, where the beach was no more than ten feet wide. To the left of the beach was a wooden dock, white paint peeling slightly.

It was almost exactly as she remembered. The only thing missing was her grandad's pontoon boat with blue siding that belonged on a lift at the end of the dock, just off the right side. The many things that had stayed the same were a familiar blanket for her soul. She smiled at the vivid memory of her younger self bent over in the shallow water, hunting hour after sun-drenched hour for distinctively speckled Petoskey stones or minnows that she could scoop up in her brightly colored bucket if she was fast enough.

She turned hesitantly toward the house, not looking up until she was facing it. When she did, her eyes went wide and she inhaled sharply, light-headed from the rush of emotions flooding her all at once.

Anywhere else, she could have appreciated this modern house with wide, steep stairs leading up to a large porch, but not here. It was beautiful, but it looked absolutely nothing like it once had, and her brain screamed in protest.

Because of the slope of the land, the two-story house looked much taller and grander than it would have on a flat property. That was the only thing this one had in common with its predecessor. The older house had been built in the

1960s or 1970s, but the house in front of her screamed "New!" This house had deep blue siding instead of plain white. The windows were larger and newer, the trim wide and decorative. In her memory, a narrow set of stairs had led up to a screen door at one end of the porch, which had been surrounded by a wall of windows. On this house, a grand staircase stood in the middle of the space, open to the weather.

Thick pillars flanked the stairs, and soft yellow cushions complemented the homey yet obviously expensive dark wooden porch furniture. If she hadn't known that this sophisticated lake house stood on the spot where 'her' house should've been, she would never have recognized it.

It was gorgeous, and she had never hated anything more.

How dare they? How could they change what was absolutely perfect?

It doesn't matter. It doesn't.

She closed her eyes and she could still see herself sitting on the porch, playing cards with Mal and their dad. Or sitting in the chair with the metal frame and pillow soft cushion—the one they'd been forbidden to put their feet on—where she'd watched the hummingbirds visit the hummingbird feeder. How those tiny creatures could hover in mid-air, drinking with their pointed beaks, had seemed like magic.

It doesn't matter. If she said it enough, maybe she would believe it.

"It's..." Her breaths were quick and shallow as she stumbled forward across the grass, unable to take her eyes off the monstrosity in front of her. "It's wrong. It wasn't... It's not..." Her voice shook as her chest compressed, and holding herself up became increasingly difficult. The team had remained on the sidewalk, giving her space, but they may as well have vanished. Everything but the unfamiliar house had disappeared from her view. Agent Donnelly suddenly materialized a few feet away from her, his eyes full of concern. Behind him, the other two agents now wore that expression she knew all too well—the same one people had directed her way as she'd stood alone at her mother's funeral. The look she hated.

"Poor Ella, now she's lost both her parents. Still no boyfriend. She just keeps to herself. Now she has no one." They'd whispered it to each other when they thought she couldn't hear them.

She didn't want pity any more now than she had then.

All at once she was charging back down the path toward the village. She stumbled more than once, narrowly avoiding hitting the ground each time.

"Ella!"

Her name ricocheted through the trees from behind her as it echoed over the water. She'd already flown by two houses, fleeing as fast as she could. From somewhere on her left, a muffled conversation stopped abruptly, followed by the slam of a door. These sounds, like all the others around her, registered only in the back of her mind. By the time she heard them, she'd already passed their sources.

Though quickly winded, her muscles burning with exertion, she didn't slow down. All she knew was she had to get away. This version of Walloon Lake was so like the one she remembered, but still wrong. She was a time traveler who'd returned to the right year, but the wrong reality. Or, more accurately, the right reality in the wrong year. Either way, her past had been dangled in front of her just long enough to pull her in, only to slap her so hard that every inch of her stung.

By the time she reached the village main street, her lungs were on fire and she couldn't run any farther. She stopped, bent over with her hands propped on her knees, for just long enough to catch her breath before pushing onward. She ended up at the same public beachfront she'd been drawn to earlier.

It's not fair.

She heard the words in the same gentle voice in which Agent Donnelly had said them earlier. That was the last straw, and her composure finally broke, her grief erupting in heaving sobs as she dropped into the sand. She pulled off her shoes and socks and threw them angrily to one side, digging her toes defiantly into the sand as if someone was there to stop her. This place had been the closest thing to a home she had left, but now she saw that it, too, was already gone.

It was too much.

She hadn't thought it was possible, but the pain in her chest was even greater than it had been after she'd watched her house—and her life—explode before her eyes. A hundred times more.

Though only moments ago she'd needed to be alone, away from the agents' looks of pity, suddenly loneliness crushed her from all sides. She couldn't win. This was exactly why she didn't give in to remembering. It never ended well.

A sound behind her told her she had company, but she kept her eyes on the water, feet burrowed in the sand and her arms tightly hugging her knees. Still fighting back the sobs that pounded at her insides, she didn't care who it was. The agents would be furious with her for taking off. Or maybe it was whoever had blown up her house. She couldn't even bring herself to care. If they meant her harm, so be it.

Agent Donnelly lowered himself onto the sand beside her, and she braced herself for his reprimand. At the same time, some part of her was glad to see him.

"A little warning next time?" As always, his face was serious. "You're pretty fast."

"Sorry," she whispered.

"I'm sorry, too."

Her eyes were glassy when she looked at him.

"I wish you didn't have to go through any of this," he said softly.

The urge to smile forced her eyelids closed, pushing out a few more tears. She rested her forehead on her knees, too tired to pretend to be okay. "I just want to go back to the way it was."

"I know." Something in his voice told her he wasn't just saying that.

There was nothing else to say.

She wasn't sure what she expected him to say or do, but she relaxed slightly when she glanced over and found his attention on the lake. The minutes ticked on as they sat quietly, and the panic leaked out of her little by little, replaced by exhaustion. She released her grip on her knees, keeping her focus on the sun setting over the water. Though this wasn't the exact spot from which she'd watched it as a child, the view was similar enough to remind her of summer nights when she'd watched the sunset with her family. The vivid flashback was comforting, even as a bittersweet pain tugged at her insides. As horrible as it all was, at least she wasn't alone for once.

She chided herself as the urge to rest her head on his shoulder came out of nowhere. He wasn't a friend or a significant other; he was an FBI agent here to protect her—apparently despite her complete lack of self-preservation instincts. The only thing that would come of taking comfort from his presence was disappointment when he was gone. She knew that.

And yet. She couldn't quite make the feeling of relief at his presence go away completely.

They'd been silent for going on fifteen minutes, both staring out at the horizon, when she emerged from her thoughts and asked, "Where are the others?"

"Canvassing the neighbors for any sign of Mal and the mystery man."

She looked away and pressed her lips together until they hurt, then released them. Filling her lungs with air, she tried to breathe in courage along with it.

"Thank you." *For not looking at me with pity. For following me both times I ran away. For not talking to me. For just being here.* She didn't elaborate aloud, but she had the strange feeling he understood. He didn't ask questions, for which she was also thankful.

They stared out at the water again, lost in thought, until his phone buzzed.

"Yeah," he barked at the caller. After long seconds of silence, he nodded. "Okay. See you there." He turned to Ella. "The others had some luck. Someone who saw Mal and her companion thought they were staying at a rental house along the path. But it's late..." He shook his head. "As frustrating as it is, we have to call it a night and start again in the morning."

She exhaled, looking out at the lake again as every muscle in her body tensed. *Don't cry.*

"I wish I could tell you everything is going to work out okay."

She looked up at him. "I don't need you to lie to me."

"No, I mean I wish I could believe it myself. I'd be more convincing when I lied to other people if I believed in happy endings."

She couldn't tell if this was honesty or deadpan humor, but either way, she didn't have it in her to react. It was ridiculous to think that any of this would be okay anyway. "Don't worry about it. I don't believe in them either."

Gazing out at the lake again, she sighed. "Once in a while, I convince myself I'm not hopelessly broken, but it never lasts. Life always smacks me in the face again." Her fingers clasped and unclasped in front of her knees. "But this... it's too much. How can I ever get past it?"

Reluctantly meeting his eyes, she found something a lot like empathy for the second time. For several seconds, something unspoken passed between them. "It feels like you're dying, but you're not. I promise you. Just keep going."

She opened her mouth to speak, but nothing came out. Too emotionally spent to be mortified for putting her vulnerability on display, she shook her head. "I should remember that from experience, right?" The words didn't come out in the light, funny tone she'd meant them to. She heard her own bitterness and cringed.

Stop talking. Her eyes went back to the water.

Again, his voice was as soothing as the sight of the lake. "Don't beat yourself up. Sometimes it helps to hear it from someone else, even if we already know it."

He was right, and the sadness pressed down on her with just a little less force.

"The others are going to meet us at the car, and Agent Martin is finding us a hotel. The one here in town is not in our budget." He stood, brushing sand off himself, and then held out his hand to help her up. She hesitated only a second, telling herself that the rush she felt as he pulled her to her feet was simply because she was emotionally spent.

With her shoes in hand, she walked to the water's edge and stopped within an inch of where it lapped the shore, the faint sound an echo from her past. She focused on the feeling of her toes in the sand, and just like that, a childhood of summer memories once again flooded her mind's eye—an explosion of sunburns, popsicles, brilliant sunshine, and happy squeals. She had long since edited out the unpleasant parts.

Calm descended over her. The stillness of the evening was interrupted only by the chirp of insects, and the intense emotions of the day drained from her, leaving her empty.

Sam was waiting for her where the sand ended and the concrete began, and she stopped in front of him.

"How old were you the last time you were here?" he asked.

"Fifteen, I think." The sight of the atrocity that had replaced her grandparents' cottage flashed behind her eyelids, and she looked down at the sand under her feet with a heavy sigh. She lifted one foot, brushing off the bottom and wrestling it into her sock. When she almost lost her balance, she instinctively grasped the only solid object within reach—Sam's bicep.

"Oh—sorry," she said. Her cheeks burned and she tensed as she looked up at him, expecting irritation but finding what looked like amusement.

"Don't be." He reached over and plucked her other shoe and sock from where she'd been holding them under her arm, as if helping her was an everyday occurrence.

She finished getting her shoe on without looking up again, already feeling awkward enough this close to him, then switched feet and repeated the process. Only when both feet were in her shoes and back on the ground did she reluctantly release her grip on his arm.

"Thanks," she whispered.

He frowned at her as if trying to read her thoughts. "Are you okay?"

Do I look as miserable as I feel?

She wanted to pretend to be fine, but she just didn't have it in her. "No." Her voice cracked, and suddenly the tears were back.

No. Do not cry. Do not cry.

"Do you... need a hug?" The question came out with great reluctance, as though he was hoping she would say no, or he expected her to shove him backwards and run.

No, she thought, but the message failed to transmit to the rest of her. By the time she understood that she'd nodded yes, his arms were moving awkwardly around her. It was only then that she admitted to herself just how badly she had, in fact, needed a hug. Her head fell against his shoulder, her thoughts turned off, and she exhaled a shaky breath as she held onto the only person who hadn't left her yet.

Yet.

Another shiver moved through her. *But only because it's his job to be here.*

His arms tightened around her ever so slightly in response, and along with a pain in her chest came a sob. She bit her lip to keep any more from escaping as her body shook silently.

Eventually her tears ran out, her breathing slowed down, and after a few more minutes, she lifted her head and let go of him, at which his hold on her loosened, as well.

"Better?" he asked, moving back and looking into her eyes with genuine concern. She could only give him the slightest nod in reply.

Not good, but not as bad.

They fell into step side by side, moving away from the beach.

By the time Ella and the three agents left the General Store with sandwiches and drinks, Agent Martin was in the agents' ears again.

"Our hotel is in Petoskey," Agent Donnelly told Ella as they settled themselves in the front seat of the SUV. "I assume you've been there."

"Yes, many times," she said, her voice wavering slightly.

She could feel the weight of Agent Donnelly's stare as he studied her reaction, but she avoided eye contact, not speaking the rest of the way to the hotel. Instead, she gave in to the rare indulgence of remembering: building sandcastles on their little beach, swimming in the shallow water, or enjoying her favorite pirate-themed mini-golf course. Her dad had always won, despite claiming every single time that he'd never played mini golf before. Afterwards, they always stopped for huge ice cream cones at a nearby family-owned shop before heading back to the house.

Before parting for the night, the four agreed to meet at seven o'clock the next morning. If Ella hadn't been so exhausted, she might have been intimidated when Agent Donnelly stomped to the window of the room she would be sharing with Agent Jacobs and tugged the heavy blackout curtains across them. He swung around to address both Ella and Agent Jacobs with the same accusatory tone. "Make sure the curtains stay closed at all times. Under no circumstances do you open them. Got it?" Only when they mumbled agreement did he mutter, "Goodnight," stalking across the hall.

"Wow," said Ella, raising her eyebrows. "Even for him, that was..."

Agent Jacobs watched him go, amused. "He's extra protective of you. I'm a little surprised he didn't insist on sleeping on our floor."

When Ella's eyes widened at the thought, Agent Jacobs laughed.

"I'm not offended. It's cute. He's been the least grumpy on this case that I've seen him for a long time, if you can believe that." She paused to let her words sink in. "But enough about him. You look like you're about to pass out. You take the bathroom first."

While Ella wished she could've been alone, she had to admit that she felt safer with an FBI agent in the room with her. Even so, she tossed and turned for a long time, tensing with every sound from the hallway, no matter how small. She bit her lip and pulled the blankets over her head, eventually falling into a restless sleep.

Chapter 16
Mal

SUNDAY

ONE MINUTE MAL HAD been relaxing on the deck of their rented lake house, gazing out at the water, and the next, she'd jumped out of her chair and bolted inside. She was still pacing back and forth, mumbling to herself, when Jimmy followed her inside.

He stepped in front of her and shook her by the shoulders. "What the hell is wrong with you?"

"I think I just saw my sister."

"Do you mean the woman who just ran by with that chap yelling her name behind her? Ellen or something?"

"Ella. Yes. I can't believe she came…" Mal stopped and gazed into the distance, lost in thought.

"I'm sorry? Did you… *invite* her? To our hideout?"

"What? No. Of course not. I just… It was a game we used to play. I've been trying to get her to play for years."

"What the hell are you talking about?"

"Forget it. It doesn't matter."

"The hell it doesn't. You wanted her to come here?" Jimmy spoke slowly and precisely.

"No! I mean… I left a Petoskey stone on her doorstep…"

"Mallory, speak English."

"It's a thing we did when we were kids. I'd give her a clue to where to come and find me. We… didn't get along as teenagers, and stopped speaking to each other for a long time. But I've been giving her clues for ten years, and as far as

I know, she's ignored them. I never thought..." She shook her head. "God, it figures this would be the time... I just can't believe it. I haven't seen her in twenty years."

"Somehow leaving her a rock tells her to come find you in the middle of nowhere in Michigan?"

Mal sighed. "We used to come here as kids. Petoskey stones are unique to this area. I left it for her before the house blew up. I was going to come here anyway. Of course, I didn't know..."

"So let me get this straight. We pulled off our biggest job yet, and you told your sister where we were going to hide out?"

Mal dragged her hands over her face. "She has never once reacted to anything I sent her. How would I have known that her house would blow up? Or that this would be the time she'd follow me?"

"Bloody hell, Mallory. This was monumentally stupid of you."

Mal's face hardened, but she said nothing.

"So you don't think she saw you out there?"

"No. There's no way. She was looking straight ahead. I didn't even realize it was her until she was two houses past us. If that guy hadn't yelled her name, it never would've even occurred to me."

"We have to go. Today. Now." Jimmy, the member of the pair who was always calm, looked shaken.

"What? No! She ran away. They didn't see me. It's fine."

"It *was* fine. Before she was here. But she brought the police with her. Didn't you see those other three? They were feds, probably FBI. Even if this was a coincidence, they're not going to leave without poking around, asking questions. We should not be here for that."

Mal grinned at him as if he'd told a joke. "I did not take you for someone with a paranoid side."

Jimmy's eyes went wide. "Paranoid?" He screamed the word with full intensity, but at a low volume, which was somehow even more terrifying. Pinching the bridge of his nose, he closed his eyes and dropped his hand, then looked at her and exhaled deliberately. She'd never seen this emotional side of him, and she found it very amusing.

He spoke as if explaining it to a child. "Bri is dead. She was with Ray when she was shot in the head. He said only one shot was fired. It had to have been a sniper. So that's why I'm saying we do not need to be anywhere near any kind of trouble, and especially not if there are cops or feds around."

She stepped backwards, sitting on the bed as her knees buckled. "Bri... what? You didn't tell me."

"I just found out. Bri is dead. That's why she's not answering you."

All three of them had done plenty of things to make enemies, so it didn't necessarily mean they were also in danger... but it could.

"And that's why I'm telling you I'm not taking any chances. Five minutes, Mallory. Stay if you want to, but I'm going."

Still in a daze, she shook her head to clear it. There was no time to be shocked. "OK. We'll go." She thought back to the uneasiness she'd felt since they'd arrived here. Were they being watched?

Jimmy was already packing their things, tornado-style, jamming them back into their suitcases.

"I'll clean up downstairs," said Mal, standing up robotically. "It'll be as though we were never here."

"Good." Jimmy was too busy erasing all traces of them to look up. "Get on with it, then."

Chapter 17

Ella

MONDAY

E LLA STIRRED IN HER hotel bed, squinting in the darkness. *Please don't let it be time to get up yet.* The clock read 1:47 am. Plenty of night left.

She turned over to go back to sleep, cursing the hotel mattress that was somehow both too firm and too soft. Just before she dropped back into unconsciousness, the hair on the back of her neck prickled, and she froze, listening. There was a faint *thump* from the direction of the door, and Ella rolled over, eyes now wide, expecting to see Agent Jacobs padding to the bathroom.

But the outline of Agent Jacobs was still in her bed. Ella jolted to high alert, holding her breath as adrenaline coursed through her veins. *Did I imagine that? Did it come from another room?* Her eyes struggled to focus in the darkness.

The shape of a man appeared, advancing steadily. He was not one of the FBI agents, but he was familiar to her.

The contractor, the one the sketch artist drew.

His eyes glowed an unnatural blue, reflecting the light from the digital alarm clock, which also illuminated his menacing scowl and the wire stretched between his hands.

She opened her mouth to scream, but no sound came out. In the other bed, Agent Jacobs stirred but showed no sign of waking up.

If I don't do something, I'm going to die.

Finally reacting, Ella kicked at the covers, scrambling towards the far side of the bed. The covers twisted around her as if to prevent her escape as she gulped for air.

"Help." Her cry was weak, and she couldn't take her eyes off the man to see if Agent Jacobs had heard her. She pushed herself across the bed without looking behind her, even though getting away from her attacker seemed less and less likely. "Help," she said again, louder this time.

Ella fell backwards off the bed with a loud thump, and she lost sight of the stranger. When she looked up a second later, he had sprung across the bed with surprising agility and was inches away and closing in.

As fast as she could, Ella flattened herself against the floor and wiggled her way into the narrow space under the bed. Her screams were coming out louder, and she kicked her feet furiously against hands that grabbed at them as she pushed farther under the bed.

For an instant, the hands stopped reaching for her, and she squirmed toward the middle of the queen-sized bed, hyper-ventilating as she repeatedly hit her head against the bottom of the frame. There were sounds of a scuffle and the *thud* of a heavy weight—probably a person—hitting the ground nearby made Ella flinch.

She'd done her best to make herself tiny and silent, hoping it would save her, but suddenly a hand wrapped firmly around her ankle. Despite her most powerful kicks, it did not let go. Her stomach dropped. This was it.

With nothing solid to hold on to, she could only claw at the carpet in vain as the hand dragged her out from under the bed.

She screamed at the top of her lungs.

"Let her go and put your hands behind your head."

Ella was so relieved to hear Agent Jacobs' voice, she almost cried. But the man did not let go of her. As if he hadn't even heard the agent, he kept his foot planted painfully over her midsection and bent down towards Ella with the wire between his hands again. Just before Agent Jacobs sprung towards him, he snapped up again, and was now aiming a gun at her.

The moment the man let go of Ella, she immediately squirmed her way back under the bed. Sounds of a struggle that she assumed to be between the agent and the man reached her from what felt like far away. The noise ended abruptly, seconds later, with a gunshot and then a loud thud. Ella winced, squeezing her eyes shut even though she couldn't see what was going on. When the door opened, she heard another loud confrontation before it slammed again. Footsteps retreated, and less than a minute later someone was pounding on the door. Ella stayed put under the bed, gasping for air and unable to stop the torrent of tears.

"Ella! Jacobs!"

She almost cried with relief when she heard Agent Donnelly's voice. It boomed even louder than the hammering on the door or her thundering heartbeat.

From the hallway, there was swearing, then a soft beep and electronic click as a keycard unlocked the door. Agent Donnelly burst in, shouting, though Ella couldn't make out the words. Something about 911. The voice was loud, agitated. He was talking to Agent Jacobs, though he wasn't getting any responses that Ella could hear.

"Ella!" he screamed.

She couldn't move, only lay where she was under the bed and cry. He stopped calling her name long enough to locate her by her whimpering, and the next moment he was on the floor beside the bed, murmuring words she couldn't decipher over the noise in her head. Even though her brain recognized his voice, when a hand landed gently on her shoulder, her whole body shuddered. The hand lifted away.

"Ella, it's me. Agent Donnelly."

She exhaled raggedly, curling her body toward the voice and bumping her shoulder against the underside of the bed. Trapped, her exhales became sobs, but still she did not open her eyes.

"Hang on," he said. "If I lift the bed up, can you scoot out?"

She nodded, assuming he could see her, and almost immediately, the bed frame lifted into the air.

"All right, come on," said Agent Donnelly, his voice strained. "I can't hold this too long."

She scooted forward until she was lying between the beds, curling onto her side. He grunted softly as he replaced the bed frame on the floor, then kneeled in front of her and leaned closer. "Are you hurt?"

His hand had found her shoulder again, but this time she didn't flinch. She took a breath and opened her eyes to find his face only inches away. She didn't bother to wipe her tear-stained cheeks. "I... I don't think so."

"Good."

"Is Agent Jacobs okay? I heard a gunshot."

He inhaled as if to steady himself. "Agent Jacobs is okay. Looks like he just knocked her out. I called 911 already. Can you tell me what happened?"

He nodded throughout her retelling, looking like he wanted to say something but keeping his lips pressed together. "I'm glad you're safe," was all he said when she'd finished.

"Did you get him? The man?"

Agent Donnelly's face turned stormy. "He got away, but he won't get far. Agent Jacobs must have shot him, which would have been the gunshot you heard, and there was blood down the hall that I assume is his. We'll find them. The cavalry should be here any second. Can you sit up?"

There was a knock on the door, and the sound of commotion in the hall. Agent Donnelly helped her sit up against Agent Jacobs' bed, facing away from the door, and looked at her seriously.

"Don't move, okay? Just rest right here."

"Okay," she said.

She listened as Agent Donnelly opened the door, but the chaos remained outside when it closed again, muffled.

The door clicked open again, and the crackle of radios entered the room, stopping behind her.

Agent Donnelly came around the corner from the direction of the door. "Just us, Ella. The EMTs are going to take care of Agent Jacobs, then they'll check on you."

"Okay." She settled against the bed, glancing back to see him standing behind the paramedics, his face grim.

Once the EMTs began loading Agent Jacobs onto a stretcher, partially conscious, Agent Donnelly sat on the floor beside Ella.

As was becoming her habit lately, she pulled her knees to her chest and wrapped her arms around them.

"Are you cold?"

She shook her head. "No."

"You're shivering."

He moved away only far enough to throw the blanket off the end of her bed and yank the flat sheet off, then wrapped it around her.

"This may not be as warm, but those blankets are disgusting," he mumbled, spending longer than necessary adjusting the sheet around her and tucking the ends together. When he finally deemed the sheet's folds acceptable, he met her eyes and gave her a weak smile.

"Is that any better?" he asked.

She nodded, still shivering.

"Good."

"What's wrong?" she asked.

Before he could answer, the EMTs were standing above them.

"Ready for us?" one of them asked.

Agent Donnelly got out of the way, retreating to talk to other agents in FBI windbreakers and a few uniform-clad police officers who'd streamed into the room, but his eyes continuously bounced back to hers.

The EMTs crouched in front of Ella. She answered their questions distractedly, the buzz of conversations around her blurring together. Every time anyone made a sudden move, she cringed. When their work was finally done, the EMTs gathered their things and departed. Ella hugged her legs to her chest again, resting her cheek on her knee. From a few steps away, Agent Donnelly mumbled something to the other agents he was standing with and made his way back to her.

Closing her eyes to escape the now-noisy room, Ella tensed as a slow-motion replay of her assailant's approach played behind her eyes: the pale, lanky but muscular man with short dark hair advanced toward her. His icy, florescent blue eyes glinted maliciously in the light of the alarm clock. He held the wire between his hands and grinned.

She gasped as she pushed her eyes open to get rid of the image, still hugging her knees. Agent Donnelly reached her then, resting a hand on her shoulder, and Ella focused on him.

He stared into her eyes and didn't have to ask if she was okay this time. The answer was pretty obvious.

She exhaled slowly, holding eye contact with him as though it were a life raft.

"Why don't you go get changed?" he said. "Here's your backpack."

When she re-emerged from the bathroom in a clean T-shirt and jeans, face washed and teeth brushed, she was still just as shaken. Her head felt foggy, and her movements unnaturally slow. Ella wondered if this was the adrenaline wearing off, or something more serious. Maybe she was going into shock.

Agent Donnelly was only a few feet away, standing with two other agents, but not appearing to listen to what they were saying.

"Ella, come and sit down," he said, waving her back toward the bed. "We need you to tell us exactly what happened." The other agents, whose names she didn't know, gathered around, while Agent Donnelly sat down next to her. "Start from last night when we split up and tell me everything you remember."

She focused on her hands in her lap and ignored the sea of faces around her. While halting at first, her retelling of the events of the night picked up speed as she went.

When she'd finished, Agent Donnelly looked almost as shaken as she was. "How confident are you that it's the contractor who came to your door the day your house blew up?"

"As sure as I can be." Though he'd been much nicer to her recently, she still paused, wondering if he would again chastise her for letting a stranger into her yard. He did not.

Her mind was reeling by the time she'd answered all their questions, and she wanted to curl up and take a nap.

The agents were in a huddle by the far wall, and they all leaned in to listen to Agent Donnelly. One agent raised her eyebrows in surprise, peered at Ella, and then back to him. Agent Donnelly shook his head sternly, mumbling something else before leaving the group and returning to Ella.

"Come on, let's get out of here."

"Wait," said Ella. "What aren't you telling me? Where's Agent Harrison?"

His face changed, and he looked at the floor with a heavy sigh. "Last night we took turns being awake to watch for trouble in your room," he said. "He knew I wouldn't sleep otherwise. He was the one awake when it happened. Maybe he looked away for a minute... I don't know how the guy slipped in unnoticed. From what I can tell, Harrison probably heard the gunshot when Agent Jacobs shot the assailant. That was what woke me up. I imagine he was on his way into your room—we both had keycards for it, in case of trouble."

He took a deep breath. "We think Agent Jacobs just grazed the guy, because he had plenty of fight left in him. He left your room swinging a knife just as Harrison was on his way in... I saw the guy run around the corner to the stairs, but Harrison was in rough shape. I had to choose. I couldn't leave him to bleed out."

Even as Ella sucked in air, for a few seconds she had the lightheaded sensation of suffocating.

"I was too late. Again." His words shook, bringing her back to reality.

Her chest squeezed painfully. "You did the right thing," she said, but he didn't react. She put a hand on his arm. "Sam."

He finally looked down at her.

"You did the right thing."

He nodded, though he didn't look convinced.

"Is Agent Harrison going to be okay?"

His foot tapped fast against the floor, and he took a deep breath. "I don't know. He'd lost a lot of blood by the time the ambulance got here. They're on their way to the hospital now."

Her tears welled up again, spilling down her cheeks. "This is because of me."

"No, Ella. Not because of you." The vehemence of his response surprised her. "It wasn't even because of Mal. The assassin who tried to kill you and whoever hired him are the only ones responsible for this."

She sniffled, unable to rein in her tears, and pressed her face into his shoulder. Agent Donnelly wrapped his arms around her, and she nearly broke apart from the relief.

They sat that way for a few minutes, until he leaned down to speak into her ear. "Come on. We have to keep moving. This doesn't stop until we solve it."

A group of them left the room in formation, stepping carefully around the large blood stain between the two hotel rooms, where the techs were still working. Agent Donnelly was in front, then Ella, then two new agents replacing the two who'd been hurt protecting her. Behind the four of them were two vaguely familiar agents whose names she didn't know.

All six of them crowded into the elevator. When they emerged into the lobby, two of the replacement agents flanked Ella, and the other two followed behind her.

From the reception desk, the Manager led them down a narrow hallway to the hotel security office. The middle-aged woman who answered the door looked as exhausted as Ella felt, though it was not yet 6:00 am. "I'm Maria, the Security Manager. It'll be tight, but come in, if you can fit."

"Watson, Rappaport," said Agent Donnelly. "Inside with me. Jackson and Ruiz, stand watch out here."

The two agents who'd been at the back of the group stayed in the hallway, their backs to the door, while Ella and the other three squeezed into the closet-sized room. Inside, two chairs faced the wall of monitors, leaving a narrow space behind them and even less on the right. Maria took the chair on the left of the console, in front of the wall of screens, and Agent Donnelly took the one on the right. Ella came in next, squeezing herself into the front-right corner so that the other two agents could come in behind her and pull the door closed. Agents Watson and Rappaport squeezed behind the chairs, their backs against the wall, and Ella was wedged between the side of Agent Donnelly's chair and the now secured door.

"I've rewound to the timeframe of the attack," said Maria. "This man," she paused the video and pointed to a man whose face was hidden by the bill of a baseball cap, "made his way in through a side entrance. Watch this." In the video, a man approached the keycard scanner at a side door, holding out a phone-shaped device to the pad before pulling the door open and continuing out of the frame of the video. Maria paused it again.

"Did you see the device he scanned? We don't use that type of technology here. We only issue keycards. Even our staff uses cards. But this man knew exactly how to outsmart our security."

The agents asked questions, but Ella's heart drummed in her ears, drowning them out. She stared at the image, the video already replaying behind her eyes as another waking nightmare she could not unsee.

She hadn't realized that she was clutching the arm of Agent Donnelly's chair, but when something brushed her hands, she released them in surprise, jumping backwards. With only a few spare inches behind her, her shoulder blade collided with the door frame and she yelped in pain.

All eyes were now on Ella, and only Agent Donnelly had any idea what had just happened. "Sorry, I didn't mean to startle you," he said. "That sounded painful."

Her face flushed, she shook her head even though her should blade was throbbing. "I'm fine." It was the easiest thing to say to make them all stop staring at her.

"Would you rather not see this?" he asked.

"No, I need to know what happened. I just..." She closed her eyes and counted to three, then opened them and managed a weak smile. "I'm okay." Attention shifted back to the monitors.

"Next, look over here." Maria pointed to a different monitor. The digital counter in the corner of the screen ticked up a few seconds, then a few more. This time, Ella clutched the arm of Agent Donnelly's chair on purpose, squeezing until her knuckles turned white.

The man appeared in the video again. He strode with purpose down the hall to her room as if he belonged there, stopping outside her door to glance over one shoulder, then the other. His baseball cap blocked his face, but in one frame the light in the hall hit him at the right angle—that's where Maria froze the screen.

Chapter 18
Mal and Ella

AGES 9 AND 10
(29 YEARS AGO)

RAIN DANCED AGAINST THE windowpanes as Ella snuggled into her favorite place in the house, the reading nook in their living room bay window. She had her current favorite book, *Junie B. Jones and Her Big, Fat Mouth*, the soft pink blanket her grandmother had bought her when she was a baby, and a giant stuffed moose as a pillow. It didn't get much better than this.

"Ella! Let's play The Breadcrumb Game!" Mal said as she bounded into the room.

Ella sighed. "I'm reading now. Let's play later."

"Please?" Mal batted her eyelashes, giving Ella her most innocent, pleading face.

"Fine. One round. But make it really, really hard. Think of a hiding place you haven't used before."

Mal nodded enthusiastically, vibrating with excitement. "Okay. I'll go find a good one. Don't count yet!" She bounced out of the room as if she had springs under her feet, and Ella went back to her book. From time to time she heard doors opening and closing, and the sounds of someone walking through the house.

Thirty minutes later, Mal was back, bursting with excitement. "I've got the best one ever!"

Ella eyed her skeptically. "Are you sure? You said that last time."

"No, it's *way* better than last time. I promise. This time count to 100. The clues are in the hall outside the door, but don't look until you finish counting."

"Okay," said Ella. She stuck her bookmark in her book and closed it. "1... 2..."
Mal squealed in delight and shot out the door. Ella smiled and kept counting.

"98... 99... 100. Okay Mal, ready or not, here I come!" In the hall, she found three items in a row along the wall. The first one was a purple crayon drawing of a doll sitting in either a suitcase or a box. Or maybe it was a laundry basket. Next, there was a plastic spider on a ring. Mal had a collection of them. Even though Ella knew it wasn't real, she still took a step back and eyed it suspiciously. The last item in the lineup was a tiny purple flower that Ella recognized as a wildflower that grew along the fence at the back edge of their backyard.

Mal's clues were usually simple. But these? Ella had no idea what they had in common. *Oh well. Might as well start looking and think about it as I go.* Starting with the most obvious clue, Ella set off for the backyard.

An hour later, Ella still hadn't solved Mal's clues, nor had she had any luck finding her without them. She'd looked everywhere twice, but it was as though her sister had just disappeared into thin air.

"Ella, please get Mal for lunch," her mother said, breezing into the kitchen.

"I don't know where she is. We were playing The Breadcrumb Game, and I've been looking for her for an hour. She said she had a really good hiding place this time."

Valerie frowned. "Hmmm. Okay, well, what clue did she leave you?"

"She left me three clues this time." Ella led her mother back to where the three items were still sitting on the floor in the hall.

Valerie stared hard at the clues, getting no farther with them than Ella had. She sighed in frustration. "I don't know what they mean, Ella. Where have you looked?"

"Everywhere! I've looked in every single place she's ever hidden, plus every other place I could think of, even if it didn't seem to match any of the clues. She's not anywhere!"

"Well, I'm sure she'll come out when she gets hungry. In the meantime, we can have lunch."

"Can we have hot dogs?" Ella asked hopefully.

"Sure. Can you find your dad and ask him if he wants a hot dog or two?"

"Yes. I know where *he* is." Ella disappeared out the back door to find her dad watering the plants on the side of the house, relieved that she could stop looking for Mal.

Around 3:00, Ella was sitting in her reading nook, and overheard her parents talking in the hall. Her mom was telling her dad what Ella had told her about Mal, the game, and the clues.

"Ella," her father said, as her parents rounded the corner into the room. "Are you sure you don't know where Mal is?"

Her mother's voice held more than a hint of worry. "You girls weren't playing in the attic, were you? The door was open earlier."

"No," said Ella immediately, then froze. The three of them stared at each other for a count of two and then moved all at once, running for the half-door in the wall of Ella's parents' bedroom closet. The padlock was on, as usual.

Her mother's hands shook as she fitted the key into the padlock—the padlock she had insisted they install so that neither of her girls ever got into the attic.

They stepped back to let the door swing open and gasped as out tumbled Mal. She fell to the floor with a thud, sobbing hysterically.

"Mal!" cried Valerie.

Sweat dripped down her face, and her cheeks were pink and puffy. Their father scooped her up and carried her to the wide bed, setting her down gently, while their mother got a damp washcloth to put on Mal's forehead. "Ella, go downstairs and get a glass of water."

Ella scampered to the kitchen and got the biggest cup she could find—it had a pink elephant on it from a trip to the zoo. She added ice, then water, and hurried back upstairs, only spilling a little on the carpet. Their parents were sitting on the bed, their mother murmuring soothingly and holding Mal on her lap. Ella handed the water to her father, who helped Mal take a sip.

Mal was calming down little by little, but a sick feeling was growing larger and larger in the pit of Ella's stomach.

"Mal, does anything hurt?" asked her father.

She clung to her mother's arm. "My hands." She held out her hands, the sides of which were red and raw where she must've pounded on the door.

"Why did you go in the attic?"

"Ella said I had to think of a better hiding place. A hard one! She knows all the other ones."

The knot in Ella's stomach tightened. She had told her that. If she hadn't, Mal might not have gone into the attic.

Their mother smoothed Mal's hair, speaking calmly but firmly. "The attic is off limits for a reason, sweetheart. It doesn't even have a floor all the way back. You could've hurt yourself. That's why you're not allowed to play there. You know that."

"I didn't move! I stayed right by the door, where it's safe. Who locked the door?" She looked from one of them to another, betrayal written all over her face.

"I did," said Valerie. "I'm so sorry, Mal. I didn't know."

Their father nodded. "It was my fault it was open. I was looking for something in there and forgot to lock it when I was done."

Mal looked directly at Ella, becoming agitated. "You were supposed to find me! You told me to hide somewhere hard to find, and then you left me there!" Even though Mal's version of events wasn't quite true, Ella felt guilty enough to accept it as if it was.

"I'm sorry," Ella whispered, blinking back tears. "I tried to solve it! Mom tried, too. Even Dad didn't know what it meant. I looked everywhere..." Mal narrowed her eyes at her. "Except the attic." As if it would change anything, she added feebly, "Because we're not allowed to go in there."

"I do not forgive you," Mal said. "I will never forgive you."

"Now, now, let's not be so dramatic. Of course we forgive each other. We're family. Mal, I know it was dark and hot and scary in there. I'm sorry I closed you in."

"I was screaming," said Mal, sniffling again. "I was screaming and pounding on the door and the floor. And no one came."

"We couldn't hear you," said their father. He stroked her head. "We thought you just didn't want to come out of your hiding spot."

"I gave you awesome clues. A picture of an old doll in a box—she was in storage, because she was *old*! Storage is in the attic. And a spider ring because, duh! Spiders live in the attic. And a flower, because of the book!"

The other three looked at each other, confused.

"You know! The one on Mom's bookshelf!"

Understanding dawned on Valerie's face. "You mean Flowers in the Attic? You didn't read it, did you? That's a scary book for a kid."

"I read the first page, but it was boring," Mal said with a shrug.

Ella's eyes widened, and suddenly she was shouting. "I've never seen that book! How would I know that clue? And the doll didn't look old to me!"

"She had *wrinkles*!"

"Where?"

"Those lines under her eyes!"

"You're such a bad artist! How was I supposed to know?"

"Alright," said their mother. "Let's stop now. It's not going to change anything. All's well that ends well."

Mal sniffled, grumbling under her breath.

"Why don't we rent a movie and just relax tonight? I'll go pick it up. What movie do you want to see, Mal?" their father asked.

Mal tilted her head in thought. "Home Alone?"

Ella was about to protest. They'd already rented Home Alone five times. But as soon as she opened her mouth, she snapped it shut again. Today was not a day when she should start a fight with Mal.

"Home Alone it is. Ella, why don't you come with me to get it?"

"Okay," said Ella, more than happy to get away from Mal's icy stare. She followed her dad to the door and turned back for one more look at her mother and Mal, still cuddled together on the bed. Mal was watching her every move, and narrowed her eyes at her. Eager to escape her sister's glare, Ella jumped through the doorway into the hall to catch up with her father.

Chapter 19
Ella
MONDAY

A GENT DONNELLY HAD BROUGHT up the sketch artist's rendering of the man who'd come to Ella's door the day her house had blown up, and the likeness to the man on the screen was undeniable.

"This is the only clear shot of his face in all our footage," said Maria.

Breathe, Ella told herself.

"He's a match for our suspect," said Agent Donnelly.

He pushed his phone back into his pocket and, without looking at Ella, sat back in his chair and rested his right arm on the armrest, the end of which Ella was gripping firmly. His fingers spread out just enough that his hand rested lightly on top of both of hers. This time, instead of jumping back, she glanced down in surprise. Her exhale was still shaky as the agents conferred in low voices.

"Ready to continue?" Maria asked.

"Ready," said Agent Donnelly. He still hadn't looked in Ella's direction.

In motion once again, the man who was definitely not a contractor held up the same device to the keycard scanner beside the door to Ella's room, then turned the door handle.

But we bolted the door. I'm sure of it.

Maria paused the video again. "This next part brings up obvious causes for concern for the safety of all our guests, not only Ella." The look on her face was pained. "Rest assured that we are addressing them."

The video started again, and the door opened several inches before stopping—the bolt on the inside had engaged.

Ella exhaled slowly, waiting.

The man had a piece of string a foot or two long in his hand, and he pushed a loop of it through the opening in the door, his fingers working quickly in the small space. He knew what he was doing. Whatever it was, he made it look easy, and in under two minutes, he pulled on the string and pushed the door open.

He opened a locked and bolted door from the outside with a phone and some string.

Ella's blood ran cold and her hands tightened on the armrest. Agent Donnelly didn't look at her, but his hand tightened over hers ever so slightly. Her eyes locked onto his hand, and she sealed her mind in a vice-like grip so it couldn't wander back to what had happened after the man had entered her room.

Maria grimaced at her audience. "I'll just fast forward to the last part..."

The door to Ella and Agent Jacobs' room remained closed. Ella's stomach clenched, realizing what she was about to see. Agent Harrison emerged from the room across the hall, his gun ready, and Ella squeezed her eyes shut. She already knew what would happen. Seeing it would only give her another nightmare she couldn't unsee.

There was a collective gasp in the room, as even these trained professionals who'd seen this sort of thing many times before reacted in dismay. She let go of the armrest, tugging her hands out from under Agent Donnelly's, and turned around so she could press her forehead against the door. She wanted nothing more than to escape from this closet, which was getting smaller by the second.

"And then, his exit from the building," said Maria. Ella stayed frozen, her back to the monitors.

"That's all there is." Maria said after a painful silence. "We've never had an incident like this. Are there any other feeds you'd like to see?"

"We'll need the ones you just showed us, and everything else taken at the same times, plus an hour before and an hour after, sent to FBI headquarters," said Agent Donnelly, standing carefully so his chair didn't crush the agents behind him. "I'll have Agent Martin give you instructions on submitting them."

Ella had thought she'd wanted to know what happened, but after seeing the footage, she wished she hadn't. *Don't throw up.*

"Ella?" Agent Donnelly asked. His hand landed on her shoulder, warmth spreading through the fabric of her shirt. When his thumb brushed her skin along the shirt's neckline, she slowly looked back over her shoulder at him. Pausing with her chin only a few inches above his fingers, she glanced at his hand as he dropped it back to his side. She continued turning until she was facing him again, her momentary panic nearly gone.

"Come on," he said, but his eyes said, *"I know."* He steered her back into the hall, and the group resumed their positions around her, past the elevators and around two corners. After crossing a wide, empty lobby, they arrived at a door with a sign that read *Conference Room A*. A man in a suit with a comm device in his ear blocked the doorway. "All clear, sir," he said as he stepped aside, to which Agent Donnelly nodded.

"Wait here," he told Ella. Even surrounded by five alert FBI agents, watching Sam disappear through the door into the conference room made her long to follow him, and she immediately glanced over her shoulder for impending danger.

None too soon, he was back at the door, motioning for Ella to come in. She followed him inside to a standard windowless meeting room. This one was small, and the walls were not movable partitions—which was probably one reason he'd chosen it. She settled herself at the conference table and studied her hands, looking up with a wince when the door lock clicked. Agent Donnelly was the only one there, and she watched him, willing the panic inside her to settle.

She turned her chair to the side, leaned forward to rest her head in her hands, and made the mistake of closing her eyes. There he was again: the man with the wire, and her eyes flew open as she straightened, checking over both shoulders.

"It's just you and me," Sam said as he pulled out the chair next to hers. He turned it to face her, then sat down facing her. She deflated, slumping forward again and studying her hands.

Eyes open. No, don't cry again. Suck it up. Breathe.

He matched her position, his forearms against his knees, his fingers dangling inches from hers.

"Ella, it's okay. I mean, of course, it's not *okay*... it's completely fucked up. But..." He shook his head with a sigh. "I'm sorry. I suck at motivational speeches."

The sound that burst out of her was somewhere between a sob and a laugh, and her chin trembled. "Yeah, you do." For some reason, his inability to give her even a crappy pep talk actually made her feel a little better.

She gave him a weak smile as her eyes flicked to his and then down again.

As if realizing how close they were sitting, he straightened, pushed his chair back, and turned to sit up to the table. Ella did the same, but folded her arms on the cool surface and rested her head on them, squeezing her eyes shut only to have her attacker's face flash in the momentary darkness again. Her eyes popped open, and she rested her chin on her hands, keeping her eyes on the wall ahead of her, and focused only on inhaling and exhaling.

An eternity later, a knock at the door disturbed the tense silence. Agent Donnelly strode across the room and unlocked the door for Agents Watson and Rappaport, who had brought four coffees and several paper bags of food. They joined Ella and Agent Donnelly across the table.

"Two agents outside the door?" Agent Donnelly asked.

"Yes, sir," said Agent Rappaport.

"Good."

The mood in the room was somber; Agent Jacobs' injuries had been declared non-life threatening, but they were still waiting for word on Agent Harrison's condition. Even with her eyes open, Ella was stuck in a loop, her mind replaying the video of the assassin unlocking her door, every second of his attempt to kill her, then attacking Agent Harrison. Her bagel remained untouched in front of her, but she sipped her coffee.

"Ella, we've learned a few things," said Agent Donnelly. "First, there were multiple contracts taken out, one on each member of Mal's team, but the one assigned to Mal targeted you instead. These hitmen are part of a sophisticated global network that we've been tracking, so it's crucial that we not only apprehend the one coming after you, but that we also bring down the larger system." When Ella squeezed her hands into fists in her lap, he added, "Which we will."

Ella did not miss the look exchanged by the other two agents. What Agent Donnelly was promising wasn't a certainty, and they all knew it. "How?" she asked skeptically.

"There are many more people working on this than you know. We're just one part of the operation. Our team has two primary focuses: first, finding Mal, which we hope will not only stop the assassination attempts on you, but also get us the answers we need, and second, keeping you safe until then."

"If it's such a sophisticated network, why couldn't they figure out I'm not Mal?" Ella asked.

Agent Donnelly sighed. "That's the million-dollar question, isn't it?" he asked.

He stood abruptly, avoiding Ella's eyes. "Watson," he said, "Stay with her. Rappaport, let's step outside."

Agent Rappaport nodded, and the two men left, closing the windowless door behind them and leaving Ella more flustered now than ever.

A few minutes later, Agent Rappaport returned and signaled to Agent Watson to trade places with him.

"What's going on?" asked Ella.

Agent Rappaport's expression was apologetic, but he said only, "He said he'd tell you himself."

Time ticked by, but the other two agents did not reappear. Agent Rappaport's phone buzzed, and he read the message and set the device back on the table but said nothing, despite Ella's exaggerated sigh.

Two hours had passed. She didn't know at what point she'd put her head down, only that suddenly she was waking up, disoriented, her cheek resting against her arms. Opening her eyes in search of Agent Donnelly, she found Agent Rappaport across the table from her. Not long ago, it would've been a relief to find anyone but Agent Donnelly, but not anymore.

Her nap had been just long enough to make her groggy. Muffled voices came from outside the conference room, and she glared at the door, willing herself to see through it. When the other two agents entered, Ella narrowed her eyes at Agent Donnelly, whose face was impossible to read. She had a feeling she would not like whatever he was about to say.

He stopped a few feet from her, folding his arms across his chest. "Now that we know for sure someone is tracking you, and they know where you are, we have to be more careful. What happened this morning is my fault, and it will not happen again." The warmth she'd been getting from him more and more often was nowhere to be found.

She was out of her chair and standing in front of him before she knew what she was doing. "What are you saying?" The other two agents looked on with concern, as if ready to jump in, but Agent Donnelly shook his head slightly at them.

"I'm saying that you need to stay out of sight for now."

"Is that why you left me in here for hours? Is your solution for me to hide in a windowless room for the rest of my life?" Her tone had escalated to hostile, which was completely unlike her. It felt good to stand up for herself for once.

He gave her the same hard look as he had the first day they'd met. "I'm going back to Walloon Lake with Agent Rappaport. You're going to stay with Agent Watson..."

"No! Don't leave me here! I can help you!"

He continued calmly, as if she hadn't interrupted him. "I'm not saying you can't help us, but this is for your safety. It's not a punishment."

Ella opened her mouth to yell back at him again, but his expression quickly darkened.

"This is not a game. It's not a TV show. We're talking about a professional assassin here!" He gathered steam, becoming louder and angrier. "He's incompetent, because otherwise you'd be dead by now, but I'm not letting him get another shot. Will you please stop being impossible and just let me protect you?"

Ella took a step back, speechless.

Agent Donnelly held up his hands towards her, putting an obvious effort into calming down. "You're going to stay with Agent Watson. But not here.

Agent Martin has a more secure location picked out, and you're going to wait there until we're done."

The only reason she didn't scream back at him was the bottleneck of furious words in her head had reduced her to sputtering, her face hot.

"Please, Ella." For a second his expression was pained, before he managed to smooth his features back to neutral. "I know you're angry, but I was wrong to bring you along. You're not safe here."

"But you said..." Again, she wanted to scream but couldn't make her mouth cooperate. *He said I was right to insist on being here.* Logically, she shouldn't have felt betrayed, but that didn't change the fact that she did.

"The most important thing is that you're safe."

All her anger, frustration, sadness, and loneliness of the past days—even years—crystallized, and the words came out loud and fast. "I'm not safe anywhere! If Agent Jacobs hadn't been in the room with me last night, I'd be dead! I'm not any safer back in DC than I am here. You said so yourself! If you're tired of protecting me, just say so!"

Breathe. She wanted to cry, but also to punch him in the face, and to run as far as she could away from him—but none of those would solve anything.

Agent Donnelly stiffened. His face was blank again, his calm infuriating. She turned her back on him and folded her arms, fighting to hold back tears.

"Ella, I don't think..." Agent Watson started from across the room.

"Give us a minute, please." Agent Donnelly said, his tone firm but not unkind. The other two agents nodded and filed out.

For several more tense seconds, neither of them said anything as she sniffled, fighting to regain control of her emotions.

"I'm not tired of protecting you," he said to the back of her head. "Protecting people is why I took this job. It's the reason I keep doing it, even after it cost me so much." His voice had softened and he continued in barely more than a whisper, sounding unusually emotional. "I need you to be safe. That's all I care about. I can't lose anyone else."

She sucked in a breath as if she'd been burned. He'd insisted that what happened to Agent Harrison hadn't been her fault, but she still felt entirely responsible. *How many other people has he lost over the years?*

She wheeled around to face him. "Well, I need you to..." She broke off at the look of distress on his face, and the realization that she had no idea how to finish the sentence.

What do I need from him?

She shook her head. "Never mind." Her thoughts were a jumble. Anger was so much easier than the rest of what she was feeling, so that's where she focused her energy.

She expected hostility from him in return, or at least that bland, empty expression, but he gave her the opposite.

Any other time, his smile would have been a pleasant surprise, but this was the wrong time.

"Why the hell are you smiling at me?" She had the urge to punch him again, but the longer she stared at him, the more her anger drained away even without an answer.

"I'm sorry," she whispered. "I feel like I'm losing my mind."

He took a tentative step towards her, and when she didn't tense or flinch, he took another one. "It's okay to be angry. You have a lot to be angry about. That's not why I was smiling. I'm sorry if that's how it looked. Even I'm not that much of an asshole. It's just... You remind me of someone."

He did not elaborate, and something in his eyes told her not to ask any follow-up questions.

Only a few feet separated them, and neither of them looked away.

This time she was the one with the hardened expression, but her voice came out more sad than angry. She looked at the ground. "So you're really going to send me away?"

"Not far. I'll see you in a few hours. I told you, the most important thing to me is your safety."

She'd wanted nothing more than for him to be nicer to her, but now that she'd gotten her wish, she found his kindness terrifying and his caution infuriating. Neither of those was acceptable to her. No, she'd have to do this on her own.

I'm the only one who can warn Mal. I owe her at least that much... Besides, no one else will be able to get close enough to her. I can't just sit around waiting. I guess I have to do it on my own. Now I just have to think like Mal...

Thinking like the sister she hadn't spoken to in over twenty years wouldn't be easy, and neither would escaping from the chokehold of protective custody. It wasn't the smart thing to do, but she'd done the smart thing all her life, and look where she'd ended up.

A shiver ran through her at the thought of that morning. Agent Jacobs had been injured, though superficially. She still didn't even know if Agent Harrison was dead or alive, but either way, she'd put them all in danger just because they were with her. She desperately wanted to ask Agent Donnelly about Agent Harrison's condition, but she was determined not to speak to him. In the back of her mind, it occurred to her that if she snuck away, no one else would get hurt because of her. That was for the best.

She'd keep her eyes open for the right time.

For now, she was done dealing with Agent Donnelly. She stalked to the far end of the room and leaned against the wall, crossed her arms and pretended he wasn't there. Yes, she was being ridiculous. Childish, even. She didn't care.

Her mother's voice called to her from the past, as it sometimes did.

I, for one, am glad he's finally showing some sense. How can you be upset with him for wanting you to be safe? Is it because he's going to let someone else protect you? He has a job to do. Why are you so angry?

She saw the logic in the argument, but refused to give in to it. *He's being unreasonable. I can help them. How is he going to find Mal's clues if he doesn't know what he's looking for? He's an idiot.*

She took out her phone, opened the notes app, and started to organize her thoughts.

If I was Mal, where would I go?

Chapter 20

Mal

MONDAY

AFTER TEARING ALONG THE back roads to get away from Walloon Lake, Mal and Jimmy had driven south as quickly as they dared. Mal had been at the wheel when they reached the southern border of Michigan, just after midnight, and she steered east into Ohio. They still hadn't picked a specific destination, though they'd proposed and discarded many possibilities.

"I know you don't love the idea, but I still say we should go to Virginia Beach."

Jimmy tipped his head to one side and wrinkled his nose. "That's the third time you've suggested it. If I didn't know better, I'd think you have a secret boyfriend there. What makes it so special?"

"The whole sleepy, middle of nowhere thing didn't work. Let's go get lost in a crowd."

He sighed. "There are lots of places with crowds, Mallory."

"I have connections there. I'm waiting to hear back from a few of them so... Oh, I got a text. What does it say?"

He took her phone from the center console and read the notification on the screen. "It's from someone called Daz, who says, 'You got it! Lemme know.'" His imitation of an American accent made Mal shake her head and laugh.

"Who's this Daz?"

"Friend of a friend."

"How close is this friend? Please tell me you're not contacting anyone who can link us back to everything we're trying to disconnect ourselves from."

"I'm not stupid. This friend goes much farther back. High school." She tilted her head and smiled at him. "Nothing to worry about."

"Right then," Jimmy said with a sigh. "We'll go see Daz."

"The best kind of road trip... one that ends at the beach." Mal cranked up the volume of the radio and rolled down the window. "If we don't stop much, we can be there by lunch time."

The blue car that had been behind them on the road pulled off at the next exit, and Mal let out a sigh of relief. She'd been trying to shake a growing paranoia—it was the only other car they'd seen on the road in either direction for over an hour, and it had been behind them for the last 90 miles. With that car gone, she could be sure no one was following them.

Smiling to herself, she envisioned the sandy beach she'd be seeing later that day. Just maybe, she'd see Ella, too.

***

Hours later, Jimmy was driving. He kept his eyes straight ahead, his fingers clenching the steering wheel.

"What's your problem? You've been wound up for hours." The irritation in Mal's voice made him clench the wheel tighter.

He paused before answering. "Well, forgive my asking an obvious question, but why are we still doing this?"

"Doing what?"

"This whole 'catch me if you can' thing with your sister. It's ridiculous."

Mal's face clouded over. "You wouldn't understand."

"Did you ever get along with her?"

Staring out the window, she shrugged. "Occasionally."

"What was the problem between you?"

Her head snapped to the side, and she glared at him. "What are you trying to say?"

They'd stopped at a traffic light, and he turned to look at her. "I'm trying to figure out why it's so important to torture your sister that you're willing to risk being arrested. We could be on a tropical beach by now."

Mal crossed her arms. "There was... a game we played as kids."

"So this is you being sentimental? That's pretty fucked up."

She rolled her eyes as the light changed and he turned back to the road.

"And Virginia Beach is the last stop, yeah? Before we get the hell off the grid?"

"Yeah. It should be."

"What clue did you leave her this time?"

Mal huffed. "Nothing! Okay? I didn't leave her anything. I just have an old contact there I need to talk to."

Jimmy exhaled loudly and shook his head, cursing at the top of his lungs as another driver cut him off. He let the subject drop for the time being, focusing on the road.

When he checked the rear-view mirror, he did a double take. The black car three cars behind them looked familiar, but it was a popular model.

"What's wrong?" asked Mal.

"Nothing," he snapped. "I'm just ready to be done with this nonsense."

Chapter 21
Ella

MONDAY

AN HOUR LATER, ELLA was still standing against the conference room wall, still angry with Agent Donnelly. She hated that she'd thought—wrongly—that she'd felt a connection with him, and that she'd fallen apart in front of him numerous times. She needed to get herself together.

"Time to go."

She said nothing, but followed him into the hall, her security team immediately in place around her.

The hotel lobby buzzed with police activity, and the driveway outside was awash in flashing lights. Ella tightened her grip on the strap of her backpack, doing her best to avoid looking at Agent Donnelly in front of her.

An unfamiliar man in a suit nodded to them at the curb, flashing his badge. Ella watched out of the corner of her eye as he and Agent Donnelly conversed nearby.

"Ma'am." The newcomer dipped his head slightly in acknowledgement. Following the man's gaze, Ella found the back door of one of the black SUVs open and climbed in. The door closed behind her.

She looked up when Agent Watson got into the driver's seat, glancing over his shoulder with a sympathetic expression. "I know you're pissed off, Ella. I would be, too. But it's for your own safety."

She said nothing, only folded her arms and looked out the window at the other vehicle as both of them departed.

Ella kept her gaze fixed on Agent Donnelly's vehicle until it turned out of view. Agent Watson focused on the road, and after forty-five minutes without conversation or even the radio, she couldn't stand it anymore.

"Are we driving all the way back to DC?"

The agent spoke matter-of-factly without taking his eyes off the road. "No. We're almost there, actually."

"We're almost where?"

"Look for yourself. This is it."

They'd entered the parking lot for a large police station, a building with one strangely placed, steep point interrupting an otherwise normal roof. "Michigan State Police District headquarters?"

"It's the safest place in the area we could come up with."

"So what? I'm under arrest now?"

Agent Watson let out a deep sigh. "Ella, come on. You know that's not what's happening here, and you know I'm not the one you're angry with. Don't make this harder than it has to be. There are much worse things in life than having someone want you to be safe."

She clamped her mouth shut, not trusting herself to reply without bitterness or sarcasm. It was especially annoying that he was right—he wasn't the one she was angry with.

Ella stomped towards the station entrance with Agent Watson at her side. His calm demeanor only annoyed her more.

"Unless you want them to mistake you for someone in custody, tone it down."

Hating that he might be right, she forced herself to take a deep breath and dropped her arms to her sides.

Agent Martin had called ahead, so the young officer who greeted them from behind a low counter knew exactly why they were there, and escorted them to a windowless conference room that required a six-digit code to open the door.

"It's only locked from the outside," the officer explained. "Hopefully, this will give you some peace of mind. We only had the code installed last year." He handed Agent Watson a card with a string of numbers on it. "The restrooms are around the corner, so if you need to leave and get back in, that's the code. I'll get you some coffee. You need anything else?"

"No, this is great. Thanks very much," said Agent Watson. The door closed behind the retreating officer with a loud click.

Ella took a seat at the table, letting her backpack fall from her shoulder onto the floor. She fished her phone out of her jacket pocket and woke up the screen, but found no notifications—not that she usually had many. *So much for a distraction.* Setting the device on the table with a heavy sigh, she contemplated how long she and Agent Watson were going to be spending together, sitting in silence, being absolutely useless while Agents Donnelly and Rappaport were actually doing something.

"Let me see your phone." Suddenly, Agent Watson's tone was as stern as his expression. She slid it across the table to him, and he peered at it closely. "Agent Martin gave you this one?"

"Yes, why?"

He ran his fingers along the edges, then held it only inches from his face and examined it as if he'd never laid eyes on a smartphone before. When he finally handed it back to her, he shook his head. "There must be a way they keep finding us so fast... I wondered if it was bugged. I don't see anything unusual, but I'll have Agent Martin do a diagnostic check, just to be sure."

She set the phone down carefully on the table, as if it might explode if she used too much force. Of course, phones were trackable—everyone knew that. But the FBI had given it to her, so she'd assumed it was safe.

I'm not safe anywhere! she heard herself yelling at Agent Donnelly.

Don't be such a baby! A younger version of Mal yelled at her. *What're you so afraid of?*

A clip of a memory appeared, in which she sat by the edge of a hospital bed, teary-eyed. The image lasted barely a second before she was swimming with Mal at Walloon Lake. She recognized the memory a split second before she remembered being pushed and held under the water, flailing her arms.

Without warning, her thoughts jumped back to the attack in her hotel room that morning. Squeezing her hands into fists as she tried to get her mind under control, she focused on a montage of clips of happy memories: her mother's joyful smile. A bear hug from her father. Belting out her favorite song as a teen. They were edited versions of the summer days at Walloon Lake in her childhood.

No longer frantic, she tensed at the appearance of a new lakeside memory. Her heartbeat hammered in her ears as she was once again tearing down the path blindly, as she'd done the day before. She collapsed in the sand at the public beach, and she felt the despair just as vividly as she had the first time.

When Agent Donnelly sat beside her, her thoughts of everything else stopped.

As angry as she'd been at him for the past few hours, seeing him in her memory lightened the crushing pressure of her life to something she could almost handle. She wasn't used to having anyone there to help pick up the pieces when everything shattered around her. The feeling that, for once, she had someone in her corner brought her peace—at least until she remembered the rest of it.

It's his job to follow me around, to protect me. He's not doing it because he cares. And now he's not even here.

The thought that he'd been kind to her only because it was his job left behind an ache that made her wish he hadn't followed her. It was horrible to go through this alone, but it was a thousand times worse to feel hope, and then realize it was all a lie.

Again, she heard her mother's refrain as clearly as if she was in the room. *Oh Ella, don't be so dramatic.*

A loud click brought her out of her thoughts. A young officer with bright red hair and a pale face full of freckles had entered the room. In a travel carrier, he balanced two large cups of coffee and a third cup piled high with small packets and flat wooden sticks. "We thought you two might want some coffee."

"Thanks," said Agent Watson, and the officer disappeared as quickly as he'd arrived. The click of the locking mechanism echoed in Ella's ears, and in her head, she was once again locked in the interrogation room at the FBI.

"Ella, you look pale. Are you okay?"

Suddenly, she was too tired to be angry with the world. "Yeah," she said automatically, before adding. "No."

Agent Watson had been the good cop so far, so she was afraid he was going to launch into something inspirational or sympathetic. Instead, all he said was, "Have some coffee," and slid a cup towards her, along with the collection of miscellaneous packets.

He sighed. "You know we're trying to help you, right?"

"I know." The former, timid Ella had automatically apologized for things that weren't even remotely her fault, but this new Ella had to force herself to say those two words. "I'm sorry."

"I know this sucks. You just have to hang in there and let us do our jobs."

She nodded, then let her mind wander. Time moved at a crawl, slower every second.

After refusing to eat a single bite of the greasy hamburgers Agent Watson had ordered for lunch, at some point later she was sitting with her head on the table, half-asleep, when her thoughts again drifted back to the day before. Though she didn't want to, in her mind she tiptoed slowly along the path, pulled by an invisible force as she gritted her teeth and braced herself against impending distress.

As she had the day before, she looked out at the lake, the dock, her little beach. The tension left her, and happiness crept its way through her veins. But she had learned long ago that nothing this good could last, so the feeling immediately put her on edge.

This time, when she looked up at the house she observed the scene as an impartial witness, noting the horror in her own face in the seconds before she fled. Now floating above herself, she saw the things she hadn't the first time. The way the light danced through the trees and the gentle lapping of the water were exactly the same as they'd always been, even after so many years. Then came Agent Donnelly's call from behind her, bellowing her name and breaking the quiet.

Sloppy. We're dodging assassins, but he yells my name in public?

She must have mumbled some part of her thoughts aloud, because Agent Watson looked up at her. "Everything okay?"

She shrugged. "Okay" wasn't how she'd describe herself.

Agent Watson's phone buzzed an hour later. He mumbled into the device, not saying more than a few words before hanging up again. Ella sat rigid, growing increasingly impatient.

"Please don't say you can't tell me anything. Did they find her?"

He shook his head. "They found the house where Mal and her friend were staying. They talked to the neighbors, who didn't notice anything except that someone had been there. The management company said they checked out unexpectedly yesterday, though they'd been scheduled to stay through next week. I'm sorry, Ella. They're not there. No one had any information about where they're headed next."

She focused on the worn surface of the table and breathed through her disappointment.

"It's only a matter of time, though. We got this far, didn't we? You gave us a major lead. We'll find another one. Also, Agent Donnelly sent me the pictures they took of the house where Mal was staying. He asked me to ask you to look at them to see if anything you see means anything to you."

He clicked the screen of the tablet he'd brought with him, then handed it across the table to her. Still reeling from missing Mal so narrowly, she stabbed at the screen as she clicked through the pictures. They'd photographed what looked like every inch of every room in the house.

There must be something here. Focus.

"You can study those in the car," he said.

"Are we going back to DC?"

"Yeah. We'll meet the other two at the airport. The jet's waiting for us."

"Wherever the next lead sends the team, he's not going to let me come along."

Agent Watson paused. "Probably not. Then again, I never thought he'd have brought you here. What I do know is that he has good instincts. He's not perfect, but he's right a hell of a lot more than he's wrong."

That's a nice way of saying he's going to leave me in a random agent's protective custody, "for my own good." The thought made her even more miserable than before.

"Don't get ahead of yourself. For now, let's get out of here." His chair scraped the floor as he got to his feet.

"Finally. It's so claustrophobic in here. The world could end and we wouldn't know."

He didn't speak until she looked up at him. "Do you want to be entertained, or do you want to be safe? Because none of the rest of it will matter if you're dead. Keep that in mind, all right?"

For a second, she swore he was reading her mind. *Don't be paranoid.*

"Right. Of course. I... I don't mean to be difficult. It's all just been... a lot."

He held the door open for her but said nothing.

A few minutes later, Ella was back in the car, once again in the back seat at Agent Watson's insistence. "You know he'll kill me if anything happens to you." She nodded, almost smiling.

Funny how you're in no mood to argue unless Agent Donnelly is around.

Agent Watson had unlocked the tablet again, and Ella scrolled through the pictures, now examining each one in painstaking detail.

Halfway through the pictures, Ella yawned and stretched. So far, nothing looked out of place as far as she could tell.

"How's it going back there?" asked Agent Watson, glancing at her in the rearview mirror.

"Nothing so far," she said. "But I'm not done yet."

She'd reviewed nearly every image when she came to the ones taken inside the back door. While the houses opened in the front to the lake, the backs of the properties faced the road, with clusters of trees between many of the properties. The photo of the back door area included some dead leaves and a few twigs that must have been tracked in from outside.

In the far corner of the room, beside the rocking chair and a side table that held an owl statue sitting atop a pile of six old books, one twig lay on the floor. It looked like a stick drawing of a duck's webbed foot. Ella paused and narrowed her eyes, then rotated the photo on the screen. Just like that, it became a tiny trident—the three-pronged spear used by Poseidon, or Neptune, depending which version of mythology you were reading.

Bingo.

Ella said nothing, keeping her face neutral as she took her time studying the rest of the pictures. Nothing else jumped out at her. She clicked the off button on the tablet and set it on the seat beside her.

"Anything?" asked Agent Watson.

"No." She leaned back against the seat and closed her eyes. Nervous energy hummed through her veins, and her foot bounced against the floor.

Having spent several family vacations in Virginia Beach, Ella knew that there was a statue of Neptune there that was large enough to be seen from nearly the entire length of the three-mile-long boardwalk.

The smart thing to do would be to tell Agent Watson what she'd found and let them handle it, but for once, she didn't care about doing the smart thing. She would somehow get herself to Virginia Beach and look for Mal. Agent Harrison had been stabbed because she'd insisted on tagging along with the team, and she would never forgive herself. She was the only one with a chance of warning Mal about the danger she could be in. No one else needed to get hurt because of her. The question was how to slip out of protective custody.

Once we get back, I'll figure something out.

Chapter 22
Ella

MONDAY

The sun was low in the sky by the time the jet touched down at Ronald Reagan Washington National Airport, just outside of DC, and Ella still had no idea what the plan was. Agent Donnelly herded her along with them into a waiting vehicle without a word. Agent Jacobs had been well enough to fly back with them, but Agent Donnelly had sent her home for a good night's sleep. To replace both her and Agent Harrison, they had borrowed Agent Rappaport and Agent Watson from their regular assignments for the time being.

The more time that elapsed with no one telling Ella what was going on, the more it annoyed her, but she was too stubborn to ask.

At the federal building, they headed directly for Agent Martin, who sat at her keyboard and shook her head at their approach. Without further prompting, Agents Rappaport and Watson peeled off towards nearby workstations. This left Ella standing awkwardly beside Sam. He turned his attention to her for the first time in hours. Maddeningly, his face was back to being unreadable.

"Nothing new since my last update. But I got what you asked for." Agent Martin handed him a white letter-sized envelope.

He unfastened the clasp on the back and looked inside, then nodded. "Good work. Thanks." He pushed the contents back in and handed the envelope to Ella. "These are for you."

Caught off-guard, she peered from the envelope to him and back several times before reaching out to take it. "What is it?" She pulled out the stack of papers and a smaller envelope. Affixed to the papers, she found a new copy of her driver's license, her bank card, and her credit card, addressed to her care of the FBI. In the smaller envelope, there was cash—a small pile of $1s, $5s, and $10s.

"Remember those papers we had you sign?"

No, I really don't. She shook her head.

"Agent Martin got all this in record time. It's not everything, but it's something, at least. The most important ones. Plus a little cash, just in case."

She hated to admit that it had been thoughtful of them. They could've made her do it herself, though she wouldn't have known where to even have these things sent—she doubted the post office would deliver mail to a pile of rubble.

Speaking of which, where is the rest of my mail? But that was a problem for another time.

"Thanks," she said to Agent Martin. She detached the cards from the gummy strips that had held them in place, then shoved them in her pocket.

"Come on." Without further explanation, he walked away. She rolled her eyes and sighed heavily. Yes, he'd made sure she got her new IDs, but she was still mad at him.

"Bye," she said over her shoulder to Agent Martin as she followed Agent Donnelly out.

They ended up back in the garage, heading for the SUV. When she opened the back passenger side door, he turned around in surprise from the driver's seat. "You can sit in front." His tone made it clear that he wasn't feeling any friendlier than she was, so she climbed in the back.

She crossed her arms tightly and sunk down against the seat, as though she'd reverted to a moody teenager. After a painfully long crawl through rush hour traffic, they parked in front of a nondescript strip of row houses. It wasn't the same part of town as her last, ill-fated safe house, but upon inspection of the interior, it may as well have been the same place. Nothing was falling apart, but signs of wear and tear were everywhere. The only thing that appeared to be less than ten years old was the alarm panel on the wall by the door, which Agent Donnelly disarmed with a six-digit code.

Was there an alarm panel in the last place? She honestly couldn't remember.

Everywhere she looked, she saw the things a person would use to 'make do,' but nothing anyone would choose on purpose. It was probably because she was an interior designer that these places depressed her so much. It wouldn't have been difficult or expensive to improve them, but no one had bothered.

Only after Agent Donnelly had inspected every inch of the property did he speak to her. "So, this is your new place. I've also had it inspected by four different agents besides me. It's secure. I need to run home for some clothes..."

Ella's brain perked up. *Maybe I can—*

"...but I'm not leaving you alone here." He checked his watch. "I'll wait for your security detail. They should be here any minute."

At the front window, he pushed back the curtain just enough to look out. "I've told your detail to stay inside with you until I get back. I know it's more intrusive than having them at the curb, but after everything that's happened, I'm not risking it. They'll be stationed outside when I get back. I shouldn't be more than an hour and a half."

When she didn't respond, he let out an exasperated sigh, but said nothing.

Fifteen tense, silent minutes later, there was a knock on the door. Despite the friction between them, Agent Donnelly's eyes went to her at the same instant hers flew to him, and he held up a hand that could either have meant *stay there* or *don't panic*. Maybe both. Or maybe she was imagining it.

"Relax," he said. "Bad guys don't usually knock."

She was about to point out that someone who had tried to kill her had knocked on the door of her first safe house a few days before, remembering just in time that she still wasn't talking to him.

Agent Donnelly ushered the two imposing men in suits inside. They wore earpieces and serious expressions.

"Ella, Agents Nichols and Fernandez." She tilted her head toward them at the introduction, then crossed the room to the couch.

The three agents conversed in low voices, and Ella did her best to ignore them.

"I'll be back soon," said Agent Donnelly. He paused, as if waiting for a response, but her eyes stayed glued to her phone.

As the newly arrived agents confirmed that the access points were all locked, she stretched out on the couch, trying to pass for tired even though it wasn't yet 7:00. They'd stationed themselves at the dining room table, and she waited only five minutes before she yawned loudly, stretching her arms above her and getting to her feet. "Well, I'm exhausted. I know it's early, but I'm going to bed."

They stood as well, and she shook her head quickly. "Oh no, you don't need to... you're not going to watch me sleep, are you?"

"No ma'am. We'll just verify once more that your room is secure."

She bit back her annoyance as they followed her up the narrow stairs. Her plan could still work, assuming she could find a way out her window.

When they reached the bedroom, however, she discovered heavy bars running from top to bottom outside both windows. She hadn't noticed those when she'd traipsed behind Agent Donnelly.

She kept her expression neutral as the agents diligently inspected every nook and cranny of the room, and gave them her most innocent smile when they nodded at her on their way out.

"We'll be downstairs. Let us know if you need anything."

"Thank you. Good night." The door closed behind them and their footsteps retreated.

She could already hear her time ticking down. It occurred to her that if the agents were competent at their jobs, they would rearm the security system, in which case her plan was destined for a loud and spectacular failure. Still, no one had touched the panel after Agent Donnelly left, so she'd have to hope they wouldn't arm it now.

If I set it off... I guess I could say I wanted some fresh air. That I didn't notice the alarm. No one pointed it out, or said I shouldn't open the window.

It would be the lamest of lame excuses, but it was the only way.

She swallowed her apprehension and twisted the metal piece toward her, pausing before tugging the window open. She had less than an hour and a half to escape.

This was only the first of many opportunities for her plan to fall apart.

Chapter 23
Mal and Ella

AGES 10 AND 11
(28 YEARS AGO)

MAL HAD REFUSED TO speak to Ella for two weeks after the attic incident, except to fight with her even more bitterly than before. After that, they had grudgingly de-escalated; they began talking to each other again, and another few weeks later, their games of The Breadcrumb Game resumed. Everything seemed to be back to what had been normal for them—until a little more than a year later, on the morning of Ella's 11th birthday.

Ella had scored the trifecta of birthday luck. Her birthday was on a Saturday, which meant not only that there was no school but also that she could have her birthday party on her actual birthday. The weather was perfect, and every single friend she'd invited to her party had said they'd come. She was wearing her new purple sundress, which she'd picked out especially for the party. She was on cloud nine, and not even Mal's sulking could bring her down.

"Want to play The Breadcrumb Game?" Mal asked hopefully as the rest of the family rushed around her.

"I can't, Mal. I'm helping Mom and Dad get everything ready for my party. We can play after."

"We'd love to have your help right now, Mal," said Valerie.

Mal grumbled something as she walked away, and they didn't press her. It was almost a given that a day focused on Ella would make Mal grumpy. Even the fact that Mal had been allowed to invite a friend over to play with during the party hadn't made a noticeable difference in her mood. Her mother let her go without forcing the issue.

They didn't see Mal again until her friend, Beth, arrived, and the two immediately disappeared to the far corner of the backyard. They stayed out there, deep in conversation, for most of the afternoon.

At last, it was time for the cake. "Happy birthday to you…" Ella's guests and family sang, and Ella's face shone with happiness. Her mother stood across the table and took pictures of her as she blew out the candles.

All at once, Mal shot forward out of nowhere from behind Ella, arms flailing as she tumbled smack into the back of her. Flailing clumsily to regain her balance, Mal shoved Ella's head forward.

All the way into her cake.

For half a second, there was shocked silence, and then chaos erupted.

Mal jumped back, a look of horror on her face. Ella lifted her face out of her cake slowly and let out a wail. Every one of her friends sat in silence, their mouths forming perfect Os. Both parents leaped into action. Her mother grabbed the roll of paper towels on the table and moved around the table to Ella, and her father reached Mal in only a few strides. He hustled her back inside, away from the chaos.

"Mal, are you okay? What just happened?"

"I was running because I was afraid I was going to miss the cake, and I… I tripped." There were tears in her eyes now, and she was hiccupping. "I couldn't stop. And then I crashed into Ella." She looked at the ground, taking shaky breaths.

"Okay. Calm down. Everyone makes mistakes." He paused. "But I think you can understand that Ella is going to be pretty upset with you."

Mal nodded, still staring at the ground. "I know."

Valerie had wiped most of the cake from Ella's face by the time Mal and their father stepped back outside.

"Ella's going to go wash her face and change," said Valerie. "Good thing we have a big cake. We'll have some of the non-smashed part as soon as she's ready." To the guests, she added, "Why don't you girls go play? Ella will be right back."

Chairs scraped the floor loudly as Ella's classmates left the table all at once and headed back out to the grass.

Mal had taken another step back, out of Ella's path.

"I'm sorry, Ella. I was rushing, and I tripped. It was an accident. I didn't mean to fall on you."

Ella said nothing. She pretended she hadn't even heard her and continued into the house.

Her father grimaced at her sympathetically. "You and Beth go play for now."

"Okay." As she and Beth walked back to the corner of the yard where they'd been before, every one of Ella's guests stopped to stare at her, then moved farther away, to the other end of the yard.

That night at bedtime, Mal knocked on Ella's door.

"Who is it?"

"Mal."

"Go away."

"I need to tell you something."

"Fine."

Mal opened the door to find Ella glaring at her.

"What do you want?" Ella demanded. "You can apologize all you want. It won't help. You ruined my birthday."

Mal raised her eyebrows. "I don't want to apologize. I want to tell you two things."

"Spit them out and get out of here."

Mal held up one finger, and then a second. "One, it wasn't an accident. And two, now we're even for the attic."

She closed the door as she left, leaving Ella sitting up in bed open-mouthed, and scampered back to her room as Ella yelled, "MOM!" at the top of her lungs.

Chapter 24

Ella

MONDAY

ELLA TUGGED UPWARDS ON the safe house window with all her might, but nothing happened. She checked the lock—it was unlatched. It should have opened.

What the hell?

She tried again, pulling harder. This time there was movement, but not much, and she took a step back to consider her options. If the window was stuck, this plan had already failed. After heaving against the stubborn wood one more time without success, she walked to the window on the adjacent wall. That one wouldn't work—not only was it on the front of the building and therefore obvious from the street, but there was no fire escape. There was nowhere to go but straight down.

Back at the side window, she braced her hands against the wooden lip and channeled all her frustration into this one task. Little by little, the window inched upwards. By the time it was halfway open, she was sticky with sweat and stopped to catch her breath. She needed to get it all the way up to have a chance of fitting through it, and she had to do it fast.

At least the alarm didn't go off.

Emboldened by her slow but steady progress, she found another burst of energy. This was enough to get the window past whatever it had been stuck on, and all at once it slid up the rest of the way, hitting the top of the track with a loud *thud*. She grabbed the windowsill to steady herself, muttering curses. Steady again, she froze, cringing at the thought of what the agents had heard from downstairs. As expected, footsteps thundered up the stairs, and they were at her door in seconds.

"Ma'am, are you alright?"

She dashed across the room to get to the door before they opened it, pulling it back enough to show she was unharmed and was not attempting to hide anything. She could only hope they wouldn't be able to see the window from that angle. "Yes, I'm so clumsy. I swear, I trip over my own feet more often than anyone I know." She shook her head at her own alleged clumsiness.

"Are you sure?"

Giving them her most sincere smile, she nodded. "Yes. I'm sorry I worried you."

Their skeptical looks eased. "Sorry to bother you, ma'am."

"No problem. Good night."

Her relief at not being caught made her momentarily giddy—until her eyes fell on the now open window. Her next problem was the metal bars. There had to be a simple way to open them—it wouldn't be safe in case of fire otherwise.

Agent Donnelly had been gone for fifteen minutes. She needed to keep moving.

The window didn't have a screen, so there was one less thing to remove. But what was the trick to the bars? She inspected them inch by inch and found a keyhole in the bottom left corner.

So where's the key?

She swung around, her eyes darting over the sparse room. It had to be there for emergencies. Most likely, it would be somewhere in the room.

The walls were bare and the furniture was minimal. An inspection of the closet yielded nothing. However, at the back of the top dresser drawer, behind some of the plainest clothing she'd ever laid eyes on, was a tiny key.

Seconds later, she swung the heavy metal grate open carefully, making sure it wouldn't snap back at her or hit the wall outside. A noise from downstairs as she lifted a leg to climb through the opening made her freeze and listen, her heart in her throat. She waited thirty seconds, and then a minute, but no knock came at her door, so she continued contorting herself to fit through the window, pausing only to work her sweater free when it snagged on the metal.

She paused on the fire escape landing, sweaty and sore but relieved. Her head buzzed with adrenaline, and she bit her lip, hesitating. Her chances of success weren't great, but she knew what would happen if she stayed, and her anger with Agent Donnelly bubbled back to the surface. *For once in my life, I'm going to take a risk.*

Her determination restored, she tiptoed down the metal stairs with everything she owned in her backpack and her recently acquired driver's license, bank card, and credit card jammed in her pocket. Her descent went smoothly, and she hesitated for only a second before gritting her teeth and letting herself drop the last eight feet to the ground.

Ella clamped her mouth shut to hold in a moan as she landed, wincing as pain from her left ankle radiated up her leg. She hadn't even made it out of the shadow of the safe house and things were already going wrong. Managing to stand, she limped down the alley past the townhouse behind hers, then across the quiet street parallel to hers and back into the shadows.

She made it down the alley to the next block, her ankle throbbing more with every step. Leaving an obvious trail for the FBI by ordering a ride through an app was out of the question, but she wouldn't make it much farther on foot. From the alley, she ducked down a silent residential street.

Just as finding a ride seemed like a lost cause, a bright yellow taxi stopped at the red light at the end of the block. She waved her arms wildly, hoping the driver would pull over, but it barreled past her and was out of sight in seconds. The silence of the deserted street pressed even more heavily around her in its wake.

Keep moving. Limp-jogging on her throbbing ankle, she rounded the corner, moving by darkened shops with her head down. She jumped back when a door swung open only a few feet in front of her, releasing a burst of light and laughter as a group of tipsy twenty-somethings spilled out of a restaurant. The fragrance of spicy food wafted out to greet her, and Ella ignored her grumbling stomach. She wasn't sure when she'd last eaten.

Only when her ankle threatened to give out did she hobble to a worn-out bench under a covered bus shelter at the end of the block. The adrenaline of her escape was fading, and the pain in her ankle made the path ahead of her even more daunting. *This was either incredibly brave or incredibly stupid.*

Yes, she still had a long way to go, but she'd snuck out of FBI protective custody. Not bad for a woman who, until a few days ago, had been so shy and obedient that she didn't even jaywalk.

Headlights swept over the buildings across the street and an engine rumbled. Ella looked up as a black and red taxi barreled around the corner. She expected it to drive on like the last one, but it stopped at the curb and the passenger side window rolled down. "Miss, you need a ride? No bus coming here for a long time."

"Yes, thank you." Glad that at least one thing had gone right, she limped to the beat-up sedan. Maybe accepting an unsolicited ride from a stranger while assassins were chasing her was unwise, but she was out of options.

"Where you going, miss?"

"Union Station." It was already after seven, and she wasn't sure where in the city she was or how long it would take to get there. "Please hurry."

"Should not be too bad traffic at this time." The driver programmed his GPS and swore at it in disgust. "Useless garbage machine!" Over his shoulder to her, he added, "You don't worry. I know a faster way."

Her ankle throbbed even more than before as she limped briskly toward the station twenty minutes later. A police officer on duty stood outside the main doors, and part of her expected him to stop her. He didn't, but she still didn't relax until she was out of his line of sight.

In the wide entry hall, travelers' conversations echoed up to the cavernous cathedral ceiling. Even though her ankle was now screaming, she limped briskly, dodging off-hour commuters who walked with purpose and more casual travelers who did not. Her determination got her to the middle of the large room, where without warning her ankle simply failed to support her and she hit the marble floor with an embarrassingly loud *thud*.

Far too many heads turned in her direction, and the three people closest to her responded: two women who'd just passed her going the opposite direction and a man who'd been walking behind her. They all squatted around her to ask if she was all right.

"I'm fine. I twisted my ankle earlier and it's acting up."

The man and one of the women helped her to her feet, and Ella thanked them all profusely. One tentative step told her in no uncertain terms that her ankle would not hold her weight. When she shuddered forward, hands reached out and caught her again.

"Are you heading to Amtrak?" the man asked. Ella looked at him properly for the first time then. He was bald, thin but muscular with a serious air about him. He resembled a TV character whose bad side you wouldn't want to end up on.

"Yes."

"May I give you a hand to get over there? You might not make it otherwise. I'm going that way, anyway."

He's not an assassin. I'm being ridiculous. He's a guy who walked into the station behind me.

Annoyed with herself for not even being able to execute the first and easiest part of her plan without complication, she thanked the two women for their help and allowed this stranger to help her the rest of the way to the Amtrak ticket line.

At the ticket counter, she held her injured ankle off the ground and leaned on the counter as she talked to the ticket agent.

"The closest you can get to Virginia Beach is Norfolk. The next train to Norfolk is at 7:20 tomorrow morning."

She envisioned Agent Martin calling Agent Donnelly to tell him they'd caught her on surveillance video from the train station—she couldn't wait there for twelve hours. With the belated realization that the FBI could track her phone, she hastily turned it off. Even though TV had taught her that Agent Martin could probably still track her with it, she couldn't afford to throw it away. She didn't have a TV character's unlimited bank account.

Think. You can figure this out. You have to figure this out.

"Okay, thank you." She limped away from the counter to a seat nearby.

What about a bus?

Accepting the risk it involved, she turned her phone back on and did what she should have done before running to Union Station. A quick internet search for *bus DC to Virginia Beach* gave disheartening results.

The next bus left the following morning at 6:05 am.

Not ready to give up hope, she typed *bus DC to Norfolk* and held her breath, releasing it with a smile when the schedule listed a bus leaving for Norfolk at 11:30 pm. Her mission accomplished, she powered her phone down and put it away.

Gritting her teeth against the pain as she got to her feet, she set off toward the bus waiting area, wincing with every step. Thankfully, the only law enforcement she encountered was a security guard on patrol who didn't look twice at her.

She spent her four-hour wait on the hard metal bench, tired, hungry, and in pain with nothing to do but think. If she stopped herself from remembering the moment her house had blown up, she pictured the man with the wire who'd tried to kill her, his cold eyes staring into hers and a sick grin on his face. If she got her mind off him, she saw Mal sneering at her. When she crowded Mal out of her mind, there was Sam breaking down her door, berating her for her carelessness, staring at her in irritation, or glaring at her with intense hostility.

Sam's going to be so angry with me...

According to what she had learned from TV, the FBI would flag any transactions on her account, so she waited until 11:20 to buy her ticket for the 11:30 bus. From the moment she swiped her card, she half expected Agent Donnelly to fly through the door and knock her to the ground. It was almost anti-climactic when he didn't.

As she waited to board, glancing nervously behind her, she imagined what might be happening back at the FBI. If they had flagged her accounts, then Agent Martin would have noticed her transaction by now. The agents would've discovered her missing hours ago, because there was no way Agent Donnelly wouldn't have checked on her when he got back to the safe house. To say that he'd be upset with her felt like a significant understatement.

Her shoulders ached from the tension flowing through her by the time she took a seat halfway back in the bus, against the window. There was still no sign of the flashing lights that would've meant the FBI's arrival, but that could change at any moment. Ella's attention was torn between watching out for Agent Donnelly's team and monitoring the other passengers as they boarded. She gave a forced smile when a man about her age carrying a small gym bag sat down beside her. He was casually dressed, with curly brown hair, and after a quick nod at her, his attention went to his phone.

After multiple recent attempts on her life, being sardined between complete strangers was not ideal. Still, even as stressed as she was, every moment that elapsed without incident felt like a victory.

At 11:29, the driver closed the doors. At the last second, a tall man wearing a baseball cap jammed his shoulder into the door, squeezing himself in. He apologized to the driver, then took a seat in the first row. Even though she never got a good look at him, something about him made Ella's skin prickle. She ducked down in her seat, trying to be as small as possible.

Don't be paranoid. All at once, she longed to be surrounded by FBI agents. Doubt about her plan hit her like a ton of bricks. Agent Donnelly's face, flushed with anger, appeared in her mind to read her the riot act.

Sam Donnelly was taking up far too much space in her head. Never mind that he would be furious with her, and rightly so. He'd probably take himself off her case, but that was tomorrow's problem—if it was even a problem. It might even be for the best. Right now, she had to get herself to Norfolk, and then somehow to Virginia Beach. After that, well, she'd worry about it when she got there. Maybe then she'd call the FBI once she'd looked around by herself.

The bus swung around a corner and out onto the road. Everyone in Ella's line of sight either had their eyes closed, or were engrossed in a book, magazine, or electronic device. Still, as they picked up speed en route to Norfolk, she remained on high alert, all too aware that danger waited for her in the darkness.

Chapter 25
Ella

TUESDAY

E LLA DISTINCTLY REMEMBERED FORBIDDING herself to fall asleep on the bus. The problem was that the driver had dimmed the interior lights and, exhausted as she was, with the adrenaline from her escape now gone, there was nothing left to keep her from drifting off.

She woke up with a gasp, her head jerking up from where it had rested against the window. They were still on the highway, and she was still clutching her backpack against her. According to her watch, they'd been on the road for less than an hour.

The man in the seat beside her had dozed off as well, and he was falling towards her little by little. She pressed herself against the window, but there was no escape. In minutes, the man's head landed heavily on her shoulder, but he didn't even stir. With a shudder, she attempted to shake him. "Hey. Excuse me... Hello?" Her voice was low but insistent, but it did no good. She cringed as he let out a loud snore and seemed to snuggle against her.

The good news is that this guy is probably not the assassin.

In another situation, being trapped like this could have been funny. Maybe it would be later. *Just make it to Richmond.* That was where she would change buses. Giving up on pushing the man off her, she resigned herself to several awkward hours.

At least he doesn't smell. Come to think of it, his hair smells good. Like some kind of berry. The rest of it came back to her then—the man at the front of the bus whose presence had made her so uncomfortable. *I wonder if that guy's awake.* She craned her neck, but couldn't see him from her angle.

In Richmond, the guy Ella had nicknamed Sleepy woke up and was mortified to have been sleeping on her shoulder. Ella wished him a good night and limped towards the bus waiting area. Upon inspection, she found her ankle to be swollen, but slightly less painful after a few hours of rest.

After a tense wait in Richmond, she boarded another bus bound for Norfolk. She hadn't spotted the man who'd jumped onto the bus in DC at the last second, but that didn't mean he wasn't there.

She took a seat near the front of the bus this time, and examined each passenger as they boarded, but she didn't recognize anyone.

Again, she imagined what Sam might be doing. *Pacing. A lot of swearing. Driving fast. Standing by Agent Martin at the screens and demanding an update.* She smiled at the caricature images before realizing that she shouldn't be smiling about this. She wouldn't be smiling when he caught up with her—which he would.

Imaginary Sam was so worked up, she almost felt sorry for him—until she remembered how infuriating he was, and then her guilt evaporated. She wrapped her arms more tightly around the backpack in her lap and stared out the window for the rest of the drive, attempting not to think about him.

The bus arrived in Norfolk on time, at 4:40 am. According to the fastest internet search she could manage before she switched off her phone again, there was a rental car company around the corner that opened at 8:00 am, and a coffee shop nearby that opened at 5:00 am. For the next three hours, she waited at the coffee shop, nursing some desperately needed coffee and scrutinizing everyone who walked through the doors for signs that they meant her harm.

At 8:01 she limped through the car rental's door, and after completing the painfully slow check-in process, she was on her way.

The morning sunshine was bright, but staying up all night was catching up with her quickly. Less than fifteen minutes after she got on the road, her eyelids were sagging and her head was pounding. Even though she'd had two coffees, she scanned the roadside signs for somewhere for another one.

Every part of her ached when she limped into a gas station moments later, the leftover pain in her ankle no longer her biggest complaint. The movement

helped wake her up a little, but what she needed was sleep. Since that would
have to wait, she headed back to her car with coffee and the sweetest donut
she could find, balancing both in one hand and unlocked the door with the
other.

Something small and solid pressed against her lower back, and strong
fingers curled securely around her arm just above her elbow.

"Don't move," a menacing voice hissed in her ear.

She froze, her heart thudding in her chest as every smart idea about what to
do in this situation immediately vanished. *Could I throw my coffee in his face
before he stopped me?* Considering what felt like a gun at her back and the fact
that the coffee had a lid on it, it seemed unlikely.

"Don't turn around and don't make any noise. Act like everything's normal
and walk with me." Without looking back, she let him steer her, recoiling as an
arm wound around her waist. "Easy." His voice was low and gruff as he led her
away from the building, toward the edge of the parking lot, somehow walking
beside her but just outside her peripheral vision, so she couldn't see him.

How is no one else seeing this happen? Try as she might to stay calm, she was
hyperventilating.

The seconds ticked by as single frames in her mind, like some sort of movie
special effect. The man's ever-tightening grip and the jab of metal in her back
made her wince as he pushed her toward a white work van sitting off by itself,
away from the other cars. Rounding the corner to the far side, she gasped.
The back door was open, so she could see that the van's back seats had been
removed and the floor was covered in plastic, as if he was prepared to do
something messy and clean it up without leaving a trace. A large metal box
and bottles of chemicals stood just inside the door.

Do something! Her brain screamed.

Gun or no gun, it might be her last chance to save herself, and she flailed
against him with all her might.

At that moment, a truck horn blared loudly from across the back of the
parking lot to their left. She used the man's momentary distraction to her
advantage, wiggling out of his grip. She'd worried that he would shoot at her as

she tried to escape, but he didn't need to. Before she was out of his arm's reach, he grabbed her wrist and yanked her back.

No!

She was struggling against his hold and calling for help now, and heads were turning. Not too far away, a loud male voice was yelling.

Despite her thrashing, something sharp pricked her neck and the ground rushed up to meet her face, ending in a painful collision. A door slammed beside her, then another one, and the van peeled away. She lay on the concrete, dizziness overcoming her as the light tunneled to a pinprick and then disappeared.

Chapter 26
Mal

TUESDAY

M AL WAS DOZING OFF again, ignoring the light creeping in through the cracks in the curtains of their hotel room. Her face was half buried in fluffy, white pillows, as Jimmy stirred beside her. His fingers gently tangled in her hair, and his voice was low. "So, how are you enjoying your beach vacation?"

"Mmmmm," Mal hummed, her eyes closed. "It's even better this time, without my family here to spoil it." She opened her eyes and grinned at him. "You are much more fun than my sister." She leaned forward to kiss him, but he backed away from her, blinking as he digested her last statements.

"Bloody hell, Mallory, you didn't mention that you came here with your family, too!" Sitting up in bed, he glanced around the room as if seeing it for the first time. Their takeout containers from earlier lay open on the table, and their towels sat in damp piles where they'd dropped them, along with their clothes.

Turning onto her back, she gazed at him and shrugged. "Didn't I? Okay, but so what?"

"So what?" His voice bled disbelief. "Mallory, why did you insist we come here?"

Defiance flashed in her eyes. "I told you. I know the area. I have some connections here, and I happen to like it."

"You don't think your sister would come looking for you here? Or was that the point? Did you invite her, as well?"

Mal frowned, not looking him in the eye. "No. Of course not. It's not like she can read my mind." She reached a hand around to his lower back, tugging him toward her.

"Besides, she never even saw us at Walloon Lake. She went right by us without looking up." She'd gotten him to move toward her as they talked, and now he was on his side, an elbow propped against the pillows and his face only inches above hers.

Sarcasm had replaced Jimmy's usual carefree attitude. "Did you leave her another rock?"

"Of course not! That wouldn't have anything to do with this area."

"What exactly did you leave her, then?"

"Nothing!"

Jimmy raised his eyebrows. "I don't believe you."

"It was just a stick."

"A stick? What stick? How does a stick make someone think of the ocean?"

Mal sighed. "It was in the shape of a trident." When Jimmy still looked lost, she huffed and added, "A trident is the staff that the statue of Neptune is holding... the giant one that's on the boardwalk."

Jimmy stomped to the window and shoved the blackout curtain aside, momentarily blinding them. Mal hid her head under the pillow, hissing. "So much for being paranoid enough to keep the blinds closed." She peeked out from under the pillow, giving him a sarcastic look.

Jimmy ignored her and peered out at the statue, which was easily visible from only a few buildings away, then flung the curtains closed again. The room dropped back into darkness as he spun around to face her. His voice had turned uncharacteristically low and menacing.

"Are you insane? Seriously. I think you may have lost it. Not only are we on a tour of your childhood vacation spots, but you're telling your sister where we're going. You do understand that we're trying *not* to get caught, right?" He stood in front of her, tension flowing through every inch of him.

Ignoring his question, she reached for his hand, pulling him toward her. "You're pretty hot when you're all worked up. Did you know that?" She stood slowly, leaned forward until their lips made contact, then ever so slowly moved back until the back of her legs bumped the edge of the bed. Hooking her arms around Jimmy's waist, she let herself fall backward on the bed, taking him with her. Thanks to his fast reflexes, he landed on his forearms and didn't crush her—they never even broke the kiss.

Mal's attempt at distraction had succeeded, and both Jimmy's bad mood and the discussion about whether they should or should not have fled to Virginia Beach were behind them for the time being.

Chapter 27
Ella
TUESDAY

Ella woke up lying on the concrete of the parking lot, gasping for air. She had no idea how long she'd been unconscious, only that she was in more pain than she'd ever been in her life, her arms and legs heavy.

A spotlight shone on her from somewhere nearby.

"Miss, can you hear me?" A scruffy older man with a long red beard leaned into her field of vision.

She nodded, sending a spasm of pain down her back.

"A guy in a work van injected you with something and left you here. I already called 911. Just hang on a couple more minutes."

She tried to make some kind of affirmative noise or movement, but she was pretty sure all she'd done was continue taking the most difficult breaths of her life. It hurt everywhere. She tried to pull an arm over her face to block out the light, but she couldn't seem to bend her elbow. She tried the other one, with no luck.

What's happening to me?

Her panic did not help her breathing, which was getting even more difficult.

What felt like hours later, she heard a siren, and after that, finally, flashing lights flashed in her peripheral vision. She closed her eyes and focused.

In. Out. In. Out.

Tires squealed. Voices came closer. The red-bearded man was explaining what he'd seen. After that, her heartbeat pulsed in her ears, blocking out every other sound. *Thump thump. Thump thump. Thump thump.*

I'm sorry, she thought, focusing what little energy she had left on beaming her thoughts to Sam. *I'm sorry. Help me.*

Car doors slammed. The EMTs' voices carried across the short distance from the ambulance, their radios crackling. They were standing over her. Lifting her. Strapping her onto the board and lifting her again. Talking to her.

She was nowhere near strong enough to open her eyes. She had no choice but to let it all happen, to hope that these strangers would get her to safety.

"Ella!" She heard her name, but had no idea if it was only in her imagination, or if it was real. It sounded like Sam, but how could he possibly have gotten there so fast? How would he know to be there at all?

Before she had time to wonder any more, she felt a wave of pain roll through her, and then she went still.

Chapter 28
Ella

TUESDAY

T HE STEADY BEEPING CAME from nearby, and Ella stiffened. That sound had been a part of the soundtrack of agonizing visits with her parents in hospitals years ago. The speed of the beeps increased as her breathing became uneven.

So I'm in a hospital. But why?

Her eyelids were too heavy to open. Panic set in, and the beeping sped up even more. Murmurs ricocheted around her, but nothing else she recognized.

She willed herself to relax, then tried again. This time she succeeded, only to find that the world around her was out of focus. A blurry shape approached her, and she had a lingering sense of being in danger. Her first instinct was to get away, but when she attempted to move, the shape pinned her down by her shoulders with ease.

"Ella..."

The shape held her in place as she squeezed her eyes shut and flailed wildly. "Let go of me!"

It took a few seconds to process why the firm but gentle voice was familiar.

"Ella, it's okay. It's Agent Donnelly." A pause, and then, "Sam." The words sank in as he continued. "You're safe. I won't let anyone hurt you."

She stopped struggling, breathing hard as her panic receded. His hands relaxed on her shoulders, then let go when she offered no further resistance. She inhaled deeply once more and opened her eyes slowly, squinting against the light as her vision cleared. As she'd suspected, she was hooked up to a heart monitor, with a sensor clamped to her finger.

In the chair beside the machine was Sam. She sighed heavily as their eyes met, able to admit that she was the tiniest bit glad to see him there. It wasn't bad enough that she felt safer with him around. Even worse, he was developing the irritating habit of saving her life, which made it harder to hate him.

"You again," she said in a raspy voice.

She'd expected his anger, and found it in his face. But there wasn't just anger. "Ella, I swear to God." His voice was lower than usual, and he looked much older than he had the day before. Or maybe just far more tired.

The single chair in the room scraped the floor as he pulled it closer to the bed. He looked down and took a slow, deep breath.

He looks like he's seen a ghost. Ella waited for the explosion she knew was coming.

His words came out with what looked like a great deal of effort. "I'm relieved that you're not hurt. But I'm also so angry with you I don't even know where to start."

She tilted her head up so she could stare at the ceiling. Anything was better than looking at him while he lectured her.

"Do you even understand...? What you did was so unfathomably stupid." His voice rose with each word. "And dangerous. And selfish. What the hell were you thinking? And why did you run here, of all places?"

Overwhelmed at the barrage of questions, the unexpected emotion behind them, and a flood of emotions of her own, she was dismayed when several tears streaked down her cheeks.

You are not a child. Why do you keep crying when things go wrong?

Ella's hands clenched into fists at her sides on the bed. She focused on the ceiling, and though she willed herself not to cry, more and more tears trickled down her cheeks.

The weight of his stare continued to bore into the side of her face as they each fumed silently for several minutes—the only sounds were the beeping of the heart monitor, their respective breathing, and the sniffles she couldn't avoid. He thrust a tissue at her and grumbled when she hesitated to take it. The word 'stubborn' was in there somewhere. In the end she took it, blew her nose, and wadded the tissue into a ball. She wanted to throw it at him, but she resisted. Steeling herself for a fight, she glared at him.

His expression wasn't what she'd expected, and she studied him as if she'd never met him before. She knew he was here because it was his job, but the man in front of her looked like he'd been through much more than a frustrating night's work with a difficult—whatever he considered her. If she didn't know better, she'd say he'd been worried sick—which implied that he cared about what happened to her.

That didn't make sense. Sam didn't even like her, much less care enough about her to worry.

If something bad happened to me, there would be extra paperwork for him. Everyone hates paperwork. That must be it.

When he spoke again, the anger in his voice was gone. "I'm sorry. That wasn't... helpful of me."

"Or nice."

His glare held no bite, and it disappeared almost immediately, giving way to exasperation. "It's hard to be nice to someone who has no regard for their own safety and runs headfirst into danger when I'm trying to protect them. Do you run into burning buildings, too?"

"So what was your excuse for being a jerk when we first met, then? Before I did that?"

The muscles in her face tightened and she turned her head toward the other side of the bed, wishing she'd kept her mouth shut.

Another loud sigh sounded from beside her. "I used to be good at this." His voice faltered, and he continued in a more formal tone. "You took some profoundly stupid chances, and I didn't react well. You had to have seen that coming."

She nodded, one corner of her lips tilting up as she wondered how much of what she'd imagined him doing had actually happened.

"But... I am sorry the precautions that keep you safe are frustrating."

"That's not really an apology." She crossed her arms over her chest.

"Our protocols are in place because they work."

"They work. Great. Freaking out over your protocols might keep me alive, but for what? It won't give me back anything worth having," she snapped. The rush of emotion inside her made her voice shake. "Nothing will."

Anger seeped into his voice. "So that's it? Your pity party makes you go out and do the most dangerous thing you can think of?"

Her volume increased to match his. "That's not what happened and you know it! Why are you such a pain in the ass?"

She slammed her fists down on the bed on either side of her, angry with him for his lack of sympathy and with herself for needing his help. He was infuriating, which made it even stranger that now and then she got the feeling that he cared what happened to her. Of course, after the stunt she'd pulled, he was probably going to wash his hands of her. While she didn't like the meek person she'd been for most of her life, she didn't like this new person she'd turned into who made such poor decisions, either.

Focusing on the far end of the room, she fumed.

Exhaling loudly, he ran a hand over his face. "How about we start this conversation again?"

She haltingly met his eyes. "Yes, please."

He looked at her for a few seconds, his expression smoothing out. "It was irresponsible of you to go out on your own. I'm angry at you because I'm trying to protect you, and you're actively making my job harder. You could have died—the assailant at the gas station injected you with strychnine, which is highly poisonous. You're lucky to still be alive. I hope now you understand that I'm not exaggerating the danger you're in." She was about to respond when he added, "I don't want to stop you from helping us, but keeping you safe is more important than anything else."

"I know. That's your job." Her tone was acidic.

The look on his face said he wanted to argue, but he didn't.

She willed herself to calm down. "I'm sorry for running away. But... you don't understand. No one understands. Every one of you gets to go home when this is over. It's just a job. This is my *life*. My problem. Every single thing I had is gone."

His expression changed, his face tightening. "I know what it's like to feel like you've lost everything."

From his expression, Ella got the feeling there was a lot more he wasn't saying, but when he didn't continue, she did. "Anyway, after what happened in Michigan, I knew you wouldn't let me come along the next time. But I needed to be there, I mean here, so I felt like I didn't have a choice."

His expression was stormy. "No matter how frustrating it is, this is not something you can fix by yourself. You have to trust me."

She cringed at the word *trust*, hoping it hadn't been too obvious, and gave him a sad smile.

As if reading her mind, he added, "It's hard, I know."

Her gaze moved back up to his in surprise, color rising in her cheeks. "Not because of you. I don't..." She sighed and looked away. "I couldn't stand the thought of anyone else getting hurt because of me... At least this way, I was only risking my own life, no one else's."

Whatever he'd been about to say stopped on his lips, and his expression softened. "What happened to Agent Harrison was not your fault." His hand landed on her forearm, applying gentle pressure. "Please look at me."

She stared at the blanket covering her legs, trying to blink away her tears as a burning sensation flared inside her. He would never convince her it was not her fault.

"Hey," he said, and she hesitantly made eye contact. "Just promise me you won't do that again. You scared the hell out of me."

That wasn't an unreasonable request, all things considered. "I promise."

The door to the hallway opened and a nurse stepped into the room. "Good morning. My name is Helen." She looked down at the tablet in her hands, then up at her patient. "You must be Ella. My shift just started, so I'll be with you for the next twelve hours. I hear you gave some folks quite a scare. Let's see how you're doing."

Sam stood and headed for the door without waiting to be told, and Ella stiffened. He glanced over his shoulder before turning the handle, and they locked eyes.

She'd risked her life to get away from him, but her first instinct as he left the room was to panic. *Dammit.*

"I'll just be in the hall," he said, and then he was gone.

When Helen opened the door to go on to her next patient, Sam was blocking the doorway. He moved aside to let her out, then let himself back in and closed the door. "If you're thinking you'll be rid of me anytime soon, you're wrong... especially after what you pulled. You're going to be very sick of me before I leave you alone again."

A strange combination of embarrassment, defeat and relief overtook her and she sighed softly. "Yeah, I was afraid of that. I clearly can't be trusted." She'd said it jokingly, but the thought that he no longer trusted her gnawed at her insides. All her life, she'd been the pinnacle of responsibility. She hated that she'd failed at her mission, but she hated that she'd made herself a burden to him even more.

He watched her from the bedside chair, back against the wall. The silence between them lasted only a minute. "So, tell me... why here?"

She stared down at her hands. "You're not going to like the answer."

He pulled the chair forward again, and when she hazarded a glance at him, the annoyance she'd expected on his face wasn't there.

"Talk to me." It was unsettling to hear kindness in his voice.

For her own protection, she didn't let herself get close to anyone—especially not someone whose presence in her life was temporary. The more she let him in now, the worse it would be when the case ended and she no longer had him around.

The problem was, she'd already started.

A fluttering sensation in her chest that was both pleasant and terrifying made her think back to when he'd hugged her on the beach in Michigan. She wished he would do it again—not that she would say so.

"You're going to be mad," she whispered.

He raised his eyebrows. "Thanks for the warning. I think it's a bit late for that one, though, so you may as well just tell me."

Ella's hands clenched and unclenched in front of her, and she nodded. "Mal left me another clue. In Michigan. One that only I would understand." She waited for him to yell or stomp, but he remained seated, leaning forward in the chair and waiting for her to continue. "In the pictures you sent for me to look at, there was one with a pile of twigs by the back door. There was also one twig off by itself. It was shaped like a trident. Just like the trident that the Neptune statue on the Virginia Beach boardwalk holds."

He'd pulled his lips into a tight line, and he was breathing deliberately, as though it was taking a lot of effort to control himself. Knowing him, it probably was.

"My family went on a couple vacations here, so I was almost sure that was what it meant. It was stupid not to tell you, but if I had, you would've made me stay in DC with some random agent and you would've checked it out without me. I needed to be here. I know you think it's too dangerous, but..."

"You're right. After what happened in Michigan, I realized that bringing you along was selfish of me." His expression bordered on desperation. "You have to understand..."

Sadness filled her voice, knowing what he was going to say. "I know. I have to stay in the shoebox."

"It's not a punishment. You understand that part, right?"

In theory, she understood, but that didn't make it any easier. "It may as well be one, though. And I helped in Michigan... didn't I?" She was proud until she remembered the details more clearly. "At least when I wasn't being attacked or freaking out?"

"You did. That's not the issue. Victims don't help investigate their own cases for a reason. No, several reasons. We're trained for it. You can't just..."

She tensed as he spoke, not waiting for him to finish. "But I can..."

He held up a hand to stop her, shaking his head and sighing heavily.

"Ella, I don't want to argue with you. For now, please tell me you didn't come here solely because of a twig Mal may or may not have left on the floor."

She narrowed her eyes at his dismissal of what was, to her, a significant clue. "Not just because of that... that's just what made me make the connection. When we were teenagers, Mal decided Walloon Lake was boring. My dad had been sick, and my mom thought Virginia Beach would be a more teenager-friendly vacation. Mal loved it. There were more people and more trouble to get into. It made sense to me that she would come here."

He said nothing, just looked at her as if to say, "Keep talking," and she rolled her eyes and continued.

"I told the agents at the safe house I was going to sleep, snuck out the window on the fire escape, and immediately sprained my ankle jumping the last few feet to the ground, which I guess I deserved. I took the bus to Norfolk last night and then rented a car to drive the rest of the way."

He nodded, still saying nothing.

"I was exhausted after being up all night, and I needed to stop for coffee. And then…" She thought back to the night before at the gas station, telling him about it in as much detail as she could. The whole time, she braced herself for his reaction.

"Is your ankle okay? Did they look at it?"

She looked up at him in confusion. "After everything I just told you, that's your first question? I expected more yelling."

"I care if you're okay, believe it or not," he said, his expression wounded. "And I thought we were done with yelling."

She drew her leg out from under the blanket, setting her tightly bandaged ankle down for his inspection. He leaned closer, but did not touch her, and studied it for a few seconds before looking back up at her.

"It's feeling a little better."

"Good." He reached down and tugged gently at the blanket until she lifted her foot, and he tucked the blanket back over it. "That trucker who honked his horn while you were being poisoned saved your life. Your attacker didn't give you the whole dose in his hurry to get away. Several people there called 911, and the trucker stayed by you until the ambulance arrived and told the police what he saw. You were lucky you got to the hospital in time, and that they had the treatment you needed. You could have died."

"What can I say? It's my lucky week." The sarcasm was thick in her voice, and she looked up at him and sighed. "I haven't been feeling so lucky the past few days, but I guess you're right. It all sucks, but it could've been worse."

He'd taken out his phone, and now he tapped the screen rapidly before stuffing it back in his pocket. "I told Agent Martin the situation, so she can work her magic and find out if Mal's here. We were still looking for another lead when you, uh, slipped out, so your guess is as good as any right now. In the meantime, you need to get some sleep."

"What about you? You look like crap. I mean, you're still hot, but..." She clapped her hands over her mouth and stopped, wide-eyed.

His surprise at her blunt assessment morphed into amusement.

Her face heated up. "Sorry. Uh, apparently, I have no filter anymore."

"Yeah, I'm sure I do look like crap. I'll rest until Agent Martin finds something. Agent Rappaport and a local agent are outside the door, but as I promised, I'm not leaving you alone here. Unlike at the safe house, this time you're really going to get some sleep."

Her eyes darted down to her lap. "I'm never going to live that down, am I?"

"Maybe... Eventually." There must have been something on her face that betrayed her, because he added, "What else is wrong?"

She pressed her lips together, debating whether to tell him the other thing. "It's just that..."

Spit it out.

All she could manage was a whisper. "Every time I close my eyes, it all comes back. The explosion. The assassin. At the hotel. *Agent Harrison...*" Her voice broke, but she steadied herself. "At the van. Just all of it. Over and over. If I manage to sleep, I have nightmares about everything jumbled together."

"Are you planning to climb out the window?"

She grimaced. "No."

"You see? You're already safer than you were yesterday." His voice held a touch of humor, and his eyes twinkled despite the seriousness of his expression. "I promise you, you're safe. I'm going to be right here." Before she could respond, he added, "No, not watching you sleep like some creepy stalker. Just... here. So go to sleep."

He hadn't reacted to his partner's name a moment before, so she had to ask. "You never told me. Did Agent Harrison...?"

He shook his head and looked down at the floor, and it was as if she'd been punched in the stomach.

"In our line of work, we know the risks going in."

Fresh tears made their way down Ella's cheeks as she recalled how kind Agent Harrison had been to her in the immediate aftermath of the explosion, when Agent Donnelly had been actively hostile.

She rolled onto her side so she was facing him, sniffling and hugging the thin blanket tightly. He perched on the edge of the chair, his arms resting just above his knees. To her surprise, he unclenched his hands and reached up to smooth her hair back from her forehead.

"You can do everything right, and things can still go wrong," he said in a voice thick with emotion.

She nodded, sniffling.

His face clouded over, as if he'd only just absorbed the news he himself had delivered. "We worked together for fifteen years," he said, then sighed heavily.

"I'm sorry." She shifted, almost taking his hand but then stopping herself. That felt too intimate.

"I can understand why you don't want to sleep," he said. "At least try to rest."

He looked so sincere that she gave him the best watery smile she could. With a yawn, she sat up to move the end of the adjustable bed down until it was flat and turned onto her side to face him once more. "You're bossy, you know that?"

"So I've been told. And you are stubborn and infuriating." His words didn't match the warmth on his face.

"I'll take that as a compliment," she said. It felt good to smile, even sadly.

"Go to sleep, Ella. I'll be here."

Chapter 29
Mal

JIMMY PACED THE CRAMPED hotel room, alternating between staring at Mal with his mouth ajar and avoiding the sight of her.

"Whatever you have to say, just say it," she said.

"Explain to me again how any of this makes sense to you."

She rolled her eyes. "I told you. I want to talk to Ella. We make one more stop. Then it's over, and we're off to the Caribbean. I promise."

"And you couldn't have talked to her before this job? Met for coffee or something, like an adult?"

"It's too late for that now. I need to go back at the beginning before we leave for good."

"I've mentioned that I think you're being ridiculous, right? Every time we go out in public, we risk being caught. And don't get me started about the stupidity of starting a bar fight."

"I did *not* start that!" She clenched her fists at her sides.

"The point is, I know you're smarter than this. Do you want to end up like Bri?" He paused, and Mal's stomach turned at the reminder of Bri's death. Jimmy kept going.

"You're being reckless again. You suddenly need a heart-to-heart with your sister? For what? We need to cut our losses and leave the country while we can."

"One more stop, I swear. Just like you insisted we do one more job."

He stared at her in disbelief for a few seconds before reacting, his voice louder with every word. "*That was for a ton of money.* This is for... nothing. Your entertainment. Or closure. Or whatever it is." He tone was mocking.

Her face clouded over. "You wouldn't understand."

"You're right, I don't," said Jimmy. "But do whatever you want, because I'm done. Make as many stupid choices as you'd like. I'm leaving the country tonight, with or without you."

Mal sputtered. "You're what?"

"You heard me. If you want to get arrested, go ahead. If you make it to the Caribbean, you're welcome to join me. But don't bring any feds with you this time."

Mal's face hardened into a scowl. "You wouldn't."

"Oh, but I would, darling. You may be sentimental, but I'm not."

Her voice took on the same hostile tone she'd once used with Ella. "Fine then. Go. I don't need you."

Jimmy shook his head and tried one more time. "Mallory, she's not worth it. I don't know your history, but I know we're pushing our luck every moment we stay here. Stop sabotaging yourself."

"Very fucking deep for a thief, aren't you?"

What little sympathy he'd had for her dissipated, and he made one last sweep around the hotel room to grab the suitcase he'd packed earlier. He strode to the door, pausing before opening it.

"Good luck, Mallory. I hope you accomplish whatever it is you're hoping to get out of this." Holding the door open with his foot, he wiped both handles with a washcloth, tossed it back inside the room, and left without a backwards glance.

Mal watched Jimmy's retreat, stone-faced. When the door closed behind him, she let out a shriek and picked up a large, glass paperweight from the desk. She hurled it at the window, where it shattered the glass into thousands of spiderweb cracks and fell to the floor with a thud. Walking in a circle around the room, she knocked over the heavy bedside lamp and launched a half-finished container of takeout at the wall, moving faster and grabbing anything within her reach, hurling it away indiscriminately with all her might. When she was finally still again, the room looked like a tornado had blown through.

"I don't care," she said to the empty room, and then again, at the top of her lungs. "I don't care!"

A sharp cracking sound brought her back to reality, and she looked around in surprise at the mess. Sheets and towels littered the floor, the heavy standing lamp lying on the floor with a crack in the middle, and the bedside lamp was on its side, missing a large chip. A half-full takeout container had splattered on the wall, and the rest of the contents on the floor below. There was a dark scuff mark and a scratch on the wall, and a series of cracks running across the TV.

Grabbing her bag as she headed for the door, she wiped the fingerprints off the door handles just as Jimmy had.

A buzz filled the air the moment she stepped off the elevator in the lobby. Something was wrong. The commotion came from the large windows that faced the boardwalk; a crowd had gathered there, murmuring loudly. A knot formed in Mal's stomach. Though she was anxious to get on the road, she squeezed through the cluster of onlookers, keeping her head down and fighting a wave of dread.

Out on the concrete, the police had the area in front of the door roped off. They were surrounding something—no, someone—on the ground.

"What happened?" Mal asked the woman standing next to her.

"They're saying the guy out there got *shot*," the woman said, her eyes wide. "No one even saw who did it. It just happened a few minutes ago. The first couple cops happened to be nearby, and they called in back-up. See, more are just arriving." She pointed through the windows, where sure enough, the swarm of officers had grown. Mal had a bad feeling about all this, and not just because she needed to avoid law enforcement. Despite her need to disappear, she stayed rooted to the spot where she stood.

"Were you here when it happened?"

"I was across the lobby, talking with my friends. Someone screamed, so we all ran over..."

It's not possible.

Except that it was. Jimmy could always talk a good game, and he was easy on the eyes, but neither he nor Bri were any good at defending themselves. Neither of them would've lasted long in a fight. That's why Mal, who had spent two years with *Bratva*, aka the Russian mafia, had been in charge of security for the trio.

The police had blocked off the revolving door that led to the boardwalk, so she pressed on along the window in search of a better view.

Where are you? she typed to Jimmy, but got no response.

Unable to get a good view from inside, she used the street side doors and went around the building the long way. She didn't get far. The entire section of the boardwalk in front of the hotel was blocked off, and passersby were being directed either down to the sand or to the side street behind the row of hotels. Most people, however, were not walking by—they were standing behind a line of police tape in a growing crowd, watching.

Mal squeezed through the group until she was at the front. None of the officers were moving with any urgency, and the EMTs climbed into the ambulance, deep in conversation. Her stomach tightened. This was not a good sign.

One officer stepped to the side, and that was when she saw them—the red sneakers. The person who'd been shot was wearing the same red sneakers she'd teased Jimmy mercilessly for buying a few weeks ago.

A van with "Coroner" in bold black letters pulled in nearby, and Mal swallowed an urge to throw up.

Looking up at the tops of the other hotels in the strip along the ocean, Mal suddenly imagined herself in the crosshairs of a sniper. If that really was Jimmy—and he was dead—she was next.

Her breaths started coming quickly, and she tripped backwards without looking, causing grumbling from the people behind her. The urge to sprint away was strong, but she forced herself to walk—back around the hotel the way she'd come, to the street, and then to the cab waiting area on the next block.

Only once she was speeding through the night away from the scene did she stop to think about what this meant. Bri was dead. Jimmy was most likely dead. Had the clues she'd left for Ella put Jimmy, and now even herself, in danger? Was she next?

Chapter 30
Ella

W HAT FELT LIKE MINUTES later, Ella opened her eyes to bright light streaming in through the window. She'd survived another night.

Sam had not moved from the chair at the edge of the bed, where he'd been when she'd fallen asleep. His head was propped heavily against his hand and his eyes were closed. A few seconds later, he toppled forward.

She stifled a laugh as he caught himself just short of face-planting into her blanket. His momentary disorientation morphed into alarm as he jerked awake, then changed to relief as he focused on her.

Her voice was raspy. "I think I got the better sleeping arrangement here."

"Sadly, this isn't the worst one I've ever had, thanks to this job."

"It sounds like your job sucks."

"Sometimes. Others not so much."

He held eye contact with her for a few beats, until Ella cleared her throat and glanced away. "Is there any news?"

"Not yet. It's barely morning now, so Rappaport and Watson will head down to Oceanfront soon. Agent Martin doesn't have a lead in the area yet. Is there somewhere specific you were planning to look first?"

His eyebrows arched and she blushed, staring at her hands on the thin blanket.

I can't believe I thought I could do a better investigation than the FBI.

"We always stayed at a hotel near 20th and Atlantic, overlooking the beach. It was nothing fancy, and it may not even be there anymore... It's stupid to think she'd go back there, I know..."

"Maybe not. But we're here, so we might as well check it out."

Her eyes met his again, and she managed a tight-lipped smile. "Thank you. And... I'm sorry again."

"Let me talk to the others. They should be right outside." Before he opened the door, he peered over his shoulder. "I'm going to be right outside. If they're not there, I'll come right back in here."

A few days ago, that would've been a threat, but now it sounded more like a promise. She nodded, curious who he was trying to reassure—her, or himself, or maybe both of them.

The muffled voices from outside the door were comforting, even if she couldn't make out the words. When the voices stopped, he opened the door again. "They're going to canvas the area and show Mal's picture around. Agent Martin is still digging."

"And you?"

"I told you, I'm staying here." He dropped back into the chair by her bed, leaning back as if to get comfortable.

"You're stuck here, babysitting, because of me." *I'm such a moron.*

He shrugged, looking uncharacteristically relaxed. "You're good company when you decide to be. And after everything that's happened, I don't trust anyone else to keep an eye on you."

She cringed. "You mean you don't trust me not to do something stupid."

"No, I think you've learned your lesson. At least I hope so. But if anything happened to you and I wasn't here..." He was trying to hide it, but she heard the anxiety behind his words. "Besides, everyone's always telling me I should rely more on my team, and delegate more of the work. I'm not so good at that. So this is good practice." His face remained serious despite a twinkle in his eyes.

A small, nervous smile twitched on her face, but she said nothing.

"How are you feeling, anyway? They said you were extremely lucky that you didn't get more of the poison than you did."

"I feel... okay. After, what are we up to? Three attempts on my life?"

"Four."

"I guess just being alive is an enormous accomplishment for me. I'm... numb. Embarrassed. Grateful. And... scared."

"All of those make sense." His scrutiny made her avert her eyes again. "You still look tired."

At that moment, a yawn escaped her. "I guess I am. You still look pretty tired yourself."

Ignoring her observation, he shook his head. "You should get some sleep now, while you can. Once you're discharged from this place, we're going to be busy."

"We? As in both of us?"

He sighed. "For now."

"What about you?" she asked. "Are you finally going to sleep?"

"I have work to do right here. Every time I leave you alone, something bad happens."

He gave her a teasing smile, and she rolled her eyes. "Hilarious." She reluctantly closed her eyes, and for two minutes, she blocked out the things she dreaded by picturing him sitting right in front of her.

As much as she hated to admit it, she felt safer with him there. The hallway noises faded into the background, but when they did, her mind wandered back to the things she only wished she could forget. Her eyes snapped open, panicked, and she propped herself up on her elbow.

"Still here." His words were laced with amusement, but his face changed when he looked up from his phone and saw her distress. "What's wrong?"

"Just... I was falling asleep and when it got really quiet, for a second I was back in the hotel room and that man was coming after me with the wire..." She shuddered.

He leaned forward in his chair, closing the space between them, his eyes fixed on her intently. "You trust me, right?"

She nodded. *It would be so much simpler if I didn't.*

"Nothing's going to happen to you on my watch."

Ella didn't look away from Sam as she settled back against the pillows. He was close enough for her to study the tired lines around his eyes, even as hers began drooping again. She didn't fight to stay awake, knowing he would keep his word.

The next time she woke up, her eyes tiny slits against the light, she found him still sitting near the edge of the bed, engrossed in something on his phone. She lay still, a sleepy fondness filling her as she watched him. His stubble had grown thicker over the past few days, but did not yet suggest neglect. As calm and focused as he was, she guessed from his scowl that he was unhappy with what he was reading.

When she shifted, the sound drew his attention. "Hey. How are you feeling?"

"Less tired. What about you? Do you ever sleep?"

"Not much. I'll catch up later."

"When you finally solve this case? Or as you jump headfirst into your next one? Because I get the feeling that neither of those is going to happen soon."

He shrugged. "You're pleasantly snarky. You must be feeling better." He sounded amused.

"Does that mean it's time to go?"

"Easy there, tiger. The doctor hasn't cleared you yet. You got pissed off at me for being impatient to spring you free the last time."

She scoffed. "You were a jerk about it. This is different! We should be out looking for Mal, not sitting around and doing nothing. We don't have time to waste like this."

There was a knock on the door, and Helen, the nurse on duty, entered the room. "Good morning. How are you feeling?"

Agent Donnelly stood suddenly, his eyes glued to his phone. "I'll be right back," he said, heading for the hall.

Ella turned back to Helen. "I'm ready to get out of here. No offense."

"None taken. Let me just check a few things. We just need to make sure you're stable and didn't have any adverse reactions before we can discharge you."

Helen chatted as she read Ella's chart, took her temperature and blood pressure.

"Everything looks great. I'm going to ask the doctor to swing by, and maybe we can get you out of here soon."

When Helen stepped out into the hall, Sam took her place. His eyes were wider and he suddenly looked more alert.

"Everything okay?" asked Ella.

"I think so. Agent Martin has two potential leads."

Chapter 31
Ella

"WHAT KIND OF LEAD?"

"On our way down here, we contacted the Virginia Beach Police to see if they'd gotten anything that sounded like a match for Mal. They hadn't at the time, but they just got back to us. It's a grainy video from an altercation in a bar in Virginia Beach just before they closed a few hours ago. There was a possible match for Mal. It happened near the area you suggested we check. Their security footage is low quality, so Agent Martin is working on enhancing it."

"What happened?"

"We don't know anything for sure."

Without her noticing, Sam had moved the chair up to the bed again, and now he broke through her racing thoughts. "When we're done here, we'll go see the footage for ourselves and interview the owner of the bar."

She took a deep breath.

"Don't assume the worst."

"I'll try," she said. "What was the other lead?"

"A shooting on the boardwalk outside a hotel at 20th and Atlantic."

"Who was shot?" Desperation crept into her voice.

"A middle-aged male of undetermined ethnicity. That's all the information I have."

Ella exhaled, nodding in relief. Neither of them spoke as Sam got up and paced back and forth, appearing to be working something out in his head. He stopped when a woman in a white coat entered the room, smiling at Ella. Her dark hair was pulled into a mass of tiny braids, which were tied back in a long ponytail. She identified herself as Dr. Wilkins as Sam headed for the hall to wait.

"All your tests have come back clean," she told Ella after examining her. "You tolerated the treatment well, and there's no trace of strychnine in your system. I think you're ready for your discharge paperwork. I'll get a nurse to bring it in and go over it with you. In the meantime, you can get dressed."

Once the doctor was gone, Sam paced back and forth across Ella's room. He stopped abruptly when she emerged from the bathroom in her own clothes. She'd just pulled her hand out of her pocket, and she stared down at something in her hand as if in wonder.

"What's that?" he asked.

"The only thing I saved from my house, I guess," she said without looking up. "I forgot it was in my pocket."

He walked closer and saw what looked like a small, flat silver padlock with rounded sides. It had a raised heart in the center and lines coming out all around it, like a child's drawing of the sun would have.

"My mom gave it to me when I was seven. I had a necklace for it, but it broke and I didn't replace it. I liked to hold it in my hand, so I would stuff it in my pocket." Putting it back where she'd found it, she looked back up at him.

"Why don't you sit? You must be tired," she said. Taking her own advice, she sat back down on the bed and leaned against the pillow. As she did, her phone's ring pierced the quiet of the room, demanding to be let out of her bag.

"Stay there. I've got it." He grabbed the bag from the floor and set it on the bed beside her. When she fished it out, she smiled at the name on the display. It was Anthony, her neighbor and the father of Mason, the teenager who'd helped her out of the street immediately after the explosion.

"We heard about the explosion the other day. Mason said you were injured, and we've all been wondering what happened to you. Sue said she'd left you a couple messages. Are you all right?"

"Please tell her I'm sorry I haven't called her back. I'm okay. The FBI has been looking out for me. They're working on unraveling what happened. It's... more complicated than I could have imagined."

Sam shook his head firmly, and she got the message loud and clear.

"I can't say anything about it, though. You know, ongoing investigation and all that."

"Just like on TV?"

She chuckled. "Sort of. Anyway, it's going to take a while to get back on my feet, and there's a lot to sort out. But I'm in good hands."

"I'm glad. And Sue and Mason will be glad to hear it as well. You know Sue, she'll tell everyone on the block."

"It's sweet of you all to worry. I'll come by soon. I'm just not sure when."

"Okay. Take care of yourself. Let us know if you need anything. We're always here to help." Ella closed her eyes and fought back a wave of nostalgia. Though quite a bit younger than her parents, Sue and Anthony had been among their best friends. They'd been nothing but supportive of her, but she'd spent most of her adult life pushing them away. They were another reminder of what she'd lost.

"Bye." She glanced up as she ended the call, her gaze meeting Sam's.

"Friend of yours?"

There was something about his expression. *Is he... jealous?*

"My neighbor. His son helped me out of the street after the explosion. His wife is the self-appointed block captain. He was just checking on me."

Sam's features relaxed, but before she had time to analyze his reaction further, Helen was back with her discharge paperwork.

Just after 1:00 pm, Helen parked Ella's wheelchair at the curb outside the hospital. "I'll wait here with Ella while you get your car," she told Sam.

"That's not going to work. If she's not able to walk, I can use the wheelchair to take her to the car. She's under FBI protection after multiple threats on her life, and there's no way I can leave her here."

His words sounded strangely protective, but she reminded herself it was his job. After assuring them both that she could walk from there, Ella followed him slowly to the parking lot and his borrowed SUV. This time, he matched her slow pace without complaint.

Once they were in the car, she asked, "Do you have any more news on the lead from the bar?"

"Nothing new. They're waiting for us. We're meeting the others by the bar."

"Are you sure I should be there?"

His voice had been flat a second before, but now it was charged with annoyance. "Are you changing your mind? Because after what you pulled to get here…"

"No, of course not. I want to be there. I just didn't think I'd be allowed. The closer we get, the more nervous I am about what we'll find." She stared down at her knees, listening to the engine hum.

"Whatever it is, we'll get to the bottom of it. I'm stubborn, or so they tell me."

"You? Stubborn? You don't say." She grinned, and he cracked a hint of a smile in return.

"You really are a pain in the ass," he said, doing a weak impression of his former surliness.

She'd never been called a pain in the ass before. It shouldn't have been a good thing, but it made her chuckle.

"It's better to be sure of what's going on than to wonder, right?" he asked, and her head snapped up. "Then we know what we're working with and you're not imagining the worst."

Is he reading my mind?

"Yeah." It made sense logically, but it wasn't enough to comfort her.

As they approached the Virginia Beach Visitor Center, the knots in Ella's stomach tightened. She'd held this place frozen in her memory for decades, so the changes were jarring. They were still blocks from the beach, but the signs of civilization spilled much farther from the ocean than they had twenty-plus years before.

Agent Donnelly didn't waste time finding a parking spot, pulling up on the sidewalk at the edge of the wide plaza between two hotels at 24th Street and Atlantic Avenue. From there, they had an unobstructed view of the water.

As they had in Michigan, the sights and smells of Ella's past assaulted her the moment she stepped out of the car. Yes, the hotels in the strip between Atlantic Avenue and the concrete boardwalk were now bigger and newer, but when she inhaled the sea air, she was seventeen again. The rest was the same. The blue of the ocean. The squawking seagulls. The crashing waves. The tourists clogging the sidewalks.

Just like at Walloon Lake, the passage of time had air-brushed the way she remembered Virginia Beach. No matter what the reality had been or what strife her sister had caused her here, in her mind this was mostly a happy place.

When Sam cleared his throat beside her, however, she was flung forward through time, crashing into the present without landing gear. Not that she minded his presence, it was just that he was a reminder of when and where she was, and why. If not for him, it would've been so easy to look around for her parents, though she knew they were long gone.

She hadn't realized she was grinning until her face fell at the sight of him. In response, he frowned even harder than usual. She got the feeling he'd taken her shift in mood personally.

"Sorry, I..."

"No." The sudden hardness in his voice stopped her apology before it could go any farther.

No longer meeting her eyes, he scanned the surrounding area.

She let out a heavy sigh. Sam's attention flicked back to her, the lines on his face deeper than usual. When he spoke again, the familiarity in his tone was gone.

"The bar is across the street and a few doors down. This way." He pointed her away from the ocean, toward Atlantic Avenue. Agents Jacobs, Rappaport, and Watson materialized beside them and the five of them crossed the street, drawing curious stares from the tourists around them. Agent Donnelly jogged to catch up with Agent Watson, while Agents Jacobs and Rappaport walked on either side of Ella.

"How are you feeling?" she asked Agent Jacobs, grimacing. It was strange not to be on the receiving end of that question for once.

"I'm good," Agent Jacobs said with a grin. "How's it going with you, Houdini?"

Ella stared at the concrete at her feet. "Feeling like an idiot."

"Not your smartest choice, but I get it." Agent Jacobs smiled sympathetically. "Agent Donnelly, on the other hand..."

"He was really pissed off at me at the hospital, but we came to an understanding. Things were actually good and then... I think I just offended him by accident."

"Ella, he has two settings, Growl and Bite. Don't take it personally."

He isn't always angry at me, though.

Partway down the block, they opened the door of a dark, hole-in-the-wall bar. As soon as she crossed the threshold, beads of sweat formed on Ella's forehead. The three fans rotating half-heartedly on the ceiling provided no relief. Without the benefit of the ocean breeze, it was at least ten degrees warmer inside.

A man of average build with short black hair and several tattoos visible on his arms emerged from behind the bar.

"Miles Kranzer?" Agent Donnelly asked.

"That's me. What can I do for you?"

The agents introduced themselves and followed Miles to a table by the window overlooking the street. His gaze landed on Ella and recognition flared in his eyes. She had a feeling they were in the right place.

Sam took the lead. "We're looking for this woman's sister. Was someone who resembles her here last night?"

"Oh yeah, and she was trouble. She won't be allowed in here again, that's for sure. Her or the guy she was with, either."

"What exactly did they do?" Agent Donnelly asked.

"I didn't notice her until after she'd already had a lot to drink. Of course, I'm not against drinking. If people don't wanna drink, I got problems. But those two got out of control. Seems like they were arguing about something, then the guy got up and went to the bathroom. While he was gone, the woman was talking to some other guy. No big deal. Except the new guy didn't react well when her guy came back. The two guys got in each other's faces. She screamed at both of

them, which pissed off another chick, uh, woman. From there, it escalated
to the guys throwing punches and the women lunging at each other. Even
during spring break, we don't get many fights like that in here."

Even after many years without contact, the behavior he described
sounded like Mal. Confrontational. Aggressive.

"Security escorted all four of them out. The other two went quietly, and
your sister's friend was cooperating, but your sister did not. Before they
made it to the door, she used some kind of judo moves on my guys, and she
knocked one of them on his ass before the others got her under control, or
so they thought. On their way out, she grabbed a beer bottle out of a guy's
hand and hurled it at the bar. It smashed the display." He motioned to the
bar, where there was a noticeable gap in the line of glass bottles filled with
different colored liquids. "Those are not cheap. She knocked over six of the
bigger ones like dominoes. Those fuckers cheered when they all shattered
on the floor."

Miles paused and took a deep breath. His jaw was tight, and he clenched
and unclenched his hands. One by one, he met the eyes of the agents, who
studied him calmly.

As usual, Sam was cool and detached. "You didn't call the police?"

"I did," said the bar owner, "but by the time they got here, we had them
all out. I don't know if they caught up with them."

"And you have the video footage of the altercation?"

"Yep, got it saved on my laptop. I sent the file to the police and the FBI."

Sam nodded. "Yes, our techs are enhancing it. We'd still like to see what
you have."

Miles retrieved the device from behind the bar and set it up on the table.
The grainy video of the scene played out exactly as he'd described.

It could have been Mal and her accomplice, but it also could have been
someone else of similar build and coloring. It wasn't until the very end,
when Mal grinned into the camera, that a shiver of recognition ran down
Ella's spine. The poor-quality footage and the fact that they hadn't been
face to face in twenty-one years meant nothing. Ella would recognize Mal's

smirk anywhere—the same one she'd worn every time she'd knowingly done something wrong.

"That's her." Ella shuddered. Her voice came out in a hoarse whisper, and everyone at the table turned in her direction. "She's made that face all her life. It's the same way she looked at me when she ripped the stuffing out of my favorite stuffed animal when I was eight. Or when she told me she'd left my parakeet's cage open on purpose so it could escape when I was eleven. Or after any of the times she held my head under water when we were swimming at Walloon Lake—jokingly, she said. Or about a thousand other times."

Miles' expression of horror made her wish she'd kept her mouth shut.

All at once, the pieces clicked into place. "If she knows I'm following her, that I'm finally playing her game, she'll want to milk it."

The conversation continued around her, but Ella tuned it out. Her heart thudded in her ears, so loudly it seemed strange that no one else could hear it. No one had ever understood just how much her sister's cruelty had affected her. Her parents had told her she should just let it go, but she'd never been able to. When Mal had done something nice, it had been either to get something from her in return, or so she had something to take away later.

Ella was suddenly conscious of four sets of eyes on her and looked up to find the group standing and watching her expectantly. She scrambled to her feet.

Agent Donnelly thanked the bar owner, and the group stepped back out into the sunshine. As they did, all four agents straightened at once. Sam put a finger against the comm in his ear. "What's up, Ayanna?"

After a brief conversation with Agent Martin on his comm, he turned to Ella. "We may have something. Come on." That was all he said to her as the group stalked back across the street, between the hotels toward the concrete boardwalk.

"What? What's happening?" Ella walked sideways beside him, staring into his face.

He moved with purpose, and she had to work hard to keep up. "There's..." Sam looked down at her and his answer stalled. They'd emerged from between the buildings onto the boardwalk, the beach stretching out before them, and

Ella's attention had shifted to the horizon. A few seconds later, with the pull of the ocean drawing her forward, she veered away from him.

In one swift motion, he darted in front of her so he stood between her and the ocean, blocking her view, staring down at her with fire in his eyes. She tried to push him out of her way, but before she could, she saw the look in his eyes and the words died on her lips. His face was red, every muscle tight, and his eyes wide.

Oh no.

His voice was low, and from the intensity radiating off him, she could tell he was making a supreme effort not to lose his temper in public. "Let's get one thing straight. You. Are. In. Danger. No matter what happens, you don't run off on your own. Not even a few feet. Understand?"

"I wasn't..."

He glared at her. Realizing nothing she could say would help, she decided not to fight him. "I'm sorry. I saw the ocean, and I..."

"Because it only takes a second and..." He snapped his fingers inches from her face. Startled, her attention jumped from the sudden hand in her face to his expression; she'd expected anger, but what she saw was pain. "Just like that, it's all gone." Before she could react, his empty-faced mask slipped back on.

"I'm sorry." She wasn't sure whether she was apologizing for having walked ahead, for escaping the safe house, for Agent Harrison, or for whatever had happened to him in his past. Maybe all those things.

His face didn't change, but his hands were balled into fists, relaxing only gradually as they stood and watched each other.

As they passed between the hotels and rounded the corner onto the boardwalk, she put him between her and the water. She glanced up at him and their eyes met, and for several seconds neither of them looked away. By the time they reached the hotel, she got the feeling that things between them were once again okay.

A swarm of agents waited for them outside the beachside entrance to a medium-sized, mid-level chain hotel, but even then, Sam scanned their surroundings for danger.

Inside, the woman at the desk directed the group towards a couch across the lobby, where a forty-something man in a hotel uniform with dark hair and glasses waited. His nametag read *Hugo*. He jumped to his feet as they approached, growing increasingly fidgety as FBI badges were produced. His eyes darted nervously between them.

The agents sat on the couch across from Hugo, who was now perched on the edge of the seat, foot tapping rapidly on the floor. "So, uh, you guys wanted to talk to me?" She empathized with him—it was only a few days ago that the FBI had shown up to question her.

"Yes." Agent Rappaport held out his phone toward Hugo. "Have you seen this woman in the past few days? We think she's traveling with a man with a British accent."

Hugo surveyed the group nervously. "I... I think so. The guy's accent stuck out. We don't get a lot of Brits. He was complaining about something, and she shushed him really fast. Glared at him like he was giving away some big secret, when all he was doing was being a pain in the ass."

The agents asked more questions and made notes of his answers, but Ella focused on the ocean out the window, once again losing herself in her memories.

In this one, she and Mal were about fifteen and sixteen, leaning against the metal railing at the edge of the concrete boardwalk. Mal was wearing a black bikini and Ella a purple one piece. Ella sometimes covered for Mal when she wanted to do something their parents objected to if it didn't put her in obvious danger—but this time Mal had wanted to meet up with an older boy she'd met on the beach and Ella had refused to be involved as soon as she said he wanted her to meet him at his hotel. The problem was, no matter how logical the arguments presented to her, Mal never saw the things she wanted to do as bad ideas.

In Ella's memory, her parents came up to them then. She inhaled quickly as a tsunami of emotions washed over her. Things hadn't been perfect, but at least she hadn't been alone.

Damn you, Mal, for making me come back to these places. It was so much easier not to remember.

The agents thanked Hugo for his time and instructed him to call if he thought of anything else.

As the group passed the front desk on the way out, a woman called after them. "Sir!"

Ella stayed at Sam's side as he detoured to the desk.

"You're with the FBI?"

"Yes," Sam grumbled, flipping his badge open. "Agent Sam Donnelly."

"I went through our records. The guests you're looking for appear to have left this morning. I'm sorry."

Ella's stomach dropped. A near miss was still a miss. Being so close was actually more frustrating. She turned to face away from the desk, leaning back against it for support and staring at the floor as she fought the sting of disappointment. Without breaking eye contact with the woman behind the desk, Sam inched closer to Ella, laying his hand on the desk beside her so that his forearm had the slightest contact with her arm. At first it seemed like a mistake, but he didn't move it away. She focused on the warmth flooding her body from the spot where their arms connected.

"Has their room been cleaned?" he asked.

"I'll find out for you," she said. The woman spoke into a walkie talkie, and a reply crackled over the device almost immediately. "No sir, it hasn't. I was called up to this particular room earlier to see the condition they left it in, and I can tell you that those guests will be paying significant fees for damages. Would you like to go up and see it?"

Chapter 32
Mal and Ella

AGES 13 AND 14
(25 YEARS AGO)

"IT'S NOT A BIG deal." Mal glared at the three girls in front of her, keeping her voice down to a threatening whisper. They were behind the dumpster beside the convenience store, blocked from the view of passersby. "They'll never miss this stuff. We're not hurting anyone."

Only the bravest of them, who stood an inch taller than Mal and studied her skeptically, dared to speak up. "I can't afford to get in trouble again. My dad threatened to take away my phone privileges for a month."

Mal's eyes narrowed as she focused directly on her challenger. "That's fine, Becka." Her tone made it clear that Becka's hesitation was anything but fine. "I don't care what you do. But don't think you can sit with us at lunch tomorrow if you chicken out."

The other two girls' eyes widened, but they said nothing.

Having reconsidered her options, Becka took a step back and glared at Mal.

"Okay, good. Any other objections?" Neither of the other two girls had ever dared to defy Mal, and they shook their heads. "Everyone remember the plan?"

When the three mumbled their agreement, Mal's devilish grin spread across her face. "Then let's go shopping."

They rounded the corner and strutted into the small convenience store with the swagger of newly unchaperoned middle schoolers. Mal gave the owner her most innocent smile as they passed, calling "Good morning," and heading directly for the candy aisle. This was the third time they'd been to this store to fill their purses with candy. They'd also done the same thing twice at the branch in the next town over. None of them needed to steal—it was just for fun.

They'd just closed their bags when Ella rounded the aisle and stopped in front of them. The sisters exchanged hostile glares but said nothing, and Ella spun around and marched back the way she'd come.

"Shit. I think my sister's going to rat us out. Let's pretend we're looking at the drinks and chips."

An employee turned down the aisle from the opposite end as they were leaving it, eyeing them suspiciously but saying nothing. They stalked back and forth in front of the refrigerator doors containing bottled sodas, juices, teas, and coffees before pretending to peruse the chips. They made stiff idle chit chat, growing more confident every moment that no one was the wiser.

"Alright let's go," said Mal. "Act natural. Just do what we planned."

Their purses loaded but not bulging with candy, they sauntered towards the exit empty-handed. "Are you sure you don't want anything, Mal?" Becka asked.

"No, they don't have the kind I like." Mal could feign innocence alarmingly well.

Ignoring the watchful eye of the man behind the counter, they passed through the doors and were barely on the sidewalk outside when their path was blocked by two police officers.

"Hi, Officer Duncan. How's it going?" Mal's tone was a mixture of confidence, fake cheer, and defiance.

"Hello, Mal. How are things?"

"I'm great, thank you. We need to get going, though. We'll see you around."

Officer Duncan made no move to get out of the girls' way. "I'd like you to show me what you've got in your bags, girls," he said.

"Just lipstick, wallets, hair ties... and, you know, girl stuff. Why? You want to borrow something?" Mal held his glare, daring him to call her bluff as the other girls shrank back behind her.

The officer glared at her, his eyes darting to each of the others and back to Mal. "Bags. Now."

One of the other girls held her purse forward, her hand trembling as she hid behind a curtain of mousy brown hair. Mal shot daggers from her eyes over her shoulder at the other girl, who just shrugged. Their friend with the corkscrew curls followed her lead, as did Becka the Brave. Opening the bags one by one and peering inside, Office Duncan whistled. After showing the contents to the shop owner, who was hovering nearby, Officer Duncan handed them off to his partner.

"Your turn, Mal."

Her defiant glare hadn't wavered. She threw her purse at him with all her might, mumbling under her breath. He caught it easily. Contents inspected, he spoke calmly.

"Mal, you and your friends have had your warnings. You leave me no choice."

"You always have a choice," Mal said in a mocking tone. "Isn't that what adults are always telling me?"

Mal and assorted accomplices had been caught at numerous other acts of mischief before, and they'd been let off after a stern lecture on each occasion. The last time, officers had delivered Mal and two others home to their angry parents in a squad car. This time, Mal's friends were escorted to one car, while she was led to the other.

As the car drove away, Mal spotted Ella and a freckled girl with an unfortunate haircut staring at them from the sidewalk. Mal scowled hard at her until the car turned a corner out of sight.

The police station was only a brief ride away, and unlike the other three, who were petrified, Mal's expression was more annoyed than fearful.

In the interrogation room, Mal rolled her eyes at the reverse mirror, knowing they were watching her. Drumming her fingers against the table to show just how bored she was, she didn't show a shred of concern for her situation.

When Officer Duncan and his partner joined her, she sat slumped in her chair, glaring at them defiantly.

"Mal, you've met Officer Meeks, right?" Mal only rolled her eyes again, and Officer Duncan pressed on. "You want to tell me why I'm finding you stealing now?"

"If you don't want to find me stealing, stop looking."

He ignored her heavy sarcasm. "Or you could just not do it."

Mal grinned, as if it was all a joke. "True. But that's no fun." When Officer Duncan just continued to stare at her, she added, "Am I supposed to be scared because you brought me in here this time? Because I'm not."

"I hoped you would take the consequences of your actions more seriously than you have in the past."

She shrugged. "Whatever."

"This isn't what you want to do with your life, Mal."

Her smile fell away. "Right, and you know exactly what I want out of life."

Officer Meeks arched his eyebrows. "No, we don't. Do you?"

"Do I need a lawyer? Because I passed Civics class. I know my rights."

"Time to call her parents?" asked Officer Meeks. When Officer Duncan nodded, Officer Meeks left the room, shaking his head, while the other two glared at each other in stony silence.

Chapter 33
Ella

WEDNESDAY

THE ELEVATOR DOOR OPENED on the third floor and the agents filed out after the hotel manager, but Ella found herself frozen in place. Sam put out his hand to stop the door from closing and lifted an eyebrow ever so slightly at her with an unspoken question. *You okay?*

She was definitely not okay, but she nodded and followed him into the hall.

At the far end, the manager and the other agents were nearing number 301. Ella slowed as she and Sam approached the door, but Agent Jacobs blocked the doorway, shaking her head at them. Over her shoulder, Ella glimpsed a room in disarray.

Agent Jacobs shook her head. "She shouldn't be in here yet. We need to have a look. It's messy."

Agent Donnelly turned to the hotel manager. "Is there an open room we could sit in for a few minutes?" The manager tapped the screen of her phone rapidly, then led them three doors down the hall and in under a minute, a man in a hotel uniform emerged from the elevator with a key card. She swiped it to open the door, then handed the card to Sam. "Let me know if you need anything else," she said, and walked back down the hall to stand outside the room Mal had trashed.

An eternity later, at least to Ella, Agent Donnelly's phone buzzed with a text. After reading it, he fished out examination gloves from his pocket and offered them to her. "Let's go. Your turn."

The mess that greeted them was impressive. A sheet was draped over one side of the TV and hung down to the floor. The rest of the bedding was twisted together, half of it hanging over the side. A wet towel had landed on one lamp, while another lamp had toppled over and the base had cracked. Empty alcohol bottles littered the floor, as did empty takeout containers. Large globs of food were on the carpet, the bed, and had dripped down the mirror and the wall.

Even if no crime had been committed here, there was likely valuable DNA from both Mal and the man with her. Ella fought the queasiness that had been growing since they'd arrived, heading for the balcony door overlooking the ocean.

Before touching the handle, she asked, "Is it okay if I go outside? I need some air."

Sam looked up. "Yeah, as long as you're not planning to make a Spiderman-style escape."

Ouch. She rolled her eyes at him. "Funny. I'll try to resist." He nodded, his expression registering the tiniest hint of amusement, then went back to work.

Ella was glad to put a sliding door between herself and the chaos. The afternoon sun glittered on the water and she blinked against the glare as a large ship sailed slowly across the horizon. Overhead, the deafening roar of a jet momentarily blocked out all other sounds. A moment later, the seagulls called to each other, sailing on the breeze, while the braver ones stood on the beach in groups to observe the humans. The delighted squeals of children punctuated the chaos, and she shaded her eyes, searching for the source of the happy sound.

Below her, the concrete boardwalk was about the width of a three-lane road, and people strolled by in both directions—some with children, some dressed for the beach, others in athletic gear. On the closer edge, just in front of the hotels, was a narrow bike path on which bikes and pedal-powered vehicles went by. Ella smiled at the memory of the bearded man she'd once seen riding down the bike path while obviously intoxicated. He'd been good-natured about crashing into a nearby bench, and had asked the bench if it would like to file a police report for the accident. Luckily, the path and the boardwalk had been mostly deserted that evening, and the bench had not pressed charges.

The sensation that she was being watched prickled the back of her neck. She was still alone on the balcony, and the room behind her was still full of FBI agents. Her eyes roamed over the crowd below her until she settled on a man in sunglasses who was crouched behind a black bike, fiddling with the chain. He was by the metal barrier at the far edge of the boardwalk. Ella had trouble keeping track of him, with other people constantly walking by and blocking her view. Still, what made him stick out from the crowd was that he wore jeans and a gray sweatshirt with the hood pulled up over his head, even though the day was sticky with humidity and most people were dressed accordingly.

Now on his feet, the man mounted the bike, his gaze sliding over Ella. *Did I imagine that?*

As he rode into the crowd, Ella backed away from the railing. Had he been watching her, or was she paranoid? Stepping backwards, she collided with the small patio table and lost her balance. The sound of the plastic furniture scraping the concrete startled her and, as if on cue, Agent Donnelly opened the sliding door and joined her outside as she righted herself.

"Everything okay?" By now his controlled facial expression and serious tone of voice were so familiar, they were almost comforting.

"There was a man down there. He..." She searched the sea of faces, but it had swallowed him.

"What man?"

"He's gone now, I think," she said.

Agent Donnelly frowned, scanning the boardwalk below for threats. "Let's get back inside," he said after finding none. They carefully bypassed the mess to the clear area by the door to the hall.

She leaned her back against the wall and exhaled a shaky breath.

"Ella?"

He was standing in front of her, closer than usual, staring intently into her eyes. She focused on him, and the panic gradually subsided.

"Tell me what happened." Unlike the gruff demands he'd issued when they'd first met, his voice was calm, with a hint of something else.

Concern?

A shadow of emotion flitted across his face, but it was gone before she could figure out which one it was.

After her account of the man and the bike, Sam was noticeably tense. He quizzed her until he had a more detailed description of what the man looked like and which way he'd headed, and then conversed quietly with the other agents. A moment later, Agents Rappaport and Watson nodded at Sam and left.

I shouldn't have gone outside. Just like I shouldn't have snuck out of the safe house, and I shouldn't have gone to Michigan. Somehow, every decision I make is wrong.

Sam was across the room, making notes. Her heart rate accelerating once again, Ella slid down until she was sitting on the floor, slouching until her head was even with her knees.

Loud thuds broke her out of her miserable reverie. Someone was pounding on the door only a few feet away, and her eyes went immediately to Sam's.

He motioned for her to move away from the door, and she scrambled around the corner into the bathroom, closing and locking the door behind her as Sam checked the peephole. The tiles were cool as she curled into a ball beside the heap of dirty towels. The brave Ella who had escaped from the safe house was gone. This version of her was once again huddled on a bathroom floor.

On the other side of the door, Sam conversed calmly with a man whose voice she didn't recognize. Not focusing on the words, she was conscious only of the conversation growing louder. Sam had let whoever it was inside, which must have meant he trusted him. His tone wasn't friendly, but then again, it never really was. Except sometimes with her.

When someone knocked softly on the bathroom door, she was already on her feet, bouncing slightly on her heels.

"Ella, it's me," said Sam. She opened the door a few inches, and his face appeared on the other side.

"The techs are here. You ready to go?"

"Yeah."

She squeezed out of the bathroom, and in her haste to leave, she grabbed the handle on the door to the hall.

"Stop." His tone was sharp and his hand landed on hers, gently but firmly holding it in place. Surprised by his sudden reaction, she jerked her hand out from under his and jumped back.

"Sorry, I didn't mean to startle you," he said. "Let me go first to make sure it's clear." He leaned out into the hall and checked both directions, his attention then dropping to the threshold in front of them. When she saw him looking down, she squeezed into the doorway beside him, immediately swallowing hard. She hadn't meant to press herself against him, but that was what she'd done. His arm moved to accommodate her, and he braced his hand against the opposite side of the doorframe, his arm stretched out behind her. Blushing, her eyes darted down to what he'd been staring at.

Something neon orange and the size of her thumbnail but shaped like a fish.

He crouched down to inspect the colored speck. "Do you recognize this?"

"No, I... Maybe. It's familiar somehow." A memory nagged at her, but she couldn't quite get to it.

He put on a new glove before reaching down to collect the fish. "It looks like one of those erasers kids like to collect, but that doesn't really erase anything. My friend's daughter loves those things."

She studied the fish intently, willing herself to remember where she'd seen one before. Her sense of déjà vu was strong. "It wasn't here when we got here, right?"

"I don't believe so, no." He frowned as he dropped the eraser into an evidence bag and sealed it, then handed it to Ella.

Someone left it there while we were in the room.

"Please, can we get out of here?" She thrust the bag at him, and the back of her hand rested against his chest for several heartbeats before he took it from her and slipped it into his pocket.

"Let's go," he said. Neither of them spoke after that as they started down the hall, making their way back to the lobby.

What had been a calm space when they'd arrived was now clogged with tourists. Ella was barely off the elevator when she froze in place, overwhelmed by the crowd. Sam put his left arm gently around her back and urged her forward, clearing a path through the throng with his right shoulder. She was surprised that not only did she not mind his touch, but the section of her back where his arm rested sparked through her clothes. Once through the door facing the boardwalk, they stopped beside a huge planter overflowing with delicate purple flowers flapping in the breeze. His arm dropped to his side, and a surge of disappointment that she immediately squashed tugged at her as she gazed at the horizon.

"I never should've come here."

He scanned for danger around them, looking everywhere but at her. "You weren't wrong, though. Before. I wouldn't have felt safe leaving you with anyone else. I would've been worried."

"About me?"

"Yes, about you." He exhaled loudly, turning in her direction but looking past her.

Instead of saying something that would make things even more awkward between them, he asked, "What's that giant statue?"

She knew without looking what he was talking about. The statue was visible from most of the three-mile expanse of beach and boardwalk. "Neptune. God of the Sea. It wasn't built when we used to come here, but my mom would've loved it. She would've made us take our picture in front of it, like she did with everything." She smiled sadly.

"Oh, right. I read about that statue." Their eyes met, and he shook his head. "I know what you're thinking, and the answer is no."

"Oh yeah? What am I thinking?"

"You want to go down there, and I get it. But not today."

He's right. Even though she knew it would have been too risky, she would've been there in a heartbeat.

"Let's get back to the car...we're too exposed out here. How many times have people tried to kill you in the past few days?"

She scoffed, averting her eyes. "I don't even know anymore."

When she forced her gaze back up to meet his, she was surprised to find sympathy in his eyes, and even more surprised that it lessened her heartache just a little—which set off her internal alarm bells.

Shaking her head to dislodge the unwelcome thoughts before they had formed completely, she steeled herself. "Do you really believe you can solve this?"

"Damn right I can. And I'm going to. And then you get your life back."

Pain flared in her chest, and she deflated. "Right." Her voice was suddenly flat, and she hoped he didn't notice.

His phone buzzed as they made their way back to the SUV, but he didn't stop to read the message until they were safely back inside. Even when he did, his expression was as unreadable as ever.

"Agent Martin's been scouring security footage from all along the boardwalk and the shops on Atlantic Avenue. She found a man who fits your description of the man with the bike, but she lost him. Agents Rappaport and Watson found no sign of him, though."

She slumped in her seat and scowled at her knees.

"But Agent Martin found something else. Mal's friend is James Smith, who goes by Jimmy, a British national who has a record of arrests for cybercrime. Based on his criminal record, it seems he's a little short on common sense. And he's done time for something similar to the break-in that Mal was involved in."

"It's something, I guess."

They were silent for several minutes, until Agent Donnelly asked, "What's on your mind?"

"I was thinking. So far, everywhere they've gone has been places we visited as kids. I don't know why I remember that fish eraser, but I think..." All at once, it flooded back to her. *Wait.* "May I see it again, please?"

As she turned the evidence bag over, a memory reconstructed itself. Ella and her family had been standing by the edge of pale blue water, where dozens of tiny fish erasers bobbed up and down below them.

"Mommy, look!" The cries of a much younger Ella echoed across the years.

"Excuse me, folks," a man with a large net said as he scooped up the fish, grinning at the small group of mostly children. "These fish are a non-native species, so we've got to remove them."

Neither Ella nor Mal had understood what that meant, so their mother had explained it to them.

"Boston," Ella said as she returned to the present. "We saw a bunch of these fish in the water in Boston one time. It may have been in a pool."

Agent Donnelly was already connecting with Agent Martin at headquarters. "Ayanna, check for any signs that Mal and Jimmy are headed to Boston. Ella just remembered a connection to the fish eraser we found." After disconnecting, he said to Ella, "Now that we've established a pattern, you should make a list of the places where your family has visited, so Agent Martin can focus on those areas if this doesn't pan out." When she scoffed, he raised his eyebrows.

"No, I can try, it's just... It's a lot of places."

"Lucky kid," he said, giving her a half smile. "It's worth a shot."

"Okay." She took out her phone and started composing her list in a text box addressed to him. Just as Agent Donnelly started the engine, the back doors opened and Agents Watson, and Rappaport climbed in. Behind them, Agent Jacobs carefully joined them and closed the door.

"Good, you made it," said Agent Donnelly. "We need to get moving."

"Agent Jacobs, are you okay?" asked Ella.

"They just released me from the hospital. I'm going to be sore for a little while, but I've been through much worse," the agent said with a pained smile.

Ella pressed her lips together and nodded, her eyes stinging. The air was heavy with unspoken words. *Agent Harrison hadn't been so lucky.* Ella couldn't stand the sudden silence.

"So, where are we going?" she asked.

Agent Donnelly glanced at her, understanding written across his face. "Back to the airport. Apparently, our next stop is Boston."

Chapter 34

Ella

WEDNESDAY

FOR A FEW SECONDS, Ella gaped at him in surprise.

"You okay?" asked Agent Donnelly.

"I'm going with you?"

"Seems like we might need you. In case you recognize anything else. And like you said, I can keep an eye on you."

While relieved that she wasn't being sent back to DC, Ella couldn't decide whether she was elated or terrified that he was bringing her along when the danger was still so real. Maybe both.

Is it because he trusts me, or because he doesn't?

She forced out a barely audible, "Okay." Her stomach flipped as they watched each other, but she pushed the feeling down. Whatever stupid crush she was developing on him was all in her head. Besides, she was here because he felt like he had to babysit her while trying to do his job, nothing more.

Her face burned, and she concentrated on making the list he'd requested. For once, he turned on the radio, scanning the channels until he found a station playing music that wasn't quite old yet, but was also long past new.

"How's the list coming?" They were pulling onto the airport grounds and would be at the curb for departures momentarily.

"I have twenty-six so far."

"Wow," he said with genuine surprise. "I thought you meant eight or ten."

"My parents liked to travel."

Back onboard the jet, she took the same seat as always—the first one, by the window. Sam disappeared into a small, curtained area outside the cockpit just as the other three agents entered the cabin. Agents Watson and Rappaport nodded at her and sat down at the table across the aisle, while Agent Jacobs sat beside her.

"Hey. How are you holding up?"

"Tired," said Ella. "I don't understand how you do it. It's only been a few days, but it feels like years."

Agent Jacobs grimaced. "Coffee is a big part of it. And we have a lot of practice going without sleep. Also, it's your case. The emotional component takes more out of you than you realize. That's why agents don't work cases that deal with their own family members or friends. They're too close to the situation to be objective."

Ella's eyes darted around the cabin. Sam was nowhere to be seen, and the other two men were engrossed in something on a tablet. She leaned towards Agent Jacobs and dropped her voice to a whisper. "Can I ask you something?"

"Of course."

"Back in Michigan, Agent Donnelly said I reminded him of someone. It was in the middle of an argument, and we were both pretty worked up. Do you know who he was talking about?"

Agent Jacobs gave a pained smile. "I think so."

"You can't tell me anything, can you?"

"No, I'm sorry. I'm surprised he even said that much. He must like you."

While Ella wished the agent could have told her more, she respected her loyalty. "At first I was sure he hated me, but it's gotten better. Sometimes I feel like he and I understand each other. And then he closes up again."

Agent Jacobs sighed. "Yeah. Solving other people's problems helps keep his mind off his own. For a while, anyway. Our job gives us a lot to distract us from our own baggage. His baggage is still pretty heavy."

As if on cue, Agent Donnelly reappeared at the front of the cabin, motioning to Agent Jacobs to join the other agents at the table.

"Well, duty calls. Don't worry about him. I told you, he likes you better than any of the rest of us, trust me." She gave Ella an encouraging smile before standing.

Ella didn't try to listen to the agents' conversation this time. She was exhausted, and no one could say for sure when or if this odyssey would ever end.

Once it's all over... then what? I have nothing left. I can't win.

Closing her eyes, she tried to focus on something besides this wild goose chase Mal had them on or her empty future. But what? There was nothing in her life not in flux. Her muscles tightened in frustration. Mal had done terrible things to her, but she was her sister, and Ella couldn't stop believing that should mean something.

You must be stupid to still be hoping to reconcile with Mal after all these years, she chided herself. *She's a criminal, and you of all people know she's never going to change.* Ella was angrier with Mal than ever, but even angrier with herself for being unable to stop hoping.

Not wanting to open her eyes and find herself on the FBI jet, chasing her sister around the country while dodging assassins, she stubbornly kept them closed even when a rustling and the scent of a familiar cologne told her that Sam had joined her. Besides, letting herself enjoy his company would only make her miserable later.

Though neither of them spoke, her anxiety lessened little by little. She'd begun to consider opening her eyes after all when the same rustling was replaced by silence. Opening her eyes only a sliver, she watched Sam on his way to the far end of the cabin, sitting down on the other side by the window.

It doesn't matter. I'm fine. She stubbornly ignored the sting in her chest.

The flight to Boston was about four hours long, and Ella had nothing to do but pretend to sleep, stare into space or out the window, or think. She seemed to be on tour—with the worst band ever. She smiled as she imagined the FBI agents as a band.

Agent Jacobs would be the lead singer and Agent Watson would play drums. She was envisioning Sam playing guitar when the scent of food wafted through the air.

Her stomach churned, though she wasn't sure if the gurgle meant she was hungry or nauseated. It had to be dinner time already, and they'd had nothing to eat since before 8:00 am. She swore morning had been weeks ago. Her plan was to keep pretending she was asleep, but when Agent Jacobs called her name, her eyes popped open out of habit.

Dammit.

The agents waved her over to the table, where they'd set up the food.

"No, thanks." She shook her head, then turned back to watch the clouds. Tears pricked at her eyes for no specific reason, and she clenched her fists.

What I wouldn't give to be alone right now.

As if her inability to escape wasn't bad enough, Agent Donnelly took the seat beside her again.

"You're not even pretending to be asleep this time, so you may as well eat." Before she could deny that she was hungry or that she'd pretended to be asleep before, he'd lowered her tray table and set a paper plate and a large sandwich on a wheat roll. "You think I've been annoying up to now? I advise you to eat, or you'll find out how annoying I can be."

A spark of warmth flared inside her. Since she wasn't breaking free of Sam anytime soon, she surrendered and picked up the sandwich. She hated to admit it, but she liked that he cared enough to force her to eat—even if it was just part of his job, and even if he was a real pain in the ass about it.

"Where'd the food come from?"

"The others picked it up before they got on the plane."

"Smart. Why didn't I think of that? Oh right, because we're being chased by an assassin and running after my criminal sister."

"It's been a busy week," he said. His expression was serious, but there was laughter in his eyes, and she smiled despite herself, enjoying having him only inches away from her, his attention focused on her.

After a few bites, she put her sandwich down and sighed, having barely made a dent in it. Out of the corner of her eye, she saw him watching her, but continued to avoid eye contact.

She sighed. "Is it possible to be numb but to also feel everything way too much all at once? Because I think that's where I am."

"People who haven't been through it might not think so, but it's possible."

She turned to look at him in surprise, but he didn't elaborate. It was strange how sometimes he was infuriating, and other times just being around him temporarily lightened her emotional baggage. "So what do I do now?"

He shrugged. "Keep going."

"You know, I was really hoping for something a little more specific."

"Sorry. I got nothing." His face was serious, but his tone was light.

"What good are you, then?"

"Absolutely none."

Even when she burst out laughing, he held himself in check. "Thanks, I needed that," she said, and faced forward again. For a moment they sat in silence, and she sighed heavily.

"Alright, tell me what's wrong," he said.

"I'm just so tired of always being afraid."

He set down his phone. "Afraid of what?"

She sighed. "Change. Taking chances." *Letting people in,* she thought. "Just... everything." Her eyes darted to the table, to the far side of the room, and then back to him. "Mal never worried about failure, or what other people thought, or the consequences of her actions. Maybe because I'm the oldest, or because she never did, but I worried about them all, constantly. I'm not saying I want to be like her. She's a criminal. But I'm tired of being so... weak."

"Being sensitive doesn't make you weak." When she turned towards him again, their faces were even closer together than she'd expected, his eyes on hers. It was hard to focus on his words when he continued, their eyes locked on each other.

"Besides, I don't think you're giving yourself nearly enough credit. I seem to remember you breaking out of a safe house and leading the FBI on a multi-city chase, even though you were aware of a contract out on your life. That doesn't scream 'weak' to me." Before she could reply, he added, "Not that I'm saying you should do it again."

"Okay, so I'm not weak, just stupid." She winced as her voice cracked and she studied her hands, fidgeting in her lap. "Maybe I am like Mal," she said.

His hand landed lightly on hers and she went still, not daring to take her eyes off them. "No. Let's get one thing straight," he said. "You are determined. Brave. I'm not going to lie. Escaping wasn't the smartest choice. But you're not stupid, and you're not like Mal."

She blushed at the compliment, wanting to meet his eyes but too scared of what she would see. "Go big or go home, right?" Only after the words left her mouth did she hear it. *Home.*

Tears suddenly loomed behind her eyes. It was amazing the power one word had to undo any good thoughts she may have managed. "Figuratively speaking, of course."

His hand squeezed hers ever so slightly. "Just focus on your exciting and glamorous life on tour with the FBI. I promise, no singing is involved. It's not that kind of tour."

She was sure she hadn't spoken her thoughts about her FBI tour out loud earlier, but his comment made her wonder. To cover her surprise, she scoffed. "You're making jokes now? Who are you, anyway?" Resisting the competing urges to bolt and to squeeze his hands for dear life, she made eye contact with him again.

He let out a breath, pretending to take offense, but his expression didn't fool her. It wasn't a smile, but it was close. "Oh, you'll wish you never got me started making jokes. Just wait."

She stifled a yawn and leaned her cheek against the seat, looking up at him. "I swear today has been a week long."

"You have about two and a half hours until we land, if you want to take a nap for real."

"No, I..."

"I know. Nightmares. But I have good news. I've put in a stop order on those."

A tired smile lit her face. She got the feeling that if it had been within his power, he would've done just that.

"In that case, I guess I'll try to sleep. If nothing else, it's something to do." She expected him to get up and go back to the others, but as she closed her eyes and reclined her seat as far as it would go, she was aware of him still beside her. His hand still rested on hers, and she didn't dare move it.

Maybe I'll sleep a little. The noise in her head wasn't as loud when he was there.

And then suddenly she was waking up. Her eyelids fluttered for a few seconds before the cabin came into focus around her.

I slept better than I expected. And no nightmares for once. I guess it was—

She froze, horrified to find her head on Sam's shoulder. As nonchalantly as possible, she lifted it inch by inch, side to side to stretch the kinks out of her neck as if nothing out of the ordinary had happened.

Don't say anything. Please don't say anything.

He had reclined his seat at the same angle as hers, and he slouched so that his face was level with hers, only inches away. "Good nap?"

The proximity of his face to her ear made her shiver and blush harder. "Uh, yeah."

"You looked comfortable."

She turned to face him, so much closer than ever before, and she could tell from the glint in his eyes that he was enjoying her mortification.

"Sorry about that. I..."

"Don't be. It didn't bother me."

She watched him, mesmerized by his rare, unburdened smile.

Stop it. You're the only one having that fantasy.

"Go back to sleep. You still have an hour. At least in here, I know you're safe."

Her insides twisted. It was part of his job to keep her safe, yes. But damn, it sounded so sweet when he said it like that. Too bad that wasn't how he meant it.

When she closed her eyes, he let out what was clearly a fake cough. She considered pretending she didn't understand what he meant, but it would've been silly—even though she would've liked to hear him say it. So, without opening her eyes, she let her head drop until it rested against his shoulder—lightly at first, as she fought both sleep and the idea of letting herself lean on him, literally or otherwise. Despite the butterflies in her stomach, this was the most at peace she'd been in many years, and sleep came far more quickly than usual.

She woke up to his voice coming from just above her forehead. It was scarcely louder than a whisper, slightly gravely—

This is not helping me not get attached.

"Ella... time to wake up."

Opening her eyes and lifting her head, the first thing she noted was that they were no longer moving. The roar of the engines had stopped, and the airport was visible outside the window.

Where are we again? Oh, right. Boston.

"What time is it?"

"6:00 am," said Sam. "We parked on the tarmac for a few hours when we landed. If we'd taken the time to check into a hotel, it would've been almost time to get up by the time we went to sleep, so we just stayed here."

While the three agents huddled at the table, conferring with Agent Martin back in DC, Ella slipped into the bathroom to brush her teeth. She'd already told them what little she recalled about their family trip there many years before. Gone were her assumptions that she knew better than all their surveillance equipment and tracking technology, especially because she'd been only seven years old when they went to Boston, so her memory was hazy.

When she emerged from the bathroom, Ella listened to their discussion from a nearby chair. Agent Martin had identified the starting point for their search in Boston. Based on the few details Ella could provide, she'd located a cobblestone area by the water downtown, from which both the duck boats and bus tours departed. It would be full of tourists. There had been no sightings yet, but they didn't sound discouraged, so she tried not to be, either.

The agents stood and headed for the exit. "Come on," said Agent Donnelly, stopping in front of her. "Let's go find Mal."

Chapter 35
Ella

THURSDAY

E LLA GOT UP, SWINGING her backpack onto her shoulder. It was 6:30 am, and she dreaded the day ahead. She'd been running on adrenaline and high emotions for what felt like weeks, both chasing Mal and being chased herself. Another assassin's attempt was almost a given at this point. The only questions were when, where, and how.

A steady rain had drenched Boston for the past few hours. As Ella and the agents made their way down the slippery metal steps to the tarmac without the benefit of umbrellas, they blinked rain and sleepiness from their eyes. Sam walked in front of her, and she gripped the railing for dear life with both hands and repeated her new mantra to herself.

I am not afraid.

Now she just had to believe it.

She stumbled without warning, and for a fraction of a second she expected to land hard on the concrete below—with her luck, probably on her head. But her fall stopped abruptly when, without meaning to, she clamped onto Sam's shoulder so fast that she was holding onto him before she even knew what had happened. He tensed, turning to look at her, and she pushed herself back up. Her face was on fire.

"Sorry, I slipped. I'm fine," she insisted before he could say anything.

He gave her a look that someone else might have mistaken for annoyance, but she knew better. "You sure?" he asked.

"You think I did that on purpose?"

He held in a laugh. "No, I meant, are you sure you're fine?"

"Oh... I... I knew that. Yes, I'm sure I'm fine."

Stop talking. Now.

With her hands clamped tightly around the railing on either side as the heat in her cheeks subsided, she made it down the rest of the slippery stairs.

Inside yet another black SUV, Ella stared out the window at the gloom. Her hair was wet from the rain, and even with the heat on in the car, she shivered. Agent Donnelly was beside her in the driver's seat, and the other three agents were squeezed in the back, engrossed in their phones. No one spoke, as if they were all conserving their energy for the day ahead.

When the team reached their destination, they found several identical SUVs already on the scene. The rain had slowed to a heavy mist, making umbrellas pointless, but leaving enough water in the air that everything was wet. The agents got out of the car, but Ella stayed put, as instructed. From behind the tinted glass, she searched for her sister in every face in the crowd.

She jumped when Agent Donnelly opened her door, her head snapping to the side to look at him.

"We're ready for you," he said, then frowned. "You sure you're okay?"

"I'm okay enough."

He remained firmly planted in her way, leaning down and resting his forearm against the door frame. "Are you sure? Because we can sit this one out. Be honest. Are you up for this?"

The idea of letting someone else handle the chaos was tempting, but the only way to the other side of this was through the middle.

"I'll do as much as I can. Besides, they need you. And until this is all over, I don't have the luxury of living my own life. So let's get it over with." He still didn't look convinced, and desperation crept into her voice. "Please."

He stepped back so there was just enough room for her to climb down. With her backpack on her shoulder, she was swallowed by a sea of people she assumed to be agents, this time dressed casually but all with earpieces and somber expressions. Beyond them, tourists swarmed the sidewalk despite the rain.

She was immediately on edge. Although Sam was right there, another assassin—or the same one—could be among the hundreds of people in the throng. As Sam had told her so adamantly, it only took a second for the worst to happen. Her new appreciation for the danger she was in made her shiver, and before she could stop herself, she moved closer to him, hooking her arm around his at his elbow.

He glanced down at her in surprise, and she was already pulling away. "Sorry, I don't know why I..."

His free hand landed on her arm, and she stopped tugging it back. "It's a good idea in this chaos. I don't want to lose you." Something flared in his eyes and then was gone. The seriousness in his voice gave way to self-deprecating humor when he added, "And you're a little too fond of walking away from me."

She smiled. "Not always. Sometimes I'm running away."

He looked like he had more to say, but he only scanned their surroundings. The larger group of agents, including Agents Jacobs and Watson, were forming teams to canvas merchants and tourists nearby.

"Is this the place?" he asked.

"I think so. At least... somewhere around here."

"Let's walk a little. It might help."

Sam ushered Ella through the FBI perimeter, still arm in arm as they dodged tourists across the concrete plaza. He'd said anything she could come up with could be a clue, but so far not even the smallest detail was familiar.

Closing her eyes and letting him steer her, she focused on the day long ago when she'd been there with her family. A sigh escaped her and she opened her eyes, blinking against the light. "I'm sorry. All I remember is being in a bad mood and Mal making it worse. This almost looks right, but just not exactly how I remember it."

"When you went on the bus tour afterwards, do you remember where you went?"

"No, only that my mom was disappointed because she wanted to get off at all the stops, but it was raining by then, and she knew better than to drag little kids to too many historical sites in the rain. I was being enough of a pain. And Mal was being... well, Mal."

"Why don't we take the bus tour? It might jog your memory."

"That was thirty years ago. The tour won't be the same."

"Not exactly. But I don't think historical Boston landmarks have changed that much in the last thirty years."

She eyed him skeptically. "You really think it'll help?"

"Well, it can't hurt. And didn't anyone tell you? I'm known for my good instincts. And my jokes." He said it in such a deadpan that if she didn't know him, she would've thought he was serious.

"But everyone else is working. It doesn't seem fair."

He pulled them to a stop and turned so she was in front of him, looking at her seriously. "Trying to recover your memories counts as working. I'd say you're working the hardest."

She smiled up at him slowly, and it took an extra second for them to break eye contact. After an awkward pause, they continued across the plaza to get tickets for the bus tour.

They were just past the ticket booth when Ella felt a hand on her arm, tugging her back. She inhaled sharply, ready to scream, when she saw it was Sam. He had stopped to put away his wallet, and Ella had unknowingly gotten ahead of him.

She opened her mouth to apologize for walking away, but he spoke first, his face creased with emotion.

"I know you think I'm being overly dramatic, and I know I said it before, but I can't stress this enough. All it takes is one thing I miss..." He choked on the rest of his words, and she nodded quickly, peering down at his hand still resting on her arm. He squeezed it gently before letting go.

He's obviously been through something, and I'm making him relive it.

"I'm sorry. It wasn't on purpose. I didn't know you'd stopped," she said. His pained expression made her feel even worse, and without thinking, she stepped closer to him. "I didn't mean to scare you."

He shook his head, the light in his eyes returning. "I know." With a weak smile, he added, "Ready for the tour?"

Chapter 36
Mal

THURSDAY

MAL STOOD OUTSIDE THE souvenir shop, staring into the windows at the overstuffed shelves. Her hands clenched and unclenched in her pockets. Seconds after the clock on her phone said 9:00, a shadow appeared behind the glass door and fingers clasped the side of the CLOSED sign, flipping it to OPEN. Mal approached the door, turning the handle almost as soon as she heard the *pop* of the door unlocking.

The young brunette with heavy black eyeliner looked up, startled at Mal's sudden appearance. "Oh, good morning. You're off to an early start today."

"I am," Mal said pleasantly. "I'm looking for your postcards."

"Straight back on the left, on the rack by the check out counter," the woman said.

Mal gave the woman her best friendly smile and strode to the rack of postcards. She knew what picture she needed to ensure that Ella understood her clue, and she held her breath as she examined every image on the rack until she found it. The last copy of the perfect one.

"What brings you to Boston?" The woman asked as Mal approached the counter with the postcard.

Mal sighed dramatically, glancing around and leaning forward. She lowered her voice. "Actually, I'm hiding out from my ex. He's been stalking me. I don't want to think about what he'll do if he finds me."

The woman reacted exactly as Mal had hoped, gasping and looking at her in horror. "Seriously? Have you called the police?"

"I have. But they can't be with me all the time. I decided it was better to leave my hometown, so I ended up here."

"Can I do anything to help you?" the woman asked, glancing past Mal as if the man in question might walk through the door at any moment.

"If anyone asks, just don't tell them I was here," Mal said, her eyes pleading.

"No, of course not." The woman hesitated, then added, "Do you have someone who could help you hide out for a while?"

Something sparked in Mal's brain. *Someone who can get an assassin off my tail. Someone like... the feds who are with Ella. I wanted to see Ella anyway... And Ella and I always looked alike enough to confuse people...*

The plan was beautiful in its simplicity. Not only would it save her the headache of dodging an assassin, it would let her complete her plans for Ella's Breadcrumb Game style scavenger hunt.

The woman behind the counter finished ringing up the postcard, and Mal paid with cash. "If you need anything, just call. Our number is on the bag." She handed Mal a small paper bag containing her purchase. "My name is Marilyn."

"Thank you so much, Marilyn. I should go."

"Be safe."

Mal gave her one more smile before turning to leave, shoving her receipt in her pocket and pausing in the doorway to look up and down the street. Satisfied that the coast was clear, she stepped outside. There was still plenty of game left to play, and with any luck, she'd stay two steps ahead of Ella, the feds, and whoever might want her dead.

Chapter 37
Ella

THURSDAY

E LLA AND SAM BOARDED a bus at the end of the next block, Ella by the window and Sam beside her on the long bench. As the bus lurched around the first corner, she slid along the smooth bench into him. One of his hands grasped the bench in front of them to stop them both from sliding further, and the other went around her.

"Sorry." It was even more embarrassing than the first time she'd woken up with her head on his shoulder. He released her as she sat back up, restoring the small space between them as her cheeks flushed the color of tomatoes. The worst part was, she wasn't actually sorry.

"Nothing to be sorry for." He sounded amused, but she kept her gaze focused on the world outside.

The misty rain had finally stopped, and she stared out at the gloomy day, searching her mind for a memory. A stiff wind gusted through the open window, whipping her hair into both her face and Sam's at the same time. She was laughing as she reached back to wrestle it into an elastic, but his hands were already in her hair, scratching gently at her scalp.

His grip on her hair kept her from turning to face him, which was just as well. Heat surged through her as he gently gathered the flying strands into a ponytail. Yes, it had been a method of self-preservation for him, she knew, but for the space of a heartbeat, the flip-flopping feeling in her stomach took her breath away.

Stop it. It's not like that.

"Do you have an elastic?" he asked in her ear over the wind.

She reached over her shoulder to hand him the elastic she'd had on her wrist, then tried in vain not to enjoy it as he finger-combed her hair one more time before securing it.

"Thanks," she said, peering at him sheepishly. "You're good at that."

"No problem. It's not the first time long hair has attacked me." His eyes sparkled with laughter.

After that, they were quiet, watching the scenery go by. The bus was only a third full, and the young tour guide chatted with the riders near the front.

"We'll arrive at our first stop in just a moment," said the tour guide.

Sam leaned closer to her so she could hear him over the noise of the microphone and the wind. "If you recognize something, let me know and we'll get out and have a look."

She nodded but didn't turn in his direction, intensely conscious that his face was still mere inches from hers.

More than once, the driver took a corner sharply or they hit an unexpected bump, sending one of them sliding into the other. The first few times she was flustered, but eventually she gave up on apologizing.

They were almost at stop number six for Cambridge, MIT and Harvard, when she gave up on restoring the space between them. He had draped his arm along the top of the bench behind her, and she tried not to overthink it as she let her shoulder rest lightly against him.

The sense of déjà vu hit her out of nowhere as the bus rolled to a stop, and her eyes widened.

"Here?" Sam asked, speaking into her ear.

"Yeah."

"Let's go." They joined the line of tourists and students exiting through the back doors. On the sidewalk, Ella and Sam waited as the crowd around them dispersed.

"What do you remember?" His voice was gentle.

She was stuck halfway between desperation to remember more and fear that she would do just that. "Wherever we went from here looked like the pictures I've seen of Harvard online."

"That's this way." He pointed at a sign and took her arm, but she didn't move.

"What's wrong?" Before she could answer, he was standing only inches in front of her.

"Do you feel like we're being watched?"

His eyes darted around quickly and then back to her. "No. Do you?"

"Yeah. But maybe it's more déjà vu. I don't know what it is, but it's creepy."

He studied their surroundings critically. "I don't see anything out of the ordinary, but stay close."

She turned to stand beside him and threaded her arm through his, glancing up when he patted her arm once with his free hand before dropping it back to his side. It was hard to decide what she was most afraid of: the next attempt on her life, discovering another of Mal's clues, or finding Mal herself. The growing rapport with Sam was pretty terrifying, too.

"What's the worst thing you know of that Mal ever did?" he asked.

"The worst thing she did... that's a hard one. Legally, I'm not sure. I think the worst thing she did to me was when she held my head under the water when we were swimming at Walloon Lake and I thought I was going to drown. The worst thing she did to someone else..." Her stomach knotted. "When we were in middle school, there was a shy girl who wore these funny pants with ducks on them. She wore them constantly. Her name was Misty. She and Mal were in sixth grade, and I was in seventh. Mal teased that poor girl mercilessly. The guidance counselor got involved, but Mal didn't stop. She just got sneakier about it. It got so bad, Misty... tried to kill herself. Slit her wrists."

Ella's gaze wandered down to the sidewalk, as she tried not to remember the day she'd overheard her parents' hushed discussion from the next room. Even now, thinking about it gave her a nauseous, guilty feeling. It had taken years for her to let go of the certainty that she should have somehow been able to make Mal stop.

"It took hours of begging to get my mom to take me to the hospital to see Misty. When we got there, Misty's mother freaked out, even though Mal wasn't with us. I never got the chance to talk to Misty. Her mom withdrew her from our school immediately afterwards. The guidance counselor told me to write her a letter, and that she'd pass it along. No matter how many times I tried, all I could come up with was, *I'm sorry.*"

Only then did she glance up at Sam, who shook his head slightly.

"I'm sorry I didn't tell you about that before. I just hate to remember it."

"You're very careful with your memories."

"I have to be. They're a minefield... and they're all I have left of them." Her eyes burned, and she looked at the sky to stop them from tearing up. She laughed nervously, not daring to look at him. "I know, I know... I probably need therapy. Isn't that the answer to everything these days?"

Ella had just regained control of her emotions when she looked around and stopped short, the arm threaded through his tightening involuntarily. Beside them, the bars of an imposing iron gate were open, and through them was a grassy area surrounded by a tall redbrick wall.

"It was here..." Without warning, the scene from her childhood played out like a grainy film in her mind.

"We stood there, in front of the gate. My mom wanted to take a picture, but Mal wouldn't smile. I remember wondering why she had to spoil everything. It would've been so much easier to just get it over with."

"Did you go through the gate?"

The memory faded, and she was embarrassed to be leaning against him. She was about to step back when his arm squeezed hers slightly, and the corners of her mouth tipped up.

"I think so."

"Okay. Well, let's look by the gate first, then we'll check inside the fence."

Her déjà vu was stronger than ever as they approached the brick wall, but there was no sign of anything unusual. She bit back her disappointment when a careful inspection of the wall near the gate and the surrounding area came up empty.

Sam had slipped back into work mode, though he still held tight to her arm. "Let's walk a little in each direction. Maybe we'll find something."

They found nothing in the thirty feet to the left of the gate, and they'd gone almost as far to the right of it. Ella was ready to give up and move inside the yard, but Sam tugged on her arm. "There's something here."

She squatted beside him and saw that he was right. He'd found something.

"See? Someone scratched an arrow." The arrow in the dirt pointed at the wall. "It could be nothing. A bored student. A mark that means something else."

Her right hand landed on his shoulder to help her keep her balance. "Or it could be something."

"But what if...?" Sam mumbled to himself and took a picture of the arrow with his phone. They stood, and he took several more shots of the arrow from further back. After snapping one showing the wall all the way from the gate, he motioned to her.

Ella watched him with interest. "Find something?"

"Maybe. I have a hunch. Come on." He tilted his head towards the gate.

Sam counted his steps under his breath as they went back the way they'd come, and they ducked through the gate and turned right. Searching along the wall, he mumble-counted his steps again, slowing when they neared the right distance. Laser focused on the patchy grass by the wall, Sam crouched and examined the dirt.

"There we go," he said under his breath, pulling gloves and an evidence bag out of his jacket pocket.

He pulled a two-inch long piece of paper tightly rolled around a twig out of the soft mud. Ella watched him, frozen in place, as he stood up.

"Breathe," he said, and she met his eyes to find them with genuine concern. "Whatever it is, we'll handle it."

She nodded, and their attention returned to the tiny scroll he held between his fingers. Smudges of dirt marred the half that had been in the ground, but as he gently unrolled it, the words were still legible, and the handwriting was familiar. She moved around to his side to read it.

E— You didn't think it would be that easy, did you? This game is too much fun to let you catch me so soon. —M

A game? This is a game to her? Dismay pummeled her, though she shouldn't have been surprised. It was so very Mal. Apparently, she hadn't changed much, if at all.

Ella slumped against the brick wall. Nothing in the note described where she was going next, and Mal hadn't left anything else with it. It was a dead end.

We're never going to find her. Or if we do, it'll be too late.

Sam pushed the paper into the evidence bag and tucked it safely into his pocket. After removing his gloves, he slid a hand lightly between her back and the wall to steer her to a bench a few feet away. They sat side by side, Ella staring at her shoes and Sam staring at her.

"We know she was here, and that it was today. We're close, Ella."

She raised her head and looked into his eyes, giving him a limp nod before looking away again. "But that's all we know. It's not enough." The exasperation in her voice had melted into bitterness. "She's in control, just like always."

"She's going to make a mistake, and that's when we'll catch up to her."

"I hope I'm still alive then."

She hadn't meant it as an attack, only a statement of her own fear, but Sam looked like she'd slapped him. With a sigh, she turned and rested her forehead on his shoulder, too tired to be self-conscious. "I'm sorry."

His hand landed lightly on her back. "Let's get back to the bus. We're on the right track. There may be another stop that jogs your memory." When she looked skeptical, he added, "It's not time to give up."

"Will you tell me when it is time to give up?"

"I never give up."

That made them opposites, because time and experience had taught her that hope was a waste of time. Even worse, it kept you from letting go of things or people—or memories—you were better off without. No matter how hard she tried, she couldn't make herself give up hope completely, even after years of disappointment. She saw it as her biggest flaw. He, on the other hand, was proud of it.

When her eyes strayed back to his, she found him watching her as if waiting for something. The breeze blew several tendrils of her long, dark hair across her face, and his hand appeared in her peripheral vision. Her eyes left his face to follow that hand, and her stomach somersaulted as he reached up in slow motion to push the wayward strands behind her ear. The tiny patch of skin he touched sparked, and her eyes locked on his as his hand withdrew just as slowly as it had approached. Judging from his expression, he was as surprised as Ella herself.

The sole explanation her mind could accept for whatever was happening between the two of them was that she was reading too much into it. Her hair had been in her face and he moved it. Nothing more.

He's just doing his job. Besides, he'll only be around long enough to solve this case, anyway.

She focused on the ground, and a heavy silence fell between them. The longer it dragged on, the louder her thoughts became. When she forced herself to look up at him, he met her gaze with an uncertain expression and an awkward smile. "You can do this, Ella."

Even though she didn't believe it, she nodded. Suddenly restless, she pushed herself to her feet, and he was immediately at her side, a hand resting gently on her arm to keep her in place.

"Hang on a second."

He scanned the surrounding area. "Looks like we're clear. Come on. Let's keep going."

Seated among chattering tourists on a more crowded bus this time, Ella stared out the window, pretending to ignore Sam's arm stretched out behind her. All she could come up with as the bus wound through its route was that Mal remembered something she didn't. If that was true, they might never solve the case.

They were nearing stop number fourteen, Beacon Hill and Boston Common, when she sat up straight.

"This one?"

"Yeah."

Ella allowed herself to enjoy one more second sitting lightly against Sam, taking a deep breath to prepare herself for the next round of personalized torture. She followed him once more off the bus and into her memories.

Chapter 38
Ella

THURSDAY

They stood on another busy sidewalk. Jostled by impatient passersby, Ella instinctively stepped closer to Sam. He put a hand on her shoulder and tugged her to the strip of grass between the sidewalk and the curb, out of the way of traffic, then let his arm fall back to his side.

A fuzzy memory was coming back to her. "I remember a lot of grass. A lake. And... swans?"

"That's an easy one. Boston Public Garden. Come on." He nudged her arm with his elbow to get her attention, then hooked his arm through hers. She smiled at him as they started off again.

A sign on a wrought-iron gate announced their arrival at one of many entrances to the famous park. Inside the gate, he tugged her to the side of the path and waited so she could lead them, but she looked around and shook her head helplessly.

Misunderstanding the dismay on her face, Sam asked, "Do you remember something?"

"No! That's exactly the problem. This place is massive. I could walk for days and not find anything. It's another dead end."

He moved in front of her so that he was blocking her view of the large open space, remaining calm and meeting her eyes. "I disagree. We're here because your instincts told you it was the right place. You've been right every time so far. I trust you. Trust yourself."

She looked away. "You're the one who's gotten us this far."

"We'll argue about that later. Let's focus on what you remembered: 'a lot of grass.' Well, we found that. You also said, 'a lake.' That's on our map." Pulling out the tour bus company's map, he shifted so he was beside her, then found their location. "Here we are. And 'Swan Boats' is a huge landmark. I'll bet that's it. If you don't have another specific memory, we'll head for that."

Her eyes were on the grass at their feet and her voice was flat. "Yeah, I guess so."

"Come on." The gentleness in his tone made her look up. Having Sam around to bolster her strength was bittersweet, because she hated to think about how empty her life would be once the case was closed.

They kept up a brisk pace, and finally the Swan Boats loomed ahead. The area was surprisingly busy for the middle of a weekday, and Ella studied each person. There were families with not-yet-school-aged children in tow, mothers pushing infants in strollers, men and women in pairs or alone, dressed in workout gear and weaving through people, or carrying food or coffee and looking for a place to sit.

So many people. They had friends and families and things to do. They had homes and routines—they had lives. It made her feel even emptier than she already had, because she had none of those things. Maybe she never would.

They'd almost reached the Swan Boats when a commotion broke out somewhere over her right shoulder. There was a loud pop, and she gasped as she was slammed to the ground.

Flat on her back, Ella struggled to breathe as a heavy weight pinned her firmly in place. With her eyes squeezed shut, she flailed her arms and legs, attempting to push away her attacker, but to no avail.

She didn't have to see whoever it was to know she was about to die.

A sob choked out what little air she had left in her lungs. That was when a voice reached her ears. "Ella! Hey, it's me."

Sam.

She stopped fighting, her tensed muscles turning to jelly with relief.

"Stay still so I can figure out what's going on." His chin hovered just inches above her face as he surveyed their surroundings, and Ella used the opportunity to study him up close. Her dislike of him had colored her initial impression. While he might not have been heart-throb material, he was handsome in a less flashy way—especially when he wasn't scowling at her.

He pushed himself to his hands and knees above her, checking their surroundings. Though she was still boxed in by his forearms, she tried to sit up along with him, stopping abruptly when he leaned back down, bringing their faces within less than an inch of each other. "Not yet," he said. Without moving back, he made one more sweep of the area, then tilted his head down to look at her, the tip of his nose brushing hers.

"Sorry," he mumbled, as her head tilted back in surprise, her face suddenly pink. Awkward as it was, she immediately wished she hadn't moved away. Seconds ticked by and he didn't push himself back up or break eye contact.

"Let me make sure it's safe," he said, just loud enough for her to hear.

"What happened?"

"I'm not sure. Please stay down until I'm sure it's clear. Okay?"

Only when she nodded did he push himself up to look around again. Glancing to one side, she saw nothing amiss—except strangers gawking at them. That made sense, considering that he was lying on top of her in a public park.

"We're clear," he said. He met her eyes again just before closing his and leaning his forehead down to rest against hers, deflating with what looked like relief.

Warmth flowed outward from his forehead into hers, and she closed her eyes as well, calmed by whatever was happening between them.

From across the grass, the same popping sound she'd heard just before Sam had tackled her came again, and their heads snapped apart, eyes wide in the direction of the noise. A family with two small children were gathered around a plastic toy that made the sound two more times as they whacked it with a mallet.

"I thought the pop was a gunshot," Sam said, pushing up to kneel beside her. "I overreacted." She pushed herself up on her elbows, then sat up the rest of the way and smoothed her hair, brushing leaves off her shirt.

The few people who'd been watching them with raised eyebrows had moved on. Snippets of conversations floated in the air and police sirens wailed in the distance. Above them, birds called to each other. The day had returned to normal.

Ella had still been sore from the injuries of the past few days, so being knocked to the ground hadn't helped—there was no part of her that didn't ache.

"I'm sorry I body slammed you," he said.

"Don't apologize. I'd say it's better safe than sorry."

"Are you hurt?"

"My back will be sore for a while. At least we weren't standing on concrete." Despite her joke, her smile faltered.

"I know what you're thinking. Don't. We're going to get to the bottom of this."

"You can read my mind now?" She raised her eyebrows.

"You're afraid I can't protect you. I would be, too. Am I wrong?"

She stared hard at her shoes. "It's not that. I'm safer with you than with anyone. I just..." She shook her head. "My head is a mess."

"Let's find the Swan Boats. We still need that clue."

She scoffed, shaking her head. "Do you really think there's a clue to find?"

"Yes, I do, and I'm almost never wrong. Come on." He stood and held out his hands to help her to her up. Her back screamed in protest, as did her mind, but she ignored both and let him pull her to her feet.

And after the case is over?

Even if he could save her life, he couldn't save her *from* her life. In the long run, letting herself enjoy his help would backfire, but in that moment she just could not make herself care about what came later.

They walked across the grass again, but Ella was much jumpier this time. When a child yelped with delight, she froze.

"Easy." Sam's voice was near her ear, and it brought her back to reality. "Just a happy kid."

Once again recovering from the jolt of adrenaline, she squeezed her hands into fists at her sides.

Get a hold of yourself.

Sam put his arm through hers. "Let's just be two people out for a walk, okay?" he said, leaning close.

It sounded so good, even though it was a lie.

They'd nearly reached the Swan Boats when her steps slowed. She felt him watching her even as she kept her attention straight ahead.

Ten people who were almost certainly tourists stood in line for Swan Boat tickets. One boat waited at the dock, while several others slid through the water at various points along the circuit around the small lake. After examining one boat as it floated by, they agreed that Mal wouldn't have been able to leave clues on them—the rows of bench seating meant anything left behind was immediately visible and would have been discarded as either trash or as a potential threat.

Near the boarding area was a much more likely bet. They examined the baseboards of the ticket booth, but found nothing out of place. A security guard approached them to ask what they were doing, and Sam flashed his badge, answered a few questions, then got back to work. Ella's spirits dropped steadily, but Sam simply widened his search radius to include the nearby trees.

That was when she spotted it: a speck of gold in the otherwise green and brown underbrush. Moving toward the spot without thinking, she jumped when he gripped her arm—gently this time—to stop her.

"Wait—don't touch it." His tone softened as he added, "Please."

Donning a new pair of gloves, Sam reached carefully between the leaves, and seconds later, he pulled out a postcard. He stood slowly, and Ella stared at it, remembering to keep her hands to herself.

In the message section, it said simply, "Wish you were here!" When he turned it over, Ella gasped.

"I've been there!"

They stared down at a picture of a stately brick building with columns across the front and on top, a golden dome gleaming in the sunshine. The text at the bottom read, "Masachusetts State house." Sam carefully slipped it into an evidence bag.

"So do you think that's the clue? Do we go there now?"

He studied her for several beats before responding. "Let's make sure there's nothing else here first, in case that wasn't the real clue."

Forty minutes later, having found only a few discarded food wrappers and two plastic bottles, Sam was finally satisfied that there was nothing else with any real chance of being a clue.

"Let me guess, before we go to the State House, we go back to the bus?"

"That's right. There are a few more stops to go. You never know..."

Children's happy squeals echoed in the air, and a memory tugged at her. They hadn't gotten far when her feet came to a halt. She'd once again stumbled into the middle of a hazy memory.

As it cleared, the first thing she saw was Sam, concern written across his face. "Another one?"

She breathed through the sting in her chest. "Nothing relevant. I was standing in the Swan Boat line with my family. Mal was being... Mal. She was so mean. That was the day she punched me in the face because she thought I was laughing at her. We were six and seven." She pushed her hair behind her ear. "My parents were so frustrated. I was so frustrated. Still, if I could go back there, I'd do it in a heartbeat. Stupid, right?"

He opened his mouth to answer, but she continued before he could say anything.

"I know I've made Mal out to be horrible, and I hate to sound like I'm blaming everything on her. I was no angel or anything, but..." She bit her lip.

"It wasn't just one mean thing that she did. No matter how much you've airbrushed your memories over time, she was unnecessarily mean," he assured her.

Her head bobbed in agreement. "Yes, but..." She focused on counting the blades of grass at her feet. "But what if she was the way she was because of me?"

"Impossible. Siblings fight. Some more than others, sure." He grew more insistent with each word. "But you couldn't have made her do those things if you'd tried, which you wouldn't have. You may not have been perfect, but you can't carry that guilt yourself. There were too many other factors. Okay?"

Logically, it made sense, but that didn't mean she believed it. She looked up at him, wishing it was that simple.

"Besides, look how well you turned out."

A noise that was half laugh and half sob burst out of her. "You're kidding, right? Look at me. I'm a mess." She resisted the urge to lean forward and rest her head on his shoulder.

"A mess? No. You're..."

He stopped and shook his head.

Was he blushing?

He exhaled a chuckle and started again. "We're all a mess, in our own way. You're having a rough time, but you're going to be fine." The fondness in his voice surprised her, and the corners of her eyes watered even as she smiled up at him, her cheeks heating up in embarrassment. How anyone could see her as anything other than a disaster was a mystery to her. It was only now that she had Sam by her side that she realized how long she'd been holding herself together by a thread.

When he spoke again, his voice was almost nostalgic. "Trust me, I know what it's like to wish you could go back in time. But you've read the Harry Potter books, right?"

She nodded.

"It's like that mirror that shows you what you want to see. If you spend too much time reliving the past, you can't live in the present."

"No offense, but the present sucks right now." She immediately felt guilty. *Not everything sucks right now...*

A hint of a sad smile crossed his face. "I know. It's going to get better, I promise."

The future meant no home and no family, and no Sam, either—her life was bad now, but it was going to get worse, not better. And yet, closing her eyes, the face she saw was his.

They rode past the last few bus stops, without triggering any more of Ella's memories, and they disembarked where they'd boarded. Agents Jacobs and

Watson were working with the local agents for the time being, so Ella and Sam headed to the Masachusetts State House.

It can't be a coincidence.

Ella held onto that thought all the way back to their borrowed SUV, when doubt began to creep into her mind. She rested her temple against the window and closed her eyes, focusing only on the cadence of Sam's voice as he talked to Agent Martin over his comm. The cool surface of the glass, the gentle rocking of the car, Sam's voice, and her exhaustion quickly overcame what had become the pounding headache that had been building slowly for hours.

She awoke to the sound of Sam's voice. "Ella, wake up. We have a lead."

Chapter 39
Ella
THURSDAY

E LLA'S EYES FLEW OPEN.

"Look who's awake," said Sam.

She narrowed her eyes at him, in no mood to joke around. "What's happening?"

"Agent Martin got a hit. They had a BOLO out—be on the lookout—for Mal. There's security footage of her leaving a building not too far away. The footage is a few hours old, but we have agents converging there, and others working outwards from that point in a grid."

She paused to process this information. "Wait, something isn't right. She has almost completely avoided surveillance cameras until now. Why would she walk outside right into the path of one? And what happened to the guy she was with?"

"Maybe she wanted us to see her and only her. That's my theory. She could have left something for us to find."

"So, are we going there?"

"No. Not yet."

"But there's a lead!"

"We already had a lead, remember? We'll go to the Massachusetts State House first, and then we'll see if anything comes from the new one."

She scowled at him.

"We don't know what we'd be walking into at the new scene. It could be anything." He shook his head. "I'm not willingly putting you in a dangerous situation, even if you're mad at me for it. Let the other agents figure out what we're dealing with. If it's safe, then we'll go, too."

"Fine," she said with a heavy sigh. The silence between them stretched on, heavy and thick.

His voice was much quieter than usual when he spoke next. "If I could be sure it was safe, I'd take you there now."

Just like that, her anger deflated in one shaky breath.

The silence that followed was less charged. Ella focused on not thinking of anything—not the assassin or her sister or the man sitting beside her.

They'd almost reached the State House when Sam's phone buzzed, and she looked up to find him holding it out for her to see. She took the phone from him as they entered a wide intersection, waiting to make a left turn. At the same instant, everything went into slow motion as, in her peripheral vision, a dark shape barreled toward them. One second she was facing forward, the next something slammed into them and she was spinning, flailing wildly for something stable to grab onto. Their SUV spun into other cars, propelled into oncoming traffic in the middle of the intersection before lurching to a stop.

Ella's seatbelt whipped her back against the headrest as she felt the airbag in front of her knock the air from her lungs. Finally still, she opened her eyes, disoriented, the pressure inside her head making her wince.

The sight of Sam unconscious against the airbag nearly knocked the air out of her lungs all over again. She knew she had to get her brain to stop spinning and figure out what to do, but in that moment, she was at a loss.

"Sam, wake up." Still dizzy, she reached over and poked him roughly in the shoulder. He did not respond. "Dammit, Sam, this is not the time to be stubborn!" In her head, she was on the verge of hysterical, but she couldn't be sure she'd even said the words aloud.

I have to get help.

She turned to the door, trying to focus enough to make everything stop spinning so she could find the door handle. At first, the door stuck, bent out of alignment in the crash. After unbuckling her seatbelt, she leaned back to use her foot to kick at it while she pulled the lever, and finally wrenched it free.

Detangling herself from her deflated airbag, she slowly climbed down from her seat, losing her balance and landing hard on the concrete below. Pain zigzagged through her. As if all that wasn't bad enough, she peered up to find herself at the center of traffic snarled in all directions.

"Hey, are you all right? Don't move." A fuzzy shape with a calm voice loomed in front of her, and she immediately tensed.

Her first instinct was to run, but she wouldn't have gotten anywhere in her current condition. "I don't know. I think so..."

"If I didn't know better, I'd say the car that hit you actually sped up." The stranger was still indistinct, a blurry mass of dark curly hair. When she came closer, Ella could see that her clothing was all the same shade of light blue. The stranger peered past Ella into the car. "Is it just the two of you in here?"

Ella tensed, wondering if this woman was another assassin.

Undeterred by Ella's silence, the stranger continued. "I've seen at least five people call 911, so I'm sure an ambulance will be here momentarily. My name is Wendy. I'm a med student. Does it hurt anywhere specific?"

"No, not really. I'm just a little dizzy."

"That's probably the adrenaline. Stay where you are. The EMTs will need to make sure you're not injured. I'm sure they'll be here any minute."

"Could you please make sure Agent Donnelly's okay? He was driving." Her chest squeezed at the thought of him not being okay.

"Of course." Wendy climbed up through the open door into Ella's seat and reached over, blocking Ella's view of what she was doing.

Meanwhile, panic rose inside Ella. Sam would've lost his mind if he'd known she was sitting out here, completely exposed on the pavement by herself. If anyone had wanted to take a shot at her, this would've been the perfect time. She scooted back until she was sitting against the step below her seat, hugging her knees.

Not nearly soon enough, Wendy climbed back down. "He's unconscious, but his pulse is strong." Sirens wailed in the distance.

"Thank goodness." Ella could see her more clearly now.

The other woman surveyed the wreckage again dubiously. "You two were lucky. Your car's probably totaled. You could've been killed."

"Yeah."

I think that was the idea.

When the EMTs arrived, Wendy reported her observations about Ella and Sam before fading back into the crowd. The medics got Sam out of the car and onto a stretcher. Local FBI agents showed up as well, pulled from the scene where Mal's note had been discovered. Ella answered their initial questions, and then the EMTs were ready to take them both to yet another hospital. Agents Jacobs and Watson were on their way, so a tall, light-haired agent rode with Sam and Ella. He nodded at her as he took the seat in the corner of the cramped ambulance.

From her seat, Ella kept a death grip on the side rail of the stretcher as she stared at Sam, silently pleading for him to open his eyes. She winced at every bump in the road, but he didn't stir. The middle-aged EMT across from her had assured her that his vital signs were good, but the longer he remained unconscious, the more agitated she became.

You have to be okay, Sam. You can't leave me, too. Not yet. She sniffled, swiping her fingers under her eyes and willing herself not to cry.

After one particularly large bump, Sam groaned and opened his eyes. "What the hell?" His voice was raspy, but all at once he was conscious, and she was light-headed with relief.

"Agent Donnelly, it's okay. We were in an accident. A car slammed into us when we were turning left."

"Seriously, Ella? Aren't we on a first-name basis yet?" His eyes were only half open and he spoke with difficulty, but there was humor in his voice. She bit her lip, holding back a flood of emotion.

Yes, he's okay.

Their eyes locked on each other as a pained smile spread across his face.

His left hand inched haltingly across the thin blanket towards her, coming to rest lightly on her white knuckles, where she gripped the rail. Her eyes darted to his hand and then back to his face, and her fingers loosened. As if they had a mind of their own, her fingers laced themselves with his. The simple gesture filled her with an equal mix of relief and terror.

Back away, her mind screamed.

Even knowing for certain she would lose him sooner than later, she could not have made herself let go of his hand if her life had depended on it.

Leaning forward, she sandwiched his hand between both of hers, balancing her elbows against the edge of the stretcher, and held their hands together against her forehead. Squeezing her eyes shut, she blocked out everything else and held on for dear life all the way to the hospital.

After another long wait in the ER lobby, it was almost 3:00 pm before they had separate curtained-off beds in which to wait to see a doctor. The tall, silent agent whose name she still didn't know shadowed her.

Ella was normally a patient person, but from the moment she sat down on her assigned bed, she felt like crawling out of her skin. Thanks to the curtains, she couldn't look out for an attacker, and while he was surely qualified, she did not trust the agent who was not Sam to protect her.

Her feet tapped against the bed, overflowing with nervous energy. She jumped when her phone vibrated on the blanket with a message notification from Sam.

You okay over there?

Yeah, but I've somehow ended up with the wrong FBI agent. Where can I trade this one in?

I will put in the request for you. It may take a little while, though.

Stupid bureaucracy.

Familiar voices rang back through the ER.

Another bubble popped up on her screen. *Here comes the cavalry.*

The voices grew louder, until the curtain beside her bed moved to one side and a harried looking nurse appeared, followed by Agents Jacobs, Rappaport, and Watson. They nodded at the man behind her. "Hey Ella," said Agent Jacobs. "Agent Donnelly made me promise to ask you if you were okay as soon as I got here. I think he has separation anxiety." Her tone made it clear that she found her team leader's behavior amusing.

Ella pressed her lips together as warmth flooded her face. "I'm fine. Is he okay?"

Agent Jacobs gave her a knowing smile, and Ella wondered exactly what Agent Jacobs thought she knew. The other woman's thumbs danced across her phone as Ella gritted her teeth. "Don't worry, it's nowhere near his worst injury, as he mentioned several times when he felt like I was 'making a fuss.' He's a little banged up, but he's as tough as they come."

"Has the doctor been by yet?" Agent Watson asked Ella.

"No, not yet. Soon I hope. I've never liked hospitals, and I've been in way too many this week. I feel like a trapped rat in here."

"Well, lucky you, because we've been ordered to stay right here with you until you're discharged." Agent Jacobs turned to the unnamed agent who'd accompanied Ella to the hospital. "We've got her. Thanks." He inclined his head slightly in acknowledgement and shifted out of the crowded space.

A new text from Agent Donnelly popped up on her phone. *Better now?*

Not yet. I'll let you know.

She leaned back and closed her eyes as Agents Jacobs and Watson conferred in low voices.

She must have drifted off, because the next thing she knew, an older man with salt and pepper hair and a matching beard was pulling back the curtain. The three agents were on alert, and the man in the white coat cast a curious glance in their direction. "Hello, I'm Dr. Shah. You must be Annabella Madson?"

"Yes."

The doctor motioned toward the agents. "And they are...?"

The agents showed their badges, and Agent Jacobs spoke for all of them. "Agents Jacobs, Rappaport, and Watson, FBI."

"My security detail." Ella couldn't get over how strange it was to say that.

"I see," said Dr. Shah. "I don't suppose they'll wait outside?"

"They're under orders not to leave me alone, from a very demanding boss who's also a patient around the corner. We were in the same car accident."

"I believe I heard about someone who fits that description."

Ella enjoyed the image of grumpy Sam, mostly because it was Sam.

Next, Ella impressed Dr. Shah with her long list of recent injuries and answered his questions. After a quick exam, followed by what felt like an endless wait, a nurse went over Ella's paperwork, warned her to take it easy, and then officially discharged her.

From there, she and the three agents walked back to Sam. His expression changed instantly when he saw her, from brooding to intense relief. He had a nasty cut on his cheek and bruising down the right side of his face, and who knew what else? Still, he was conscious and in one piece, and she momentarily forgot everything around her except him.

Smiling self-consciously as her cheeks burned, she looked down at her phone and typed quickly in response to his previous text. *Better now.*

The other three agents crowded shoulder to shoulder near the end of the bed, while Ella stood by Sam's side, her eyes fixed on his as if an intense enough stare could extract information from him.

His voice wavered when he said, "Hey. You okay?"

Those three little words contained more concern than anyone had shown her in years. She nodded, her response momentarily sticking in her throat, and then coming out in a whisper. "Yeah. Are you okay?"

Only now did he look down at the message she'd sent from a few feet away. "Better now," he said with a pained smile.

Hoping against hope that she was not blushing, she raised her eyes from the floor back up to his. "I heard you were getting a little antsy."

He shrugged, admitting nothing. "This wasn't exactly part of the plan for today." The corner of his mouth tilted up mischievously.

The curtain whipped to one side, and a stern, white-haired nurse appeared. She did not look happy to find four extra people crammed into the small space. "Please keep in mind that this is not a lounge. If you don't need to be here, see yourselves out." She disappeared as quickly as she'd arrived.

The five of them were still exchanging amused looks when the curtain moved aside again. Instead of another reprimand, a friendly face appeared.

"Hi Dr. Shah," said Ella.

"Hello again. I heard there was a party over here." He consulted Agent Donnelly's chart. "So, young man, it's been a few hours. Still feeling all right?"

"Good as new."

The doctor looked from Sam to Ella sternly. "What are the odds you two will take it easy for a few days?"

"Less than zero," said Agent Jacobs with a grin. "Outside the hospital, Agent Donnelly might manage an hour, if we're lucky."

Ella and Agent Watson exchanged a smirk while Sam rolled his eyes but didn't bother feigning annoyance. "Funny. But probably true. In my defense, we are in the middle of a case."

"I thought as much," said Dr. Shah, turning back to Sam. "I can't force you to stay here. I'd normally send you home with strict orders to rest for two or three days. In this case, I get the feeling that to even have a chance of getting you to rest that long, I'd have to admit you and keep you here. Seeing as both would be losing battles, as a compromise, I'd like you to stay for observation for another three hours. Some rest is better than none."

All eyes were on Sam, and Ella was certain he was going to tell the doctor bluntly that it was out of the question.

"If I agree to stay, do they need to leave?"

Ella wondered if he meant that he wanted them there, or he didn't.

Dr. Shah shook his head. "No, they can stay. Though I don't think we can squeeze more than one chair in here. They may be more comfortable in the waiting area. The nursing staff may be a little less agitated by that, as well."

"Rappaport, Watson, go check in with the team and then stay in the waiting area," said Sam. The two stepped out through the curtain.

"I'll likely see you again before you're released," the doctor said. "Sit back and relax for a while."

"I can take Ella over to the scene to see the note," said Agent Jacobs once Dr. Shah had squeezed his way out of the cubicle.

"No, I can wait," Ella said quickly. "It's only a few hours."

Once again, Agent Jacobs' knowing smile as she looked from one of them to the other made Ella uncomfortable.

A different nurse arrived with a chair, which she put near Agent Donnelly's feet to be the least in the way. Agent Jacobs stepped back to make room, motioning to the chair. "Take a load off, Ella."

"No, you take it. I'm too wired to sit."

Agent Jacobs shrugged and sat down, and for a while, Ella paced the two-foot-wide strip of floor beside the bed.

Finally growing tired, she stopped by the bed to study Sam for signs of discomfort. "How are you feeling?"

"The same as last time you asked, ten minutes ago," he said good-naturedly. "Just as sore as when we came in." He scooted over in bed. "Why don't you sit down? We've been up almost all night. You're going to crash soon." He patted the space he'd made beside him.

Against her better judgement, she let herself perch on the edge of the bed, her legs hanging off the side. She was immensely grateful that Agent Jacobs was typing into her phone and at least pretending to be ignoring them, even though she was undoubtedly still aware of every awkward glance between them.

"We're going to be here a while. If you pass out sitting over the edge like that, you're going to fall face first on the floor," Sam said, scooting farther over in bed. "Turn this way and lean on the pillow. I don't bite, despite popular belief."

He threw a look at Agent Jacobs, who made a skeptical face before breaking into a grin. "Not a word," he warned her.

"I didn't say anything," she said in mock indignation.

Ella leaned back against the pillow, glancing at him sheepishly when their shoulders touched.

"Good. Now stretch your legs out and relax."

She was sure he saw her blushing as she settled next to him with her legs extended in front of her.

"Isn't this more comfortable than the seats on the plane?" He used the remote control on his right side to tilt the bed back a little farther, and she straightened in surprise. "Sorry. Let me just make it a little easier to sleep."

Embarrassed that she was about to go from sitting on the bed next to him to *lying* on the bed next to him, Ella's eyes went to Agent Jacobs. She would've given anything for the other agent not to be there to witness this very innocent but extremely awkward scene, but the other woman smiled at them as if this were perfectly normal.

"We have about two and a half hours. Take advantage of it." To Agent Jacobs he said, "You okay over there?"

She nodded. "Rest up. I got this."

The next thing Ella knew, she was waking up. Her head had landed on Sam's shoulder while she slept, just as it had on the plane. Careful not to disturb him, she sat up and swung her legs over the side. Ella's cheeks grew warm as she let herself gently down from the bed and glanced up at Agent Jacobs, who'd definitely seen her sleeping on his shoulder. Oh well.

"Do you know where the bathroom is?" Ella whispered.

She knew exactly when Sam woke up, because her phone buzzed as they made their way back to him.

Are you with Agent Jacobs?

Yes

His expression relaxed at the sight of them, but before they could say anything, Dr. Shah squeezed in, as well.

"So, how are you feeling?"

Thirty minutes later, they climbed into another FBI standard black SUV. Agent Jacobs was driving, Agent Rappaport was beside her, and Sam held the door for Ella to squeeze into the middle of the back seat beside Agent Watson, then got in after her. The SUV was officially crowded.

"Where are we going now?" Ella asked. "The Massachusetts State House?"

"No," said Agent Donnelly. "We're going to see this." On the screen was a picture of a note. For the second time that day, Ella recognized Mal's handwriting, and her eyes went wide.

E—You were always a good sport about following my clues when we were kids. I guess you liked this game after all. —M

Next to the paper was a coin. It was slightly larger than a dime, and though the words stamped into it—*No Cash Value*—gave nothing away, a memory tugged at the back of her mind. *Where do I know it from?*

They pulled up in front of a yellow brick building that filled the entire block, with a street address emblazoned in black on an awning above the door. The only remarkable thing about the building was the small army of police cars with their lights flashing surrounding it. The entire perimeter was ringed with caution tape, and while the other agents headed directly for the door, Sam stopped beside Ella when she hesitated on the sidewalk.

"You don't have to go in." He stood closer to her than usual, and she could sense him watching her as she stared at the entrance ahead of them.

"No, I need to see it." Squaring her shoulders, she exhaled.

I can do this.

Her pulse sped up all over again as she walked through the main door, Sam close behind her.

They moved farther inside the entry, which was set up as a lobby, and Ella clenched her teeth. Sam leaned down to put his face near her ear. "If you don't want to be here, we can leave. It's up to you."

The gesture, like the words, made her wonder how he could be the unbearable man she'd met the day her house had exploded. She shook her head. "I'm okay." His face was so close to hers that if she'd turned, their noses would've brushed.

They continued into a spacious inner room, which was set up in two sections—the right side as an office with a large wooden desk facing two armchairs, the left side with a conference table surrounded by six upholstered chairs and an oversized whiteboard.

Sam's voice was in her ear again. "Does this location mean anything to you?"

"No."

"It's possible that this building isn't what's important. They may have chosen it simply because it was the easiest to get in and out of without getting caught. We'll keep digging. Agent Martin and her team will go over it all. Take your time."

An officer approached them, introducing himself as Officer Lowe. He escorted them to the far end of the room to see the evidence.

Mal's note sat in the middle of the conference table, now sealed in an evidence bag, and the coin was beside it in a matching bag.

"Is this where they found the evidence?" Agent Donnelly was back in work mode, a stark contrast to the soft way he'd just spoken to her.

"Yes. The light in this corner of the room was the only one on in the entire unit. Look for yourself." Officer Lowe handed them gloves, which they put on as he retreated.

"She wanted you to find it," said Sam.

Ella swallowed hard at the certainty in his voice. Snapping the edge of one glove against her skin, her eyes darted to him. When he nodded, she reached down to pick up the small slip of paper.

Even through a layer of plastic and a layer of latex, holding it and rereading Mal's distinctive scrawl made her shiver.

E—You were always a good sport about following my clues when we were kids. I guess you liked this game after all. —M

She'd seen a picture, but this was different. Her eyes were glued to the paper, and though she wanted to put it down, she found her hand frozen in place. Her fingers clamped down tighter, creasing the paper.

Please take it away from me.

She couldn't tear her eyes away from it. What was worse, someone had vacuumed the oxygen from the room, but she was inexplicably the only one affected.

It came as a relief when Sam tugged the note out of her hand and returned it to the table. Her lungs refilled as she managed a quick, grateful look in his direction. The glint in his eyes and the faint hint of concern made her look away as he took a step closer to her.

For what felt to her like an hour, she scrutinized the two pieces of evidence, not daring to get any closer lest the note's gravity suck her in again. Sam didn't speak, just stood perpendicular to her, surveying the scene. After a long hesitation, she picked up the smaller bag to examine the coin in more detail.

"Does it remind you of anything?"

"Yes, but I can't think of what it is..."

Agent Donnelly called to an officer nearby. "Alright if we sit down?"

"Yes, sir. Let us know if you need anything."

Sam pulled out a padded chair from under the conference table for Ella, then one for himself. Ella sat back far enough from the table that she could lean forward and hold the bag containing the coin loosely between her knees. Becoming increasingly agitated, she willed herself to remember something. Anything.

It was no use, and after several long minutes with her eyes squeezed shut, she had to admit defeat. "The memory is there. I just can't quite reach it," she said.

"Give it time. It may still come back to you. In the meantime, we have another lead to check out... if you're ready to go."

"Yeah." This time she set down the evidence bag herself and stepped back from it, feeling a weight lift off her.

Leaving the other agents to work with the local team for now, Sam and Ella took the SUV and headed to the Massachusetts State House. They exchanged awkward looks, but said nothing as, outside the windows, the city went by in a blur.

The next moment, a slamming door jolted her awake. Her eyes flew open, and panic shot through her veins when Sam wasn't beside her. Had their car been hit again?

A tapping only inches to her right made her jump, and there he was, grinning at her through the window. "Ready?" His voice was muffled by the glass, but his amusement was obvious. Standing beside him a moment later, she stretched her stiff muscles after a nap that had been far too short.

Across the street, the golden dome atop the Massachusetts State House gleamed, standing out against the overcast sky. Her jaw dropped, and she stared up at the building. "We were here. That roof... I remember it."

Chapter 40
Mal and Ella

AGES 14 AND 15
(24 YEARS AGO)

E LLA STOOD ON THE empty beach, staring out at the horizon. The sand stretched as far as she could see in both directions under a cloudless sky that was tinted pink by the impending sunrise. During the day, the beach would be wall to wall tourists, but at that obscenely early hour of the morning, the only other beachgoers were seagulls. Her mother had gone for a jog on the sand, growing smaller and smaller until she was nothing but a bouncing dot in the distance. Ella had never shared her mother's love of running. She preferred to stand and gaze out at the water, relishing the peace and quiet.

Icy waves washed over her feet, interrupting her thoughts, and she shrieked, hopping backwards. Now out of the water's reach, she burrowed her toes down into the warm sand as she squinted, tracking her mother's path down the beach. She tucked the flyaway strands of hair that had escaped from her ponytail behind her ears. The morning was about as perfect as it was possible to be.

Once again, the icy water hit her feet. This time, when she jumped back with a squeal, she collided with something solid.

Not something, she realized. Someone.

Flustered, she scuttled to one side. "Oh, I... I'm sorry. I wasn't..."

She raised her eyes to gaze at a handsome boy who she guessed was about her age. She attempted to finish her sentence but suddenly could not put words together properly. "I don't... I mean, it's not... I wasn't paying attention. Then the waves surprised me..."

"No, that was definitely my fault," he said. "You'd think on an empty beach, I could walk without bumping into anyone, but the wind blew my hat off my head and I had to chase it."

She was mesmerized by the laughter in his blue eyes. "But you're not wearing a hat," she said, immediately feeling like an idiot.

He held up a dark blue baseball cap with a capital M filled in with yellow. "Not anymore. I learned my lesson."

She hated how painfully awkward her laugh came out, and that she couldn't think of a single intelligent thing to say in response.

"I'm Drew." He stuck out his hand, and she hesitated before shaking it.

"Ella," she said. "Nice to meet you."

His smile was so intense, she had to look away, studying the sand by her bare feet and only glancing back up at him with an awkward grin.

If Mal was here, she'd be flirting with him, and I'd already be invisible.

"So, what are you doing out on the beach this early?" He spoke as if he was genuinely interested in her answer, which was confusing. She couldn't remember the last time an attractive boy had cared what she had to say.

"Oh, well, my mom was getting up to go running, and I love the beach, so I came out with her. It's not nearly as much fun later, when I have to share it with thousands of people." *Or when my sister's here.*

"So you're not a runner?"

"Me? No. Not unless I'm running from danger." She focused on him longer before looking away this time, emboldened when he chuckled at her joke. "What about you? What are you doing out here so early?"

"Well, our hotel room is a little cramped. I was sharing a double bed with my little brother, but he always ends up sleeping sideways. He's six. So then I slept on the floor. But that wasn't too comfortable, so... I figured I'd just get up. My mom is probably watching me from the balcony." He looked back and shaded his eyes with his hand, peering up at the hotel behind them. "Yep, there she is." With a wave at the distant woman in a white t-shirt and shorts who waved back at them, they turned to face the water again.

Though she'd been a dot in the distance a few moments before, Valerie Madson arrived beside them then, out of breath and glistening with sweat.

"Hi Mom. How was the run?"

"Great. I see you found a friend."

"I'm Drew, ma'am. Nice to meet you."

"Hi Drew. I'm Valerie. So you're an early bird, too, huh?"

"Not usually, but four family members sharing one hotel room has made me one this week."

Ella and her mother shared a look. "We understand that, don't we?" Valerie asked. "So, are you out here alone?"

"Well, yes and no. My mom is up on our balcony." Drew grinned and waved at his mother again. His mother waved back.

Valerie waved as well. "And how old are you?"

"Mom!" Ella's face flushed.

Drew was unruffled.

"Fifteen, ma'am. We're here for the week from Ohio."

Satisfied with his answers, Valerie turned to her daughter. "I'm going up to shower and see if your father and Mal are ready to eat. If I don't see you in the room before then, we'll meet you in front of the hotel in half an hour for breakfast, all right?"

Ella nodded. "Okay."

"See you then."

As Valerie jogged back toward their hotel, the two teenagers walked along the sand. "So, Ella, tell me about yourself."

"Oh, well, I'm from Maryland." She faced into the wind to get her hair out of her face, and over her right shoulder she caught sight of a figure in black on a balcony of their hotel, which was the building next door to Drew's. It wasn't just any balcony, it was hers, and it wasn't just any figure in black.

It was Mal.

Returning her attention to Drew, she pushed her sister from her mind.

***

It was almost dinnertime that same day, and Ella had been looking for Mal for twenty minutes. She'd combed the beach and the boardwalk for blocks on either side of their hotel in the unforgiving summer sun, and had now resorted to looking in dark corners, grumbling to herself that she probably should've started there.

Ella recognized her sister as soon as she turned into the alley around the side of the hotel—the tight black shirt, skimpy denim shorts and ridiculously high wedge-heeled sandals were her signature look, which set her apart from most of the beach town full of light-colored t-shirts. There was also no mistaking what she was doing—she was pressed up against a very tan and muscular someone, whose hands were all over her. Ella rolled her eyes and steeled herself for the impending confrontation, walking just close enough to call out to her.

"What the hell, Mal?"

Mal didn't react to Ella's voice, but her companion did. He immediately went still, peering around Mal's head as his eyes widened in recognition.

Ella's breath caught in her throat. On the outside, she was perfectly calm, but inside she was screaming.

Why am I even surprised? After breakfast, she'd spent six hours hanging out with Drew, until they'd both had to meet up with their respective families. *How did he end up kissing Mal only a few hours later?*

Drew's eyes darted between the two girls, then down at the street. "Oh, uh, hey... Stella. What's up?"

Ella was momentarily speechless at being called the wrong name, on top of everything else. Mal let out a sharp peal of laughter, and Drew's expression changed from sheepish to perplexed. She forced the emotion out of her voice. "It's Ella." She pronounced her nickname carefully, as if he was a small child. "And what's up is you're kissing my sister."

Drew's eyes darted back and forth between the two of them. "Oh man, wow. Uh, now that you mention it, you two do look alike."

Ella rolled her eyes, no longer acknowledging Drew's existence. "Mom says to meet them in the hotel lobby. Now," she told the back of Mal's head.

"I'll be there when I'm ready." Mal's voice was icy against the oppressive heat, which flashed even hotter on Ella's cheeks. Done with their conversation, Mal leaned forward to kiss Drew again, even as he gaped at her in surprise.

Disgusted, Ella swatted at the tears leaking down her cheeks as she spun around to leave. When they kept coming, she gave up and crossed her arms over her chest, storming back toward the hotel lobby to find her parents.

Chapter 41
Ella

THURSDAY

E LLA STARED AT THE golden dome, trying to sharpen the hazy memories she had of her last visit long ago.

"What else do you remember?" Sam asked.

"I used to love anything sparkly or shiny, so it makes sense that my parents must have brought us here. Of course, that meant Mal would have decided in advance that it was stupid, because anything I liked was stupid."

He stuck close to her side as they crossed the street, and she pointed at the gate at the bottom of the stairs leading up to the second-floor entrance. "My mom had us stand right there, in front of the gate, so she could take our picture. And of course, Mal pinched me, so I was making a horrible face. It was way before digital cameras, so we didn't…" She trailed off, momentarily lost in thought.

"I'll say it again: your sister really sounds like a lot of fun." The lightness in his tone brought her back to the present with a smile, her jaw relaxing, and she made a face at him.

"Do you have siblings?" It had just occurred to her how much he knew about her, but how little she knew about him.

"No siblings. Just me. I went back and forth on how I felt about that for most of my life, but I think now I'm erring on the side of being grateful."

They'd reached the base of the stairs, and she wound her fingers around the wrought-iron gate where she'd stood years before.

"What about your parents?" It was nice to talk about something besides her screwed-up life, and she wondered how much he would indulge her. They looked up the hill at the building.

"They live in Northern Virginia, on a street that reminds me of yours, in the house they bought when I was eight. About an hour from your place."

She squashed the spark of jealousy over his still-intact family. Needing to change the subject, she peered up the stairs and said, "I'll race you to the top."

He shook his head. "That's not a good idea."

"Why? You afraid I'll beat you?" She grinned.

"Because someone wants you dead."

"You're definitely afraid I'll beat you."

"Afraid? No."

"Prove it." She didn't expect him to change his mind. He was right, after all. They shouldn't.

"If you insist." There was a glint in his eyes that hadn't been there before, and another of his rare, genuine smiles replaced his frown like the sun breaking through the clouds.

"Really?" She had not seen that coming.

"Let's do it before I change my mind. Just don't say I didn't warn you, okay?"

She narrowed her eyes at him, waiting for the signal.

"On your mark. Get set. Go!"

The stairway had four sets of seven stairs, each with three or four feet of concrete landing before the next set. They flew upwards, arriving at the top winded and laughing. He'd beaten her, but barely. Never having been athletic, she called this a success.

Their cheeks had flushed with exertion as he closed the distance between them, his grin giving way to a frown. "I shouldn't have let you talk me into doing that. We need to stay alert."

"I know. It was fun, though."

Though his expression was serious, his eyes still held the same sparkle they had a minute before. "Okay, I'm putting my foot down. Now that I've defended my honor, no more racing up flights of stairs until you're out of danger. That's fair, right?"

Her face grew serious as his words sank in. Once the case was closed, they'd go their separate ways. Looking out at the view and hoping he didn't notice that her face had fallen, she nodded. "Yeah, that's fair."

After scanning as far as he could see in all directions, Sam was satisfied that they were still safe. He started towards the door with Ella close behind him.

"Anything left out up here would either be considered littering or some sort of attempted terrorism. Making any marks on the building or the concrete here would be removed immediately, so I doubt there'll be anything out here."

Inside at the security checkpoint, Sam conversed briefly with the guard before they were allowed to proceed. "Let's look around in here before we head back outside to check the grounds," Sam said.

The building's interior was filled with ornate features, and as a designer, Ella was fascinated. Marble floors, columns, and elaborately patterned iron banisters along the stairways and landings gave way to high ceilings with intricate murals, complicated molding and, of course, the dome they'd seen from the outside.

"Wow." The word was not nearly big enough to express her wonder.

"It's quite a place."

Her head snapped back toward the sound of his voice. There he was, ten feet away, with a hint of a smirk on his face.

Even though he was smiling at her, she hurried back to him. "Sorry. I didn't mean to go that far. This place is mesmerizing. I just…"

She was now standing only a few inches in front of him, bracing for an explosion.

The fondness in his eyes was confusing. "Ella, it's okay. We're practically the only ones here. But thank you for taking what I said seriously."

Only slowly understanding that he wasn't upset with her, she said, "Oh. Well, I'm trying."

"I know. Let's look around."

They started with the floor they'd entered on, finding nothing that looked like a clue. A large section of the floor above that was empty space, with the grand staircases on the far walls leading to a balcony overlooking the first-floor foyer—if such a cavernous opening could be called a foyer. Ella marveled at the intricate design of the centuries-old building, reminding herself repeatedly of their purpose there. They finished checking the top floor without finding anything clue-worthy, so they stepped into the elevator to go to the ground level.

Ella kept her eyes on the ceiling as the metal doors closed. Sam pressed the button for the lower floor, watching her.

"What are you looking at?"

"If this were a movie, someone would be on top of the elevator. They'd burst in and take us by surprise." The elevator jolted slowly to life as the ridiculousness of what she'd said hit her. She chuckled and glanced at him before her eyes went back to the ceiling again. "My luck has been pretty bad, so I guess I can't be too careful, right?"

Her face heated up when he laughed as well, and said, "I'm pretty sure that's not going to happen here, but I'm not going to discourage you from being cautious."

It was silly, but knowing that no one could surprise her from above made her less anxious.

That is, until the elevator jerked to a stop.

Chapter 42
Ella

THURSDAY

IN A FLASH, SAM had pressed Ella into the corner of the elevator behind him, his arms spread wide. Neither of them looked away from the ceiling, and Ella's heart thundered in her chest. The seconds ticked by, but nothing happened. She became very aware of how little space there was between the walls of the elevator and Sam's back.

The metal box jolted back to life and continued downward toward the lobby as if it had never stopped. Still standing inside her personal space, he dropped his arms and turned to face her. They exhaled loudly, their cheeks still flushed from the surge of adrenaline. They were so close that she would barely have had to move to lean into him, and the urge to do so unnerved her. She tilted her head back against the corner instead and stared up into his eyes. Their color reminded her of coffee with the slightest splash of milk.

He's just being protective. It's his job, she chided herself.

Something about the intensity in his eyes made it impossible to look away. "See, nothing to worry about," he mumbled, without taking his eyes off her or moving back.

"I guess not." She was still cornered in the elevator, looking up at him. This time, she didn't want to run away.

"Just a malfunction," he said.

They stood frozen, staring at each other. For a few seconds, she forgot all about the elevator malfunction. She licked her lips, then immediately kicked herself inside her head. *How many hundreds of romance novels have you read? That's what you do when you want someone to kiss you! But I don't want him to...*

The image came all on its own, and her traitorous mind decided she did not hate it. This, of course, was terrifying.

The elevator's *ding* mercifully cut off these thoughts, and they broke eye contact without getting any closer as the doors opened. Sam smiled at her bashfully before turning away, and Ella followed a few steps behind on shaky legs. *Was I blushing? Was he blushing?*

Stop it. Don't make something out of nothing. She forced those thoughts away. They had work to do.

The ground floor was just as devoid of clues as the others. However, Sam's FBI credentials earned them access to the concrete patio that wrapped around the base of the building. The stairway they'd raced up moments before now towered a story high above them, but their meticulous examination of the back of the building turned up nothing out of place on or along the exterior wall.

Ella swallowed her disappointment, reminding herself that they weren't done yet. She shadowed Sam as he checked the landscaped yard around the building, starting in the back and moving inch by inch toward the sloping grounds in front. He examined every single one of the evenly spaced shrubs, not stopping until an hour later when they reached the wrought-iron fence that bordered the plaza where they'd started. They'd learned nothing.

"We're missing something," he said. "I don't know what, but she's led us this far. There's something here." They stood in the shade of a tall tree beside the building, Sam lost in thought, while Ella stewed. He paced a six-foot line in front of her, back and forth.

"So you think it's inside?" she asked.

"No. It's out here... somewhere."

She blew out a breath and gazed upwards, her eyes locking on the tree above them as if seeing it for the first time, then darting to the two others nearby. "The trees."

Sam came to a halt and spun in her direction, waiting.

"We should look in the trees," she said.

"Okay. Any reason in particular?"

"Yes. One thing she could beat me at was climbing the tree in our backyard. She would brag about how she could climb higher than I could, as if it was a good thing that she was fearless to the point of stupidity. I would only go so high because I was afraid to fall. Not Mal. She fell out of the tree and broke her arm. Twice."

"That's a great thought. Let's take a look." They started with the tree closest to them, Ella hanging back as if it might suddenly decide to bite her. Of the two on the closer side of the building, this one was larger, the branches far too high for anyone without a ladder. On the smaller tree, the branches were the right height, but a thorough search by Agent Donnelly turned up nothing.

They moved to the tree on the other side of the building, and when nothing was immediately obvious from the ground, Sam hoisted himself up into the lower branches. Ella stood on her tiptoes to get a better look. After what felt like hours, he called down, "I've got something."

"What is it?"

Balancing in the branches so he could once again put on a latex glove from his pocket, he picked up the object and studied it in the palm of his hand. "A marble."

By the time he was standing beside her with the small blue and orange sphere, Ella's face was set in a tight line.

"Does this mean something to you?"

"Two different things. There was a summer when we were visiting my cousins in Pennsylvania. I was ten, so Mal was nine. The boys had to be seven and nine, I think, and they had a huge marble collection. Even though she'd never once played marbles and didn't care about them at all, she bet them all their marbles they couldn't beat her in a race. She probably saw how important the marble collection was to them, so she wanted to take it from them." She grimaced at the thought.

"They were both soccer players, and they were pretty fast. But they made the mistake of saying they were faster than any girls anywhere, and she got this evil grin on her face. They took her bet without knowing how fast she was. Mal won the race, and their entire marble collection. It must have been in the hundreds.

My aunt told them they had to give her all the marbles, even though my mom protested. I think my aunt was secretly happy to get rid of the marbles, because she said the boys never cleaned them up. She used it as a lesson on why they shouldn't gamble, and why they should never underestimate what girls can do."

"What did Mal do with all those marbles?"

"She kept one as a souvenir and threw the rest of them in the trash as soon as we got home."

Sam shook his head. "That shouldn't surprise me by now. What's the other thing?"

"Mal had this expression she loved to use when someone annoyed the hell out of her and she wanted them to go away. The polite version of it was, 'Take your marbles and go home.'"

"So the clue could be directing us to Pennsylvania, or back to Maryland."

"Yeah."

"Which one do you think it is?"

"Well, so far, all the clues have led to places we visited when we were kids. I think she wants me to go to Pennsylvania, but I don't think that's where she's going."

"You think she's going back to the house?"

"Yeah. 'Take your marbles and go home.' She always loved to feel like she was outsmarting people."

"We can send agents to Pennsylvania just in case, and we can go back to the house."

Every cell in her body screamed with exhaustion, and she slumped as it all hit her at once. "Whatever her reason, she's bringing it full circle."

He took a step closer. "We're close, Ella."

She allowed herself to meet his eyes. *And once it's over, I'll lose you, too.*

Her insides knotted at the reminder that Sam, the only constant in her life, was as temporary as everyone else, and as always, there was nothing she could do to change that. The familiar ache ricocheted around inside her chest.

"Let's go. I need to check in with the team." He handed her the marble, secure in an evidence bag, as his phone buzzed. Glancing at the screen, he added, "Looks like Agent Martin has something for us."

He spent several minutes with his phone to his ear, pacing back and forth and saying very little. Finally he said, "Thanks. We'll see you later," and ended the call.

"So?" Ella asked.

"Agent Martin's team has been analyzing the breadcrumbs Mal has fed us, along with facial recognition from CCTV cameras all over the country and bits of computer code left behind from the hack that started all this. There were some algorithms involved and an analysis of data from all over the place... you really should've gotten to hear this from her, sorry. Anyway, the point is, she knows the name of the guy who's been trying to carry out the hit. Not the guy who came after you, but the go-between who takes the money and dispatches the assassins."

"So that's the guy who was paid to set it up?"

"It appears so."

Maybe she should've felt better knowing he'd been identified, but she just felt sick. "Can the FBI pick him up?"

"She's working on it. His name is Brett Kingston. Apparently he goes by 'Mr. K.' Ring any bells?"

Ella thought for several seconds and then shook her head. "No."

"He's been slipping up lately, and we're connecting a lot of things back to him with the information we've found so far. He's known to be ruthless, but not nearly as smart as he thinks he is. So if nothing else, you've helped us track down a dangerous criminal. A lot of good will come from this mess." His expression was apologetic.

"That's good, I guess." The FBI saw this as a win, of course. Ella wanted to be happy to have helped them, but all she saw was the looming emptiness of her future after the case was over, stretching wide enough to swallow her whole.

"We'll find him. Right now, let's get back to the jet and meet up with the others."

Chapter 43
Mal and Ella

AGES 16 AND 17
(22 YEARS AGO)

ELLA STOOD ON THE balcony of her hotel overlooking the ocean, leaning against the railing and staring out at the waves. Without warning, someone was pushing her over the railing by her shoulders—not hard enough to make her tumble over the edge, only to think she would.

It was Mal. It was always Mal.

"Don't fall!"

Ella gasped as her hands clamped onto the railing for dear life and glared at Mal, who was grinning from ear to ear.

"You should see your face right now! It's priceless."

Ella was not in the mood to attempt diplomacy with her sister. She'd begun to dread their annual family trips to the beach—they'd been bringing out the mean side of Mal more and more. "What do you want?"

"Who says I want something?"

"You're talking to me, so obviously you want something."

"That's rude."

"Am I wrong?" Mal's lack of a scowl made Ella even more suspicious.

"I had an idea," said Mal, ignoring the question. "I heard about a party tonight a couple blocks away, and I think we should go."

Ella narrowed her eyes. "Why do you care if I go to a party?"

"Because Mom won't let me go unless you go."

"I wonder why."

"Shut up. Don't you want to have a little fun?"

"What if I don't want to go to the party?"

"Then go hang out on the street. Go get pizza by yourself. Go stare sadly at the ocean. I don't care! Just tell Mom you're going with me."

Ella frowned. Ever since the day Mal had accidentally been locked in the attic, there was a tiny part of Ella that wanted to say yes when Mal asked her for something. Never mind that her parents said that it hadn't been her fault—Ella had goaded Mal into finding "the hardest hiding place." Thanks to her guilty conscience, Ella sometimes said yes to Mal despite her better judgement, hoping the two of them could get along. Too bad it never seemed to work.

Putting aside the meanness in Mal's tone, Ella shrugged. "Okay."

***

Even before the automatic doors of the hotel lobby parted with a *whoosh*, Ella was having second thoughts.

"I don't know how I let you talk me into this," said Ella as they walked into a wall of hot, sticky air.

"Because you're seventeen years old and you don't want to spend a Saturday night in a beach town playing cards with Mom and Dad."

"Maybe I should have."

"Oh my God, shut up! If you're going to whine, then go hide in a closet and cry, like you always do."

Ella fumed silently as they worked their way through the mobs of tourists, but her curiosity won out. "Where are we going, anyway?"

"A couple more blocks."

Ella noted each street sign they passed, doing her best to keep track of where they were. The farther they walked, the more she regretted agreeing to this outing.

The party was in a small corner house, the yard of which was jammed with college students. Weeds and dead plants filled what might once have been a beautiful flowerbed, and the peeling paint hinted that this was a rental property whose inhabitants didn't much care what it looked like. Music blared from inside.

Ella surveyed the scene uneasily, crossing the overgrown lawn. With the crowd and loud music, Mal was in her element. Ella wrapped her arms around herself, at maximum awkwardness levels around the other partygoers.

The guys in the crowd wore shorts and t-shirts, most of them scrubby and unshaven. The girls were the opposite, dressed in short shorts and tight tops. Mal had hidden her black bikini top under a t-shirt when they left the hotel, but she'd stuffed her shirt into her purse before they'd arrived. Combined with her short shorts and her platform sandals, Mal's legs looked a mile long. All eyes were drawn to her, just the way she liked it.

Ella wore a simple V-neck white t-shirt and khaki shorts that reached half-way to her knees. Uncomfortable with the attention Mal was drawing in their direction, she stopped in the grass, biting her lip. Meanwhile, Mal talked and flirted her way toward the door, the masses parting to make space for her as she approached the house. She accepted a beer from a muscular, scruffy twenty-something dressed in a faded t-shirt and cargo shorts, smiling as the throng pressed them against each other.

She's only sixteen! Ella wanted to scream.

She flinched as someone bumped into her, looking up at a very good-looking and very tipsy someone holding out his hands to get his balance.

"Sorry," he said with a laugh. "You want a beer?"

"No, thank you," said Ella, stepping away.

"Suit yourself." He disappeared into the fray as Ella craned her neck to see past him, but Mal had disappeared inside.

Torn between following her sister and her own intense discomfort, she stood gritting her teeth, invisible, as the party went on around her.

After thirty painfully long minutes of ignoring drunken advances and watching people make fools of themselves, Ella had had enough. She pushed her way into the house, where the air was even hotter and more stagnant than outside. The farther in she went, the more crowded it became. She shoved her way through the wall of bodies, recoiling every time a phantom hand landed on her. At last, she found Mal perched on the lap of a muscular frat-boy type on a loveseat in the basement.

Mal didn't notice her. She was too busy laughing at something the frat boy had whispered in her ear. His hands were all over her, and the bow on the back of her neck that held up her bikini top looked suspiciously askew, as though it had been recently re-tied by someone who'd had too much to drink—which didn't narrow it down at all.

The guy next to Mal on the couch gestured down to the coffee table. Following his hand, Ella saw lines of white powder.

Despite her relative innocence, Ella knew exactly what was happening. "Come on Mal. Don't." Ella whispered the words aloud, but even if she'd yelled, Mal wouldn't have heard her over the din in the house. Knowing Mal, if she'd heard Ella, she would've done it on purpose, just because she knew it would bother her.

Mal slid off the man's lap, landing on the floor and then laughing uproariously before repositioning herself with her face close to the table. Only a few inches short of doing exactly what Ella was hoping she wouldn't do, Mal looked up and locked eyes with her, Mal's malicious smile spreading from ear to ear.

The room was spinning around Ella, and she fled, desperately pushing people out of her way.

"Hey! How drunk are you?" a male voice called after her.

Outside, the sweltering night was a relief. When she stumbled on the single step by the front door, hands belonging to a man at least twice her size caught her clumsily. "Hey, baby."

"No, thank you," she said, swatting him away. Safely on the sidewalk, she turned around to observe the disaster of a party as she caught her breath.

Across the street, she sat down under a tree and leaned back against the trunk, glaring at the house—she couldn't bear to be inside to see Mal destroy herself, but she also couldn't bring herself to leave Mal there alone. Imagining all the horrible things that Mal wouldn't think twice about doing, Ella squeezed her hands into fists, oblivious to the tears on her cheeks.

Chapter 44
Ella

THURSDAY

I T WAS DUSK WHEN Ella and the agents got back on the jet and headed home to DC, and she fell asleep against the curved wall of the plane in her favorite seat before they even took off. When she woke up, Sam was sitting beside her.

"Hey."

The day he'd walked into her hospital room and glared at her, she would never have been able to imagine that he could muster a fraction of the warmth that radiated off that one word. He handed her a snack-size bag of pretzels and a bottle of lemonade.

"Hey. Thanks." She gave him a sleepy grin and took a drink, ate two pretzels, and stowed it all in the seat pocket. "Are we almost there already?"

"Nope. We just reached our cruising altitude. We have another hour to go."

"Good. I'm not ready to be there yet. Or ever." Her eyelids drooped, and he chuckled softly as she rested her head on his shoulder.

"Sweet dreams," he whispered as she fell back to sleep.

The next thing she knew, Sam was saying her name. A smile tugged at her mouth, but her eyes remained closed. When his fingers smoothed her hair, she couldn't breathe. *No one wake me up from this dream.* But it was too late—her eyes blinked open.

Her head was on his shoulder and he was inches from her face, giving her a smile that made her forget everything else.

However, the moment was broken by the plane bouncing onto the runway. She flinched, jerking her head up and squeezing the armrests.

"Welcome home. We're in DC."

"Thanks," she said, hoping she wasn't blushing.

"So, did you enjoy being on tour with the FBI?"

"Well, I suppose it was exciting, but there was this one agent who kept bossing me around. Wouldn't leave me alone. Followed me everywhere. Very bossy."

"That guy sounds like a stalker. You want me to have him investigated?"

"No, he kind of grew on me. I'm lucky he was there. He saved my life so many times, I lost count. I'm going to tell them he deserves a raise, even if he is sort of annoying."

That earned her a chuckle. The plane slowly taxied and parked on the tarmac. The other agents got up, but Sam didn't move.

Ella let out a sigh. "Are we going straight to my house?"

"Yes. Maybe we'll get there ahead of Mal. She'll think she has time to kill while she waits for us to go to your cousins' house."

Forcing herself to stand, she walked behind him down the aisle of the small plane. "I don't know. Mal wouldn't blow off her plan after going to all this trouble. If anything, she'll be bursting with anticipation to get another jab in at me. Just catching her at my house sounds too easy."

Sam paused at the door, glancing back at her. "You're calling this easy? I do this for a living, and I wouldn't call anything about this week easy."

"Sorry, I know that was partially my fault."

He raised his eyebrows at her, and she bit her lip to hold in her laughter.

"Okay, it was mostly my fault."

His eyes twinkled, but his expression remained neutral. Still, she swore she heard him chuckle as he stepped through the doorway, before the wind outside filled her ears.

"So, we're going to Ella's house?" asked Agent Rappaport once they were in the SUV and underway.

"Yes. We'll see what the situation is there and take over surveillance."

"And if Mal's not there, we wait?" asked Ella.

"That's right. One of the less glamorous parts of our job is surveillance. We can call in back up to help with that, since we don't know how long it'll be. And we've had a team monitoring the area while we've been out of town. They said it's been quiet."

Agent Jacobs leaned forward between the front seats. "Did you get chewed out by Barker for bringing Ella along in the first place?"

"Yeah." Sam kept his eyes fixed on the road ahead as he spoke. "But we came to an understanding." After several seconds of silence, he said, "Ella, there's one more thing."

"What?" she asked.

"The man who tried to kill you... the one who..." The words hung heavy in the air.

The one who killed Agent Harrison. Ella swallowed hard. "What about him?"

"They found him dead early this morning."

Ella took slow, deliberate breaths. "Does that change anything?"

"Well, that depends. They didn't find any evidence of who killed him. The police said it was a drug overdose. They found him in a hotel room that had been wiped clean. No fingerprints or personal items anywhere. However he was tracking you, the police didn't find it... which means someone else may have."

"Do you think it's a coincidence?"

"That our hitman turned up dead after he missed you multiple times? I think it means he's been fired."

Ella scoffed.

"It also means they're probably sending someone else. Someone we won't recognize, and therefore can't look out for."

She nodded, staring at her lap. "I was afraid you were going to say that."

Though the temperature in the car was comfortable, she looked out into the darkness and shivered, dread creeping down her neck. The closer they got to her neighborhood, the more on edge she became. If their plan worked, she was nearing the end of this ordeal. It would be a relief not to be running for her life, of course, but she also dreaded what came after.

However, she had more immediate things to stress over, like whether her neighbors would come out of their houses and blow what needed to be a quiet operation.

The FBI knows what they're doing. It's going to be over soon, and then... I'll move on. On my own, like I always have. She ignored the urge to look at Sam. He wouldn't be around long, and she needed to be okay with that.

Chapter 45
Ella

Thursday

T HEY PARKED AROUND THE corner from the pile of rubble that had been her house. The dim streetlights illuminated the sidewalk but left the yards and the thirty-something year old houses in shadow.

Ella watched Sam from inside the car as he conferred with Agents Watson and Rappaport. She was queasy with anticipation as he approached her door and pulled it open.

"You ready?" he asked.

She was and she wasn't in equal parts, and she tried and failed to plaster a smile on her face.

He held out a hand to steady her as she got out of the car. "Come on," he said. His tone said, *I've got you.*

She climbed out of the car and stood in front of him, waiting for instructions. "Arms up," he whispered, and when she lifted them, he slipped a bullet-proof vest that matched the ones the FBI agents were wearing over her head. He adjusted the fit and checked every inch, to the point that she was pretty sure he was stalling. If he'd been anyone else, she would've already put more space between them, but the magnetic pull she felt around him was stronger than ever. When he finally met her eyes, the intensity in his startled her.

His voice was lower and gruffer than usual. "This doesn't make you invincible. Stay close to me."

That made sense to her—the agents each had special training, a flashlight, and a gun, but Ella had none of those things.

They'd put plain windbreakers over their vests, and she expected him to tell her it was time to go. Instead, he rested his hands on her upper arms and took a deep breath, as if he was going to say something important. But no words came. He just stared at her, his eyes filled with a conflicted mix of emotions. She had the urge to lean into him, and she got the feeling that he would've wrapped his arms around her if she had. It was exactly what she needed at that moment—of course, that was all the more reason to stand up straight.

Someone coughed nearby, and Agent Donnelly glanced up, breaking the spell. "Let's go," he said, squeezing her arms quickly before letting go.

Agents Jacobs, Rappaport, and Watson disappeared around the block to approach the property through the yard behind hers, while Sam and Ella headed for the front. Before rounding the corner, they stopped to scan the block. Everything was still.

When he bent down to whisper in her ear, his forehead rested against the side of her face, making her pulse race. "Whatever happens, promise me you won't do anything stupid. No matter what. She's your sister, and I get that it's complicated. But it's my job to solve your case, and to keep you safe. No one else. Only you."

If only he hadn't said 'it's my job' again for what felt like the hundredth time, reminding her that she was only a case to him, the sweetness behind his words might not have hurt so much. She was thankful for the darkness, so he couldn't see the pain that was almost certainly blazing on her face. She stamped it out immediately. There would be plenty of time to feel sorry for herself later, when it was all over and he was gone.

She exhaled evenly to steady herself, her eyes glued to the darkened street. "I promise." Hoping she sounded confident, she added, "Let's do this."

He made a loop with his elbow, nudged it against her side, and she threaded her arm through it.

When Ella tugged on Sam's arm to pull him down the sidewalk faster, he leaned down near her face again and whispered, "Slow down. I know you're anxious, but just relax." And then, in a voice that sounded suspiciously emotional, "Trust me."

Her pounding heart filled her ears.

Can't you get one thing right in your life? Mal's voice from long ago echoed in her head, and the resulting surge of anger helped her focus.

Calm descended on her—not because she was confident in what was about to happen, but because she had decided enough was enough. She was no longer the woman who'd spent years feeling so broken. Whatever happened, she could handle it.

The houses were on their left and the street on their right as they moved down the block. Hers had been the third house from this direction, and she slowed as they neared the mailbox. It was the only thing still standing.

The moment of the explosion rushed back to her without warning. Even though she'd watched it happen a hundred times since that day, she recoiled as she saw it all again. Being thrown backwards into the street. The smell of smoke filling her lungs. Ash covering her and everything else. Her life erupting into a fireball before her eyes.

As if reading her mind, Sam seemed to anticipate it when her knees buckled, folding her into a tight hug. They stayed that way for several seconds, Ella trying to recover from having the wind knocked out of her. "I've got you," he murmured. "Breathe with me."

Thanks to the arms wrapped securely around her, holding her up, and the sincerity of the man those arms belonged to, the tight feeling of desperation in her chest lessened. She didn't know how to put her thoughts into words, so she settled for, "Thanks." He slowly released her, and they turned to face the pile of debris that had yet to be cleared.

Half her front yard was scorched, and the willow tree that sat between her house and her next-door neighbors' house had a section of black, shortened branches near the back. Soot clung to the siding of the house on the left. The house on the right must already have had their siding cleaned, because it looked like nothing at all had happened there. It was unbelievable that somehow her neighbors' houses were intact at all.

As they listened, a noise came from behind the wreckage, faint but growing louder. From the shadows, something shifted. In a swift motion, Sam lifted both his gun and his flashlight, illuminating the source of the disturbance.

Agents Jacobs, Rappaport, and Watson shielded their eyes from the brightness, stopping in their tracks until Sam clicked the flashlight off and lowered his weapon. "It's all clear up there," said Agent Watson in a low voice as they approached. "What do you want to do?"

"You three go back to the car and watch the block from there," said Agent Donnelly. "Tell the beta team to be ready to move in on my signal."

Agents Jacobs and Watson shared a look.

"Are you sure you don't want one of us to stay here with you, and the other two to take Ella back to the car?" Agent Jacobs asked Agent Donnelly. "Or back to headquarters? She'd be safer—"

"No."

Agent Watson opened his mouth to protest, but Agent Donnelly beat him to it, keeping his voice down. "First, this whole thing has been personal. Mal is looking for Ella, not us. We're more likely to find out why it's happening if Ella's here when Mal shows up. Second, I'm not giving anyone else the responsibility of protecting her. Period."

Agent Jacobs nodded, and Ella got the feeling she'd just missed something, even though she'd heard the entire exchange.

"Alright, call if you need us," said Agent Jacobs. The three agents melted back into the blackness.

Sam now focused on Ella, keeping his voice low. "Let's find somewhere to wait where we can't be spotted."

Despite some shortened branches, the weeping willow in the yard between her house and the house to the right still presented the best place to conceal themselves. She'd spent many hours under it as a child on scorching summer days, and had always seen it as a haven.

Ella gestured toward the tree, which still had enough low-hanging branches to give the space underneath the feeling of a cave. "What about under that tree?"

They crossed the yard to it, and he pushed the curtain of leaves aside and peered inside skeptically. "We don't have a good line of sight from down there."

"No, but we can sit with our backs against my neighbors' house so no one can sneak up on us from behind."

"Fair enough. I guess we're short on options."

When she ducked down and entered her childhood hideout, it was as though she'd gone back in time again, and she was almost surprised not to have instantly become her younger self. Crouching under the lower branches, she walked all the way in and sat with her back against the cool siding of her neighbors' house. Unlike by the beach, she smiled at the sight of Sam shuffling in behind her. He was the only person she didn't mind sharing this space with. His presence actually made it better.

Sam lowered himself to the ground beside her, and she told herself she shouldn't be enjoying the scent of his cologne as much as she was. As they settled themselves, something rustled nearby, and before he had a chance to reach for his gun, a ball of fur streaked out of the darkness, running full speed toward them and jumping into Ella's lap.

"Domino!"

Ella quickly rested her hand on Sam's arm, speaking softly. "It's okay. This is Domino, my neighbors' cat. She loves everyone." Feeling instantly self-conscious about touching him, she let go of his arm and stroked the cat's fur, as Domino purred contentedly.

Sam relaxed, chuckling softly. "She's fast. What do you think my chances are of recruiting her for my team?"

"I'm not sure how much of a team player she is. She's more of a lone wolf. She goes where she wants to when it suits her." She looked down at Domino in her lap, now purring in her sleep.

She pointed at the now sleeping cat before continuing in an even softer whisper. "Growing up, I spent at least half my time every summer under this tree, mostly reading. Mal didn't usually bother me here."

Sam leaned closer to her as she spoke quietly, and he replied in the same tone. "Why not?"

Ella sighed. The memory didn't hurt, exactly—at least, not any more than any other memory—but she knew how it sounded. "Miss Rosa, who still lives across the street, was always out working in her garden, and she got really upset when she saw Mal giving me a hard time. Mal wasn't my neighbors' favorite."

"Shocking," said Sam, more than a little sarcastically.

Ella grimaced and continued. "If Miss Rosa saw Mal come in here, she knew there would be trouble and marched right in after us. Mal called her nosy. Some parents might not have appreciated a neighbor correcting their kids, but she and my parents were close, and when it came to Mal, they were grateful for help wherever they could get it. I think Mal decided it was easier not to fight that battle, so she usually left me alone under here."

"Thank goodness for nosy neighbors."

"Yeah." She had a nosy question of her own, one that she'd told herself she wouldn't ask him, but her mouth betrayed her. "Can I ask you a question?" She focused on petting Domino, and on not looking at him at all.

"Of course. And that was a question." The darkness was thick under the willow, where almost none of the moonlight or the dim streetlights could reach them, and her eyes were still adjusting as he turned towards her and smiled at his own joke. She could barely make out his face, much less the expression playing across it.

I'm going to miss him after all this.

Suddenly, she wished she hadn't brought it up. "I've been wanting to ask you this for a while... But it's okay if you don't want to answer."

He was serious now, lines of genuine concern gathered on his forehead. "What is it?"

"Do you remember in Michigan, when we were arguing, and you said..." She bit her lip. It was too late to take it back now. "You said that I reminded you of someone?"

He inhaled a slow breath, looking away. Though she could barely see him, she felt the happiness drain from him. He sighed heavily, and his next words came out with what sounded like great difficulty. "Yes, I remember."

She knew him better now, and at some point she'd learned to read him better, too. When he turned to look at her, even in the dark she could see that he was barely holding back a tidal wave of emotions.

"Who did you mean?"

He had paused long enough that she was about to apologize for asking when he said, "My wife."

The bottom dropped out of her stomach.

He's married?

All she could say in response was, "Oh."

Whatever the story was, there was clearly a lot going on in his head, and it wasn't taking him to a good place. "I'm sorry. Forget I said anything. It's none of my business."

He stared out the opening of the tree with his mouth ajar, as if stuck in the middle of a thought.

She cursed her nosiness, hoping she hadn't ruined things between them.

His next words came out even more quietly than before, and he leaned over to pet Domino's head. "No, it's okay. Julia was... self-assured and opinionated and never sat still."

She froze. *Was?*

Silence stretched long enough that she didn't think he was going to elaborate. When he did, his voice was low and sad. "One night about two years ago, I was with my team, working late on a case, and a guy broke into our house. Julia wasn't the type to submit to anyone, even a guy twice her size with a gun. According to the investigation, he shot her point blank. I got a call from our neighbor about a gunshot even before the police had logged it, but... By the time help got there, it was too late. I was too late."

The only sound was the crickets chirping. So much about him now made sense.

"I wonder sometimes if something about me, or my job, made her feel invincible. Like she could stand up to him. Maybe if I'd prepared her better, or..." He shook his head, abandoning his thought mid-sentence. "Anyway, another team tracked the guy down, and he eventually went to jail. Life goes on.

I keep catching the bad guys, so other people don't have to live through what I did. Too little, too late."

What little light there was under the tree reflected an ocean of sadness.

What a horrible thing to live with, especially for an FBI Agent.

"I'm sorry," she said. Her face twitched as a tangle of emotions pulsed through her. "I can't even imagine how horrible that was. I'm... We're all lucky you're still here, protecting us. You do so much good for so many people."

"Not enough." His gaze darted back out the opening in the tree again. His hand moved gently against Domino's fur, and when his fingers brushed Ella's on the cat's back, their eyes met

"I wish I could be more like that. Stronger," said Ella.

"You've been through your own set of nightmare scenarios. You're not exactly like her, but you're strong in your own way. But now that I think about it, I misspoke in that moment... we were both a little wound up." He almost smiled at her, his eyes darting away and then back. "The thing that's the same... isn't you, it's me."

"What do you mean?"

He looked down at his lap, then back out at the night. "It's... the feeling I get when I'm around you. I just feel... better. Like the things that weigh me down aren't as heavy. I used to feel that way around her." He shrugged and glanced at her again before releasing a ragged breath as he averted his eyes.

"Oh." No other words would come, and her chest felt lighter and heavier at the same time. She simply didn't know how to process his confession, much less how to respond. She continued stroking Domino's silky fur while she tried not to be overwhelmed by relief, fear, affection, the need to run, and the need to hold on for dear life. It was exactly what she was most afraid of and exactly what she most needed, all tangled together.

"I'm sorry, that was very unprofessional of me. Completely inappropriate." The blank mask descended over his features again.

She imagined he would've bolted if he'd had the luxury, and she was thankful that their situation forced him to stay, even though the tension between them was unbearable.

He was right in front of her, but still inaccessible. After spending many years closing herself off in a similar way, she knew how it felt, and she wanted to help.

"Sam." His name came out so low she barely heard it herself, but his head turned and his eyes locked on hers.

Her heart pounded as if it was trying to break free. She wanted to comfort him, but didn't know how. As empty as she was herself, what could she give to anyone else? Still, somehow he made her want to try.

The corners of her mouth tilted up, but that was all she could manage when confronted with the sadness in his eyes.

He looked away again, back out at the darkness. "I'd blocked off that part of me for so long. I had no idea how much I'd missed that feeling until it was there again. I'd thought it was gone forever. Maybe that's why I'm so over-protective of you. I've known all along that I should've taken myself off your case, but after you said you didn't want me to, I couldn't make myself do it. I didn't trust anyone else to protect you."

At a loss for words, she laid her hand on top of his, where it sat on his leg, curling her fingers around it and holding on tight. He studied their hands before bringing his gaze back up to hers. Her heart thudded as she waited for his reaction.

When he let go of her hand, she was sure she'd made a grave mistake. But instead of pulling away, he turned his hand over beneath hers and laced their fingers together.

"To be fair, your so-called overprotectiveness is probably the only reason I'm still alive. So I'm grateful."

He opened his mouth to say something, but stopped, and she dropped her head against his shoulder, momentarily forgetting where they were and why.

She spoke without looking up at him. "I'm sorry. That it happened, and that I brought it up."

"I don't talk about it, though I've been told that I should. I haven't been able to. But it's different with you. It hurts a little less now. So, thanks." He squeezed her hand, and they fell into comfortable silence.

Their hands were still clasped a few minutes later when her phone buzzed in her pocket.

"I should check that." She told herself to move, but her muscles weren't listening.

"You probably should."

She shifted reluctantly to fish her phone out with her free hand. When a glance at her screen made her gasp, jolt upright, and let go of his hand, he leaned in closer.

"What is it?" He gently lifted her hand to get a look at the text as she stared urgently out of their hiding place.

The text she'd received contained only a picture of their SUV, still parked where they'd left it. The silhouettes of the three agents inside were visible, and while there was no reason to believe they'd been harmed, she shivered. Judging from the image, they hadn't even noticed anyone watching them.

Fear clenched Ella's stomach. "Mal's here." As if she knew what that meant, Domino jumped off her lap and scampered into the darkness.

It was time.

Chapter 46
Mal and Ella

AGES 17 AND 18
(21 YEARS AGO)

ELLA STEPPED OFF THE front porch and stopped. Mal leaned against the back bumper of their parents' very packed car, smiling at her. Mal's smiles always meant trouble, and Ella braced herself.

Their parents' cheerful voices floated out to them through an open window from inside the house.

"Hey," said Mal, as if she greeted Ella with a smile every day.

Ella narrowed her eyes at her. "What do you want?"

"Today's the big day. I just wanted to say congratulations before you left."

"Yeah, sure you did. More like you wanted to see if there would be any chance to push me in front of a moving car before I go."

Mal scoffed, shaking her head. "Well, that's rude. But you're right, I'm glad you're leaving. I hope I never see you again. I mean it. You're just as useless and pathetic as you've always been."

The remark had been harsh, even for Mal, and Ella stared at her sister. "Why are we doing this? Why have we been doing this for the past ten years?"

"You haven't figured it out?"

"Figured out what? That you're pissed off? Got it! That you hate me? Yeah, I know. Why? Because Mom accidentally locked you in the attic when you were nine?"

Mal crossed her arms. "Of course not. Don't be dumb."

"Well then, give me a clue, Mal, because I don't know."

With a shake of her head, Mal rolled her eyes. "Never were too good with clues, were you?"

That was the last straw for Ella. "I was ten years old! I'd never heard of that stupid book!" she shrieked, then took a deep breath and counted to five, composing herself.

At that moment, two police cars pulled into their driveway. Both girls froze.

"What did you do this time, Mal?" Ella raised her eyebrows.

"Let me think... Well, I slept with Ethan last week. Guess he wasn't good boyfriend material after all." She shrugged, as if sleeping with her sister's boyfriend was no big deal. "But I don't think they're here about that."

Mal's casual remark caused Ella exactly as much pain as she'd intended, but just before the officers were within earshot, Ella whispered, "If I had to guess, I'd say they know about your drugs."

Now it was Mal's turn to look stricken, and her head whipped toward her sister. "My...? What did you...?" Unlike her usual cool demeanor, Mal looked visibly panicked.

Ella smiled at her without a trace of malice and shrugged.

"Good afternoon, girls," said Officer Meeks. "Are your parents home?"

"I'll get them," said Ella, already halfway to the front door.

"Just stay right here, Mal," said Officer Donovan when Mal moved to follow Ella inside.

When her parents came out of the house a minute later, eyes wide, Mal was surrounded by the four officers, a scowl on her face and her hands balled into fists at her sides.

"Ma'am, Sir," said Officer Meeks. His tone gave away nothing. "We have a warrant to search your residence." He handed the papers to the girls' father, who stared at it uncomprehendingly for two seconds before handing it to his wife.

"What are you looking for?" Valerie asked.

"We have evidence that Mallory has quite a drug stash, and that she's been selling to kids in the neighborhood."

Valerie gasped and covered her mouth with one hand, looking like she'd been slapped. Her husband tensed beside her, his hand resting tightly on his wife's shoulder. Mal, usually quick to lash out, just glared at the officers.

The parents glanced from Mal back to Officer Meeks. "Do what you need to do," said their father. They stepped back to let the officers pass.

Officer Meeks turned to the two officers whose names Ella didn't know. "Keep an eye on Mallory. I'll let you know if we need you." They nodded, and Ella watched Officer Meeks and Officer Duncan disappear into the house, her parents following them only as far as the front door, where they stood outside and peered through the screen door after them.

Mal's scowl burned into the back of Ella's head, and when Ella turned to look at her, she saw pure hatred in her sister's eyes.

Neither girl dared to say a word in front of the officers, but they almost didn't need to. Their glares spoke volumes.

I hate you.

I hate you more.

Hours later than planned, Ella and her parents took the thirty-minute drive to the University of Maryland campus in College Park. They were nearly there, and Ella still hadn't said a word.

"You okay, Bella?" Her father's face was lined with concern.

"I'm fine." Her voice said the opposite.

Her parents looked at each other, and her mother sighed, reaching into the back seat to take Ella's hand. "I know today has been upsetting, but you can't let that spoil the day for you. You're finally going to college. That's something to celebrate." She squeezed Ella's hand.

Ella nodded as her mother's attempt to comfort her failed. "She said... she hoped she never saw me again. I guess it should make me happy never to see her again, but... I just don't understand. She's still mad at me over that stupid day in the attic." She took deep breaths to steady herself. "And she said she slept with Ethan."

Her mother's face betrayed her surprise at the last part, but she smoothed her expression and squeezed Ella's hand tighter. "Oh, honey..." Valerie looked as stricken as Ella felt, and it was a full minute before she spoke again. "I'm sorry. About Ethan, and about Mal. I hope that being away from home will be good for you. You can meet a whole new set of people. It's a fresh start. We'll miss you, though."

Ella nodded half-heartedly for her mother's benefit, glancing away as Valerie continued.

"I know you and Mal have had a lot of trouble, but don't give up. Growing up is hard, and people can change. Maybe she'll grow out of whatever this is. But whatever choices she makes, you're going on to great things. I know it. Don't let her spoil this for you."

Ella nodded without looking up, the words bouncing off her like ping-pong balls. She wished she could just not care that her sister hated her, but it wasn't that simple. Deep down, she still believed she deserved it, especially after she'd told the police about Mal's drug dealing. No matter what her intentions had been, she'd gotten her sister arrested.

As they wound their way through the familiar suburban streets toward the University of Maryland, Ella stared into the blinding sunshine. The numbness inside her had given way to anger.

I'm the one giving Mal the power to hurt me, even though I know better.

The scenery flew by them in a blur.

I've spent as long as I can remember wishing she would change. How could I have been so stupid? She hurts me because I let her. It's my own fault.

From the outside, Ella looked a little sad, or maybe just deep in thought. Inside, she had curled up into a cocoon, tuning out her parents' concern and attempts at idle chit chat. It had taken eighteen years, but she finally understood that she was the problem. She'd do the only thing she could do, and build a wall she hoped would stop her from feeling everything too much. This was her new start, and she was going to protect herself from now on.

I can't let this happen again. I won't.

Chapter 47
Mal and Ella
THURSDAY

"YOU KNOW HER BEST. Do you think she'll be alone?" Sam asked.

"It wouldn't surprise me," said Ella. "She was always reckless. Like you said, all the evidence suggests that she hasn't changed."

"Let's go." He typed into his phone rapidly, then got to his feet, shoulders bent beneath to avoid hitting his head on the branches. "If you get the chance to get her to admit anything, great," he said in a low voice. And then, as if he could hear Ella's thoughts when she hesitated, he added, "I know you can do this."

She took the hand he offered, allowing him to pull her up to her feet, then held on for an extra beat before reluctantly letting go. Under the canopy of the willow, Sam's hunched shoulders brought their faces closer together than usual.

"Ella..."

"I know. Don't do anything stupid. I promise I won't."

He put his hand on her arm and held it there, looking into her eyes as if he wanted to say something else, as he had before. Once again, no words came. The look in his eyes could have meant so many different things, but she knew she was seeing what she wanted to see. When his hand left her arm and he started toward the opening, she watched him walk away, the same way he would soon walk out of her life.

She bit her lip, knowing this was the beginning of the end.

When he glanced back and saw that she wasn't following, he reached for her hand again. Something in her chest compressed, but she swallowed and allowed him to tug her forward.

At the edge of the tree's canopy, Sam let go of her hand to draw his gun, pointing his flashlight into the darkness. Ella stayed close behind him and rested her hand lightly on the back of his upper arm to reassure him that she was there. He advanced slowly, not lowering the gun or flashlight.

Sam's foot hit something and he stepped back in surprise into Ella. Her heart lurched as she was suddenly flush against him, and for a moment, she held on to his arms with both hands to get her balance. The beam of his flashlight illuminated a dark shape on the ground. They squatted, and Sam kept watch, handing Ella a pair of gloves.

Mumbling to herself, she turned over the smooth statue that stood less than a foot tall.

"Any idea what it means?" Sam asked.

She traced her fingers over the curves again and again. "I think it's a miniature version of an abstract statue that's in a park down the street," she said, standing up.

"I checked the ground when we got here. Someone put it here since then."

Ella shivered, shifting as she stared into the darkness. Someone had walked only feet away from where they'd been sitting under the tree, and they'd had no idea.

"Where is the park from here?" he asked.

"About a ten-minute walk."

He tapped his ear to activate his comm and connect to the rest of his team, mumbling the change of plan.

"The other three are going to swing the car over here and monitor the property, just in case. You and I are going to the park."

She tensed.

"Ella." He rested a hand on her arm again. "Whatever happens tonight, Mal doesn't get to decide anything for you. She's pulled you into her mess, but you don't have to be part of that world anymore. You're going to be okay."

She pasted a smile on her face despite the tangled knot of her feelings. Maybe someday she'd be able to look back on his kindness fondly, but at that moment she couldn't imagine ever being able to think of him without breaking down the way she wanted to at that moment.

"I know," she forced herself to say.

He nodded toward the sidewalk and the pile of rubble that had been her house. "Same as before. Stay close," he said. "You lead the way."

Staying close was probably the easiest directive she'd ever followed, because the closer to him she was, the safer she felt. Looping her right arm through his left, in which he held the flashlight, she tried to calm her galloping heartbeat.

The last time she'd walked this route had been decades ago, and she'd never done it in the dead of night. There were no cars on the road except the ones parked for the night, no other people to be seen. The chirping of nighttime insects and the occasional owl's hoot made for a spooky walk, with Ella constantly startling.

"Easy," Sam mumbled, squeezing her arm against his side.

When a car backfired a few blocks away, Sam dropped her arm, spinning as he wrapped his arms around her and hunching away from the sound. Ella collapsed into him. They stood that way, breathing deliberately as her heart raced, until they were sure there was no danger. For an instant, Ella allowed herself to enjoy the feeling of his arms around her.

Stop it.

They laughed quietly as they started off down the sidewalk again. This time her arm threaded around his waist, and in response, his left arm draped over her shoulder, the flashlight beam swishing back and forth ahead of them. His right hand rested on his gun, secured in its holster.

"It's on the next block," Ella whispered. It was strange how a place she remembered as a happy part of her childhood could look so sinister in the dark. The closer they got, the more Ella felt like she'd walked into a horror movie, and the tighter she clung to Sam.

She stopped on the sidewalk at the edge of the park, and he glanced down at her.

"That coin... it was from here." A memory took shape, and she closed her eyes and pulled on the strings until her patience was rewarded.

Staring straight ahead, Ella's vision went slightly fuzzy, just as it had in Boston when she'd remembered something. "Mal and I were standing on the pavement near the statue, waiting for my parents to pick us up. I was twelve or thirteen. Some guy had dropped this, and she picked it up. At least, that's what Mal told me afterwards. She made a big show of picking it up and acted all fascinated by it, then asked if I wanted to see it. Typical Mal, she made me curious, even though it was nothing. As soon as I said 'yes,' she snatched it back and shoved it in her pocket, then smirked at me. I didn't see it until later, when she got bored with it and dropped it on the ground. I guess she found another one."

"She was always the charmer, huh?"

"Yeah. I know it's stupid that I still remember these things, and that they still bother me, especially after all this time."

He shrugged. "Everything's always so much more complicated with family. The things that hurt us don't have to be the important things. Besides, it's not as though that was the only unkind thing she ever did to you." He paused. "This could be out of line, but... It sounds like you were better off without her. Maybe she unintentionally did you a favor by removing herself from your life? Though obviously she's not doing you any favors right now."

Her eyes were glued to the park as it came back into focus. "Yeah. Maybe."

After that they were quiet, watching for Mal. The only sound was the rustling of the leaves in the trees. Even the insects seemed to be holding their breath. Ella and Sam proceeded cautiously towards the statue at the center of the park, the whole time on the lookout. They got as far as the concrete plaza area, which was when Mal materialized from behind the statue.

A slow clap echoed in the night, and Sam drew his gun. Ella dropped her arms and scrambled behind him, standing just to the right of his right shoulder where she had a view of Mal, and placed her hand along the edge of his vest, behind his arm.

"Mallory Madson, I'm Sam Donnelly with the FBI. Get down on the ground."

Ella heard Sam's words as if across a great distance, her eyes never leaving her sister. Mal held nothing in her hands, but Ella knew better than to assume that she was unarmed.

Mal ignored Sam's order. "Congratulations. You caught up! Wasn't this fun, Ella? And you came here instead of going back to Pennsylvania. I knew you'd figure it out. We finally get our family reunion."

Ella's free hand clenched and unclenched at her side, while the one behind Sam's arm flattened against the cloth of his jacket, reassuring him she was still there and hoping to soak in his strength under pressure.

"Get down on the ground." Sam's tone was stern, his gun trained on Mal.

"For God's sake, Ella, you don't have to hide from me."

"What exactly do you want from me?" To Ella's surprise, her voice boomed from her chest across the twenty feet separating them.

"I just wanted to talk to you. You don't have to hide back there. Agent Muscles here is easy on the eyes, but I'll watch him for you."

Ella flashed back to Mal telling her she'd slept with Ethan, her high school boyfriend, and the fingers on Sam's back gathered the fabric of his jacket tightly in her fist.

Finally acknowledging Sam, Mal said, "I just want to talk to my sister. That's all." The innocent smile she flashed at him almost made her look like Ella.

Ella let go of Sam's jacket and stepped out from behind him, her left shoulder now in front of his right.

He still held his gun and his flashlight trained on Mal. "Dammit, Ella, you promised." His voice was full of fear, not anger.

"Do you want to tell me about the data breach?"

Mal wrinkled her nose. "A data breach? Definitely not. I just wanted to see you again. It's been so long."

Ella shook her head. "You know you could've contacted me anytime over the last twenty years. Text and email work just fine. Or you could've written me a letter, if you wanted to be old school. You didn't need to use those stupid, cryptic clues."

"But that was our game! Don't you remember? I've been trying to get you to play, to have a little fun with it, for years. I thought..."

"You thought what?"

"I wanted something good between us. That game was the one thing we always had."

"You didn't have to make up some weird scavenger hunt for things to be good between us."

Mal shrugged. "It was more fun this way."

Ella's teeth clenched. "Fun? Do you know what I've been through over the past few weeks?"

"Not really... but I know you and the FBI were in Michigan. I'm assuming it had something to do with me. I'm sorry if it's been a pain..."

The weird part was, she actually sounded sorry.

"Someone tried to kill me," said Ella.

"What?" Mal looked visibly shaken.

"More than once."

"What happened?"

"Let's see... my house blew up. Someone broke into a safe house the FBI put me in and tried to attack me. I've been poisoned, a guy tried to wrap a wire around my neck while I slept, and someone crashed into our car on purpose."

"But why would... Oh my God," said Mal, covering her mouth with her hand.

"What, it was a friend of yours?"

"No," said Mal, but her voice had changed, and she looked like she'd seen a ghost.

Ella squared her shoulders. "So it's horrifying when other people do it? Do you even remember how horrible you were to me when we were kids? You tried to kill me more than once yourself."

"I remember that I wanted you to play with me," Mal said slowly. "I wanted your attention, and I wanted you to like me. But nothing I did was good enough. For you or for Mom and Dad. I know I did some bad things, but I don't remember why I thought they were a good idea."

Ella's thoughts raced back over the years'—memories of the two of them. A wave of her decades-old guilt over Mal's self-destructive path hit her hard, even as she fought it.

Seeing that Ella had nothing to say, Mal went on. "I know, I know, I was no angel. Mom once said I started my teenage rebellion from the time I could walk."

"You were awful to her. To both of them."

Mal nodded, and if the shadows were not deceiving her, Ella saw regret on her sister's face.

That's a first.

Mal shrugged. "I was. You're right. But I wasn't alone in that."

Ella's thoughts were finally coming together. "You're saying it was my fault?" Which, deep down, Ella had always feared.

Mal crossed her arms. "Maybe that's why I wanted to get you to play our game again, when I started ten years ago. It was the one thing we did together that we had fun with."

"Until we didn't," said Ella.

Mal looked at the ground and let out a sigh, and once again, Ella swore she saw someone other than the sharp-edged younger sister she'd remembered Mal as for so many years.

"I... I thought you were trying to..." Ella started. "I don't know. That you were messing with me somehow."

Mal twisted her lips in thought. "I mean, maybe at first. But it gave me an excuse to go to the places the clues were from. It was our game, but even better."

"And you weren't doing anything illegal all that time." The sarcasm dripped from Ella's words.

"Well, I wouldn't go that far."

"So you just wanted to pull me into your life of crime? Thanks, but no thanks." Ella shifted forward, and Sam cleared his throat behind her, reminding her that he was there.

Mal exhaled in frustration. "Am I proud of every choice I've made?" She glared at the darkened sky, then back at Ella. "No. Okay? Was I a terrible daughter? Yes."

"Well, at least you're self-aware. Better late than never."

"Just let me finish." Mal snapped. "Yes, I wish I'd had the chance to apologize to Mom and Dad. But I can still say it to you. I'm sorry, Ella."

The world around Ella dimmed as her thoughts thundered. Mal was a world class liar, and her words were band aids on a gaping wound.

But what if she's telling the truth?

Ella's cheeks flushed, and she had to fight to calm down. "You couldn't have told them this twenty-five years ago, when—"

"Spare me the lecture. Terrible daughter. Yada yada yada. I know. Nothing I can do about it now. I can only make it right with you. That's why we're here. I really am sorry." Her voice broke on the last words, and for the first time Ella could remember, her sister looked genuinely remorseful. "Maybe it was a ridiculous way to go about it, but I just wanted to see you again. I don't know if... I don't know when I'll get another chance."

"Why?" Ella asked, a chill creeping through her.

Mal took a step forward, but Sam was ready. "Don't move," he warned her, the gun still pointed at her.

"Can't you just..." Ella started.

"No," he said shortly. "Only you," he added in a low voice.

Mal swiped her hands over her cheeks. "I'm sorry," she said, more forcefully. "I wish I could go back and undo so many things."

She's actually sorry. It was hard for Ella to believe what she was seeing and hearing.

"Me, too," said Ella, sniffling. "I wish it all could've been different."

Mal nodded, wiping tears that were falling faster now.

"Ella, we need to move somewhere safer." Sam's voice behind her reminded her he was there.

No sooner had he said that than a *CRACK* echoed across the otherwise quiet park, and time slowed down. Mal and Ella locked eyes and froze. Only Sam moved, throwing his arms around Ella from behind as he dove to the ground.

Chapter 48
Mal and Ella

THURSDAY

E VEN THOUGH ELLA KNEW it was Sam holding onto her, she struggled against his grasp, kicking, punching, and shrieking.

Twisting her head in Mal's direction, she saw her sister lying motionless on the ground. A dark shadow had spread across her chest under the weak moonlight, and Sam spoke rapidly into his comms.

"No!" Ella's shriek echoed in the distance as she untangled herself from Sam's hold. She scrambled to where Mal lay unnaturally still. The shadow spreading over her was blood, and Ella's hands quickly became covered in it as she tried to rouse her. "I'm sorry, Mal. I'm sorry. Come on... Please!" Her voice was increasingly frantic.

"Help!" She looked around for someone, anyone, but everyone was running in the other direction, including Sam.

"Check the perimeter!" he yelled.

Ella's eyes darted everywhere—first around the park, into the darkness, and then to the shopping center across the street. On the roof a shadow moved, so quickly she wasn't sure she'd seen it at all.

On the ground beside Mal's open cross-body bag was an intricately carved stone elephant statue. It looked like it had just rolled out of the pocket of her bag. Ella had given Mal an almost identical but smaller one long ago, back before they'd hated each other, because elephants had been her favorite animals. Mal had named the smaller one Skip, and for a time, he'd been her good luck charm. A sob of recognition burst out of Ella as she stuffed it in her pocket and looked up to see Agents Jacobs and Watson disappearing at a sprint. A crowd of agents had appeared out of nowhere and were moving in every direction. Desperate to do something, Ella held her hands over the gunshot wound as blood poured out under them at an alarming rate. "Help!" she shouted again.

"Ella!"

Larger hands wrapped around her wrists and pulled her away.

"No!" she shrieked, throwing one elbow and then the other behind her at whoever was behind her.

"Ella! Stop it!" said Sam.

"Let the EMTs take care of her. Come on. Let's go." He kept her wrists in his vice-like grip, and this time she let him. Falling backwards on the pavement, she was crying, screaming and flailing to get away from him all at once. On her feet, she wiped her blood-soaked hands on her jeans, leaving smeared patches. Breathing hard, she watched the EMTs take Mal to the ambulance. Only when the door slammed and the lights and sirens started did she look back at him, eyes narrowing. She took one step back and then another.

"This is your fault!"

Sam's forehead creased in confusion. "What…"

"How could you let them get her? You're supposed to protect people!"

He didn't try to stop her as she charged him, screaming, crying, and pounding on his chest with both bloody hands as he said nothing. His lack of resistance only infuriated her more.

In that moment, she could not appreciate the irony that she was now upset with him for caring about her—the opposite of why she'd been upset with him when they met.

His words came back to her as she swung at him. *"…it's my job to solve your case, and to protect you. No one else. Only you."*

Is that what he meant? That it was okay with him if Mal got shot?

"I hate you!" She screamed it at the top of her lungs. "Do you hear me? I hate you and I never want to see you again!"

Her emotional explosion hadn't made her feel better, it had only scraped her insides raw. She'd known her time with him was nearly over, but it wasn't supposed to end like this.

She pushed off him and stumbled blindly toward the sea of people and flashing lights at the curb. An agent from the back-up team caught her a few yards away and held her steady, and she took the opportunity to shoot a murderous glare over her shoulder at Sam. Agents Jacobs and Watson now stood on either side of him, and his expression was pained.

Good.

Though she desperately wanted to shut them out, she heard the voices of the agents she'd spent the past week with loud and clear.

"You're just letting her walk away?" asked Agent Jacobs, a hint of teasing in her voice. "After keeping her within a two-foot radius of you at all times through this entire case?"

If the agent holding her hadn't had such a firm grip on her, she might have run back to confront Agent Jacobs.

"Settle down, Ms. Madson. We're here to help you."

She couldn't keep Sam's voice from intruding as he replied matter-of-factly. "No matter how complicated things were with Mal, she was still her sister. It's not the same, but I remember what it was like... After Julia."

Ella's anger flared. *How dare he think he understands?*

"Right now, she needs to blame someone. I get it."

Agent Jacobs' teasing tone was gone. "That doesn't even make sense. What does she think you should've done differently?"

"Her anger isn't rational. She just watched her sister get shot. I don't know if Mal's going to make it, but it didn't look good. Ella needs to channel her anger somewhere, so if it helps her, she can blame me. I know it's not my fault."

Ella had already wanted to punch him, and he kept making it worse. When she glared at him again, his eyes met hers. She got the slightest satisfaction out of the stricken look that made its way across his face before he took a deep breath and looked away. She whipped her head back around, her blood boiling.

"You're a good man," Agent Jacobs told him. "It's about time we got you back."

Ella clenched her teeth. *They get him back, and I lose him. Just like I lose everyone else.* It only made her angrier.

The agent holding Ella had relaxed his grip, thinking she'd calmed down. Desperate to get away from Sam and everyone else, Ella jabbed her knee upwards with all her strength to hit the unfamiliar agent where it would be the most painful, and took off running again.

She didn't get much farther before hands grabbed her, keeping her inside the tight circle of law enforcement, but this time at least she'd escaped the reach of Sam's voice. Standing between so many agents who knew nothing about her, she stared into space, barely responding when spoken to. It could not get worse than this.

"Excuse me, miss?"

Ella looked up at an EMT standing in front of her.

"You took a tumble back there. Come sit down and let me have a look."

She shook her head. "I'm fine."

"I'm sorry, but I must insist. It's my job." The man was about her age and smiled at her apologetically.

With a sigh, she followed him out of the sea of police officers to an ambulance parked down the hill at the edge of the police's roped off perimeter. The EMT glanced back at the commotion nearby, his eyes darting from Ella to the ambulance and back.

Something was not right, and she dared not look away from him as he reached up to open the ambulance's back door. His windbreaker shifted as he moved, and Ella saw a gun peeking out underneath it.

EMTs did not carry guns.

No.

The world around her fell silent as her panic eclipsed everything else. She'd narrowly escaped death numerous times already, but this time, she wouldn't be so lucky.

The man turned back towards her then, focused on something over her shoulder. Through the crack in the door, Ella could see a man wearing only his underwear propped up against the side wall. He didn't appear to be breathing. Her attention darted back to the man in front of her. He was still staring past her, and grabbed her arm hard with one hand, pulling him to her while drawing his gun with the other.

She couldn't see what he was looking at, but she could guess.

Without hesitating, she squeezed her hand tightly around the stone elephant in her pocket, pulled it out and swung it at the man's face.

He staggered to one side, momentarily stunned. Before he could get his arm around her, she went limp, letting herself fall toward the ground all at once and knocking him off balance. At the same time, he drew his gun from where he'd hidden it under his jacket, raising it as she shut her eyes tightly, squirming to free herself from his grip.

Two gunshots sounded almost simultaneously, and the hand squeezing her arm let go a split second before its owner was flung aside by a heavy weight that then landed on top of her. She yelped in surprise, the wind smashed out of her. It took her only seconds to figure out that this was Sam, but once again, she knew something was wrong. Not only was he not speaking to her, but he wasn't holding himself up. All his weight pressed down on her and, she noted in the following seconds, he was struggling to breathe.

The uproar from the nearby crowd of law enforcement was immediate, and her anger was forgotten.

No!

Someone lifted Sam off her and tried to help her up, but she scuttled quickly to one side, away from the ambulance and the man who hadn't been an EMT. She didn't take her wide eyes off Sam until an army of legs obscured her view of him. The doors of the ambulance opened and voices shouted—she imagined they'd found the man inside.

If I hadn't walked away from him... just like he told me from the beginning.

Trying to see what was happening with Sam, she shook off the officer who was helping her to her feet slowly, and stood as tall as she could.

"Ella..." Her name was the last thing he said before they whisked him into another nearby ambulance, which took off with lights and sirens blazing.

Only days ago, she'd ridden in an identical ambulance at his side after the car accident. The emotion of that day flooded back—squeezing his hand between both of hers and pressing them against her forehead, terrified that he wouldn't make it. Dread knotted her stomach as a heavy weight pressed down on her chest. Not only could she not sit with him this time, but she'd just screamed at him with everything inside her, and walked away with every intention of never seeing him again.

And he'd turned around and saved her life *again*... but had it cost him his own?

She was having trouble breathing. *Is this what a panic attack feels like?*

She looked down, and her eyes landed on the silver bracelet one of the nurses had given her on that first day in the hospital. The day she'd met Sam. Her wrist had hit the ground hard when she'd fallen. The flower charm had cracked open and half was missing. She crouched down to look for the missing piece, but stopped short of picking it up. A tiny piece of unfamiliar metal lay beside it, and she stared at it uncomprehendingly. Without being told, she knew not to touch it without gloves, because she had the feeling it was going to be evidence.

The weight of everything that had happened to her over the past week hit her hard then, and she sat down. Every bit of her strength depleted, she willed the ground to swallow her.

Chapter 49

Ella

FRIDAY

ELLA CLOSED HER EYES and wished with every cell in her body to be somewhere else—no, even better, to be someone else. She counted to ten slowly and tried to exhale the tension that held her upright in the metal folding chair. The interrogation room she was in was much like the one she'd been taken to the morning Sam had first brought her in for questioning. She swore it had been a lifetime ago.

She'd never met the two agents across the table from her. Her head was pounding, and the fluorescent lights in the room made it worse. Fortunately, she'd made it through the worst night of her life. Unfortunately, now she had to rehash it all again for the record.

The hospital had given her drugs for her pain from the gunshot, and she wondered if she felt sluggish because they were still in her system, or if she had some sort of PTSD—or if it was both. Her fitful sleep had been filled with a replay of everything that had gone wrong in the previous few hours. Her dreams had been just as vivid as when it had all happened, but everything had hurt so much more the second time.

One agent reviewed his notes, and the other asked, "Can I get you anything? Water?"

"Yes, please." Ella was sore all over, especially on her left side, where the gunshot had badly bruised her despite her bullet-proof vest. When the door opened behind them, she turned toward the sound out of habit and winced in pain.

"Thank you," she mumbled when someone set water down in front of her, not looking up this time. She took a sip, then folded her hands in her lap and kept her eyes down. "Could I ask one question?"

"Of course."

She steeled herself, keeping her voice as steady as she could. "No one has told me... Is Mal...?" She squeezed her lips together and waited.

Both agents looked away, and their expressions answered for them. The one closer to her made eye contact. "I'm sorry, she didn't make it."

Ella exhaled the pain as best she could. Using the same technique she'd perfected so long ago when things were too much, she closed her eyes and breathed through the moment. She searched for something comforting to tell herself—anything—but came up empty.

"We'll give you a few minutes," the lead agent said, and they left the room. When the door latched behind them, she was snapped back to the day at the FBI when Agent Donnelly had left her in the interrogation room that first time. He'd been such an ass. A whimper escaped her. Even remembering their first unfriendly interactions made her miss him.

Pull yourself together, she told herself as she wiped away tears from her cheeks. She'd just calmed herself down when the agents returned—they'd probably been watching her through the two-way mirror.

"Alright, Ms. Madson, let's get started. Could you please tell us for the record what happened last night?"

She kept her focus on the shiny surface of the table while she told them everything she knew about what had happened: from the time they'd parked around the corner from the wreckage of her house, all the way until she sat down beside the pieces of her broken bracelet. The only things she didn't mention were the details that only mattered to her—like the fact that she'd held Sam's hand. It was irrelevant and would only get him in trouble. They stopped her from time to time to ask questions, but mostly, they let her talk.

Even after she finished, the same images that had haunted her dreams the night before replayed in an endless loop in her head. She no longer had the strength to fight them.

She still had so many questions. *Did anyone else get shot? Who was shooting? Did they catch the shooter?* And the one answer she feared more than any other.

Squeezing her hands into fists, she gathered her courage to ask the only question that really mattered. She hated to ask, but she couldn't bear not knowing.

"One more thing," said Ella. "Is... Agent Donnelly okay?"

"Yes. He's out of surgery and has a good prognosis. It'll take some time, but they expect him to make a full recovery."

A ten-thousand-pound weight lifted off her shoulders. *At least I didn't get him killed, too.* Despite the good news, her relief melted away. *Am I safe now, or am I still in danger? Is Sam's team not here because of what I said last night? Or am I no longer worth protecting?*

Her biting words to Sam came back to her with embarrassing clarity. Of course, none of them were here after how she'd acted. The mess she'd been through may not have been her fault, but in the end she had only herself to blame for the one thing she'd feared the most—ending up alone again.

"Thank you for coming in, Ms. Madson. If you'll just come with me, we've arranged a new safe house for you..."

Tears leaked from her eyes, which only made her angry all over again. She hated Mal for dragging her into this mess, and she hated herself for being angry at Mal. The hope that they could reconcile had died with her, and now the wound would never heal. As for Sam, her feelings for him weren't that simple, and she didn't have the energy to sort them out.

"Wait," Ella said. "Agent...?"

The agent standing closer to her smiled at her kindly. "Agent Simmons."

"Agent Simmons, may I ask a few more questions?"

Agent Simmons nodded to her partner, who left the two of them alone as she pulled out the chair across from Ella and sat down. "Of course."

"Will I see Agent Donnelly and his team again?"

"All three of them have given their statements. Once the paperwork is complete, the case will be closed. You probably won't see them. Did you want me to pass along a message?"

She had known they were only there because it was their job. All of them. She'd reminded herself a thousand times. And yet, it stung far more than it should have that they hadn't even come to say goodbye. She shook her head, determined to hold herself together. "No."

The agent nodded sympathetically.

"What about the hit on me? Is it still active?"

"Not according to our sources," said Agent Simmons.

"Who was it? Who paid Kingston to kill me?"

"I'm sorry. I'm not at liberty to say. It was related to Mal's past, not yours. So with her gone, you shouldn't be in danger."

"But how can I be sure they're not still following me?"

"Besides the arrests we've made, we also found out how they were tracking you. You had a bracelet with a flower charm. Where did you get it?"

"Oh..." Ella reached for the hazy memory. "There was a nurse. When I was in the hospital after the explosion. She said I reminded her of her daughter, who she'd just lost. She insisted that I take it."

Agent Simmons nodded seriously. "It had a tracker in it."

Ella's eyes widened. "So the nurse...?"

The agents shook her head. "She wasn't a nurse. We have her in custody, so don't worry about that. They can't follow you anymore."

"Okay." Knowing that the case was closed should have given her some relief, but the gaping hole inside her swallowed all her emotions, leaving only a deep sense of loss. Her sister was gone. Though she'd only known them briefly, she and the agents on Sam's team had been through a lot together, and now they were gone, too—far more suddenly and painfully than she'd expected. At least with her parents, she'd gotten to say goodbye.

Let's be honest, you're not broken up about being deserted by the other agents. You're only thinking about Sam. Too bad you killed whatever was between you.

She was still angry at him, but an icy dread had crept from the corners of her mind inward.

When Ella and Agent Simmons arrived at her new safe house, Ella didn't even drop her backpack before sinking onto the brown couch that had seen better days. The layout was different, but the standard, worn furniture was the same. She watched as Agent Simmons opened doors and checked locks, ensuring that every room was secure.

Just like Sam always had.

She was back to square one in a drab and lifeless temporary home, but this time, she didn't even have the energy to be devastated.

"Do you need anything?"

"Just sleep. I'm fine," said Ella. She wasn't fine, but she knew that those were the words that would get rid of the agent the fastest. There was nothing she could do that would help her, and Ella desperately wanted to be alone.

"If you think of anything, here's my card. I'll be in touch tomorrow." When Ella didn't reach for it, Agent Simmons set it on the coffee table and smiled at her kindly. "Call if you need anything."

When the door latch clicked and Ella was alone, the last of her composure crumbled. Her tears were back, heaving sobs that knocked her sideways on the couch, where she pulled into the fetal position.

I'm sorry.

The thread by which she'd been hanging on for so long had finally snapped.

Not bothering to drag herself upstairs, she cried herself to sleep on the couch.

Chapter 50
Ella

FRIDAY (2 WEEKS LATER)

E LLA RESTED HER CHIN in her hand, attempting to focus on her laptop screen. It wasn't working. She'd done nothing but work for almost two weeks. When her mind was busy, she couldn't overthink everything she'd been through and everything she'd lost in the past three weeks. The plain white walls of the safe house reflected her own emptiness right back at her, but work allowed her to focus on something besides the mess her life had become.

It's only temporary had become her mantra. Everything in life was temporary, really. Home was a place that was gone forever, so her surroundings didn't matter. She could have improved her surroundings with the same easy, inexpensive tricks she recommended for her clients every day—but why bother? It took all her energy just to get through the day doing the absolute minimum.

Wake up. Shower. Eat. Work. Sleep.

Tense and sore from hunching over her new laptop from before sun-up until after sun-down day after day, she stood and stretched, grudgingly acknowledging that she needed a break. Not just the five-minute breaks she'd been giving herself to empty the dishwasher or make coffee. An actual break.

Gritting her teeth, she grabbed her phone, keys, and purse and headed for the door. There was one place where she was long overdue for a visit.

She'd driven this route in every kind of weather, in darkness and sunshine and everything in between. This time she drove it on autopilot as her thoughts barreled back to that night in the park that she couldn't stop reliving. She'd had plenty of time to beat herself up for screaming at Sam. He'd been doing his job, as he'd been doing all along, and she'd acted like a spoiled child. Her regrets could fill an ocean, and she was drowning in them.

After replaying the whole encounter in her head on repeat for the past two weeks, she'd come back to the same painful realization that she'd always feared: she'd gotten what she deserved. Her dad had told her that she and Mal were like opposing magnets, repelling each other—but it was more than that. All this time, she hadn't just been repelling Mal. She'd repelled everyone. It was no wonder that she'd ended up alone.

She couldn't imagine facing Sam to give him the apology he deserved. He would hate her anyway. What she needed to do was move on.

But how?

She'd thought she had feelings for him, but now she understood that it had really been stress and exhaustion and her desperate need for an anchor in the chaos. *I saw what I wanted to see, but it wasn't real.*

It hurt like it had been, though.

Twenty minutes later, she drove through the heavy iron gates and exhaled deliberately. This place made her uncomfortably emotional on the best of days, and today was far from one of those, but she needed to come.

I'm okay. She'd been telling herself this since the night Mal had been shot, but she was still waiting for it to be true.

Parking by the curb where the road narrowed, she'd just turned off the car when her phone buzzed in her purse. She fished it out and clicked the screen to life.

She had a text from Agent Jacobs—Lindsay, as she now knew her. Even though such things weren't exactly encouraged, they'd kept in touch after Ella's case had been closed.

Hey, how are things? Want to meet for coffee tomorrow?

Ella had never been one to ask for help, but her fingers flew over the keys before she'd consciously decided to ask.

Tomorrow works. Today would be better tho

Would love to, but can't today. Just left Sam's apartment, and now driving up to my mom's for her birthday

The mention of Sam sent a jolt through her. Nodding quickly even though she was alone, she bit her lip against an irrational stab of jealousy and disappointment.

Okay, tomorrow it is. Let me know what time works

Ella had put her phone back in her purse, and was attempting to convince herself she was fine with waiting until tomorrow for company when it vibrated again.

You should go see him

Ella stiffened, reminding herself that her friend couldn't see her clenching her jaw or the panic in her eyes. Taking a deep breath, she typed a reply, but deleted it. She wasn't going to touch the subject of Sam, even though Lindsay had been a nonstop font of information about him. One of the things she'd mentioned the week before was that while the first gunshot had only bruised Ella that night Mal had died, the second one had hit Sam in the side just below the bottom of his bullet-proof vest. Lindsay had assured her that he was okay, but that this had made him crankier than ever.

Though Ella wished Lindsay would stop talking about Sam, she couldn't bring herself to say so. She wanted to know about him, even though it stung. Besides, asking her friend not to tell her these things would inevitably lead to a discussion about what had happened between them that night. Surely Lindsay already knew how badly Ella had behaved, and Ella was too ashamed to talk about it.

Lindsay's texts continued.

I know you guys haven't talked

He's not mad at you

Anything I should tell him?

The tiny bubbles scrolled at the bottom of the screen, telling her that Lindsay was still writing.

"Lindsay, please stop," Ella whispered, resting her head on the steering wheel.

He hasn't been his grumpy self since we closed your case ;) He's... sad

Each message made her clutch her phone tighter as she grew increasingly anxious.

He misses you, Ella. It's pretty obvious

There it was.

Her fingers were still. She had no idea how to respond, but the thoughts toppled over each other. *If I believe he misses me, that's worse. It's better if he hates me—that's what I deserve. And it'll be easier for him. He should hate me.*

She forced herself to reply, but ignored the topic of Sam. *Let me know what time you want to meet tomorrow, and where.* Ella typed carefully, not trusting her fingers not to change the subject.

Thankfully, Lindsay relented. *Will do. Maybe 11? Let's confirm a time and place first thing tomorrow*

Sounds good

Ella put her phone away and looked out at the gloomy day. The gray clouds hung low, looking like they might burst at any moment—which was exactly how she felt. Unconcerned about getting rained on, she got out of the car and walked the rest of the way. Very little had changed here over the years. The slabs of rock in all different shapes and sizes greeted her with the same silence as always. By now, the names of the people who were buried along the path to her parents' graves were as familiar as if they'd been old friends. In a strange way, they were, having kept her company on every visit over the years.

"Hi Mom. Hi Dad." She glanced from one headstone to another as tears prickled in her eyes. Some days she came here and stood silently, some days she sat and talked as if they were there with her, and other days she just cried. She could guess what kind of day this was going to be.

"I don't know where to start. I just—" Her voice cracked. All at once, her face crumpled, her knees buckled, and she landed in a heap in the freshly cut grass. "I'm sorry for letting you down. I thought... I hoped... eventually she'd come around. It's my fault. I should've played her game sooner. And now..." The floodgates opened.

It isn't fair.

The sun came out from behind the clouds just as she heard her mother's voice in her head, more clearly than she had in years. *"It's not your fault, Ella."*

Shame and disappointment in herself stabbed at her, which only made her angry with herself all over again and pushed her sobs out from deeper inside. No longer only crying over Mal, she also cried for Sam and the horrible way things had ended between them. Helping her had been his job, nothing more. And how had she thanked him for saving her life five times?

Ella knew life wasn't fair. Everything ended. Everyone left. She should've been used to it by now, but it still ripped her open every time. Still, if she hadn't lost control and blamed him for everything that night, she would've at least gotten a goodbye from him.

She didn't know how long she'd kneeled there, only that by the time she looked around, the sun had traveled across the sky and now cast longer shadows. For the moment, her supply of tears was as empty as she was.

A loud chirping from a nearby tree broke her out of her reverie, and a gentle breeze stirred through the trees and ruffled her hair. She stayed a little longer in the grass by her parents' graves, waiting for her mind to be still. Finally, she pushed herself to her feet, turned around and froze in place before she could take a step. She hadn't expected to see anyone there, least of all the one person who stared back at her from beyond the next row of headstones.

"Hi," said Sam, walking forward haltingly, as if he was afraid she would bolt if he approached too quickly.

"What are you doing here?"

He grimaced, reaching an arm up to scratch the back of his neck. "Oh, I... Lindsay thought you... uh... might appreciate a friendly face."

The look on her face must have betrayed her, because he added, "I know, friendly isn't really what I'm known for, but..." He put his palms up in a gesture of surrender, giving a weak smile. "I come in peace."

She tried to give him one of her own, but accomplished only less of a frown. The warring urges to run to him and away from him did battle in her head, but she did neither. "How did you know I was here?"

He chuckled. "I work for the FBI, remember?"

"Right. Of course. Well, I was just leaving, so..."

"Ella, wait." He reached for her as she tried to brush past him, resting his hand on her arm and stopping her mid-stride.

She looked at his hand on her arm, her stomach plummeting as if she'd just dropped multiple stories on a roller coaster. It seemed impossible that he wouldn't notice that she was shaking, and she wasn't sure what to do. Pull away? Move closer? A charge zipped through her from the spot he was holding, and it made her chest ache all over again. Suddenly, she was so exhausted.

His hand didn't move, and neither did she. She didn't realize she'd been holding her breath until he finally released her arm, looking chagrined.

"I'm sorry," he said.

Her stomach was now infected with jackrabbits, hopping with all their might against her insides. She stayed perfectly still and, as he took a small step closer, she fought both the urge to put more space between them and the urge to throw her arms around him.

"How long have you been here?"

"A little while. I didn't want to interrupt."

She breathed deliberately, in and out.

"Are you okay?" he asked.

All she could do was shake her head slightly. *Not even a little.*

She looked up into his eyes, biting her lower lip to stop it from shaking, and silently cursed her tears, which were suddenly overflowing again. He moved closer again, now only inches away, and she let her head fall forward against him. When his arms wound gently around her back, the dam broke inside her and she sobbed into his soft shirt.

His cheek rested on her head as he pulled her into a hug, and her arms found their way around him without a second thought. She couldn't have said how long they stayed that way, only that when she was finally still, she'd reached a whole new level of exhaustion. Slowly her breathing returned to normal, and she turned her head so her temple leaned against his now tear-soaked shirt, as she looked out at the quiet cemetery.

"You want to sit down?" He pointed to the strip of grass in front of them. "Unless you'd rather go somewhere else."

"No, right here is fine. I've spent a lot of time here over the years." She settled herself in the grass facing her parents' graves, hugging her knees loosely. Just like when he'd sat next to her on the little beach at Walloon Lake, warmth filled her when he lowered himself to the ground beside her. He sat facing her with his legs crossed, watching her.

"Lindsay told me you got shot. That night," she said slowly, looking down at his side.

He shrugged. "Yeah. But it's not the first time, and it's practically healed now. No big deal."

She grimaced. "I'm sorry you got shot because of me. But I'm every sorrier for what I said that night. It was like... like I was temporarily insane. I shouldn't have said any of it. None of it was your fault. I know that."

When he opened his mouth to speak, she put up a hand to stop him.

"Please, I need to say this out loud."

He closed his mouth with a nod, and she continued.

"Mal and I stopped getting along when we were really young. As we got older, she was only nice when she wanted something. And maybe she did want something from me that night, or maybe she'd changed. Maybe she was about to shoot me. I'd always hoped that someday... Yes, I know it's stupid, but... I don't know. I..." Chills ran through her, and she squeezed her eyes shut long enough to count to five. His hand landed on the middle of her back at the count of three, and remained there when she opened her eyes.

"I was angry with her, for making me miserable when we were kids, but I was also angry with myself, for my part in it. We fed off each other. I wish I'd been nicer to her when we were growing up. I worry that she turned out the way she did because of me."

He tilted his head but said nothing, waiting for her to go on.

"When she was nine, she got locked in the attic while we were playing a game. It was like hide and seek, except she would give me clues, and I had to come find her. Her clues were usually too easy, but that day I told her to give me a hard one. She gave me three clues, but I didn't know what they meant. We weren't supposed to hide in the attic, so I never thought to look there. But my dad left it open by mistake, and Mal hid in there. When my mom found the door unlocked, she thought my dad had left it open and locked it, then went on with her day."

"Because I was the one playing the game, and I didn't find her, Mal blamed me, not my mom. We only figured out she was in there hours later, and she was traumatized. We hadn't gotten along great before that, but afterwards, forget it."

His fingers moved gently, back and forth, on her back, and calm slowly spread through her as she continued.

"So, that night when she was... she seemed like she wanted to talk things out, I thought, 'Finally!' And then..."

She put her head in her hands for a few seconds, took a breath, and straightened. "After she got shot, I was just so angry... not just with myself and with her. It was like a lifetime of anger hit me all at once, and almost none of it made sense. I was angry with my parents for dying, and at the friends I'd had over the years who didn't stick... even though I probably pushed them away. It's just what I do. I was angry that after almost twenty years of silence, the moment Mal wanted to talk, someone shot her. You were the only one I wasn't angry at. You did nothing but keep me safe, which was your job, and I... It..." She took a few gulps of air.

"It wasn't fair, but I took it out on you because you were the only one left. I know it wasn't your fault that you were there. It was your job to protect me. You risked your life for me so many times, and that's how I repaid you."

Her eyes were blurry with tears again, and she swiped her hands across her cheeks. The words came out more slowly this time. "I couldn't even think straight... though it's all obvious now." She sniffled. "Anyway, I'm really sorry. I'd do anything to take back the things I said."

His hand was still on her back, fingers moving slightly back and forth, so she decided his reaction couldn't be too bad. Still, she couldn't make eye contact.

She hugged her knees tightly and dropped her chin on them again. When he didn't respond, she turned so her cheek rested on her knees and raised her eyes little by little to find him smiling sadly at her. She gave him a weak smile back. Her energy was depleted, but her tears had refilled and threatened to fall.

The hand on her back reached across to her far shoulder, then tugged gently toward him, pulling her into a hug. "Come here."

Once he had his cheek pressed against her forehead, he continued. "It's okay. I get it. Everything crashed down on you at the same time, and you were doing your best to protect yourself. I know it's not the same thing, but I've been in a place that's a lot like that. No more beating yourself up over it. You didn't deserve any of it either. You know that, right?"

She clenched her jaw until it ached as chills ran through her and goosebumps erupted on her skin. "I don't deserve you."

"Nope, you deserve someone better, but you're stuck with me," he said. The lightness of his tone lessened some of the tension of the moment, and she chuckled against him. "It'll take a while to convince you that none of it was your fault, and that's okay. I'm stubborn."

She stared up at him, not daring to ask the question. Instead, she chuckled. "You? Stubborn?"

He smiled and shifted so he could push a strand of hair behind her ear, then continued, now serious. "I know the last couple weeks have been a nightmare for you. But for what it's worth, when you walked into my life, it was the first good thing that had happened to me in two years."

She remembered the moment she'd first seen him and how unpleasant he'd been. In a small voice, she said, "You're the one who walked into my life. I was trapped in a hospital bed." Encouraged by a low chuckle that rumbled through him, she added, "You were such a jerk."

Though she didn't look up, she heard the smile in his voice. "You're right, I was. That was me protecting myself. Somehow, you got through to me anyway." After a pause, his voice dropped to almost nothing, as if to tell her a secret. "I hate that I can't fix this for you. That's all I want."

Her head bobbed up and down. "Thanks." Her instinct was not to trust the idea that someone else was on her side, but this time felt different.

Affection shone in his eyes, and it made the corners of her mouth turn upwards despite everything weighing her down. For a few minutes, neither of them said anything.

"Did they tell you what happened? With the case?" he asked.

"At the hospital, an agent came to pick me up when I was discharged. Simmons, I think? She told me a little."

"Do you want to hear the rest?"

She took a deep breath and leaned into him. "Yeah."

"The trio responsible for the data breach was Mal, Jimmy, and a woman named Bri. Apparently Bri got greedy afterwards and wanted all the profit for herself. She faked her death and put out the hit on Mal and Jimmy. A separate assassin was assigned to each of them. The one assigned to Mal targeted you. Think of it as a major clerical error in the assassin world, probably because you and Mal look so much alike..." He shook his head.

"When the first assassin failed, Bri put the job up on an open board, which is why it started to feel like a free for all. It seems impossible to mistake you for Mal, but apparently it wasn't. The assassins didn't know who'd hired them or anything but the basics. When you were always with the FBI, they just figured Mal had sold the others out."

"How did you know... that night... about the EMT?"

"The man pretending to be the EMT wasn't the one who shot Mal. She was shot by a woman with blonde hair. Unfortunately, she got away. After interviewing people at the shopping center across the street, all they found was that a woman fitting her description had stopped at the coffee shop a few hours earlier. The name she gave for her drink was Stephanie, but they're still running down leads."

"As for how I knew about the EMT," he said, "I was watching out for you."

Ella looked at the ground, hating to remember how angry she'd been at that moment.

"I saw you talking to him. As soon as you started walking away with him, I was moving in your direction. Something about him was off. When he grabbed your arm, I knew he wasn't who he was pretending to be. I ran as fast as I could to take him down. Nothing in the world would've stopped me."

"Even after everything I'd just said…" She kept her eyes on her knees. "You ran directly towards danger to save me."

"Come on, you know how stubborn I am."

She laughed. "So stubborn."

His voice was sincere when he added, "I'd do it again, even knowing I'd get shot."

She looked up at him with watery eyes.

"But why did he go after me, if Mal was already…?"

"When there were two of you, and they weren't sure which one of you was the target, he decided it was better to be safe than sorry. Just in case the other assassin had killed the wrong one of you." He shrugged. "They just wanted to be absolutely sure."

"For the last ten years, Mal was trying to get me to play that game she'd loved as a kid. She kept sending me clues in the mail. If I'd just done it sooner…" She shrugged. "Who knows?"

"No," he said, with an urgency that surprised her. He gripped her shoulders tightly, and she looked up into his eyes in surprise. "Don't do that. You could second guess every decision you've made in the past ten years. It won't help. You'll just feel worse." With a sigh, he added, "Been there, done that." With sadness in his eyes, he added, "Trust me."

Without giving herself time to overthink the urge, she leaned into his chest, and his arms tightened around her once again. She had no idea what to do next.

He shifted so he could pick up her hand and lace their fingers together, just as she had that night under the tree.

"You know that now that the case is closed, you're off the hook," she said.

He tilted his head and looked at her. "What hook?"

"I'm not your responsibility anymore."

"You're right. It's no longer my job to make sure you're safe, but here I am. So now maybe I can convince you I'm here because I care about you."

She stiffened.

Is it the worst thing in the world if he's here because he cares, and not because it's his job?

"My dad used to say Mal and I were like magnets," she began. Sam looked mildly confused, but said nothing.

"Not the kind that stick together, but the ones you can't force together, no matter how hard you try. It made sense to me. I called us anti-magnetic. The older I got, the more it felt like it wasn't just with Mal. I felt like I was anti-magnetic with everyone... like I was calibrated to push other people away. I'd accepted that I was just one magnet that repelled the others."

"Ella..."

The sadness in his voice was too much, so she grimaced and kept talking so he wouldn't say anything else. "Logically, I know that's not true, but I guess in a way I internalized it so deeply that I made it true. Things went downhill with Mal after the attic incident. She had zero guilty conscience, and I had mine and hers. She was mean to me, I was mean to her back. It snowballed. I blamed myself, and I couldn't bring myself to talk about it with anyone, so it ate away at me."

She took a deep breath. If she didn't tell him everything, she'd never get past it.

"I got Mal arrested."

He didn't look shocked, and there was no judgement in his eyes, as she'd expected. He shook his head. "I'm sure you mean Mal got herself arrested."

"No. I saw her a few times in the park. Talking to younger kids. Giving them little bags in exchange for something. I started following her. Then I told the police what I'd seen and what she had in her room. I helped get my sister arrested for selling drugs. What kind of person does that?"

"The kind of person who cares. Would it have been better to let her keep doing it? Think of how you helped the neighborhood kids. Even Mal herself, no matter if she could see it or not."

She'd never thought of it that way before.

"I don't know if I did it because it was the right thing to do, or because it would make her angry, or maybe both. After that, I knew she'd never forgive me. What I hadn't realized was that I wouldn't forgive myself, either."

"You did the right thing."

She'd never realized how badly she needed to hear those words, and her lips tugged upwards sadly. "Since I couldn't open up to people, and my parents didn't understand what was going on or how much any of it had affected me, it just kept festering. They would probably send a kid today to therapy for a lot less, but back then..." She shook her head.

"So I never really got past it. Trust me, I know exactly how dumb it sounds. I'm almost forty, for God's sake! Maybe that's why I felt like friends would never stick for me. I could never open up. Or maybe that's just an excuse I gave myself. Everyone eventually fell out of touch for one reason or another: their interests had changed, they'd gotten busy with work, moved away, started families, or we'd just grown apart. The more people left, the less I wanted to let anyone else in. And then it was just me." She shrugged.

She'd blocked out how much those rejections had stung, but it all flooded back and the hollowness expanded until it felt like it might swallow her. Staring into the distance, she said, "I didn't see it then, of course, but I was pushing them away. Like I do with anyone who tries to get close to me."

"Sounds like that was the opposite of what you needed," he said gently.

"I told you. It's me. Friends, acquaintances, boyfriends... no one sticks. I've psychoanalyzed myself enough to realize that to save myself the heartache of people leaving me, I push them away first." She couldn't look him in the eyes for fear the kindness in them would make her emotions overflow. "I'm such a cliché, I know."

"You must be losing your touch. You're having no luck pushing me away."

She inhaled a shaky breath and tried to force herself to smile. He had the most genuine of intentions, and she loved that about him. But he would be no different, she knew. His good intentions made it worse, because it would hurt more in the end. "Not yet, but up until a couple weeks ago, it was 'your job' to be with me."

His free hand moved to her face, and he pressed his index finger gently under her chin, lifting it until she met his eyes. He leaned forward and kissed her forehead, then moved back to look in her eyes.

"You're beautiful, smart, thoughtful, and most importantly, you somehow see right through my hard outer shell. I'm here with you until you tell me to go away. Not because I have to be, but because I want to be. Okay?" he asked.

She nodded, then looked down, smiling despite how hard it was to believe something she'd been longing to hear for so long. When she looked up at him, her eyes were glassy, but her smile was intact.

"I never expected to see you again after the awful things I said to you. I was sure I'd done an extra thorough job pushing you away and acting like a completely spoiled brat."

His free hand slid to the back of her neck, fingers tangling in her hair as they gently massaged her scalp. "You were acting like you were in pain, because you were. I knew that. I knew you didn't mean it, even though you thought you did, and that what you needed was time... or at least, I hoped so. I had to stop myself from checking on you before you were ready."

"Is that why Lindsay kept texting me?"

"I asked her to keep tabs on you after everything blew up with us, but she said she'd already planned to. She never asked any questions, but from the way she told me every single thing you said, and grinned at me the whole time, I'm pretty sure she knew better than we did what was going on."

Ella closed her eyes and let him pull her head into the crook of his neck. "She said you missed me."

When he chuckled, it vibrated through her. His head dropped until his face leaned into her hair, and when he spoke, it was near her ear. "I never told her that, but she was right. I missed you."

She scooted to his side and carefully wrapped her arms around him. When his muscles tightened on the side where he'd been shot, she repositioned herself. "Sorry." He responded by tightening his arms around her.

"I missed you, too," she said. "Even though you sort of gave me a complex by reminding me over and over that it was your job to protect me. Of course, it actually was your job, so I couldn't be upset, but it was like you kept announcing 'I'm only here because I have to be.' With everything else that was going on, it was really confusing."

He turned his head so that his cheek rested against the top of her head. "I wanted to convince myself I worried so much about you because it was my job. That's why I kept saying it. In my line of work, I have to be objective. But with you I wasn't, and deep down I knew it. It was easier to be objective when I told myself I didn't care. Which meant being an ass."

Looking away, he frowned slightly. "I blamed myself when I lost Julia, because I wasn't there. I couldn't protect her. So the thought of not being able to protect you made me..." He met her eyes, a sad smile flickering on his face before a frown took over. "That day I lost it at you at the safe house because you opened the door without looking through the peephole... I was terrified that it would happen again."

"I'm sorry," she whispered, leaning back to look up into his face, but still holding onto him.

"I'm sorry for being horrible to you," he murmured, looking down and pressing his forehead against hers.

"It worked out okay," she said, and they both chuckled, breathing in and out in rhythm.

She tucked her head against his chest as if she'd done it a thousand times, listening to the rhythm of his heart.

"You said before that Lindsay knew what was going on with us... but I still don't know what's going on with us. Want to fill me in?"

"Well, were you hoping to join the team so you can help us chase down more bad guys?"

She rolled her eyes. "Funny. No, I've had enough of your job for a lifetime."

"So then, tell me what you were hoping for."

Her face instantly flushed, and the butterflies in her stomach beat their wings so fast it made her nauseous. He took her hand, and his fingers worked their way between hers, giving off sparks against her skin as he held on securely.

She looked from their hands up into his face. *It's now or never.*

"I was hoping you would be the first one to stick," she whispered, resisting the urge to make a joke to diffuse her nervousness.

"There's no one I'd rather stick with," he said, his face inching toward hers until the tips of their noses brushed together.

Her heart was louder than a jackhammer.

"You can trust me, you know," he said, with barely any space between them.

Her gaze flicked away, but when she met his eyes again, the warmth in them soothed some of the beating wings inside her.

"You're the only one I trust." She winced, adding, "Sorry. That sounded even cheesier out loud than it did in my head. But it's the truth."

The hint of worry on his face melted back into a smile. His arms tightened around her and he let the tip of his nose rest on the bridge of hers for only a second before it skimmed upwards to her hairline, brushed his nose along her skin until their foreheads lined up.

"Everything's going to be okay now. And this time it's not a lie."

It was a lot to hope for, but for the first time in a very long time, she believed it, too. In fact, for the first time in decades, she considered the possibility that she wasn't anti-magnetic, after all.

Trusting her feelings felt like walking off a cliff. Even so, she leaned forward the last inch until their lips met in a gentle kiss, and for a short time, not even air separated them. The rest of the world had disappeared.

A nearby bird's call brought them back to reality, and they reluctantly pulled apart, still holding onto each other and smiling sheepishly.

"Was that, uh, appropriate for a cemetery?" he asked.

She glanced around, then shrugged. "They don't look offended."

"Are we good now?" he asked with a chuckle.

"I think we're better than good."

He smiled wider than she'd ever seen in all the time she'd known him. "Good," he said. "Are you ready to go?" The sun was setting, and the clouds had surrendered the sky to a flood of colors.

It was amazing what a radical shift her emotions had undergone since she'd arrived just hours before. "Yeah."

Sam stood and stretched, then offered his hand and helped her up. Instead of letting go once they were both on their feet, he kept hold of her hand and squeezed. She squeezed back.

Pressing a kiss into the pads of her fingers on her free hand, she touched the top of each of her parents' gravestones. From the back of her mind came her mother's voice again, as if she was right there with her. *That's my girl. You're okay.* And her father's. *I'm so proud of you, Bella.*

Ella looked up to find Sam watching her and gave him a tired smile.

"You want to get some dinner?" he asked.

"Dinner sounds good." Neither of them made any moves to go towards their cars. "But first I just need a little more of this moment."

He dropped her hand and rested both of his lightly on her hips, inching closer still. "I don't blame you. It's one of my new favorites."

Her eyes were suspiciously moist when she nodded and leaned forward until her forehead rested on his chest. His arms came up around her back tightly, and she took deep breaths, determined to imprint this moment on her brain. "Just what I needed," she murmured.

His cheek pressed against the top of her head. "Good."

He planted a kiss in her hair, and for a few more minutes neither of them even thought about moving. Finally he loosened his arms and moved back just far enough to look into her eyes, his hands on her lower back. "Come on. I need to get you some dinner before you get hangry," he said fondly.

"Me? Hangry?" She grinned. "Never."

He slid an arm across her shoulders, and they started walking. "Let's agree to disagree on that one."

They pretended to argue in between peals of laughter, and for once, Ella managed not to overthink happiness, and just let herself enjoy it. Yes, the path that had led her here had wound through hell. But everything she'd been through—everything both of them had been through—only made them appreciate it more. If they'd met any other way, she never would've given him a chance. She wouldn't have been ready.

Maybe her dad's comparison of Ella and Mal to magnets had been right, and she and her sister were never meant to get along.

Or maybe, it didn't mean anything, no matter what her past had told her.

Maybe it had been more about her fear of being left than anything else.

Maybe she and Sam were the magnets that would stick together.

Maybe Sam had been right, and it would be okay now.

Just maybe, it was okay to let the past go, and to stop fighting so hard to protect herself.

It was a *lot* of maybes, and only time would tell, but the fact that she even saw the possibility represented enormous progress.

"What's on your mind?" Sam asked as they walked. "You look like you have big thoughts happening in there." He tugged her to a stop and tapped his index finger lightly against her forehead. Even that tiny contact made her smile.

"Good things," she said. "But too much to talk about today."

"That's okay. I'm not going anywhere. Except with you, to get dinner."

The sun burst through a break in the clouds just then, and Ella punched him jokingly in the arm. "Very funny."

"Yes, I am," he said. "If you'll recall, I mentioned that you would regret getting me started telling jokes."

She smiled up at him, momentarily amazed. Her decades' worth of baggage suddenly felt weightless.

"I like your terrible jokes," she said.

"Well then, you're in luck. I've got lots more where that came from."

Suddenly dropping her arms and stepping back from him, she grinned. "I'll race you back to the cars," she said, and took off running with Sam only a few steps behind her, both laughing.

They arrived beside their cars together, breathless, and Sam threw his arms around her in a hug and picked her up to spin her in a circle, her legs flying out behind her. A lightness started in her chest, spreading out through her to the ends of her limbs. All at once, the ghosts that had haunted her for decades let go and flew away.

Smiling harder than she had since she was a kid, she held on tight.

Acknowledgements

THERE ARE SO MANY people who helped me get this book from a whisper of an idea to a full-length novel!

An endless supply of thanks to my husband, Chris: for prodding me to think beyond writing fanfic and to use my writing energy on a book all those years ago; for the "editorial meetings" at every stage of this book; for being in charge of breakfast and kid-wrangling so I could escape to Starbucks on weekend mornings to write; and for finding so many plot holes, and then helping me fill them. My characters and I are eternally grateful.

Thanks to my kids for their willingness to celebrate even the smallest book-related wins.

Many thanks to the rest of my friends and family for their excitement and encouragement, especially my sister, Heather McCuen, for coming up with the name The Breadcrumb Game, and my mom, Anne Bouchenoire, for her bottomless supply of support.

All of my gratitude goes to my beta readers and critique partners for their feedback over my many, many drafts: Denise Eckert Bled, Heather Dixon, Lidija Hilje, Derrick Eaves, Rosie Bindra, Jenifer Lynn, and Krista Swanson.

To Denise Eckert Bled, one of my farthest away friends who I consistently feel the closest to. You are still the President of the fan club I don't have. One of these days we'll be in the same place at the same time again! I'm sorry I can't write a Sam for you. I would if I could.

To Jenifer Lynn, one of the best writer friends I could ask for. For dragging me to the Barbie movie when I knew nothing about it (the first time we met in person), for being CP extraordinaire, for letting me pick your brain about self-publishing, for all your feedback on my books, and for your friendship.

Thanks to my editor, Michelle Hazen. I'm so glad to have met you on Twitter back in the Pitch Wars days! I'm so happy we finally got to work together.

Many thanks to my proofreader, Noel Ruessmann, who also happens to be my aunt. I'm so lucky to have you!

Immense gratitude goes out to the people who supported my Kickstarter campaign, especially: Bonnie Blevins, Anne Bouchenoire, Linda Burnham, Christopher Cericola, Morgan Forsythe, Charles and Sharon McCuen, Heather McCuen, Ellen Montemurno, Chantal Porterfield, Roylene and David Roberts, John St. Clair, Linda Thompson, and Fiona White.

And of course, thank you so much to my readers. I hope you enjoyed Ella and Sam's story!

About the Author

Once upon a time, there was a girl named Lauren who loved to read. She wrote stories about her favorite characters decades before she'd ever heard of fanfiction. Her fourth-grade teacher set her at a round table in the hall outside her classroom and sent her classmates to meet with her so she could edit their writing. Somehow, it never occurred to her that she wanted to be a writer.

About fourteen years and a BA in International Relations and an MA International Communication later, she considered joining the US Foreign Service. Instead, she taught elementary school for ten years, spent four years as an au pair coordinator, and many more at a residential property management company. Basically, she didn't know what she wanted to be when she grew up.

She rediscovered her love of writing by accident in her late thirties, writing fanfic for her favorite TV shows while her then-young children were napping. Eventually, her husband convinced her to write a book instead.

Today, Lauren lives in Northern Virginia with her husband, two teens and one tween, and their rescue dog, Thor—who is, ironically, afraid of thunder. While her family sleeps, she writes romantic books that somehow always involve assassins.

Connect with Lauren Online

Newsletter sign-up: books.laurenkristenroberts.com
Website: www.laurenkristenroberts.com
Instagram: @laurenkrobertsauthor
Facebook: @LaurenKRoberts
Twitter/X: @LaurenKRoberts

Milton Keynes UK
Ingram Content Group UK Ltd.
UKHW010756260424
441811UK00004B/293